ABOUT THE AUTHOR

From an early age, Martin was enchanted with old movies from Hollywood's golden era — from the dawn of the talkies in the late 1920s to the close of the studio system in the late 1950s — and has spent many a happy hour watching the likes of Garland, Gable, Crawford, Garbo, Grant, Miller, Kelly, Astaire, Rogers, Turner, and Welles go through their paces.

It felt inevitable that he would someday end up writing about them.

Originally from Melbourne, Australia, Martin moved to Los Angeles in the mid-90s where he now works as a writer, blogger, webmaster, and tour guide.

www.MartinTurnbull.com

This book is dedicated to

CHERYL WALTERS

because you've filled my life with so much wonder.

ISBN-13: 978-1539823810

ISBN-10: 1539823814

TWISTED BOULEVARD

a novel

by

Martin Turnbull

Book Six in the Hollywood's Garden of Allah novels.

CHAPTER 1

Gwendolyn Brick was surprised at how different Sunset Boulevard looked from twenty-five feet in the air. Its effervescence at street level had always quickened her pulse; new stores, bars, and nightclubs were always opening to replace old ones whose time had waned or whose owners weren't the impresarios they'd imagined. But standing on the roof of 8623 Sunset, Gwendolyn discovered that in the twenty-one years she'd lived in LA, she'd never wondered what the view was like from the top.

"You're on top now," she told herself. "In a few hours, you'll be one of those guys. Let's hope you're as shrewd as you think you are."

The afternoon sunlight slanted across the traffic, catching the bold stripes of the front awning of Mocambo as the club's sign flickered to life. Several blocks east, lights illuminated the white columns around the entrance to Ciro's, whose neon "C" glowed like a halo.

Dazzling personalities had surged through this town, loaded with talent and handed opportunity like caviar on a silver tray. Gwendolyn had watched them glitter and shine, only to see their egos crash-land like the *Hindenburg*. A speck of doubt caught in her throat. Could she really compete here?

She glanced at her watch; it was now-or-never o'clock.

A brisk February wind blustered up the boulevard, whipping her emerald silk dress around her calves. She peered over the ledge to make sure the tangerine cloth she'd hung over the sign of her brand-new dress shop was staying put, then scuttled across the graveled rooftop to climb down the ladder as gracefully as her skirt permitted. A dark blue DeSoto pulled into the lot below and three figures emerged holding boxes crammed with the stuff of which successful launches were made: booze.

Gwendolyn had known Kathryn Massey and Marcus Adler since the week they all moved into the Garden of Allah Hotel. She'd arrived from the other Hollywood—the one in Florida—knowing nobody, and she didn't like to think where she'd be without them. She certainly wouldn't be opening her own store along the same stretch of road that boasted some of the most famous addresses in America.

"How many people are you expecting?" Kathryn asked when she reached the store's rear entrance.

"Twenty-five, maybe?"

"We bought four dozen bottles of champagne, so we'll just make it," Marcus teased. "And Oliver's got a surprise."

Oliver Trenton was Marcus' . . . Gwendolyn wasn't sure what to call him.

Paramour? Lover? Suitor? Beau?

Whatever the word, he was a sweet fellow who made Marcus happy.

Oliver pulled a brushed-silver hip flask from inside his jacket, unscrewed the top, and handed it to her, saying,

"I call it the Gwentini! Champagne, gin, and lemon juice, which we'll serve in a martini glass. Ice optional."

It was bubbly and lemony, and packed a wallop.

"By about nine o'clock, the glass will be optional, too." Kathryn tilted her head toward Gwendolyn's doorway. "I'm dying to see what you've done with the place."

Gwendolyn ushered her friends through the back room and into the salon.

She'd had the walls painted in mottled crème. The trim was dark turquoise to match the chintz curtains that softened the room's hard edges, and the carpet was deep plum.

The counter was on the right, a full-length tri-fold mirror on the left.

Overhead, the pale lavender glass light fixtures had a hint of pink—Gwendolyn's years at Bullocks Wilshire had taught her plenty about the importance of great lighting.

"Oh, Gwennie!" Kathryn pressed her hands together. "It's perfect! And the sign? Can we see it?"

"Not until the unveiling. Didn't you notice when you drove in? Tangerine to match my scarf—OH!"

Gwendolyn's hand shot to her neck.

"My lucky scarf! Where is it?"

Ordinarily, she wasn't inclined to superstition, but she'd lent that scarf to Edith Head on the day Howard Hughes flew his *Spruce Goose*, and when Edith returned it to her at the Garden of Allah, she saw Gwendolyn's portrait and told her it was worth a small fortune. Gwendolyn had been wearing that scarf when she learned what the painting fetched at auction, and was wearing it the day she found this store.

Marcus had his lucky purple tie and Gwendolyn had her lucky tangerine scarf. She knew it was ridiculous, but the thought of opening without it sent her into a panic.

"We'll help you look," Oliver said.

"People will be arriving soon. I need you to set up the bar." Gwendolyn pointed to the counter and let the boys start preparing for a crowd whose thirst would be as deep as Sunset Boulevard was long.

"Where did you last see it?" Kathryn asked.

Gwendolyn dismissed the question with a wave. "Never mind. I'm being silly."

"Nonsense. Surely we don't need a whole hour to find a scarf."

Gwendolyn followed Kathryn into the spacious back room that could easily accommodate the dressmakers she'd need to hire if her couture services took off the way she hoped. They searched for the scarf among dress forms, boxes of notions, bolts of material, and the worktable, to no avail. The fleck of doubt she'd felt on the roof caught in her throat again, but Kathryn grabbed her hands.

"Gwennie?" Kathryn fixed her with the penetrating look she usually saved for *Hollywood Reporter* interviews with recalcitrant movie stars. "I want to tell you how proud I am of you before things get crazy."

Gwendolyn blinked away unexpected tears. "You mean 'drunk'?"

"You came to LA with nothing but moxie and talent—"

"My *acting* talent?"

They giggled.

"Your lack of acting talent made room for your real one." Kathryn squeezed her hands. "And now you're about to open your own store! On the Sunset Strip! And it's gorgeous! I couldn't be more thrilled for you."

Marcus appeared in the doorway, waving the silk scarf. "We found this under your counter."

"Thank you!" Gwendolyn plucked it out of his hands and wound it around her neck, draping the ends on either side of her right shoulder. "So these Gwentinis you mentioned, when do I get to taste one?"

* * *

Gwendolyn and Kathryn, Marcus and Oliver had scarcely finished their first cocktail when Gwendolyn's neighbor burst through the door. Bertie Kreuger was not the type to doll herself up, so Gwendolyn was touched to see she'd put some effort into taming her unruly hair with a dozen pins clustered around the back of her head. She'd even squeezed into a pair of patent leather mules. Gwendolyn knew what a sacrifice this was for someone who spent the day on her feet.

Marcus' sister, Doris, trailed behind Bertie and held the door for Albert Hackett and Frances Goodrich, who were back in town to pen a remake of Ernst Lubitch's *The Shop Around the Corner* for MGM. Gwendolyn had missed chatting with Frances and Albert around the Garden, and she was pleased to see them.

More people showed up: neighbors and their boyfriends, her boss from Bullocks, even Chuck the bartender from her long-gone days as the Cocoanut Grove's cigarette girl. Before she knew it, her store was crowded with smiling faces and fizzy laughter, but the special guest she was hoping for failed to show.

Kathryn nudged her. "Expecting someone else?"

"Huh?"

"You keep looking at the door."

"No, no," Gwendolyn said. "I was just hoping—never mind." She clapped her hands several times. "Outside! Outside!" She herded everyone toward the sidewalk and arranged them in a semicircle around the front door.

"Wait! I don't want to miss this bit!"

Dorothy Parker was tottering up Sunset from the direction of the Chateau Marmont, waving a white lace handkerchief. She was back in Hollywood to adapt Oscar Wilde's *Lady Windemere's Fan* for Twentieth Century-Fox. Gwendolyn thought Dottie was brave to take on Wilde, but if anybody could pull it off, Dottie could.

Oliver slipped a Gwentini into Dottie's hand as Gwendolyn cast around one more time. The face she wanted most to see was still absent.

"Welcome, everybody! This is a big day for me—" an outburst of cheering forced her to pause "—and whether this store of mine is a resounding success or an embarrassing flopperoo, I want to say that your being here means the world to me."

To raucous applause, she yanked on the green ribbon she'd sewn to the tangerine cotton covering her sign. Cecil B. DeMille himself couldn't have orchestrated a more picturesque puff of wind to billow beneath the curtain and send it fluttering to the sidewalk.

CHEZ GWENDOLYN
Modiste & Couturier
Fashion for All Occasions

The sight of it left Gwendolyn dizzy with joy.

The evening flew by in a rush of roaring laughter, air kisses, and increasingly slurry toasts. A wooly haze of contentment blurred Gwendolyn's edges until Marcus gripped her elbow and directed his eyes toward the front of the store. The trim figure in a suit of midnight blue was barely over five feet tall, yet seemed to fill the doorway like a bulldozer.

Marcus slid two fresh Gwentinis into her hands and she elbowed her way through the crowd toward one of Hollywood's leading costume designers.

Gwendolyn didn't *need* the approval of Edith Head, or her blessing, but it sure went a long way toward dissolving Gwendolyn's qualms about blowing all her dough on a pipe dream.

Gwendolyn and Edith pressed cheeks.

"My dear!" Edith murmured into her cocktail, "I'm so frightfully impressed."

"Thank you. I'm glad you could make it."

"Sorry to be so late. I got caught up with William Travilla over at Warners. They've got him designing ballet costumes for an Errol Flynn-Ida Lupino picture." Edith read Gwendolyn's thoughts. "I know! So incongruous! He was having trouble with the designs and sent me an SOS this afternoon. That's when we heard about Leilah."

"What about Leilah?"

The chatter around them broke off and everyone turned to look at Edith. Leilah O'Roarke was the wife of the head of security at Warners, but more importantly, she ran a trio of swanky brothels up in the Hollywood Hills.

Edith knocked back the rest of her Gwentini. "She's been arrested! For pandering!"

The crowd gasped. Marcus' sister piped up. "What's pandering?"

"It's the legal term police use when they arrest hookers and the like."

"So it's finally caught up with her?" someone said wistfully.

"Big deal," somebody else put in. "With her husband's connections at the LAPD, she'll be out before we start staggering home tonight."

"I wouldn't be so sure," Edith replied. "She was arrested at dawn and she's still behind bars. Everyone at Warners is speculating that they must really have the goods on her."

Kathryn eyed Gwendolyn. "Maybe pandering is just a cover."

What most people didn't know, Edith Head included, was that Leilah O'Roarke and her husband were behind a shady land grab around the newly minted mobster-ruled playground, Las Vegas. Gwendolyn's ex-boyfriend had discovered the scheme and become so frightened that he ran away to Mexico. Which was all very well for Linc, but not so reassuring for everyone who had done business with Leilah, legitimate and otherwise.

"So what do you think?" Gwendolyn asked.

Edith blinked knowingly. "I think that anyone with even so much as a passing acquaintance with that noxious hellcat needs to watch out. If she goes down, you can be sure she'll take as many chumps as she can with her."

CHAPTER 2

Kathryn thanked the guard at the Warner Bros. gate and broke into a run. She detested being late — particularly to a summoning at Warners while rumors were circulating about the wife of their security chief. Imagining what Betty Bacall had discovered and how much of it she would share had whipped Kathryn into a lather. This could be the scoop of the year.

It had been two months since Leilah O'Roarke's arrest. She was still in jail, which fueled a rampage of speculation about how high her bail must have been.

When Soundstage Sixteen came into view, Kathryn slowed down, smoothed her hair, and steadied her breath, then walked onto the set of *Key Largo*.

The interior had been dressed as the foyer of a typical Floridian hotel: tall windows with weathered shutters, scuffed furniture arranged haphazardly, and potted ferns wilting on wooden stands. A crew member was scattering the white tiled floor with dead leaves.

"Kathryn!"

Bacall strode toward her wearing a simple white blouse that was open at the neck, its cuffs folded to the elbows. Her hair was pinned back effortlessly. "Thank you for coming."

"You sounded so cryptic."

Bacall led her to a quiet nook behind some balsa-wood palm trees. "We only have a short time between setups. I'm worried about Bogie. He's taking all kinds of heat for his involvement with the Committee for the First Amendment."

The committee had formed to counter attacks on the freedom of speech by the recent HUAC hearings. Unfortunately, Bogie's committee discovered too late that they were defending a bunch of men who turned out to be real-life Communists. Over the past few weeks, a whisper campaign had evolved into a full-throated crusade to brand Bogie a Commie as punishment for standing up to Washington showboating.

Betty said, "It's gotten so bad that if he doesn't counteract it, this whole ludicrous idea might actually take hold."

A lump of disappointment sank through Kathryn's chest. *So this wasn't about Leilah's arrests after all?*

"Bogie really needs your help!" Betty started to dab at her eyes with a handkerchief. If she wasn't careful, she'd need to go back into makeup.

Kathryn felt a prod of guilt for having been so single-minded about the O'Roarkes. *Try thinking like a human being once in a while.* She pulled off her gloves in the suddenly stifling heat of the key lights. "Of course! What did you have in mind?"

"I thought you could help him write a retraction? Some sort of public declaration, maybe?"

"Oh, gosh, I don't know—"

"But you're so good with words. Bogie's not bad himself, but he's paralyzed with fear, and doesn't know who he can count on. He trusts you, though."

But what if I shell out the wrong advice?

Betty steered her toward a mobile trailer in a corner of the soundstage. "You're usually the shrewdest woman in the room, and probably the most savvy person we know when it comes to the media." She rapped on the trailer.

Kathryn opened the door and climbed inside. Bogie was seated at his mirror in a white shirt similar to his wife's. He looked at Kathryn's reflection in the mirror with guarded detachment. "I knew she was up to something." He lit a cigarette. "Been recruited, have we?"

She dropped her handbag onto a counter strewn with makeup and leaned a hip against it. "Not unwillingly."

Bogie faced himself in the mirror squarely, but his voice trembled. "I'm in trouble, Massey."

"Not if you play it smart."

"A guy tries to live by his conscience, stand up for what he believes in, and it comes back to kick him in the teeth. That ain't the America I believe in, and it ain't the sort of America I want my kids to grow up in."

She dropped into a chair. "You want kids?" Bogie was nearing fifty; Kathryn wondered if he was leaving his daddy run a bit late.

"Of course."

"Then you better start practicing."

Humor glistened his eyes. "We're getting in plenty o' that."

"Now is not the time to shove your head in the sand."

He killed his cigarette. "I only have one chance to get it right."

They sat in silence until Kathryn spied the January 1948 *Photoplay* lying on the makeup counter. It featured the headline THE BIGGEST MISTAKE OF MY LIFE – JUNE HAVER TALKS TO LOUELLA O. PARSONS.

"Fortune favors the bold." She jiggled the magazine in his face. "But not like this."

Bogie cocked an eyebrow. "Maybe an interview. With you. In the *Hollywood Reporter*? We could work out a bunch of questions and answers that tell my side of things –" He broke off when Kathryn shook her head.

"My boss has seen to it that everybody over the age of consent knows his views on the Red Scare. You want to distance yourself from anything like that." She fanned herself with the magazine. "This is the right venue, but not an interview. It needs to be a straight piece."

"An editorial?"

"With a big, brash headline."

"For example?"

She raised her arms, Aimee-Semple-McPherson style. "I'M NO COMMUNIST." She started pacing Bogie's trailer. "Explain your position, but no complaints, no apologies, no excuses. You're about as pro-Commie as J. Edgar Hoover, so say that. But don't politicize it by talking Democrats versus Republicans; talk instead how this is about American-style democracy. You were exercising your constitutional right to voice your opinion. Okay, so in hindsight, you didn't go about it in the wisest way."

"I thought you said no apologies."

"America loves a humble hero."

A bell rang out. Bogie stood up and straightened his shirt. "Will you write it for me?"

An assistant director rapped on the door. "Ready for you in five, Mister Bogart."

"It has to sound like you." *The last thing you need is for word to leak out that I ghostwrote your public apology.* He shot her a hangdog look. "I can't write your words for you, but I can help shape them. How about you work up a draft and send it to me?"

"I'd hug you, but I'd get makeup all over your blouse."

"I'll take my hug later." She threw open the door. "For now, go be Bogie."

Kathryn followed him to the edge of the set, where John Huston was taking Eddie Robinson through the scene. Betty sidled up to her, murmuring, "You did good."

"How can you tell?"

"I know every walk in his book." She nudged Kathryn's shoulder with her own. "Whatever you said, thank you."

"You might want to hold off thanking me till we see what happens."

"There's something else."

Kathryn's heart gave a little start. "About Leilah O'Roarke?"

"No. Why? What have you heard?"

"Nothing that you guys probably haven't already."

"It's about Max Factor. I was at a meeting there last week to sign a deal shilling summer lipsticks."

"Congrats."

"Thanks. So when I was there, I overheard the execs talking about how Max Factor is going to start selling Pan-Stik to the public. It's their first big new product in a while, so they've got a lot riding on it. They want to launch it by sponsoring a radio show."

"But we already have a sponsor." For the past few years, Kathryn had been the Hollywood gossip columnist on *Kraft Music Hall.*

John Huston turned to them and raised his hand. "Miss Bacall?"

"They want to sponsor a brand-new show. And for that, they'll need a host . . . or hostess."

As Bacall headed onto the set and took her position between Bogie and Claire Trevor, Kathryn backed toward the perimeter.

Kraft Music Hall had burned through a succession of MCs since the war ended: Edward Everett Horton, Eddie Foy, Frank Morgan, and, more recently, Al Jolson. Kathryn took pride in being the show's sole constant, but how much more life did it have left?

The assistant director yelled, "Quiet, please. This is a take." One by one, the lights came on until the set was blinding.

The Kathryn Massey Show, sponsored by Max Factor.

She liked the way it sounded . . . but the last time she grabbed for the brass ring, she was recruited by the FBI.

"And . . . action."

The camera closed in on Bogie sitting against a banister with Bacall slumped over a step next to him. The camera closed in on her head as Bogie reached over and gently patted her hair, reassuring her that he was still there. Kathryn melted into the shadows until she felt the wall at her back.

Who'll be there for me if things go wrong?

CHAPTER 3

The perfume dealer standing in front of Gwendolyn smelled of carbolic acid, like he'd spent the last hour scrubbing floors at LA County Hospital. His face was the color of raw donuts and she couldn't bear to look at it any longer.

She shifted her gaze to the bottles he'd lined up along her counter.

They were eye-catching: some red glass, some green. One had the silhouette of a swan etched into the front, and another featured a sepia shot of the Eiffel Tower with the sun setting behind it. The trouble was, out of ten perfumes, Gwendolyn only liked two, and they came in the plainest bottles.

"Mister Logan, I don't—"

"I haven't yet mentioned the best part!"

Back in her Bullocks days, all she'd had to do was sell perfume to the wives and mistresses of Hollywood's studio execs. She'd never given a thought to the patronizing sales tactics the buyers endured at the hands of half-wits like this lummox.

"Our sales incentive guarantees you one free bottle of perfume for every hundred you sell. That's pure profit!"

It's just li'l ol' me here, buster. How many do you expect me to move?

In the two months since Gwendolyn had opened her store, she'd done fairly well with a steady stream of customers. They were mainly lookie-loos checking out the new girl on the block, but that was okay. She wanted women to think of Chez Gwendolyn as a place to seek out unusual and distinctive outfits not carried by the larger stores. But she couldn't imagine selling a hundred bottles in a whole year, and she was about to tell him as much when the little silver bell above her front door jingled.

She was surprised—shocked, even—to see an older gent she hadn't encountered for quite some time.

Gwendolyn had spent much of the war dating Lincoln Tattler, the charming but reluctant scion of an upscale haberdasher, Tattler's Tuxedos. The war years had been rough on both father and son. By the time the Allies dropped the bomb on Hiroshima, Linc had absconded to Mexico and his father had been forced into bankruptcy.

Horton Tattler's hair had turned white-gray, his bristling handlebar moustache was gone altogether, and his clothes hung from him as though he'd borrowed them from someone fifty pounds heavier. He carried a cardboard box in his hands. It was alarming to see him so careworn.

"This *is* a surprise! And such a delight!"

"Good afternoon, Logan," Horton said, his voice thick with irritation.

"You know each other?"

"Hello, Tattler. You're looking . . . " Logan cast a supercilious eye over Horton's mismatched suit and didn't bother to finish his sentence.

Horton turned to Gwendolyn. "Is he trying to force his wares on you?" She rolled her eyes. "Did he mention they're so cheaply made that they evaporate within an hour?" He deposited his box at one end of Gwendolyn's counter. "Let me guess: you only like the one in the red bottle and the one with the zebra stripes."

"How did you know?" Gwendolyn asked.

"They're the only two worth a good goddamn. He's forcing you to buy all ten just to get the two good ones because Percival Perfumes has a huge warehouse of this junk out in San Bernardino they've been trying to unload since before Roosevelt was elected. Still at it, I see."

"I could say the same of you," Logan started returning the sample bottles to his presentation case "but we all know how well you've been faring." He closed the case with a snap and sauntered out the door without another word.

As soon as the door jingled shut, Gwendolyn hugged Horton again. "You're a lifesaver!"

Horton watched the stink peddler pull into the lunchtime traffic. "The last time I saw that cretin, I threw him out by the seat of his pants." He cast around the store. "I suspected you had terrifically good taste, and this proves it. Lovely. Just lovely."

Gwendolyn wasn't sure why the approval of this funny little man mattered to her so much, but she misted over at his praise.

The smile fell from Horton's lined face. "I've come to share some unhappy news, my dear."

She stiffened. "Linc?"

"Yes. He . . . he passed away last month."

Gwendolyn pressed her hand on the glass counter and looked hard at the calendar on the wall for a long moment before she could speak. She wanted to remember the date on the slip of tear-away paper at the bottom: April 24, 1948. She cleared the sob from her throat. "What happened?"

"He took a trip down the Amazon. Caught malaria." Horton reached out to touch her forearm. "Took him down hard and fast."

"He was so happy, so relaxed the last time I saw him."

"And that's the way you should remember him." Horton tapped the cardboard box. "His effects arrived from Mazatlán the other day. This box is for you."

Linc had written her name across the top in blue grease pencil. Through a fog of disbelief, she ran her finger along the adhesive tape.

"This was in a larger box he'd marked *In the event of my death*," Horton said. "He must have known the dangers of that part of the world, although why he'd want to put his life at risk is beyond me."

"Your son wasn't afraid of life."

Horton let out a quiet moan.

"Mine hasn't turned out remotely like I expected. I'd hoped Linc's might, but that hasn't proved to be the case, either." He took her hand and squeezed it. "Your store is wonderful, and I hope your life is, too, my dear."

After he left, the salon felt still as a crypt. She turned on the radio, but Nat King Cole's "Nature Boy" came on, mournfully bleak. She shut it off and reached for a box cutter.

On the top of the pile inside the box was a menu from the Tick Tock Tea Room on Cahuenga Avenue; the words *GWENDOLYN WAS HERE* were stamped on it in red.

When Gwendolyn moved to Hollywood, she'd conceived a stealthy campaign to get Hollywood talking about her. She had a custom stamp made, and carried it around marking menus, coasters, and cocktail napkins in every venue she visited. It was an outrageous stunt, but new girls in town needed to get noticed.

Things didn't work out the way she'd hoped, but when she told Linc about it years later, he laughed so hard he nearly ran his car off the road into a Richfield gas station. As he wiped the tears from his eyes, he declared he was on a mission to find one of her GWENDOLYN WAS HERE mementos. He never mentioned it again, and she'd assumed he abandoned the search, but it seemed he'd never given up on her.

She couldn't bear to pick it up. She couldn't even bear to look at it. She slapped the top down and picked up the box. It was heavier than she'd expected. Grabbing the keys from her drawer, she ran to the front door and pressed the *CLOSED* sign to the glass, and only just made it to the back room before the tears burst from her.

CHAPTER 4

Marcus Adler placed three maps on his dining table.
The largest one showed Britain and all of Europe;
another stretched from Greece to India; the last showed
the Simplon-Orient-Express railway from Paris to
Istanbul. He laid them out side by side, stood back,
then shuffled them around until it looked as though
he'd casually tossed them there.
Marcus had a plan, for which he needed a campaign,
for which he needed music and vodka.

He'd found an album called *Twenty Most Popular
Russian Gypsy Tunes* at Wallichs Music City on Vine
Street. Seconds later, an accordion-and-guitar duet
called "Korobushka" filled the villa.

Marcus was more of a bourbon guy, but this
situation called for Russian vodka. He pulled a bottle
from the freezer and set it on the counter next to a pair
of violet-blue shot glasses he'd pinched from Café Gala
on the Sunset Strip near Gwendolyn's store.

Now all he had to do was wait.

Seven months had passed since his appearance
before the House Un-American Activities Committee
led to his departure from MGM. He'd expected to feel
bitter over the way the studio system treated him, but
he didn't.

Over his twenty years at the studio, he'd watched stars lavish obscene paychecks on sprawling homes, fancy cars, expensive dinners, furs, jewelry, and servants, assuming the tide would keep coming in. Marcus promised himself he'd never make that mistake. As head of the writing department, he could have afforded a Beverly Hills mortgage and a Duesenberg in the garage, but he stayed at the Garden of Allah and socked his money away for that inevitable rainy day.

And now, if he woke shockingly hungover, he simply stayed in bed until he wasn't.

He had time to scour the newspapers from cover to cover, catch up on his reading, drive down Sunset and swim in the Pacific, and sample every new restaurant and bar.

Marcus ogled the bottle of vodka with the unpronounceable name and wondered if he should take a nip to calm his nerves.

He'd rehearsed his speech while shaving that morning, then again over his fried eggs, a few more times as he swam his fifty laps in the pool, and twice more as he staged his living room like a movie set.

His clock showed nearly six thirty; Oliver would be home soon.

Marcus shifted the bottle and shot glasses to the table and set them beside the maps. He added a brass ashtray but it made the table look cluttered, so he took it off again just as Oliver turned the key in the door.

"Why are you playing a gypsy death march?" Oliver asked.

Marcus slid the ashtray back onto the table. Suddenly the music struck him as shrill and grating. He swapped the death march for Jo Stafford. She was sixteen bars into "In the Still of the Night" when Oliver emerged from the bedroom.

"You've got your guilty face on."

Marcus pushed his glasses back up his nose. "This isn't my guilty face."

"What is it, then? Because it sure is something." Oliver's eyes drifted to the vodka and shot glasses. "Are we celebrating? Did you get a job?"

Marcus opened the vodka and filled the glasses. "I have a proposition." He handed Oliver a drink.

Oliver's frown melted into a hesitant smile. "Even though we're technically no longer mortal enemies, I can't move in with you."

From the moment they met, they'd been stuck on opposite sides of Hollywood's philosophical trenches. It was Marcus' job to produce a screenplay free of any dialogue, action, or character motivation deemed less than wholesome. It was Oliver's to enforce the stiff-necked commandments of the Breen Office. Studio writers and Breen Office censors who got personal risked excommunication—except at the Garden of Allah, where no one pointed fingers.

Marcus refilled their glasses. "I've been thinking about next month."

"Any particular date?"

"June thirteenth, as a matter of fact." Marcus downed his second shot. It was smoother than he expected. He felt it warm his stomach and fill his chest with nerve. "It's going to be five years."

Oliver considered the table display. "Anniversaries are worth celebrating."

Marcus picked up the map of Western Europe. "This is going to sound a bit crazy, but promise you'll listen all the way through."

"I'm agog with curiosity."

"Okay . . ." The word came out breathless. "Remember when I was in front of the HUAC, and I learned that my father's family came from a place called Adler?"

Oliver looked up with the skeptical eye Marcus feared most. *Don't let him interrupt until you've spelled it all out.* He unfurled the second map.

"Adler is on the eastern end of the Black Sea. That's only a day's drive from Yalta, where Nazimova was born." He pointed to a spot just north of the Georgia border. "Right there. I've researched everything."

"You have, huh?"

"We could take the train to New York, the *Britannic* to Paris. After a few days there—or a week, if you like—we can board the Orient Express." He unfolded the brochure and ran his finger down the Simplon-Orient-Express line. "It'll take us through Milan, Venice, Belgrade, Sofia, and finally Istanbul."

"Turkey?!"

Just keep going. "From Istanbul, we'd take a train to Ankara and farther west to Tbilisi. That's in Georgia. And from there we can hire a driver to take us to this place, on the coast." He drew a line with his finger to a dot labeled Gagra. "Adler is only twenty-five miles away, and we'll have a car and driver, so he can take us there—"

"To Adler?"

"Uh-huh."

"But honey, Adler is in *Russia*."

"Barely inside the border. We'll go for the day. That's probably all we—"

"Jesus Christ! Are you even listening to yourself?" Marcus opened his mouth but Oliver cut him off. "You're talking about waltzing into Russia like it's Tijuana." Oliver backed away from the table. "Russia is now the boogieman. They're the *enemy*. We're at war with them. It might be a cold war, but it's still war. You heard Truman's pledge to Congress about containing the Soviet threat to Greece and Turkey. And now you want us to *go* there? Have you gone soft in the head?"

Marcus saw now that he should have started by explaining how learning of his Russian heritage had affected him. Not at first, in the glare of the HUAC hearings and the subsequent showdown with his father. But the past six months had given him time to think about who he was, what he wanted, where he was going, and where he came from. Was his name even Adler? The immigration officer at Ellis Island probably saw some long Russian name, like the one on the vodka bottle, and said, "From now on, your name is 'Adler.'"

"I feel a hankering." He knew how woeful he sounded. "More like a pull—a strong pull toward—"

"Toward what? Career suicide? Because that's what'll happen if anyone finds out you've been there."

"What does it matter anymore? In front of the HUAC and the entire press corps, I was accused of being a Commie largely because I posed for a photograph with Charlie Chaplin and went to a cocktail party on a Soviet battleship."

Oliver moved closer. Not near enough to touch, but it wouldn't take a lot to close the gap.

"You're not a member of the Hollywood Ten or even the Unfriendly Nineteen," Oliver pointed out. "You walking out on the HUAC was hot news for a day or two, but then Dalton Trumbo and Ring Lardner got up and said what they said, and everybody forgot about you. That's a *good* thing," he added softly. "You survived, so why risk it?"

Marcus refused to let his dream wither on the vine. He picked up the map of Eastern Europe. "Nobody will know. I spoke to someone whose family lives in Sochi. That's the next town along the coast from Adler. He said half the time the border guards don't even turn up for work, and when they do they're too busy swilling homemade hooch to check for ID. Adler's just a couple of miles inside the Georgian border. We could even walk there if the driver doesn't want to take us all the way."

"I'll go with you to Paris, and I'll even take the Orient Express with you as far as Venice. That'd be a wonderful way to celebrate our anniversary. But Turkey? *Russia?* I'm not going any farther east than Italy. And neither are you."

"I'm over twenty-one and free to do as I please," Marcus threw back.

Anger flared in Oliver's face, but subsided quickly. He laid a placating hand on Marcus' shoulder. "Lookit, if you're feeling a pull toward Russia — and I can see why you would — then go read all the Dostoevsky and Turgenev you can lay your hands on. But please, honey, no more talk of actually *going* there. It's the most ludicrous idea I've ever heard — especially in this political climate. Promise me you'll forget the whole thing."

For the first couple of months after leaving MGM, Marcus had felt liberated from the fetters of office politics and outmoded Hays Code regulations. But as winter gave way to spring in 1948, he began to feel as though he were drifting rudderless through the balmy Angeleno days, each one indistinguishable from its predecessor.

Oliver's advice was sound, but Marcus had already plowed through *War and Peace, Anna Karenina, Crime and Punishment,* and *The Brothers Karamazov,* and had a couple of Gorkys stashed in his nightstand. He'd started reading them to feel closer to Alla Nazimova, whom he was missing more and more without an arduous job to distract him. Steeping himself in her history alleviated his heartache but made him yearn to see the place for himself.

"It hasn't been easy trying to figure out what I should do next," he admitted.

"You think the answer's in Russia?"

Marcus pushed Oliver's condescending tone aside in the name of household peace and picked up the vodka. "This stuff is pretty smooth, huh? Another shot?"

He could feel the heat of Oliver's stare as he refilled their glasses, but couldn't bring himself to look him in the eye. He tipped the booze down his throat and walked into the kitchen to start dinner.

CHAPTER 5

The silver lamé evening gown was a god-damned, god-awful, god-forsaken son of a bitch.

Gwendolyn had never sewn with lamé before but she knew of its beast-from-hell reputation, which is why she'd charged double her usual rate. The material was hostile. It gathered where it shouldn't have gathered, resisted where it had no business resisting, and pinched in the places Gwendolyn least expected.

She'd been working on this fiend since two o'clock, and it was now eight fifteen. Was it any wonder her fingertips ached?

She flicked on the radio and thought about her store as she spooned coffee into her percolator. In the four months Chez Gwendolyn had been open, she'd made enough money to cover expenses, with some left over for emergencies. But once the friends, neighbors, and lookie-loos had visited, traffic slowly subsided.

Had it not been for the Licketysplitters, Gwendolyn would have started to worry. Thank heavens for them and their extravagant tastes.

The night Gwendolyn discovered that her boss at Bullocks was a cross-dresser, she offered to make him an ensemble far more flattering than the one he'd cobbled together.

It had been such a hit at a cross-dresser bar called the Midnight Frolics, that the regulars — who'd nicknamed the bar "The Licks" and themselves "Licketysplitters" — started lining up, money in hand, desperate for her to make their fantasy costumes. Better yet, most of them didn't care how much they had to fork over.

Now the Licketysplitters' commissions were keeping her afloat, and she knew this was not a sustainable situation. She was brooding over whether she'd been rash with the perfume guy when a rap sounded at the front door.

She peeked out from behind the black velvet curtain strung across the doorway into the back workroom to see a girl in a knitted navy blue top and woolen skirt standing on the sidewalk. When she glimpsed Gwendolyn's face, she waved and knocked again, and gestured for her to come forward.

Gwendolyn wished she'd turned out the lights. She still had hours of work to do on that lamé shambles. She turned off the gas under her coffee and made her way through the store. "WE CLOSE AT SEVEN!"

The girl's dark blonde hair came down into a widow's peak above one of those symmetrical faces that beauticians claimed was necessary for stardom. She pressed her hands together as though in prayer. "Please!" she called through the glass. "I've been trying to get here for weeks. I desperately need some new clothes. Orry-Kelly recommended you."

Orry-Kelly was a costume designer on par with Edith Head. Gwendolyn relented.

The girl stepped inside, radiating Chanel No. 5. "Thank you!"

She's got a definite spark about her. Deep blue eyes, a wide smile, and a full bust. "You know Orry-Kelly?"

The girl scanned the store. "I was at a party with Mister Schenck and we struck up a conversation. He mentioned your store several times."

Joseph Schenck was one of the big cheeses over at Twentieth Century-Fox. If this girl had caught—and held—the attention of one of the most powerful people in Hollywood, she was probably nobody's fool.

"You're under contract at Fox?" Gwendolyn asked.

"Was. But Columbia picked me up in March. I wouldn't let myself believe that it was going to last, but I just wrapped a picture called *Ladies of the Chorus*. The casting feller told me what a bang-up job I did. I figure they plan on keeping me, so I can afford to splurge."

Gwendolyn took a step back. The girl sure knew how to show off her hourglass. "35-22-35?"

The blue eyes popped open. "You're good!"

"Those are my measurements, too." She waved her hand across the store. "Formal? Casual? Daytime?"

"All of the above!" The blonde giggled like Shirley Temple playing a taxi dancer. She swayed her behind as she gravitated toward the cocktail dresses.

Schenck must have given this kewpie doll a wad of cash and told her to go buy herself a new wardrobe. The monster in the back would have to wait.

The first piece the girl headed to was one of Gwendolyn's Christian Dior New Look knockoffs—a tight skirt in black heavy silk faille reaching below the knee, cinched waist, deep neckline, but with extra detailing Gwendolyn had thrown in for good measure.

"Do you have this in white?"

"No, but I could. It'd take me about a week."

The girl ran her finger along the embroidery. "You made this?"

"I did."

"Could you make one to match my lipstick?" She turned back toward Gwendolyn and pouted her full lips.

Gwendolyn leaned in. *Your skin, it simply glows. If they can capture that on film, you could really go places.* "Elizabeth Arden, right?"

"Crimson Lilac. It's absolutely my new favorite. You can do *that* dress in *this* shade?"

"Certainly."

"I'll take it."

She didn't even ask the price. "Don't you want to try it on first?"

"35-22-35." She started to roam the store. "What have you got in the way of casual Palm Springs weekend—OH!" Gwendolyn had left the black velvet curtain open. The girl pointed to the mound of silver lamé. "What is *that*?!"

Gwendolyn didn't know how to explain she was making a floor-length cocktail dress for a five-foot-eleven dentist from Pacoima. "An expensive experiment."

The blonde beelined for the workbench. "I hear lamé is the devil to work with."

Gwendolyn sighed. "It's slippery as all get-out and tends to fray unless you baste it with these long stitches to hold the seams. And that's just for starters."

"Oh, but when it's done." She stroked the sparkling fabric. "Remember how Jean Harlow used to look in this?"

The dentist from Pacoima had said the same thing. "She's my inspiration."

"I adored her!" The budding bombshell with the va-va-voom curves turned all baby-doll soft. "I was only eleven when she passed away. I cried and cried."

"I went to her funeral," Gwendolyn said.

"No!"

"I didn't get inside, of course. I was just one of those people in the crowd. But I couldn't not be there."

The women fell silent for a moment, and the store was quiet except for the sound of the radio.

"Would you make me one of these?" the blonde asked.

"I'd need some time," Gwendolyn replied. "And they don't come cheap."

"Would a hundred-dollar down payment be enough?"

That was more than the dentist was paying. "What did you have in mind?"

"Remember those dresses Jean used to wear with the scooped necklines, all loosey-goosey folds at the front? Like that." She clapped her hands. "Now, casual weekend wear?"

Before Gwendolyn could point her customer toward the other side of the store, the silver bell above the front door tinkled and Kathryn marched in. "I can't believe you're still open! Isn't Winchell about to start? And look who I found wandering the streets!" She hopped to one side to reveal Marcus' sister.

"I was not wandering!" Doris insisted. "I was visiting Bertie at Wil Wright's. I can't get enough of their chocolate burnt-almond ice cr—" She spotted Gwendolyn's customer.

The blonde stepped toward Kathryn. "Your column is the first thing I turn to every morning."

Kathryn shot Gwendolyn a look: *Who the heck?*

"This lucky lady has signed with Columbia," Gwendolyn said, "and felt it was time for a new wardrobe."

"Speaking of Columbia," Kathryn yanked off her gloves in a rough way that told Gwendolyn she was more than a little tanked, "I've just come from this big bash at Columbia Records. Not the same Columbia, I know, but anyway. They've come up with a new type of record. They're calling it an LP; stands for Long Playing. Means each side can last for up to twenty minutes. Or some such. Most of us weren't paying attention; we were busy speculating about what Howard Hughes is going to do now that he owns RKO." She let out a long sigh and announced, "I'm desperate for coffee."

"I was just about to make some," Gwendolyn said. *But now I've got a customer who's on the verge of spending hundreds of dollars. I can't ignore her.*

"I would love some coffee," the girl cooed. "I haven't eaten all day."

Gwendolyn led everyone into the back room and relit the stove. Doris pulled out a paper bag of Wil Wright macaroons and arranged them on a clean plate by the sink

She was pouring the coffee as the clock hit nine and Kathryn turned up the volume on Gwendolyn's new Sentinel radio.

A second or two later, Walter Winchell's staccato voice came barking through the speaker. Gwendolyn didn't particularly enjoy his harsh faultfinding and snide blind items, but he always had his finger on the pulse of America.

"Good evening, Mister and Missus America, from border to border and coast to coast and all the ships at sea. Let's go to press. Notorious Hollywood madam Leilah O'Roarke is still languishing in jail. But in a telephone conversation I had with her only hours ago, she admitted to me that she plans on turning state's evidence against alleged mobster Mickey Cohen."

Kathryn sat up straight. "Holy moly!"

"When I asked Mrs. O'Roarke what sort of bargaining chip she possessed, she told me—and I hope you're hanging onto your chapeaux, ladies and gents—of a box of filing cards on which each and every one of her clients is listed, along with all their personal preferences and particular peccadillos."

"Leilah and her client files are the talk of the Columbia lot," the blonde said. "Most people don't believe it exists, but if it does, there's probably a card on Mister Cohen."

"But if there really is a box like that," Kathryn said, "it probably includes most of the menfolk residing within the LA city limits." She shot Gwendolyn a sharp look.

Not only did Leilah's metal filing box exist, but it was missing because Gwendolyn's ex-boyfriend, Lincoln Tattler, had stolen it from under the O'Roarkes' noses and vamoosed south of the border.

How it ended up back in Leilah's possession was anyone's guess.

"I know a hot potato when I see one," Winchell continued, "so I asked her when she plans on producing this box of cards. She told me that the box is safely hidden away in a secure location, and all shall be revealed when the time is nigh. And so, America, here is my prediction: When the preferences and peccadillos of Hollywood's gentlemen-of-means surface, there will be much scampering into the shadows. And now I turn to Belmont Park, where the horse-racing community yesterday was—"

Gwendolyn switched off the radio.

"The prosecution must be playing hardball," Kathryn said. "It takes guts to admit she even has something like that to the most powerful journalist in the country."

"I'm not buying it." Doris bit into a macaroon. In the six months since she'd moved to Los Angeles from small-town Pennsylvania, her heels had gotten taller, her dresses tighter, her makeup more subtle, and her opinions stronger. "Leilah O'Roarke has been in remand since, what, February? That's four months. I haven't lived here too long, but even I can tell that no Beverly Hills madam will spend one single night in the slammer longer than absolutely necessary. I think she's bluffing."

"You don't think she's got this box of client cards?" the blonde asked.

"She'd have produced it first chance she got," Doris said.

"Who do you think's got it?" Gwendolyn asked.

Doris shrugged. "If she says she's going to reveal it when the time is right, don't you think it means she's got a pretty good idea where it is, and is stalling for time until she can track it down?"

Gwendolyn could read Kathryn's unblinking gaze like a large-print book: *That box on the floor next to the buttons. The one Linc's dad brought to you. The one Linc wanted you to have. The one you haven't sorted through yet. What if . . .?*

Gwendolyn finished her coffee and set the empty cup in the sink. "So," she said, turning to her new gold mine, "casual Palm Springs wear." She drew back the velvet curtain. "Shall we take a look?"

* * *

It was nearly eleven o'clock by the time the girl with the baby-doll voice and the Lili St. Cyr silhouette finished making fourteen purchases, paid with a fat roll of cash she pulled from her pocketbook, and needed help bundling everything into a cab.

Kathryn let out a long, low whistle. "Five hundred and twenty-six bucks! Is that a record?"

Gwendolyn nodded.

"Let's hope she comes back," Doris said. "Are you closing up now? Can we walk you home?"

"I wish!" Gwendolyn jutted her head toward the silver goliath still heaped on her workbench. "I'm going to have to pull an all-nighter."

"Do you have enough coffee to see you through?"

Kathryn let out a strangled gurgle. "I can't stand it a minute longer!" She dashed to the corner and picked up Horton Tattler's box.

Gwendolyn joined her at the table and pushed aside the lamé. "You don't actually believe it's in there, do you?"

"What are we talking about?" Doris asked.

Gwendolyn gestured to Kathryn: *Don't let me stop you.* As Kathryn told Doris how Gwennie's ex-boyfriend had been in possession of Leilah's client cards before he absconded to Mexico, Gwendolyn pulled each item from the box and spread them out across the workbench.

Apart from the *Gwendolyn Was Here* menu, there was a souvenir photograph of her and Linc at Mocambo in a silver frame, a few books, his wristwatch, a stack of their love notes bundled together with a white ribbon, and a few other odds and ends.

Leilah's box, however, was not there.

"I don't know if I'm disappointed or relieved," Kathryn said.

"I'm relieved," Gwendolyn announced. "Howard Hughes told me Linc went around town and told each guy that Leilah had a card on them. He told Howard that he planned on burning them when he was done."

"Leilah certainly thinks they're still here," Kathryn said.

"She might actually have them."

"In which case, God help us all."

Gwendolyn eyed the lamé. "The point is, they weren't in Linc's box, so please excuse me, girls, but I really must attack the beast."

Doris picked up Linc's books: *Grand Hotel; All This, and Heaven Too; Magnificent Obsession;* and *Anthony Adverse.* "I haven't read any of these."

"You're welcome to them."

"You're going to lock the door behind us, aren't you?" Kathryn said sternly. "They still haven't caught the Black Dahlia killer, so you never —"

"SCOOT!" Gwendolyn herded them out the back and locked the door behind them. She eyeballed the mound of fabric shimmering in the light. "I'm warning you," she told it. "I have a book of matches and I'm not afraid to use it."

CHAPTER 6

Bette Davis turned her olive green sedan onto Wilshire and headed east out of Beverly Hills. "You don't have to get an Oldsmobile," she told Kathryn. "We could just as easily go to DeSoto, or Packard, or Cadillac, but I've had this one for nearly two years and nothing ever goes wrong with it."

"I can barely tell a lemon from a limousine." Kathryn fidgeted with the zipper on her handbag until she chipped her nail polish. "Thanks so much for taking me out."

Bette pulled up at San Vicente Boulevard where Beverly Hills gave way to Los Angeles. "What gets me is how you've reached forty and have never had a car of your own. Even Louella's got one, and she can't even drive!"

"Louella has a chauffeur," Kathryn replied. "That's hardly my style."

"And she has a lovely niece who ferries her about on the chauffeur's day off."

"I don't have any spare nieces lying around."

"But what the hell have you been doing all this time?"

"Ever heard of taxis?"

Between LA's extensive streetcar network, the availability of cabs, and the readiness of her neighbors at the Garden to give her a lift, it hadn't been difficult for Kathryn to dodge the embarrassing truth that she was a Panicky Paula behind the wheel.

She knew how to drive, and she could park without scraping the curb—most of the time. But the idea of negotiating her way through LA's increasingly congested streets made her go sweaty in places a lady wasn't supposed to perspire. It was easier to call a cab.

But then last week, she attended a gathering of journalists at city hall to hear the prison sentences handed down to the Hollywood Ten, who'd been convicted of contempt of Congress after six months of appeals had failed to exonerate them.

Kathryn's boss, Billy Wilkerson, had originally instigated the blacklisting of Communists—genuine and alleged, which were the same to him—and Kathryn felt obligated to make it known that not everybody at the *Reporter* felt the same way.

When someone mentioned that two of the convicted screenwriters, Albert Maltz and director Edward Dmytryk, were only forty years old, it hit Kathryn how much they'd endured—and that she herself could scarcely work up the courage to drive across town.

"You're pathetic!" she told herself in the bathroom mirror that night, and vowed to get over her fear by her fortieth birthday.

The next day, she had an appointment to interview Bette on her plans for the coming year. Jack Warner wanted her to do a movie called *Beyond the Forest*, which Bette described as "a turgid piece of shit" and was the last thing she wanted to talk about.

To assuage Bette's discomfort, Kathryn confided her revelation, and Bette promised to take her out to buy a car.

Wilshire Oldsmobile sat behind the Wiltern Theatre, a monumental palace of Art Deco glory clad in copper-green terracotta. As it loomed on the horizon, Kathryn could feel her courage leak out of her.

Bette broke the silence. "I get it," she said quietly.

"Get what?"

"I used to be a nervous driver, too."

Kathryn couldn't imagine Bette Davis being a nervous anything. "You?"

"The week before my first lesson, I was in a car that nearly got sideswiped by some stupid old drunk. Six inches to the left and it could have been an entirely different story. Just think!" She barked out a laugh. "Norma Shearer could've won that year for *Marie Antoinette* instead of me for *Jezebel*. Let's all take a moment and think about THAT!"

Kathryn wasn't sure if Bette was indulging her with an invented story, but it did the trick. The two of them snorted with laughter.

"A few days later I informed my mother I didn't want to learn how to drive, but ol' Ruthie wouldn't hear of it. Told me I was being ludicrous, and she was quite right." The Oldsmobile sign appeared ahead of them. She patted Kathryn's knee. "A month from now you'll be wondering what all the fuss was about."

Bette pulled to the curb and they got out of the car. "Why don't you wander about and see what appeals, and leave the negotiations to me."

Kathryn surveyed the rainbow of Oldsmobiles parked along the front of the dealership and wondered where to begin.

44

Bette pointed to a two-door model in dark burgundy. "That looks nice. I'm going in to have a word with Mister Ponder. He runs things around here and I want to be sure you get the duckiest deal possible."

Kathryn headed for the coupe. Its steeply angled roof cut an impressive profile, but it was too over-the-hill-bachelor-hound. She liked its neighbor, a cream four-door sedan, but it was the type of car a suburban mom with a passel of brats might choose.

She roamed the front row without spotting one that screamed, "Choose me! Drive me! Buy me!" The sun had a kick that her little straw toque offered scant protection from. The final car was called a Series 66 Club Coupe; it was an appealing shade of what the windshield sticker described as Yale Blue.

A Max Factor ad on the other side of the street caught her eye: Lauren Bacall's celebrated pout filled half of a billboard for Max Factor's new line of lipsticks. Her cool composure dared passersby not to stare. Kathryn realized this was the one Bacall told her about that day she'd summoned Kathryn to Warner Bros.

Helping Bogie craft his mea culpa for *Photoplay* hadn't been too difficult. The version that made it to print had enough of Bogie's laconic voice to convince everyone that he regretted getting caught up in politics. In private, he told Kathryn that he didn't regret it at all; what he lamented was the way the whole nasty episode played out. But his penance achieved the desired result: the buzz for *Key Largo* intensified.

What wasn't as easy for Kathryn was deciding whether or not she ought to follow Bacall's advice and let the Powers That Be know she was open to hosting a show for Max Factor.

She couldn't shake her misgivings. Her five-minute segment on *Kraft Music Hall* took her down a path she'd did not want to revisit. What might a whole show lead to? She hoped her procrastination would let the situation resolve itself; maybe the men at Max Factor would settle on someone else. But the weeks darted by with no announcement.

"Sweetie," Bette said behind her, "it helps to look *at* the cars."

"How about this one?"

"I'm not the gal who'll be driving it."

"What did the guy say?"

Bette pursed a smug smile. "When I told him who you were, he jumped up out of his chair. But then I told him that you were a nervous shopper and that he'd only scare you away. We'll go see him when you've decided which one you want to test drive." She opened the driver door for Kathryn. "You can't know if you like it until you get behind the wheel."

Kathryn got in the driver's seat and Bette went around the other side.

"I don't even know what I'm supposed to be looking for." Kathryn ran her eyes along the dashboard. "Speedometer, odometer, radio, clutch, cigarette lighter—is it missing anything?"

Bette tsked. "Who cares about that stuff? They all put the same gizmos in different places. Think about how it makes you feel. Are you comfortable? Can you reach everything? Do you like the chrome and blue? Do you see yourself navigating Sunset in peak traffic? And more importantly, are you ever going to make that pitch to Max Factor for your own show?"

Kathryn's hand slipped off the steering wheel and landed on the horn, whose boom caused her to let out a high-pitched yip. "How do you know about that?"

"I saw you looking at that billboard, and it reminded me of a party I went to at Eddie Goulding's house. He throws the best dinner parties; you never know who's going to show up. To my surprise, Bogie was there."

"Didn't he direct you both in *Dark Victory*?"

"Eddie's a little on the louche side. Not really Humphrey's thing. At any rate, there he was, and of course Betty too. She and I haven't spent much time in each other's company so I went out of my way."

Kathryn slid her hands around the steering wheel. "What was your verdict?"

"There's no bull about that girl. I liked her a lot. At any rate, we got to talking about the pros and cons of these advertising promotional deals, and Max Factor came up. She mentioned to me how she suggested you pitch the idea of them sponsoring your own show, but then never heard anything more about it."

Kathryn let out a quiet "Mmmm."

"But it's such a fantastic opportunity!" Bette took in Kathryn's impassive face. "Isn't it?"

"It certainly is."

"Please tell me you're not waiting for them to approach you. If we sit around hoping the menfolk will give us what we want, we'll be waiting till kingdom come."

"It's just that . . ." Now that she had to admit it to the ballsiest woman in show business, Kathryn suddenly felt like a lily-livered namby-pamby. "It was my spot on *Kraft Music Hall* that led to all that thorny business with the FBI. And now my own show?"

Bette settled back in her seat. "Unintended consequences?"

"That's exactly it."

"Is this about turning forty?"

"No!"

"Don't bullshit a bullshitter."

A pair of gray-haired ladies in sensible shoes and lace-collared dresses they'd probably been wearing since the Great Depression tottered toward Wilshire. "I'm not—I'm just—"

"Listen, I turned forty a couple of months ago, and let me tell you, it was like getting slapped across the face with a cold, wet fish. I woke up that morning and thought to myself, Jesus Christ! Forty? How did *that* happen? I feel like I'm just getting going, but suddenly I'm besieged with panic. Have I made the right choices? Should I have fought harder—or maybe smarter? Why am I married to a guy I don't like? I could barely get out of bed."

"Lately I find myself questioning everything I do."

"Trust me, I get it." Bette pointed to the women across the street. "We're going to be them before we know it. Do you really want to be walking around wondering, What if I hadn't been so scared?"

Kathryn had been warned against getting chummy with a take-no-prisoners slugger like Bette Davis. "She'll turn on you," they'd said. "Once you're no longer of any use, she'll pick a fight you can't win, and then she'll cut you dead." Kathryn had kept an eye out for signs of the sunlight flashing against the guillotine blade suspended over their friendship, but she'd seen no glimmer of it.

"Maybe you're right."

"Would it help if you dropped my name?" Bette asked. "Tell Max Factor you've already lined me up as your first guest."

"Don't you need to run that by Warners?"

"It's been years since I worried what those clowns think."

"But surely I can't just call up Max Factor. 'Hey fellas, here I am. Give me a radio show.'"

"Don't be a drip. Now listen, I did a lipstick campaign for them a little while back. The photographer they used, he does all the celebrity print campaigns. Max Factor, Westmore, Elizabeth Arden, Lux—he's the top guy. Real personable, too."

"What's his name?"

"All I remember is Harly." She strummed her fingernails on the dashboard. "I can't rightly recall if that's his first name or his last."

"Can you find out?"

"Absolutely. But only if you promise me that you'll leave here today behind the wheel of your own vehicle."

"Deal."

CHAPTER 7

When the silver bell over Chez Gwendolyn's door rang, Gwendolyn knew it was Marcus before she looked up. He'd called earlier to say he would be bringing her corned beef on rye from Greenblatt's Deli. When she asked him what the occasion was, he replied, "Do I need one just to bring you lunch?"

It was almost a year since he'd last worked. Socking away all that big-bucks studio money let him drift through the languid summer of 1948, but his contrived nonchalance—"I don't care if I never go back to work!"—made her wonder if he was putting up a front.

She slid the last of a new shipment of opera gloves into her display cabinet. "I hope you remembered the pickle."

"I sweet-talked Mrs. Greenblatt into an extra one. Each!" He held up a couple of glass bottles. "And Orange Crush to wash it all down."

They spread out their corned beef sandwiches on her workbench without worrying about crêpe Georgette or Chinese silk because she was between Licketysplitter outfits.

Or, quite possibly, her Licketysplitter trade was over.

Last week she'd heard a rumor about a Filipino seamstress called Cherry who was making cross-dresser outfits at half her price. She wasn't sure if this woman really existed, but it would explain the drop-off in orders. They were her bread and butter; without them, Chez Gwendolyn might not prove feasible.

"You're looking tanned and trim these days," she noted.

"I've gone back to swimming. Every other day, I do a hundred laps in the pool."

"Without stopping?"

"I take a break after every twenty laps." He shook out a paper napkin and handed it to her. "On alternate days, I drive down Sunset to the ocean and walk all the way down to the pier and back."

"The Santa Monica Pier? But that must be—"

"Eight or nine miles, round trip. Sometimes I run all the way there."

"What's the rush?"

"It just feels good."

She sank her teeth into the buttery soft corned beef; it melted in her mouth. "What do you do the rest of your day?"

"I read the *L.A. Times* and the *New York Times* cover to cover."

"That's a lot to get through these days."

That summer, the papers were thick with the story of a spy trial at which an FBI informant submitted a secret report listing Communists and sympathizers that included John Garfield, Fredric March, and Edward G. Robinson. A California State Senate Committee started dotting lines connecting the list with some of the biggest names in Hollywood: Chaplin, Hepburn, Kelly, Peck, Sinatra, Welles.

"You must be glad to be out of all that," Gwendolyn commented.

"And how!" Marcus bit into his pickle. "I don't care if I never go back to work!"

The declaration sounded hollow to Gwendolyn's ear. "I never saw you as one of those people who went to work just to earn a buck."

"Me either."

"I've seen what you're like when you get a sure-fire idea, or finish a script that you've knocked out of the ballpark. You light up like a firefly. But since you left MGM, you don't seem—"

"No need to worry about me, Gwennie," he cut in. "I'm perfectly happy."

She didn't want to come across like she was judging him. It was his life, after all. "I'm glad to hear that." The bell over the front door dinged. "That's all I—"

"GWENDOLYN BRICK?!"

The two of them froze.

Marcus mouthed, "Isn't she still in jail?"

"Gwendolyn!" Leilah demanded from the other side of the velvet curtain. "I know you're here!"

Marcus squeezed Gwendolyn's hand and mouthed, "Good luck."

Gwendolyn braced herself before pulling back the curtain. She hadn't seen Leilah since the night Bugsy Siegel opened the Flamingo in Las Vegas and Hollywood stayed away. The intervening eighteen months hadn't been kind. Her once full and fleshy face, pink with the blush of high living, was now pale and deflated like yesterday's birthday balloon.

Leilah marched toward Gwendolyn and dropped her purse on the counter. She'd lost at least a couple of dress sizes, too.

"I hadn't heard you got out," Gwendolyn said.

"The nightmare I've been through," Leilah declared, "I wouldn't wish on anyone."

"That must be a relief."

"I haven't any time to lose, Gwendolyn, so I shall come straight to the point. I assume you heard Winchell's broadcast?"

"Who didn't?"

"So you know about the box?"

"Yes."

Leilah crossed her arms. "I want you to tell me where it is."

"What makes you think *I* know?"

Leilah cast her gaze down one side of Gwendolyn and up the other. "Aren't you getting a bit long in the tooth to be playing the ingénue?" She waved her hand dismissively. "This store. It's very swanky. It must have cost you a packet to set up, not to mention the rent. You got the money from somewhere."

"I sold a painting—"

"When I heard that Lincoln Tattler died, I got my husband to put a tail on his father."

"You had Horton followed?"

"I know when Linc died, Horton received Linc's belongings. I also know that Horton delivered a box to you here at the store. Furthermore, I know that Linc drove around Los Angeles and snitched to everyone in my files that the cards existed."

"Why are you here?"

"You know more than you're letting on!" Leilah stepped close enough for Gwendolyn to smell day-old body odor mixed with cigarette smoke and a dash of desperation.

"Leilah, I can only imagine how difficult your time in jail was, but—"

"You've got my cards and I want them!"

The sharp corner of the counter pressed against Gwendolyn's back. In a heady rush, she realized she had no reason to lie.

"You know what, Leilah? You're right. I went down to Mexico to see Linc, and he told me about your cards. And when he died, Horton came to see me with a box of Linc's stuff. There was a photograph, some old souvenirs, a few books, his wristwatch, and a bunch of love letters. But your cards? They were not there."

"You're lying!"

"I'm just not saying what you want to hear."

"I know you have them!" Gobs of spit seeped from the corners of Leilah's mouth. She pounded the glass countertop and one of the curls pinned into the nest atop her head came loose and flopped against the side of her face. "I KNOW IT! I JUST *KNOW* IT!"

"I don't have them."

"Then you had them and sold them to finance this place. I *insist* you tell me who you sold them to."

Gwendolyn saw that nothing good was going to come from pouring grease onto the fire wheezing in front of her. "I understand the pressure you've been under, but it's started to affect your reason. I've told you all I know and now I must insist that you leave."

Leilah wagged a finger. "If I find out that you've been lying to me, about anything—ANYTHING!—I shall go out of my way to ruin your reputation, your business, and your entire life."

"Then I've got nothing to worry about." Gwendolyn resisted adding *However, you, on the other hand . . .* "Goodbye, Leilah. And good luck."

LA's most notorious madam harrumphed as she swiped up her handbag and marched away, not even bothering to shut the door behind her. Gwendolyn closed it, then leaned her head against the glass. "It's okay," she called out. "The coast is clear."

Marcus emerged from the back room. "You were telling her the truth, weren't you?"

"If her rotten old client box still exists, it's somebody else's problem now."

"You think?"

They returned to their corned beef sandwiches. "Do I even want to know what you're hinting at?" she asked.

"I could be wrong."

"But?"

"But if she had Horton tailed, and he led her to you. And if she thinks you still have the box, or could lead her to it, what's to say she won't have you followed, too?"

CHAPTER 8

Kathryn had passed the Hollywood Masonic Temple on Hollywood Boulevard a million times, but she'd never been inside. Its ionic concrete columns were purely ornamental, but they lent the flat-roofed building a measure of solemnity, which was probably why it was chosen for D.W. Griffith's memorial service. It hardly mattered, though. Almost no one showed up. No one of note, that is.

D.W. Griffith practically invented Hollywood filmmaking. His *In Old California* was the first film shot in Hollywood; *Birth of a Nation* was one of its first this-changes-everything blockbusters; and he co-founded United Artists with Mary Pickford, Charlie Chaplin, and Douglas Fairbanks.

When he died of a cerebral hemorrhage at the Knickerbocker Hotel, alone and ignored, he made the front page of the newspapers for the first time since before the movies learned to talk. Kathryn had expected to find a sea of celebrated faces, but the mugs gathered inside were as anonymous as the gawkers on the sidewalk.

By the time the congregation filed out of the building to a boys' choir singing "Abide with Me," the crowd had disbursed, leaving Hollywood Boulevard to its everyday bustle.

"Well, that was depressing," Kathryn said to Marcus.

"It was a memorial service. You were expecting maybe ticker tape and a clown called Whacko?"

"He was the one who came up with close-ups and fade-outs," she snapped back. "Where would cinema be without him?"

"Sounds to me like someone has already started to write tomorrow's column." Marcus raised his hands in mock surrender. "And it promises to be a lulu."

"Someone should take all those missing people to task."

"Are you headed back to the office now?"

Kathryn was too keyed up to sit at her desk. An industry titan like Griffith shouldn't have squandered his life in a fusty hotel room.

"In that case . . ." He slid his arm across her shoulder and nudged her eastward.

"Where are we going?"

"What's really bugging you?"

"What do you mean?"

"You never even met the guy. Yeah, yeah, you're quite right. He practically created a whole new art form, then got kicked to the curb when he couldn't keep producing the hits. But isn't that the story of the movie business?"

They passed the Kress five-and-dime, glancing in the windows at the new *The Voice of Frank Sinatra* LPs.

Marcus tapped Kathryn's chin. "You've been wearing that pout since the day you bought your car. Didn't you enjoy your birthday party?"

When Kathryn returned home with her new car, the Garden of Allah had been transformed into an Arabian harem. The theme was Ali Baba and the Forty Thieves, and someone had borrowed props from an Yvonne De Carlo picture called *Casbah*: Persian rugs, scimitars, ceramic urns the size of prepubescent slave girls, and a papier mâché palm tree possibly pilfered from the Cocoanut Grove.

"Are you kidding?" Kathryn replied. "It was fantastic. I had a great time!"

"Did something happen when you were shopping for cars?"

"Bette read me the riot act."

"She'd be good at that."

Kathryn shot Marcus a rueful eye. "It's just that I've become so indecisive. Bette thinks it's all about turning forty."

"I have an alternate theory."

They were at the corner of Ivar Street now. Kathryn looked north toward the Knickerbocker. The lights changed and they continued to weave their way through the throngs cramming the sidewalk.

"Nelson Hoyt," he said.

Kathryn hated the way that name could still jab her like a wasp.

Hoyt had been the FBI agent tasked with recruiting her as an informant during the war. She'd resented and railed against the maneuvering, but somewhere in the thick of all that, Kathryn and Nelson had fallen for each other. But J. Edgar Hoover transferred him to some backwater post where mail was probably parachuted in once a month from a bi-plane that didn't bother to stop.

The whole subject of her thwarted relationship had been a tender issue between Kathryn and Marcus; she was surprised he'd even brought it up.

"That's quite a theory you've got there," she told him.

"I reckon I can see a Hoyt-shaped dent in your self-confidence. You haven't quite been the same since he exited stage right. Are you feeling like time is slipping away from you? Because, you know, forty *is* the start of middle—"

She backslapped him across the chest. "Don't you dare!"

"Griffith did nothing for the last third of his life." He folded her hand over his arm and led her across Vine Street. "You're not D.W. Griffith, you know."

"He was in his seventies, you little bastard!"

"I meant metaphorically."

Across the street at the Pantages Theatre, a movie called *Cry of the City* was playing. Kathryn hadn't seen it yet and wondered briefly if a film noir potboiler might take her mind off things, but decided it was too bleak for her present mood. She sighed. "I know what you meant."

"I'm just saying if that's what you're feeling, it's completely understandable."

"What about you? You turned forty before I did."

He swiped his hand through the air as though to say, *Are you kidding?* "I was head of writing at MGM; I had a huge say in what movies the studio put into production, making tons of dough—"

"But what about now?"

"I don't care if I never go back to work!"

Gwennie's right. He does say that a lot. She thought about how often she'd returned home from the office and had barely unpinned her hat before Marcus materialized with a shaker of martinis. *Is he drinking his afternoons away?*

Marcus said, "Here we are!"

Kathryn looked around the jostling corner of Hollywood and Vine. "We're where?"

He jacked a thumb behind him. The Taft building was a twelve-story skyscraper, home to all sorts of film-related businesses, including the Motion Picture Academy. He pulled a slip of paper from his pocket. "Fifth floor, Suite 502. Someone by the name of Harly."

"How do you know about him?"

"Oliver got tickets to a sneak preview for *June Bride,* but he had to work late that night so I went by myself. Afterwards, I was standing around having a smoke and your pal Bette approached me. She told me that she'd given you the name of this Harly guy, and that he's got an in with Max Factor, but you hadn't done anything about pitching them."

Bette had sent her the guy's card. It was in her purse right now, where it'd been for three weeks.

"The Kathryn I've known for twenty years wouldn't have wasted any time jumping on the horn." He pushed the paper into her hand and nudged her toward the arched stone doorway that led into the foyer. His warm breath filled her ear. "Go get 'em."

* * *

Harly was a tiny squib of a guy—barely five foot four—who had a pleasantly open face and a ready smile. "Bette told me to expect you, but that was ages ago."

Kathryn blushed. "Stuff got in the way. Are you free now?"

He led her into an expanse that stretched the length of the building

At one end, stacks of papers arranged with military precision covered a teak desk. At the other lay a photography studio with a loveseat and a fainting couch, half a dozen chairs, and a rack of backdrops from tapestries and leopard print to plain white and black cotton sheets. He pointed to a chair in front of his desk.

As they sat down, Kathryn smoothed her gloves across her handbag. "Did Bette mention what I'm after?"

"Not in so many words."

She cleared her throat. "Lauren Bacall told me that Max Factor is planning on making Pan-Stik available to the general public."

"It's a big deal for them."

"It's such a big deal that they're thinking of launching it by sponsoring a new radio show, and I want a chance to pitch the idea of having me host it."

Harly studied her somewhat enigmatically. "*The Kathryn Massey Show.* That's got quite a ring to it."

"When I mentioned the idea to Bette, she said you do all the advertising glamour shots, so you might know someone who knows someone."

"She did, huh?" He tilted his head in surprise. "I'm sorry, but I don't. I have an agent who the advertising monkeys contact when they want to book me for a layout. Most of the time it's just me and the movie star. Every now and then a PR flunky tags along, but it's an exception."

That'll teach me to procrastinate for months and get my hopes up for nothing. Kathryn stood up. "In that case, I won't take up any more of your time." She hooked her handbag over her elbow and fanned herself with her gloves. He started to walk her to the door, but she told him she could see herself out.

The elevator doors slid open onto an empty car. She stepped inside, but as they began to close, a voice rang down the corridor. "HOLD ON!"

Harly arrived at the elevator slightly out of breath. "You're a friend of Gwendolyn Brick's, aren't you?"

"I am." Kathryn stepped into the corridor. "Have we met?"

He smiled his easy smile again. "Remember that Warner Brothers contest a number of years back, Face of the Forties?"

It was a huge publicity campaign the studio ran throughout most of 1939 to find the girl who could exemplify the dawning decade. Gwendolyn won the contest, in no small part because of the exquisite photographs taken of her by—

"You're Harlan McNamara!"

"My friends call me Harly."

"I did not put that together."

"You didn't see my name on the door?"

"I was distracted and—never mind."

"Face of the Forties was a while back," he conceded.

"Everything before the war seems like a long time ago."

"If I hadn't made the connection, it never would have occurred to me."

Kathryn pulled her hand away from the elevator call button. "Oh?"

"After Gwendolyn won Face of the Forties, Jack Warner made me an offer I couldn't refuse, and I grudgingly accepted his obscene paychecks for as long as my conscience could stand it. After three years, I returned to freelance work and they promoted my assistant. He was competent enough with the camera but better at layout. Last I heard, he went to Young and Rubicam."

"The advertising agency?"

"They have the Max Factor account. Mind you, this was a while ago. I don't know if he's still there."

"A telephone call would solve that mystery." Kathryn unclipped her purse and pulled out a business card. "In case you get lucky," she told him, and pressed the button. It dinged almost instantly; the brass doors slid open.

"Wow," he exclaimed, "that elevator usually takes forever!"

"Let's take that as a sign, shall we?"

"Let's."

He was still smiling when the door slid closed between them.

CHAPTER 9

Marcus and Oliver were halfway down Cesar Romero's driveway when Oliver grabbed Marcus' car keys.

"What're you doing?"

"You're in no condition to drive." He headed toward the DeSoto that was parked a block down Saltair Avenue under a steeply leaning eucalyptus.

"Okay, so maybe I'm not stone cold sober," Marcus conceded, "but you've hardly been Tommy Temperance this afternoon. I saw all those Mai Tais."

"I'd never had one before. I wanted to see what everyone's talking about."

"You were knocking 'em back like club soda."

Oliver spun around, catching Marcus off guard. "Do you blame me? The way you were flirting with Cesar's pool boy, Taco, or whatever his name was."

"It's Paco, and I wasn't flirting—oh my God, were you jealous?" Oliver didn't get worked up very often, but when he did, his neck broke out in patches. Marcus could see a whole mottled palette of pinks and reds. "I'm flattered!"

Oliver cast him a look that Marcus found hard to interpret. Perhaps seven bourbons ago he could have, but his head was starting to spin. "I need to sit." He landed his butt on the concrete curb.

"Wouldn't you be more comfortable in the car?"

Marcus ignored Oliver's pissy attitude. "I need a breeze. Musta cracked a hundred today." He patted the curb next to him. "Come here. Sit with me."

Oliver let out a theatrical sigh, lingered at the car for a moment or two, then joined him.

Marcus felt his pockets for a crushed pack of Camels. There were two left; bent, but smokable. He lit them and handed one to Oliver. "Am I in for some more silent treatment?"

The first cool gust of the day swathed them in a cloud of pungent eucalyptus.

Abruptly, Oliver said, "It's hard for me to stand by and watch you fritter your life away."

Marcus' head jolted up. "Is that what you think I'm doing?"

"You spend your mornings swimming, your afternoons reading the paper, and your evenings drinking. Did I forget anything?"

"I spent years working my guts out at MGM; I think I deserve a break."

"You've been at home for nearly a year," Oliver said. "Don't you miss being useful?"

He jerked his shoulder with a dismissive shrug. "I don't care if I never go back to work!"

"That's what I'm afraid of." Oliver ground his half-smoked Camel into the asphalt. "I've got to say, Marcus, reading the *Times* and swimming laps isn't much of a contribution to society." The blotches on Oliver's neck grew more prominent the snider he became. "Isn't there *anything* you want to do?"

"Yes, there is," Marcus lobbed back, "but you shot me down."

"Not that crazy Russia plan again!" He stood up and twirled Marcus' car keys around his finger. "Get in the car. We're going home." Marcus didn't budge. "Or you could walk. Good luck finding a cab on Labor Day."

He unlocked the DeSoto and slid into the driver's seat, waited a moment or two, then turned the engine over.

Marcus swayed to his feet and slumped into the passenger side. "I've done more research," he said.

"Not listening." Oliver pulled onto the road.

"Do you know how much it costs to hire a car and driver in Turkey?"

"Don't care."

"One dollar per day. We can hire a driver in Istanbul to take us to a place called Sinop. It's on the northern coast. Then we hire a boat to take us directly to Adler. It's only two hundred nautical miles; we could get there and back in a day and no border crossing to deal with. It's much easier than you'd exp—"

"Is this what you do all day?" Oliver swung onto San Vicente Boulevard. The holiday traffic was light so he picked up speed. "Pore over your maps concocting a plan to sabotage your chances of getting hired again?"

The lights ahead turned amber. Oliver floored the gas pedal and rounded the hairpin bend onto Wilshire.

"Jesus!" Marcus cried out. "We took that on two wheels."

"I asked you what you do all day."

"You know what I do. I swim, I read the papers, and then I spend the afternoons making huge contributions to the betterment of society."

"And how often do you park your car outside MGM?"

Jesus. How does he know that? "Are you having me followed?"

Oliver careered along Wilshire for several blocks before he answered. "About a month ago, Mister Breen and I were called to an emergency meeting with Mayer and your replacement, Anson Purvis. There were a number of issues over *Little Women* and it was easier for us to come to them."

"How could *Little Women* have Hays Code issues?" Marcus scoffed. "It's the squeakiest, cleanest story ever written."

"You didn't see the script they bought from Selznick. At any rate, when we were leaving the lot, I spotted your car parked across the street. In fact, I'm surprised you didn't see me."

"How the hell am I supposed to know what sort of car Joseph Breen drives?" Marcus' brave thrust at bravado came out flaccid as a used rubber.

"I happened to be back there a week later to discuss *Madame Bovary*."

"Since when does the Breen Office go to a studio?"

"Mister Breen's highest concern is the health of the motion picture industry, and your old studio is in trouble. So he helped out by promising to send someone from our office to deliver the approved script. I volunteered."

"To check up on me?"

"In a way, I guess. And there you were, parked in the same place, staring at those columns." The traffic lights on Beverly Glen Boulevard changed to red; Oliver slammed on the brakes, plunging them forward. "What the hell's going on with you?"

Marcus fell back in his seat. On his days down at the beach, instead of driving home back up Sunset, he had started to point his car toward Washington Boulevard—almost like he had no choice. Invariably, he'd end up at MGM's famous ten-column entrance at Jasmine Avenue.

This urge started when MGM announced a financial loss for the 1947-48 year. Such a declaration ten years ago—or even five—or, hell, just two years—would have been unimaginable. The Tiffany of movie studios, with more stars than there were in heaven, posting a loss?

It was hardly a surprise to Marcus, though. They only had one movie in the top five box-office earners for 1947, scraping in at an embarrassing number five with *Green Dolphin Street*. And that one barely earned a profit.

Sitting in his car that first day, Marcus pictured the executive staff meetings, L.B. Mayer at the head of the table, pounding his fist. "Find me better stories! Find me fresh stars! There must be some new angle we haven't tried!" Marcus surreptitiously parked his DeSoto week after week to watch the embattled ants scurry in and out of the studio. He told himself he'd gotten out while the getting was good, and how this wasn't his problem anymore.

He was free to while away his days doing whatever he pleased instead of pacing the office at night worrying about how to capitalize on the blossoming sultriness of a still-teenage Elizabeth Taylor or how to avoid botching Greer Garson's streak.

By midsummer, he was stopping outside MGM a couple of times a week. But recently, he was getting less and less of a kick out of it, and had started to picture his career outlined in chalk on the sidewalk like a murder victim.

The lights changed. Oliver slammed on the gas, lurching into the intersection.

"It was just a habit I fell into," Marcus said lamely.

"And you've never once thought to mention it?"

"Too embarrassed, I guess."

"So instead of going out and hustling up some work, you've been loitering around a studio that pushed you out the back door?"

"I was the one who quit."

"Before they fired you."

That hurt. "Leave me alone."

"You haven't been blacklisted, so why aren't you trying to get a job at some other studio instead of making these cockamamie plans—"

"They're not cockamamie—"

"You're talking about hiring a boat from some Turkish backwater to Middle-of-Nowhere, Russia. And for what?" Oliver jerked the car into the slow lane and revved the engine to pass a pair of motorcyclists. "I know you've got a pile of scripts buried in a drawer somewhere. Pull out the best of the bunch, polish it off, and send it out to Paramount, Warners, Fox, and RKO. Remind them that you wrote *The Pistol from Pittsburgh* and *Free Leningrad!*, and see who bites."

"Now just hold on a minute! You don't know what's involved. All you know is your Breen Office rulebook. And anyway—WHOA!" Oliver narrowly missed a jalopy that looked like it was held together with spit and a prayer. "Slow the hell down!"

Oliver eased off the gas marginally. "You put in nearly twenty years building your reputation, and now you're throwing it away for no reason."

"I'm not throwing anything—"

"If you want to dribble away the rest of your life, then fine, but don't expect me to stick around and watch you do it." Oliver veered back into the center lane.

"Are you breaking up with me?"

"I never said that."

"You kind of did. And why is this coming up now? You couldn't just tell me how you felt weeks ago?"

"Hi, honey," Oliver sing-songed in a falsetto. "Pass the salt, oh and by the way, I've been loitering like a hobo outside MGM all summer. You mean like that?"

"*Dammit!*" Marcus slapped the dashboard and braced his feet against the floorboards to steady himself as Oliver rocketed past the hedges bordering the LA Country Club. "I want to see where I come from. Is that so bad?"

"In this current political climate, yes, Marcus, it's bad. Very, very bad."

"I don't care!"

"Well, you should."

"I'll get another career—OLIVER!"

They plunged into the intersection where Wilshire crossed Santa Monica Boulevard at an acute angle. The traffic lights changed just as an Adohr Dairy milk truck lumbered across Oliver's path. He pulled a sharp left that threw Marcus against the window, and the rear of the DeSoto hit the front of the truck. Metal pounded against metal with a sickening crunch, pitching Marcus in the opposite direction.

They reeled toward the fountain on the intersection's north side and the brakes screeched as the DeSoto thundered into its foot-tall embankment. A wave of ceramic splinters hit the windshield and the passenger door swung open, flinging Marcus from the car. Icy water engulfed him; the shock pulled the air from his lungs; his glasses had disappeared. Concrete scraped against his face.

He surfaced in time to see the car flipping onto the driver's side and crashing into the inner pool, spilling out a deluge of more freezing water. The center column topped with a Native American figure keeled over, collapsing onto the front of the car.

Marcus struggled to his feet, wiping blood out of his eyes. "Oliver? OLIVER!" Somehow, the jets were still spurting in all directions. Marcus pushed against the column but couldn't shift it.

The intersection was awash with milk, the road blinding white in the sun. He could see someone running toward him, but his sight was blurred and tinged with pink. Before he knew it, the guy had jumped into the fountain.

"This column," Marcus spluttered. "It fell. On my friend. He's trapped."

The man laid his hands against the side of the column. "On the count of three, we're gonna push."

They groaned under the weight of the pylon, but slowly it began to dislodge. Abruptly, it gave way and rolled off the DeSoto. Shards of glass and tile covered the crumpled hood.

Oliver was sprawled back in the driver's seat, his face bloodied, his hair matted.

Marcus reached in through the shattered windshield and grabbed a fistful of Oliver's shirt. "Can you hear me?"

Oliver opened his eyes. They were bloodshot and unfocused, but he knew Marcus' voice. "I'm sorry — I don't know what — Why is everything so wet?"

Marcus turned to the other man. "Where's the nearest telephone? Can we call an ambulance?"

"There's a drugstore down on Santa Monica." The guy took off.

Marcus turned back to Oliver. "Honey? Honey?" Without his glasses everything was blurry. "Don't move. Help's on the way."

"I can't — I can't — "

"Stay still. Don't move."

Oliver's mouth dropped open. "I can't move my legs. Marcus, I can't even feel them."

CHAPTER 10

Gwendolyn slid the box of bagels off of the counter at Greenblatt's Deli and cradled it in her arms.

Kathryn held open the door. "You got onion and poppy seed, right? He loves those."

"One each for us and four for him."

They headed back to the Garden of Allah, letting the late Sunday morning traffic sail past them.

"He looks terrible, doesn't he?"

Kathryn nodded. "I suspect he's drinking more than he's eating, so let's force feed him if we have to."

Oliver's legs were broken in eleven places. The surgeon made a big deal about how most of the breaks were relatively clean and should mend smoothly. Oliver was strung up in traction, but refusing to see visitors.

Astoundingly, Marcus had walked away with only a mild concussion and surface abrasions down the right side of his face. It bothered him that Oliver wouldn't see anyone, but the staff at Los Angeles General Hospital were sticklers when it came to their patients' wishes.

Gwendolyn and Kathryn skirted around the pool and stood in front of Marcus' villa. He told them last night that he'd leave his front door open when he was up, but it was nearly midday and it was still closed.

"Should we knock?" Gwendolyn asked.

"Let's give him an hour. I'm hoping he actually slept. Can we go to your place? I'm all out of coffee."

"Gwendolyn, may I have a word?" It was Manny, the Garden's front desk clerk.

"Don't tell me my rent check bounced!" Gwendolyn laughed to cover her embarrassment. That big-spending blonde back in June had not been a harbinger of things to come, unfortunately.

"I encountered a couple of shady types lurking around here yesterday," Manny said.

"What kind of shady?"

"Shifty eyes, no necktie, pants that look like they haven't been pressed all year."

"What were they doing?"

"Wandering around, making out like they were lost. I inquired if I could help, and they asked me which villa was yours. They spun some story about being from out of town and looking you up on a lark."

"I don't like the sound of that," Kathryn said.

"I gave them the usual speech about the privacy of our residents and escorted them out."

"I don't suppose you saw their car?" Gwendolyn asked.

"I did."

"Chevrolet? Two-door? Red with a dent on the passenger side?"

Manny stroked his bushy salt-and-pepper moustache. "I didn't notice any dent, but yes, a red Chevrolet sedan. Gosh, I'm sorry if I was rude to your friends, but they didn't strike me as being on the up-and-up."

"They're not my friends," Gwendolyn told him. "But I sure do appreciate you looking out for me. You're a peach, Uncle Manny."

She hustled Kathryn along the path to her apartment, where she deposited the bagels on her kitchen counter and started tapping her key on the white tiling. "I've noticed a red Chevy drive past the store a lot."

"How much is a lot?"

"Once or twice a week. I thought I was being paranoid and figured they're probably just regulars at some store along the Strip. But then I got to work last week and the lock on my back door looked like it'd been tampered with."

"Gwennie!"

"There were these scratches I'd never noticed before."

"Someone tried to jimmy it?"

"Could be. I'm just glad it's a real sturdy lock."

They stared at each other, each reluctant to be the first to say it.

Finally Kathryn said, "Leilah came to the store; she threatened to ruin you."

Gwendolyn stuck her coffee pot under the faucet and filled it with water. "She was upset. Her whole future's at stake. She probably came after me because she couldn't think of anyone else to yell at."

Kathryn drew alongside her and dropped her voice to a murmur. "You don't actually have those client cards, do you?"

"No! Nor do I want them."

"But if she's sent her goons after you—"

"I'm going to have to convince her that I don't have them, aren't I?" Gwendolyn admitted glumly. "But I've already screamed at her. And I don't even know where Leilah's living now."

She went to light the stove when a low rumbling filled the apartment. The china teacups in her cabinet rattled. Outside the kitchen window, a dog began to howl. Kathryn and Gwendolyn jumped into the living room doorway as a framed print of a girl on a swing thumped to the floor. The whole place juddered like a lumbering tortoise, sending the coffee pot skittering across the stovetop.

As the earthquake reached its peak, a crash of splintering glass burst from the bathroom.

Then suddenly it was over, and the room was silent again.

Kathryn let go of the doorjamb. "That sounded like your mirror."

"It's built into the cabinet. That was my perfume allowance for the next two years. Chanel No. 5 *and* Miss Dior, gone in thirty seconds."

"I should go check on my place." Kathryn laid the Maxfield Parrish print on Gwendolyn's dining table. "You should open all your windows; your place is going to reek for a month."

* * *

A week after the earthquake, Gwendolyn was dressing a mannequin when Edith Head strode into the store. "I'm pleased to see Chez Gwendolyn survived intact."

"Would you believe hardly anything moved in the entire place?" Gwendolyn greeted Edith with a cheek press.

"And at home?"

"That was a different matter."

"We were down at the house in Laguna, so we didn't feel it. But we returned home to find we were awash in broken wine bottles." Edith tsked. "Including a 1922 Château Lafite. Wiard has tried to replace it but those heinous Nazis ransacked the vineyard, so you can't find it for love nor money." She pointed to the window display. "I adore that."

Gwendolyn was proud of her newest creation: a two-piece suit in light gray merino wool. The extra-wide lapels crossed the chest into a double-breasted jacket, with a matching mid-shin skirt that had a long slit at the back to make stairs easier to negotiate.

"I spotted it when I was driving home from Warner Brothers last night," Edith said.

"Still helping Travilla?"

Edith threw her hands up. "Bette Davis requested me for this picture she's working on."

"Kathryn tells me she's most unhappy."

"She is, and when Bette's miserable, everybody's miserable. My work on that project is done, and I aim to celebrate with—" she faced the window "—that! You really do have the most admirable taste, but perhaps I'm only saying that because it aligns closely with mine. At any rate, I want it, but in deep plum, same shade as your carpet."

"Shall I send you samples?"

"I trust you."

Without the windfall from the Alistair Dunne portrait, Gwendolyn wouldn't have had the means to open Chez Gwendolyn. But without Edith Head's encouragement, she doubted she'd have ever found the chutzpah to open a store at all. In Edith's presence, Gwendolyn felt like the bumpkin she'd been when she landed in Los Angeles twenty years ago.

And yet Edith had always treated her as a colleague. She wondered for the first time if perhaps she ought to try some advertising.

Edith squinted at her. "What *are* you wearing?"

Gwendolyn looked down at her pleated dress with the square neck. It wasn't high fashion, but comfort trumped style when she was dressing mannequins.

"No, dear," Edith said, "what *perfume* are you wearing?"

Gwendolyn reflexively touched behind an earlobe. "Do you like it?"

"Is it the new Balenciaga?" She leaned in for a deep sniff. "Heaven!"

Gwendolyn smiled coyly. "I guess you could say it's mine."

Edith stared at her wide-eyed with expectation from behind her blue-tinted glasses.

"I was at home when the earthquake hit. I heard a god-almighty crash coming from the bathroom: my Chanel No. 5 had smashed into the basin right on top of my Miss Dior. Fifty dollars' worth of perfume—pfft!—down the drain!"

"You must have been devastated."

"I was expecting a high-hog stink, but when I walked in it smelled rather nice. So I ran right out and bought two new bottles." Edith didn't need to know Gwendolyn would be living on beans and rice for the next month. "I started experimenting. One drop of Chanel to two drops of Dior; then two Chanel to one Dior; then two of one and three of the other until I got the ratio exactly right." Gwendolyn circled her hands to give Edith another whiff. "What you're smelling is Chanel and Dior mixed with a hint of orange peel steeped in vanilla essence and cinnamon oil."

"How clever you are!" Edith pulled at Gwendolyn's sleeve and breathed in. "I've never smelled anything quite like it," she declared. "So what will the bottle look like?"

"What bottle?"

"You're going to sell it, aren't you? This could be your signature fragrance. I can see the sign already: *Available exclusively at Chez Gwendolyn on the Sunset Strip.*"

Gwendolyn backed off a step or two. "I was just messing about, really."

"You worked the perfume counter at Bullocks for how many years? You must know everything there is to know about selling perfume."

"Selling, yes, but manufacturing? I wouldn't know where to begin."

Edith grabbed a pad of paper. "You'd be a fool to let this slip through your fingers." She jotted down her measurements. "I'd buy a bottle on the spot." She pushed the paper toward Gwendolyn. "I'm attending an important luncheon a week from Monday. A coterie of my fellow costume designers are getting together to talk about forming an official guild, and I'd like to wear my new suit."

Gwendolyn told her she'd have it delivered to Paramount by the Friday before.

After Edith exited the store, Gwendolyn leaned against the counter for the longest time, tapping her chin with a pencil. She'd seen a perfume bottle once in a museum display of pre-French-revolution cosmetics. It was a cross between a pear and Aladdin's lamp, and made of green glass, but Gwendolyn decided purple might be more striking.

I could have it packaged in a matching box that ties up with a ribbon. Dark green, perhaps. And I could call it Earthquake – "It'll send you staggering." Available exclusively at Chez Gwendolyn on the Sunset Strip. Gwendolyn felt her heart flutter. It might bring customers in.

She pulled open a drawer and picked up the formula she'd written out for her homemade perfume. She flipped through the pages of the address book in her mind, trying to think of someone who might know how to go about manufacturing a perfume from scratch. She stopped when she came to T.

Horton Tattler sold exquisitely crafted men's clothes, and accessories like tie clips and cufflinks. She couldn't remember if they sold toiletries and colognes, but he was the most likely person she could think of.

Last she'd heard, he was living at the Hershey Arms—a once-fancy hotel near downtown that was descending into its seedy years. She called and asked to be put through to Mr. Tattler's room, but the operator told her Mr. Tattler had moved out more than a year before.

Gwendolyn stood at her counter wondering how much a private eye might cost until a flash of red caught her eye. Not just red, but red with a dent on the passenger door.

CHAPTER 11

The towering set of *Samson and Delilah* reached the ceiling of the tallest soundstage on the Paramount lot. Aqua silk drapes threaded with gold-framed twelve-foot frescoes of pastoral scenes and vines heavy with purple grapes. The enormous backdrop showed olive trees silhouetted against a sunset that deepened into dark cornflower blue. It was Cecil B. DeMille's first Technicolor movie.

Kathryn exclaimed, "This is all very striking!"

The assistant director next to her pulled at a thread in his hand-knit argyle sweater. "Miss Lamarr apologizes for keeping you waiting. This being her first color picture and all, Mister Westmore is taking extra care with her makeup."

"That's okay."

"Not with Mister DeMille, it isn't," the assistant whispered with a grin.

Kathryn pointed to the sprawling set. "Tell me about this?"

"The villa of Delilah's father. It's where Samson turns on the Philistines after somebody throws a spear through Angela Lansbury. When Mister Westmore stops fussing with Miss Lamarr's lipstick, you could watch us film it."

He offered to find Kathryn a chair, but she preferred to wander the set and absorb the atmosphere.

Kathryn had called months ahead to arrange this interview, and it was worth the wait. By the time the invitation arrived, though, her confidence had had the stuffing punched out of it, and she arrived on set feeling uncharacteristically timid.

It was all the fault of that damned radio show. Whether or not Harlan McNamara had gotten around to putting in a good word with Young and Rubicam became a moot point when Max Factor announced that their new show would be hosted by Sheilah Graham.

The biggest contenders in the Hollywood gossip industry were Louella Parsons, Hedda Hopper, Kathryn Massey, and Sheilah Graham. Over the years, Louella, Hedda, and Kathryn had occasionally broken out into war, but Kathryn and Sheilah had never locked horns. Sheilah had been a regular at the Garden when she was dating Scott Fitzgerald, and she and Kathryn bumped into each other at premieres and award nights, and occasionally on studio back lots. She was always well groomed, polite, and professional.

When Kathryn heard that Sheilah bagged the sponsorship, she'd tried to comfort herself by telling Gwendolyn and Marcus that if she didn't get the job, then she was glad it went to Sheilah. And besides, she was still co-host of *Kraft Music Hall*.

But in the intervening month, NBC canceled her show, and suddenly she was off the air altogether. For weeks she'd pictured herself striding onto the *Samson and Delilah* set in a flurry of congratulations for her new show. But today she arrived as just another columnist.

She did her best to blend into the tumult of set decorators and lighting technicians until she heard, "Watch it, lady. You don't want to catch yourself on these."

Kathryn had almost backed into a big trash can filled with wooden spears painted to look like metal.

"These may not be bronze, but they can still draw blood."

Kathryn thanked him and inched away.

He turned to his co-worker. "You know who I saw in the commissary? Billy Wilder."

"I'm surprised he's got the energy. I heard Marlene Dietrich and Jean Arthur fought the whole time on *A Foreign Affair*."

"*A Foreign Fiasco*, more like. So he and Brackett are back working on a new one?"

"Something called *A Can of Beans*."

"If that ain't the dumbest title I ever heard."

The men picked up the trash can of spears and hauled it toward the set.

Ever since Wilder made *Five Graves to Cairo*, *Double Indemnity*, and *The Lost Weekend* in a row, Kathryn had been a fan of his work. She didn't think *A Foreign Affair* was such a fiasco. At the very least, it presented a glimpse into postwar Berlin.

Kathryn pulled a pad and pencil from her handbag and wrote down *A Can of Beans*. It had to be a phony title.

The production assistant approached her to say that Miss Lamarr could give her fifteen minutes until she was required on set.

Kathryn assumed the actress would be holed up in her trailer, but instead found her resting on a padded board set at a thirty-degree angle. Leaning boards allowed an actress stitched into a tightly fitted gown or an actor clamped into fifty pounds of armor to comfortably relax between takes.

Hedy laid aside her book: *Postwar Advances in Electromagnetic Research*. She was decked out in a two-piece costume made of a sparkling silver material. Threaded around her head like a snood were dozens of pearls culminating in an enormous crown that matched her earrings; ropes of pearls were wound around each wrist.

"I'm sorry," she said. "We're about to do a close-up where George Sanders holds a ruby next to my mouth. You wouldn't believe how long it took to match the lipstick to the ruby. And for what? One second on-screen."

Kathryn jutted her head toward the book. "A little light reading?"

"I've already read *The Naked and the Dead*."

Kathryn smiled before she realized that the actress was being neither flippant nor ironic.

During the war, someone told Kathryn at an exceptionally drunken cocktail party at David Selznick's that Lamarr had helped develop radio-controlled torpedoes. Kathryn couldn't imagine what the most gorgeous woman in American movies might know about torpedoes, and had discounted the story as one of the outrageous rumors that fed the Hollywood mill.

Hedy Lamarr appearing in her first Technicolor picture was certainly newsworthy, but Hedy Lamarr reading *Postwar Advances in Electromagnetic Research* on the set of DeMille's latest sword-and-sands epic? Kathryn knew she could sink her teeth into a story like that.

She picked up the book. "This is what Hedy Lamarr reads in her spare time?"

Hedy shook her head without smiling.

Kathryn returned the book to the table. Of course not. Back to pretty Hedy in pretty Technicolor.

"I helped write it."

"You what?"

"Perhaps that's an overstatement." A thin smile curved Hedy's forty-minute lips. "The authors consulted me on how to reduce the technical aspects to a level more comprehensible to the average man on the street."

Kathryn stared at that perfectly formed face, anticipating the moment when Hedy admitted her practical joke. But the actress maintained her Teutonic mask for so long, Kathryn felt compelled to write something down.

Lamarr electro-mag book consult man on street

She wasn't even sure she would understand what that meant back at the office. When she looked up, she found Hedy smiling.

"Are you putting me on?" Kathryn asked.

"Not at all. But I can see the puzzlement on your face. If it would make you feel more comfortable, we can talk about these." She shook her arm so that the string of pearls wound around her wrist five times caught the key lights.

"Good heavens, no!" Kathryn stepped forward to create a more intimate atmosphere in the middle of the energetic movie set. "I'd heard that you were a bit of a whiz with . . . electrical . . . "

She lacked the vocabulary for such a technical conversation and was forced to finish with the insipid, "stuff."

She made sure she didn't break eye contact as she returned her pad and pen to her purse. She'd learned a number of years ago that making a show of stowing away the tools of her trade signaled to a performer that their encounter was less of a formal interview and more of an off-the-cuff chat. "I want to hear about this extraordinary gift you have."

Hedy took a moment to consider her response. "Americans want their movie stars pretty of face, but empty of mind."

Rule number one for interviewing stars was to avoid contradicting them, belittling them, or tell them they're wrong. Kathryn was starting to see that the usual rules didn't apply to this gorgeous creature.

"I think you're mistaken," Kathryn said, and waited for a reaction. None came. "When the men went off to war, American women walked into the factories and discovered they were just as smart as the guys they replaced. If they go to see *Samson and Delilah* knowing that behind the lovely face is a brain that could trounce the smartest man they know, they'd get an enormous kick out of it."

Forget American women, Kathryn thought. *I need to be reminded that we can have it all — looks, brains, success, career.*

The assistant hovered beside them. "Mister DeMille will need you on set in ten."

Hedy nodded, then turned back to Kathryn. "Throughout my entire childhood, my mother called me an ugly weed."

"Were you a late bloomer?"

She shrugged off the question. "Looking back, I can see now that Mama telling me I wasn't attractive forced me to develop my mind. It took me more than twenty years to figure out that was her gift." A sly smile nudged the corners of her lips. "Perhaps we can save American girls twenty years of anguish."

Kathryn knew a "yes" when she heard one. "If you're free on Sunday, we could get together and you can tell me about the real Hedy Lamarr."

The actress lifted her arms, indicating that she needed Kathryn's assistance getting off the leaning board. As Kathryn pulled her upright, Hedy said, "This weekend, my children will be spending the day with their father."

"How about I pick up some chili from Chasen's and come to you? One o'clock?"

A glint of approval twinkled in Hedy's eyes. "I like to sleep in. So let's make it three. Excuse me, please, for now I must go and be decorative."

* * *

An hour ago, Kathryn walked onto the *Samson and Delilah* set dreading that someone would look at her with pity, but now that she was flush with ideas, she didn't want to leave.

Hedy Lamarr and George Sanders took their places as Kathryn cast around for a place where she could sit and record on paper the thoughts that were tumbling out of her like gumballs. She spotted an ornate mauve velvet chaise lounge outside the half-circle of production crew and headed for it.

She was so absorbed in filling the pages of her pad that she failed to notice someone approach her. "Excuse me, but you're Kathryn Massey, aren't you?"

Kathryn looked up to see a young woman — she couldn't have been much older than twenty-two — standing five feet away, her fingers intertwined as though in prayer, her bent elbows pushed against her sides.

Kathryn pressed a finger to her lips. "They're about to start rolling."

"Perhaps we could talk outside?"

Kathryn would have preferred to empty the contents of her head, but the girl's quaintly beseeching air made it hard to turn her down. The cool October air was a refreshing change from the overheated movie set.

Now that they were in clear daylight, Kathryn could see that this pert little kid had one of those heart-shaped faces that was punctuated with a cute button nose. Her dull brown hair hung dead straight from the sides of her head, but it was nothing that a touch of coloring and some rollers couldn't fix.

"My name is Ruby Courtland and — oh-my-goodness-gracious-me!" she exclaimed, a little breathless. "I must confess, I'm a bit nervous meeting you!"

"Inside that soundstage you've got Hedy Lamarr, Victor Mature, George Sanders, and Cecil B. DeMille, but it's *me* that's got you in a twist?"

The girl's eyes grew wide. "I've been reading your column for as long as I can remember, and I never, *ever* missed your radio show." A gloved hand flew to her mouth. "When they canceled it, I was distraught!"

"You and me both," Kathryn said. "So tell me, Ruby, you work here at Paramount?" She had that earnestly conscientious look that studio script girls wore as they went about recording the pertinent information about each scene.

—

88

"No!" Ruby let out a string of giggles fueled by a burst of nervous energy. "I'm a New York transplant. Been here a few weeks. Still feeling my way around town. I'm with *Variety*."

Kathryn took the girl in with a second, more serious examination. *If you made some effort with your hair, and perhaps replaced that dime-store makeup, you'd be quite pretty.* "In what capacity?"

"I guess you could say I'm a junior columnist. But I like to think of myself as an apprentice Kathryn Massey."

"That's really very flattering, but—"

"May I ask for some advice?"

The adoration on the girl's face was downright embarrassing. "About what?"

"I'm just starting out, so anything at all that you think might be useful. It would mean so much."

Kathryn thought about the woman inside who'd helped invent radio-controlled torpedoes but would only show the public her beautiful face and figure.

"I've got some advice for you." When the girl started digging into her handbag for pencil and paper, Kathryn stopped her. "Don't think of yourself as an apprentice Kathryn Massey," she said. "Or an apprentice anybody. Whoever Ruby Courtland is, have the courage to be that. Let everyone else in this town pretend to be somebody they're not."

CHAPTER 12

Marcus jumped into his car as soon as he got Oliver's note. He wove in and out of the afternoon traffic, cursing everyone in his path the whole way along Sunset. He pulled into the hospital parking lot, yanked the key out of the ignition, and unfolded the slip of paper in his lap.

It's time we talked. Please come see me. Room 209. Visiting hours 11 to 4.

It's time we talked . . . and what? Decide who was to blame for the accident? Or endure Oliver taking responsibility for an accident that was both their fault?

It was already three thirty. LA General was an enormous place. It might take him ten or fifteen minutes to find Oliver's room. He forced himself out of the car before procrastination stole the moment away.

The elevator doors squeaked open on the second floor. One whiff of ammonia brought him back to the last time he was in a hospital—the day Alla Nazimova died. A layer of apprehension coated his face as he stopped at the nurse's station and asked a redhead in a starched cap for directions.

"You must be Mister Adler." She curled a finger to pull him closer. "Mister Trenton's been with us for more than two months now. He's not healing like he should."

"Can you be more specific?"

"Some people are blessed with fast-knitting bones, but even slow knitters are usually further along than him. A positive attitude is so very helpful after surviving that sort of trauma. Don't get me wrong. Mister Trenton is recovering, but it's taking much longer than it ought."

"Is that why he didn't want to see me?"

"He's refused all visitors. When he asked for pen and paper I took it as a hopeful sign." She pointed down the stark white hallway. "Second-last room on the right. See if you can cheer him up, but mind, he'll be a bit wooly headed."

Marcus marched into Room 229 like Eisenhower storming Omaha Beach. "Hello there!"

Oliver peered at him through heavily lidded eyes. "You came." He looked as though he hadn't been in the sun for a year. New lines were etched into the corners of his mouth and his hazel eyes had sunk deeper into his skull. Marcus was at his bedside in three strides.

He took Oliver's hand. It was cadaverously cold. "You didn't have to ask me twice." He sandwiched Oliver's fingers between his palms to get them warm. "Your nurse tells me you're still in pain."

He smiled weakly. "Pills are wonderful."

Marcus ran his eyes along Oliver's legs strung up eight inches over the bed in a complicated network of ropes and slings. "Are you comfortable?"

"Do I look it?"

Marcus pulled a face that he hoped would make Oliver laugh. It didn't. "I came as soon as I got your note." Oliver slow-blinked. "I've been stewing for weeks over what happened."

Oliver turned his head toward the window, pulling his fingers from Marcus' grasp. "My memory is kinda hazy."

"What do you remember?"

A long pause. "Anger."

"Because you thought I was flirting with the pool boy?"

"I remember taking the keys off you because you were too drunk to drive."

"You were about as drunk as I was."

"You're not getting on with your life."

Marcus thought about what the nurse said. "Wait till you see my new car! Buick Roadmaster. It's got a huge chrome grill, and four portholes along each side. It purrs like a kitty cat and drives like it's floating on air. I was going to get it in black but then Kathryn spotted a yellow one." He forced a laugh. "You can see me coming for miles! And it's a convertible. When the sun's out, and the top's down—"

"So the DeSoto was a write-off?"

Marcus pictured his car as the tow truck dragged it out of the wrecked fountain: the hood crushed beyond repair; every window busted; three out of four tires punctured. He never did find the rear license plate. "It was time I got a new car, anyway."

Tears glistened in Oliver's eyes and seeped down his cheeks. He didn't bother to wipe them away. "I'm so sorry."

Marcus took his hand again. "What have you got to be sorry about?"

"I was drunk. Angry. Too busy yelling at you to pay attention to the road."

"Stop this," Marcus said soothingly. "We were drunk and angry. What happened that day was an accident, that's all."

"An accident I could have avoided if—"

"Hush." Oliver's hand was a little warmer, but it was shaking. "I could have done *this*, you could have done *that*—what does it matter? We survived. Okay, so you came through it somewhat worse than I did—"

"I was reckless. And thoughtless. I deserved all this—"

Marcus leaned forward so that their faces were almost touching. "How about we skip the finger-pointing?"

"Stop being kind." Oliver's voice was so low that Marcus might not have heard it if he wasn't so close. "I nearly killed you."

Marcus saw now it was a good thing Oliver had kept him at arm's length. He could still feel the slap of water against his face, hear the sound of screeching brakes. He'd lost count of the times he'd filled Kathryn's or Gwendolyn's ears with the ways they could have avoided everything.

The girls had been so patient, perched mutely on his sofa, letting him run off at the mouth as he slopped bourbon over his shirt. Looking back, it was surprising how long it took them to run out of patience.

Gwendolyn finally turned on him the day of the earthquake. The three of them were gnawing at onion bagels when he brought up Oliver again. Suddenly she was on her feet yelling, "So you'd rather Oliver just outright slaughtered himself?"

It was the wake-up call he needed. Of course he was glad Oliver survived. He couldn't bear to lose the single most stabilizing influence on what had been a turbulent chapter of his life.

Once he realized that, it was a grueling test of his patience to wait until Oliver was ready to see him. Now that he was, Marcus had no intention of spoiling the moment.

"The past is the past," he told Oliver. "Let's concentrate on getting you well enough to break you out of here. You must be so damned sick of hospital food!"

Oliver was still crying, but it was laughing-crying. Marcus tilted forward and kissed the tears from Oliver's cheeks. He was about to reach up and run his fingers through Ollie's messy bed hair when a male voice behind them said,

"My boy, I was so happy to hear — "

Marcus slid off the bed and took a moment to adjust his tie.

Joseph Breen stood two paces inside the room. He was a bland-faced accountant type with a three-piece suit the color of dirt, wire-framed spectacles, and long cauliflower ears that looked better on Clark Gable. The man was uncompromisingly Roman Catholic, notoriously anti-Semitic, and most significantly, Oliver's boss.

He threaded the brim of a tan homburg through his fingers as he glared at Marcus. Over the public address, someone paged a doctor and nurse to Room 218. A flurry of footsteps pounded the linoleum, but inside Oliver's room, it was like the day had arrived for hell to freeze over.

"Hello, Mister Breen." Marcus offered his hand. "I'm Marcus Adler."

"I know who you are." Breen made no effort to shake his hand. "When Mayer cleaned house last year, I was glad to see he started with you."

That wasn't even close to the way Marcus' exit from MGM came about, but this was neither the time nor place for that argument.

Marcus lowered his hand. "I was just on my way out." He turned to Oliver. "Good to see you, Trenton, ol' boy. I hope your recovery continues apace." He went to step around Breen but was caught by the shoulder and shoved against the metal bars at the foot of Oliver's bed.

"What are you doing here?" he demanded, then glared at Oliver. "Don't tell me you're friends with this guy. You know what he is, don't you?"

Marcus and Oliver flashed panicked glances at each other. *Homo or Commie?*

"I was visiting a friend," Marcus told Breen, "and I happened to see Mister Trenton's name posted outside. Over the years at MGM, Mister Trenton and I have had a number of negotiations. I always found him professional and fair-minded, and I liked to think the respect was mutual. So when I saw he was here, I simply came in to offer my best wishes."

Of course, that didn't explain why he had been kissing away Mr. Trenton's tears, but he hoped Breen hadn't seen that. The indecision in the man's eyes was about as much as Marcus could hope for. He angled his head toward Oliver without taking his eyes off Breen. "Good luck, Trenton."

As he left the room, a loud buzz over the PA system filled the corridor, followed by an announcement it was four o'clock and visiting hours were over.

Marcus reached for his cigarettes and lit up as he pressed the elevator button with his hip. That was a hell of a close call. If Breen had walked in five seconds earlier? *Yikes.* He breathed out a long plume of Camel.

The elevator took forever to arrive, and when it did, it was packed. But the operator, a wizened old turtle of a guy, reckoned there was space for one more and instructed the other passengers to shift around.

A voice yelled, "Hold the car!" Marcus looked down at his shoes for a few moments, then raised them to meet Breen's hellfire eyes just as the doors slid to a close.

CHAPTER 13

With its bright red walls, kelly green upholstery, and prancing Carnival-in-Rio figures along the walls, Mocambo was the perfect place to celebrate the dawning of 1949, but Gwendolyn wasn't in the mood.

Kathryn nudged her in the back seat of Trevor Bergin's Studebaker while up front, Trevor and Marcus talked about the fallout over Howard Hughes cutting 1500 jobs from RKO.

"Your face is like a mini Greek tragedy," Kathryn said. "Is it the store?"

"If things don't pick up soon, I might have to shut down."

"Didn't Edith send some customers your way?"

"A few big spenders, but I haven't seen any of them again."

"What about your Licketysplitters?"

"Some Filipino woman near downtown has stolen all my business. It's impossible to compete when she charges half my rates."

"I bet the quality is half, too."

Gwendolyn smiled. "My rent's going up next month. This postwar boom is all very well unless you want retail space."

Kathryn rubbed her hand. "All you need is a celebrity to wear one of your creations to a premiere—"

"They've first got to come *into* the store." Gwendolyn regretted biting off the end of Kathryn's sentence. She was only trying to be a good friend. "I still haven't found Horton Tattler."

Kathryn popped open her clutch and pulled out a compact to check her makeup. "Horton isn't the only one who can market your perfume."

"I know," Gwendolyn sighed, "but it might be a way to help him out. This sort of thing is right up his alley, and he's had such a tough time of it."

"That's all very well," Trevor butted in from the front seat, "but Chez Gwendolyn isn't a charity. You need to make the right decisions that will shore up its survival."

Trevor Bergin had been one of MGM's biggest heartthrobs throughout the 1940s. He combined the swagger of Errol Flynn with the boy-next-door charm of Jimmy Stewart; he could fill an expensive suit as well as Randolph Scott and sang better than Van Johnson.

He was also queer as a three-dollar bill, and like other contract players in his situation, had allowed himself to be railroaded into an arranged marriage to his studio counterpart, Melody Hope.

But while Trevor took to stardom like a hog to mud, Melody's ego proved far more fragile. Her recent years had cratered into gin-soaked misery.

"By the way," Marcus said, "where is Melody tonight?"

"Beats me."

Gwendolyn could tell from the way Kathryn leaned forward that she smelled a scoop. "So, you and Melody — ?"

"—are getting a divorce." Trevor swung the car to the curb out front of Mocambo. "And yes, that scoop is all yours."

The South-American-themed nightclub was always a riot of color, from raspberry red to nightshade violet, but tonight they'd added actual rainbows—streamers hung across the ceiling from one side of the club to the other.

Mocambo's maître d' was a whippet-thin gent with a Gable moustache, an implacable face, and a precise way about him broadcasting the notion that no detail had been overlooked.

Gwendolyn was surprised when he consulted his silver pocket watch and asked them to wait a moment.

He skirted around the dance floor to consult a rotund man dressed in white tie. Their heads were together in conference for what seemed like an eternity before he retraced his steps.

"Mister Bergin," he said, "it seems our reservations girl has made a most grievous error. I am mortified that we cannot offer your party a dance floor table—"

Trevor raised his hands to stop him. "Don't worry about it, Eduardo. As long as our cocktail waiter has a clear shot to the bar."

Eduardo led them to a table one ring removed from the center of the action.

According to the tacit rules of the Hollywood food chain, the whole point of going out was to see and be seen. The bigger the star, the closer they were seated to the dance floor.

Had Melody been with them, their demotion to second tier might have set off a Wagnerian aria of do-you-know-who-I-am culminating in a how-dare-you finale. But Trevor was offloading his overindulged wife, which was reason enough to celebrate as far as Gwendolyn was concerned. *With Trevor and his divorce, Marcus and his awkward encounter with Oliver's boss, Kathryn losing her radio show, and me slowly going broke, we could do with a decent night out.*

* * *

They were halfway through a second round of champagne cocktails when Gwendolyn began to suspect something was amiss. She shook it off at first, then noticed a couple of well-dressed wives hiding their mouths behind menus and looking in her direction.

Nearby, she spied an eight-top; the women clustered at one end, their husbands at the other. Three of the four women and the oldest of the men were looking at her. Or at least her table.

She motioned for the other three to lean in. "Is it just me, or are we the center of attention?"

"Are you referring to the Junior League?" Trevor asked.

"Or that group of eight who have nothing better to do than gawk at us?"

Kathryn drained her cocktail. "Have none of you noticed Harry Cohn's table? His wife nearly fell off her chair when she spotted us."

"Did the back of my dress drop off or something?" Gwendolyn asked.

"I suspect it involves Trevor's demotion to social Siberia. Sorry, old chap, but it appears to be all downhill from here."

"That's nonsense!" Kathryn made a show of looking around for a waiter as she scanned the room. "*The Sheik* was a huge hit last summer, and this war picture you've just done—what's it called?"

"*Command Decision.*"

"I was talking to Walter Pidgeon the other day. He said that even in a rough cut, the movie is a knockout." She tapped Trevor on the wrist. "He said that Sam Wood couldn't sing your praises high enough. I doubt our banishment has anything to do with Golden Boy here."

Marcus flipped a Mocambo matchbook like a coin. "Don't look at me. I'm no longer even in the biz."

"It's not *me*, is it?" Kathryn reared back. "What the hell have *I* done?"

Marcus pretended to scratch his nose with the matchbook to cover his mouth. "How many people know you helped Bogie with that *Photoplay* essay?"

"The one from last year? That article is the sole reason his career did an about-face. *Key Largo* pulled in three million."

"Speak of the devil."

None of this made sense to Gwendolyn. Bogie and Bacall appeared at the maître d's podium. Bogie looked suave in his tux, but it was Bacall who netted all the attention. As they threaded their way toward their ringside table, her shimmering emerald gown caught the lights as it swirled around her legs.

What if I offered her a free outfit? And encouraged her to wear it to someplace like this?

When Bacall turned sideways, Gwendolyn saw that she was heavily pregnant. Aside from a prominent bosom and a little puffiness around the face, she looked every bit as radiant as she did on the screen.

Peter Lorre and his wife, Kaaren, joined the Bogarts at their table. Within seconds, a waiter appeared with a magnum of champagne, four glasses, and a chrome ice bucket. Lorre made a toast and they clinked glasses. Bogie, however, froze when he spotted Gwendolyn through the figures circling the dance floor.

"Is he staring at me?"

Bacall followed her husband's gaze and noticeably tensed.

Trevor let out a strangled squawk. "Peter Lorre's wife looks as though she's bracing herself for a root canal."

Kathryn slapped her napkin on the table and shot to her feet. "If I'm not back in ten, call out the coast guard."

Half the place charted Kathryn's progress through the maze of tables. When she approached, Humphrey and Peter made half-hearted attempts to stand, but Kathryn waved them down as she crossed to Bogie and Bacall's corner. She was only there a couple of minutes, then headed back with Bogie in tow.

When he arrived at the table, he tendered his right hand. "May I have this dance, Gwendolyn?"

Bogie swung her into a clinch as the band launched into "I'd Like to Get You on a Slow Boat to China."

Gwendolyn and Bogie had a history that stretched back to *The Maltese Falcon*. She'd proved to be so bad an actress that she'd thankfully ended up on the cutting room floor. Bogie had never brought it up when he and Bacall moved into the Garden of Allah before they got married.

She asked him, "Do you have indigestion, or are you about to deliver some bad news?"

He sneered a crooked smile. "I'm surprised I even need to tell you."

Sweet Jesus on the cross. She presented him with her bravest smile. "For the love of Mike, yank off the Band-Aid."

He pulled her in more tightly, as though to steady her for what was coming. "Your screen test for *Gone with the Wind.*"

Gwendolyn groaned. Back when every actress under fifty was maneuvering for a Scarlett O'Hara screen test, Gwendolyn's neighbor, Scott Fitzgerald, managed to score her one. It was a fiasco. Not only did her dress catch fire, but in the mad scramble to get ready, she'd neglected to put on any panties. In an absurd effort to escape the flames, Gwendolyn stumbled into the backdrop, which flipped her hoop skirt up and exposed her shame in glorious Technicolor.

She dropped her head onto Bogie's shoulder. "Why on earth would that film suddenly resurface—OH!" Her head shot up.

"Did I just hear the penny drop?" She saw a depth of sympathy in Bogie's soft brown eyes that he rarely presented to the camera.

"It's Leilah O'Roarke, isn't it?"

"That would be a safe assumption."

"Please tell me what you know."

"In the past couple of months, my wife and I have been to three parties where your screen test was shown ahead of the after-dinner movie. Inevitably, someone asks, 'I wonder whatever happened to that poor unfortunate dish.' And twice now, someone else has said that you've got a store up on the Strip and that they'd heard you financed it by forcing Leilah's hand."

"How am I supposed to have pulled that off?"

"Because you've got her client cards and are sucking her dry before you hand them over."

Gwendolyn closed her eyes and gave herself over to Bogie as he guided her around the dance floor. "These movie parties you went to, were they all Warner Brothers?"

"Yep."

"Is Leilah's husband still head of security?"

"See why I told you it'd be a safe assumption?"

"I almost wish I did have them, so I could hand them over and be done with it."

"So you don't?"

"No!"

"Because if you did—"

"Which I don't!"

"—my advice would be: Hang onto them in case you need them as a bargaining chip."

She felt him tense; the fingers of his right hand dug into her back. She looked up to see alarm plastering Bogie's face. "If this box does exist, might you be in it?"

A nervous smile. "I haven't been heaven's purest angel, but no, I've never set foot in Leilah's brothels. Half the town's running scared, and if those cards fall into the wrong hands—the FBI, the police, or—God help us—Louella or Hedda—it could be a bloodbath."

"Honestly, I don't give a fig about who's gone where, but Leilah paid me a nasty visit a while back. She's convinced I have her rotten old cards, and threatened to ruin me if I didn't fork them over."

"She's made good on her threat."

"My store can only last maybe another four or five months, six at best. Leilah said she'd kill my business; I didn't realize it'd be such a slow death."

"Then you need to convince her."

"I'm more than willing to try—"

"Good, because she and Clem walked in about five minutes ago."

That explains the bear claw to my lower back. "Where are they?"

"They're ordering Eduardo to push their table next to ours."

"Whose idea was that?"

"Sure as hell wasn't my wife's. She looks like she's about to go into labor."

"Maybe she is."

"I'd better go and run defense."

Gwendolyn thanked him for his honesty and returned to her table and related the gist of her dance floor tête-à-tête to the others.

"What are you going to do?" Marcus asked.

"I'd fight fire with fire, if I had any to fight with."

"You've got all the firepower you need," he said.

"How do you figure?"

"Look around, Gwennie. If you publicly call her on her sneaky tactics, everyone here will tell everyone they know, and they will tell everyone *they* know."

Gwendolyn cast around the room.

The eyes not aimed in her direction were pointing toward the Bogart-O'Roarke table; heads were pressed together in furtive conversations behind menus.

I'm really going to have to do this, aren't I? In front of everyone.

"It's your best shot," Kathryn said.

Maybe if I pretend I'm Joan Crawford.

Gwendolyn picked up her champagne cocktail and finished it off. She shanghaied Trevor's and drained that, too. Then she hoisted herself to her feet, locked Leilah's face in her sights, and planted herself in front of their table.

"Leilah," she hollered, "you need to stop."

Leilah looked up from her Lobster Cocktail Cardinal. "Stop what?"

"This public harassment." Gwendolyn slapped the table. "I do not have — " She realized half the people within earshot might be in Leilah's box of cards, and suddenly she couldn't say the words out loud. " — anything that belongs to you!"

"I find that very hard to believe."

"You're ruining me, Leilah! And for what? A hunch?"

"I've gone to extraordinary lengths to recover my business records." Gwendolyn leaned away from the table as Leilah got to her feet, ignoring her husband's attempt to keep her seated. "I've explored every avenue available to me, and guess where every road leads?"

"If I had them, I would give them to you."

"Then hand them over and be done with it."

"I DON'T HAVE THEM!" Gwendolyn screamed so loudly that the drummer crashed into his cymbals and the band lost its rhythm. By the time they recovered, Gwendolyn could feel every pair of eyes drilling her.

"I DO NOT HAVE YOUR GODDAMNED CARDS. I HAVE NEVER SEEN YOUR GODDAMNED CARDS. THIS CRUEL PERSECUTION IS RUINING MY LIFE AND IT MUST STOP!"

"Or you'll do what?"

The question came from Leilah's husband, Clem. The head of Warner Bros. security had spent years dealing with the sordid aspects of life in Hollywood, and he had one of those whiskey-tinged mugs to prove it. He wasn't going to be intimidated by some hysterical dressmaker on the verge of messing her mascara.

Gwendolyn mustered the courage to look him coolly in the eye. "Or I'll call in a few favors of my own." His eyes flared ever so slightly.

She felt a tug at her elbow.

"Come on." It was Marcus. "We're going."

She jutted out her chin like she had one last jab but thought the better of it. She let Marcus guide her through the sea of staring faces, past Eduardo and his pinched mouth and out into the moonless night. She consulted her watch. It was nearly eleven o'clock. She turned to her friends.

"Do you think they'll have an opening at Romanoff's?"

CHAPTER 14

Thirty members of the press were already crowded into RKO's largest soundstage when Kathryn arrived breathless and hatless. *Stupid goddamned flat tire.* She had no idea how to change a tire or who she could call for help, but she'd have to think about that later. For now, it was all about Howard Hughes and Robert Mitchum.

At the end of last summer, the papers had convulsed over the news that the police arrested a movie star for marijuana use during a sting in the Hollywood Hills. Mitchum was Hollywood's new resident bad boy, which, as Kathryn wrote in her *Window on Hollywood* column, is all very well until the boy perpetrates an inexcusable crime like being arrested for smoking reefer.

The bad boy was quoted as saying, "This is the bitter end of everything." Mitchum's official sentence had been handed down, so the question was now: What does his boss have to say about it?

Hughes stood at a microphone placed on the set of a seedy hotel room. To his left, a lawyer type — conservative suit, wary look in the eyes — filled Hughes' ear with a monologue of sound legal advice. Hughes said nothing, but Kathryn could tell he was ignoring every word.

She was gently elbowing her way around the periphery when Hughes stepped to the mike.

"Ladies and gentlemen, I have a statement to make." The chatter dropped away. "I've called this press conference in light of Robert Mitchum's sentence. While I don't personally condone the use of marijuana, nor do I indulge in it, I'd like to state publicly that I feel Mister Mitchum's two-month sentence in the prison farm up at Castaic is excessive. He is clearly being made an example of. In my book, that's an abuse of the law."

Louella Parsons called out, "But you are canceling Mitchum's contract, aren't you?"

"I am not."

Kathryn watched the battle-ax draw back in horror.

Since the invention of the Hollywood star system, the studios had spent untold bucketloads of cash and hours of manpower covering up the errant behavior of their stars. Years of coddling had led the stars to assume it was their God-given right to do as they pleased and damn the consequences.

Hughes choosing not to lift a finger to help one of his biggest stars wiggle free of his barbed hook was noteworthy in itself. But refusing to cancel the contract of a convicted star heralded a new era—one in which the stars would be held accountable, but their overlords wouldn't necessarily impose on them the same behavior the Breen Office required of their screen-bound characters.

"The production code forbids the taking of drugs!" Louella protested.

Hughes looked at her for the first time. "The Hays Code states, and I quote, 'Illegal drug traffic must not be portrayed in such a way as to stimulate curiosity concerning the use of, or traffic in, such drugs.'"

Kathryn was impressed that he had taken the time to memorize the wording verbatim.

"So you are not firing Mitchum?" Louella asked.

"Haven't I already made that clear?" Hughes turned away as someone raised her hand above the heads of the crowd.

"I have a question."

When Hughes located the speaker, he smiled the sort of smile Kathryn knew he reserved for pretty faces. She craned her neck to get a better view: it was that new *Variety* columnist she encountered on the *Samson and Delilah* set.

What a difference three months made.

Back in October, the girl looked like she'd just had her first lesson in how to apply makeup and had abandoned all hope of figuring out what to do with her hair. Evidently she'd since mastered mascara, rouge, and hot rollers. Her chignon didn't suit her, but the attempt was admirable.

Hughes angled his good ear toward the girl. "And you are — ?"

"Ruby Courtland, *Variety*."

Did she just tilt her shoulders back to swell her chest?

"Your question, Miss Courtland?"

"Is it true that your romantic pursuit of Janet Leigh has been a factor in the rumored breakdown of her marriage to Stanley Reames?"

A studio head declaring his support for a convicted movie star is revolutionary, and she wants to know about his love life?

Hughes' smile widened. "Your question makes two inaccurate assumptions. That I have been pursuing Janet Leigh, and that her marriage to Mister Reames is in trouble. I can assure you that neither is the case."

Neither of those statements is even remotely likely to be true. If this is where journalism is headed, then God help us all.

He turned back to the crowd. "That's all I'm prepared to say at this time. Thank you for coming."

Typical Hughes. He drops a bomb, accepts a question from a rookie, and then takes a powder.

He disappeared out a side door ahead of a phalanx of hangers-on. Kathryn withdrew to the edge of a seedy hotel set to jot down the salient points of Hughes' shockwave. She wasn't quite done when a shadow fell across her notepad. Expecting Ruby, it took her a moment to recognize the face smiling at her. "Ramon!"

"I saw you in the crowd just now and thought I'd say hello."

Kathryn hadn't seen Ramon Novarro since he and Marcus came to a crashing end. His skin had sagged noticeably, and gray now flecked his temples.

"I haven't seen you on-screen lately," she said. "Are you a reporter now?"

He shook his head and jutted his chin toward the set. "I have a nice role in *The Big Steal*. We were to commence shooting next week, but with Mitchum's conviction, I suspect they have some rescheduling to do. A lot of the location work was to be in Mexico, and I was looking forward to seeing my family."

Over Ramon's left shoulder, Ruby Courtland had netted a small coterie of admirers, all middle-aged men in suits that needed updating and libidos that needed dampening.

That's not what I meant by having the courage to be yourself, honey.

"That's the movies for you," she said. "You can't count on anything until it's in the can. And even then."

Ramon's smile faded. "Marcus? How is he?"

Kathryn sighed to herself. *I wish I knew.*

"You heard about his appearance in front of HUAC?"

"I assume that's why he left MGM?" Kathryn wondered if Ramon was thinking of his own exit. "Tell him I said hello." He was already half turned away before he spun back. "Does he have anyone special in his life?"

The day of the hospital encounter with Breen, Marcus landed on her doorstep pale as lard and hadn't dare go back since. Instead, he filled his day reading his newspapers and going for his crazy runs along the beach. She nodded.

"I am glad to hear it." He bit into his lower lip. "I regret everything that happened. He is my one that got away."

"Shall I tell him that?"

His gaze wandered across the abandoned set. "I'll leave it up to you."

As Ramon dissolved into the crowd, she thought about her FBI agent with a conscience that did him no good in the long run.

She was still skinny-dipping in her pool of self-pity when Harlan McNamara appeared, dressed in an open-necked shirt and loose corduroy slacks.

"I did a layout with him once, years ago," he said, nodding toward Ramon. "When the advertisers got wind that he was playing an Indian called Laughing Boy, they canceled the whole thing. Friend of yours?"

"Friend of a friend."

A high-pitched giggle erupted out of Ruby Courtland.

"Oh, stop that!" she scolded one of her admirers in a voice designed to arrest the attention of everybody in the soundstage.

"Met the new girl in town?" Harlan asked.

Kathryn dropped her notepad into her handbag and pulled out a pack of Chesterfields. She offered him one and they lit up.

"I met her a couple of months ago on the *Samson and Delilah* set. She looked like she'd stepped off the bus straight from Dogpatch, begging me for advice. I suspect I've created a monster."

They chatted about Hughes' announcement and agreed that it would give Joseph Breen sleepless nights. They shifted onto MGM's upcoming silver jubilee until he pressed the back of his hand to his mouth like the villain in a penny dreadful.

"I have some rather interesting news."

"Interesting news is always welcome."

"*Naturellement*, you didn't hear this from *moi*, but Sheilah Graham and Max Factor have had a falling out."

"You don't say?"

"Ever heard of Faith Domergue?"

"Should I have?"

"One of Hughes' hopefuls. He engaged me to take some new shots of her but she was having trouble concentrating, so I took her to the Formosa for a bite.

In the booth next door were these two businessman types. My ears pricked up when I heard the words 'Factor' and 'Graham.' One of them was a lawyer for Max Factor and he was telling his pal how Sheilah got greedy — or at least her lawyers did. The Max Factor people felt her demands were excessive. She wouldn't budge so they walked away from the deal."

"The radio show is off?"

"The show's still on, but the job of host is up for grabs."

Kathryn gripped him by the lapels in mock menace. "You wouldn't kid a girl, would you?" He told her he wasn't that kind of schmuck. "Your guy at Young and Rubicam, could he get me a name?"

"Already called him."

"And?"

"They've drawn up a short list."

"How short?"

"Six names, and two of them are here right now." He jerked his head in Ruby's direction.

The girl had doubled her number of fans. She was now a crinoline away from looking like Scarlett at the barbeque.

Kathryn flicked a shower of ash in Ruby's direction. "She's younger, prettier, and busting out with work-the-crowd charm. How am I supposed to compete with that?"

"Don't sell yourself short." He hit exactly the right tone she needed to hear. "You've got masses more experience. Plus, younger and prettier don't matter in radio."

Ruby reached her punch line and her rapturous audience broke apart in overstuffed laughter. Harlan said he had an appointment with Hughes about a shampoo advertisement for Diana Lynn. She waved goodbye and stepped onto the hotel room set, finding a shadow to conceal herself in. For the next ten minutes, she watched Ruby wink and flirt, pout and twitter until she realized a stagehand was standing next to her.

"Our art director tells me this set ain't grimy enough." He lifted a bucket of dirt. "This here's genuine grime. I'm going to have to ask you to—"

"Sorry to get in your way."

Outside, she heard Ruby call her name. It was an effort to watch the girl jiggle toward her in a too-tight skirt.

"You seem to have caught the hang of things."

Ruby pulled a face. "All I did was make a fool of myself."

"I wouldn't go that far."

"Your advice was to just be me, but for some reason I turned into Blanche DuBois."

She'd slathered on the makeup with a heavy hand, but up close, the chignon looked fine. "You'll get there."

Ruby lifted one shoulder as though to say, *I'm glad you think so.* "I saw you talking to Harlan McNamara."

"You know him?"

"Did he tell you about Max Factor's shortlist?"

Get a load of little Miss Finger-on-the-Pulse. Kathryn asked, "You heard?" when she really wanted to ask, *How do you know that Harlan knows?*

Ruby nodded. "And I thought New York had a grapevine! It's a dried-up old weed compared to out here. I suppose he told you we're both on it?"

Kathryn kept her face neutral, and simply nodded.

"I want you to know that I wouldn't take the job, even if they offered it to me."

"Why on earth not?"

Ruby threw her arms out wide and dropped them to slap her sides. "I barely know what I'm doing! Making a fool of myself in front of those people in there makes me want to go hide under the covers. Why would I want to tempt fate by standing in front of a microphone connected to millions of people? I don't even know why I'm on that list, but if they're fool enough to offer me the job, I'm going to tell them they've made a wrong call and give it to you instead."

Kathryn wasn't sure how to respond. Of course, Ruby *saying* she'd knock it back wasn't the same as doing it, but the gesture was enough.

"How about we cross that bridge if we come to it?"

Ruby nodded in a demure sort of way that made her look like a twelve-year-old caught breaking into Mommy's beauty case. "Can I walk you to your car?"

Oh God. That damned tire. "I got a flat on the way over. I'm parked on Gower."

"Let's find you a payphone and call the Auto Club." Ruby took in Kathryn's blank face. "Please tell me you're a member."

"Do they let you sign up on the spot?"

CHAPTER 15

Marcus arrived at Oliver's front door and shifted the extra-cheese tuna casserole from his right arm to his left. He hesitated before knocking.

I used to just let myself in.

After the incident at the hospital, Oliver told Marcus it might be best if he didn't come again. "We'll catch up on lost time once I'm home."

Marcus had counted the days until Oliver's release, and was elated when news finally came mid-January that he would be discharged the following Friday.

Marcus spent the whole of that Thursday vacuuming, dusting, and scrubbing Oliver's apartment near the corner of Sunset and Western. He stocked the cupboards and icebox with every staple he could think of, filled a big vase with sunflowers and propped a card against it welcoming Oliver home. *Call me when you get in!* He left it unsigned, just in case.

Marcus stayed home all day, and the following one, too, but no call came. By Sunday lunchtime, he could no longer restrain himself.

A mixture of relief and disappointment welled up when Oliver answered the telephone. Yes, he'd been discharged. Yes, he was happy to be home. Yes, he noticed how nice everything looked. Yes, he got the flowers and card. Yes, goddamnit, he was going to call. *Of course* he was going to call, but it hasn't even been twenty-four hours yet. What? It's Sunday? What happened to Saturday?

Looking back, that should have been the first clue. But Marcus had been so cross-eyed happy to have Oliver back that he tried to be understanding when Oliver told him that a migraine was coming on. He'd been suffering from them since the accident. He wasn't up for visitors. He'd call when he felt better.

Oliver took three days to call, but when he did, to Marcus' boundless joy, he sounded like the pre-accident Oliver. The Oliver who had pursued him like nobody else. The Oliver who had helped him forget Ramon Novarro.

In the privacy of Oliver's apartment, their reunion was sweet and tender. He loved the sunflowers. He appreciated the full Frigidaire. He'd slept with Marcus' note under his pillow. They touched. They kissed. They chuckled about Breen.

The bliss lasted two hours.

Marcus was preparing cheese and crackers as they chatted about Lucille Ball's new radio show, *My Favorite Husband*. Oliver hadn't heard it yet and Marcus told him how the announcer introduced each episode by saying, "Now, let's take a look at the Cooper family, two people who live together and like it."

It had long been Marcus' fantasy that he and Oliver might one day live together at the Garden of Allah. Back when Marcus was at MGM and Oliver worked for the Breen Office, it was a pipe dream. But now that Marcus' situation had changed, he felt they were one step closer to cohabitation. Bringing up *My Favorite Husband* was his way of inserting the idea into their conversation, but he didn't get that far.

He was arranging the crackers on a blue glass platter when Oliver screamed "DAMNIT ALL TO HELL!" Marcus' copy of *Sexual Behavior in the Human Male* hit the wall by his head and tumbled to the floor.

Oliver was disturbingly pale; his neck blotched with crimson. Marcus asked him what was wrong.

"I can't do this!" His eyes burned with fury. "I can't stand it! The flowers! The crackers! The cheese! None of it!"

This was about more than smoked Gouda. "I just wanted you to come home to a nice place, so if I overdid it—"

Oliver started taking staccato breaths. "It's enough to drive a guy into the loony bin!"

"What is?" Marcus walked out of the kitchen, figuring if he could touch Oliver, it might calm him down, but it had the opposite effect.

Oliver grabbed up his walking sticks and hobbled backward into the corner of his living room. "You have to go!"

"Oliver, honey, I don't—"

"Now! Before I lose my mind! GET OUT!"

Marcus vowed not to return until he received an apology.

When Oliver called a couple of days later begging forgiveness and confessing that he didn't know what came over him, he promised it wouldn't happen again.

But it did. Every time.

Marcus would go to Oliver's place. They'd make dinner, and later play cribbage or listen to the radio. Everything would be fine, easy and relaxed as it always had been, until events took a ninety-degree turn. A dark cloud would thunder across Oliver's face, then a newspaper or a hat would fly across the room, or a checkerboard would be swept from the table.

One time, he said, "I know you were sleeping with someone while I was cooped up." Marcus was unsure how to respond. Oliver took his silence as an admission. "Who was it? Someone I know? Don't tell me. I don't want it shoved in my face."

It took Oliver five days to apologize for that one.

The tuna casserole in Marcus' hands had been Doris' suggestion. "Fill him with his favorite dinner, then confront him." The recipe was hers, too. Oliver loved Doris' tuna casserole, although the extra cheese and potato chips sprinkled in for crunch were Marcus' idea. He used their secret knock: two quick raps, pause, then one more, then he turned the doorknob.

Oliver was sprawled out in his easy chair, snoring softly, his head lolling to one side. On a small wooden side table, a shot glass sat next to an empty bottle of Old Forester. A copy of *Raintree County* had fallen from his hand to the rug, its pages crumpled and its dust jacket half off. On the radio, some silly soap opera was playing.

Marcus pulled off his jacket and slung it over the back of the sofa. He picked up the book, as well as the shot glass and whiskey bottle, and deposited them on the kitchen counter. The sink had days' worth of dirty dishes. As he started to scrub them, Oliver stirred in his chair. Marcus called his name, but he didn't respond.

I'll give him until I've finished clearing up.

When he was done, Oliver was still asleep.

I'll give him until dinner is nearly ready.

He lit the oven and inserted the casserole dish, then opened the refrigerator to look for ice cubes, but the inside smelled like a can of three-bean mix open since last Thanksgiving.

The source of the stench was in a dessert dish looking like melted Velveeta coagulating beneath a carpet of blue mold dotted with orange heads. When Marcus returned from the trash cans out back, he opened every window in the place.

Although Oliver could get around, his legs still gave him trouble. Anything that involved bending at the knees or hips crippled him with pain. Marcus set about straightening the messy bedclothes, pulling the sheets tight, and fluffing the pillows. As he did, a trio of pill bottles on the nightstand caught his eye. He picked one up.

Dr. J. Kramer – Specialist in pain relief and ease of mind. The contents of this bottle are a proprietary blend of ingredients and medications.

"Are you snooping on me?"

Oliver stood in the doorway gripping his walking canes in both hands, his mouth set in a grim line.

"I was making your bed—" Marcus wished he didn't come off sounding so defensive. He held up the bottle. "What's in these?"

"How should I know?" Oliver shuffled into the room and swiped it from Marcus' hand. "I'm in real bad pain. All the time. One of the orderlies at the hospital told me to go see this guy. He was very sympathetic. Told me, 'I've got just the thing.'"

"But—"

"They work, Marcus. That's all I care about." He tipped the last of the pills into his mouth and forced them down.

Marcus said nothing more. He didn't want to risk triggering another outburst. Especially not tonight.

The aroma of the casserole reached them. "Dinner's probably fifteen minutes away. You need to wash up?"

Oliver nodded. "Smells good." He threw one of his canes onto the bed and reached out for Marcus' hand. When Marcus took it, his boyfriend's skin was dry as three-day-old bread.

He helped Oliver into the bathroom and stayed there until Oliver closed the door.

"You'll find some wine in the Frigidaire," Oliver called out. "It's not very expensive but the guy said it's halfway decent."

Marcus opened the nightstand drawer; ten more pill bottles were inside. He closed it and returned to the kitchen.

He was pulling the casserole out of the oven as Oliver made his way to the small round dining table. "I'm starving!"

Marcus' worries about the contents of those pill bottles melted away. A healthy appetite was a very good sign.

They'd downed several forkfuls when Oliver said, "Did I tell you Mister Breen has been paying my salary this whole time?"

The accident was back in September of 1948; it was now January. That was a long time to pay the salary of someone too sick to work.

"He's been like a father to me. I'd be on skid row without him."

Marcus wanted to tell Oliver that was ridiculous. Even after buying the new Buick, he still had tons of his MGM money. He would have been happy to support Oliver until he got back on his feet—financially and literally.

"He called me today." Oliver pushed his half-empty plate away. "Specifically to talk about that day at the hospital. It was a tense conversation."

"I can imagine."

"He wanted to know what you were doing there. And how I knew you. And how long. He asked me if you've ever talked to me about Communism. And if you've ever tried to seduce me."

Marcus suppressed a laugh. "Into bed?"

"I got the impression he meant seduced me into Communism as a route to your bed."

"That's ironic," Marcus laughed into his wine glass. "Considering it was you who pursued me in the beginning."

He winked conspiratorially, but got a steely look in return.

"I told you—he's been like a father to me."

"He's been very generous, continuing to pay your salary the way he has."

"Don't think I can't hear the 'but' in your voice."

Marcus debated how best to voice his concern. "I've been thinking. Back when I was at MGM, you working for the Breen Office meant we were political enemies."

"We found a middle road."

"We did. But I no longer have to play by MGM's rules and if you left the Breen Office, you wouldn't have to play by theirs. We could do what we liked. Nobody at the Garden of Allah looks sideways at anybody's living arrangements. We could live there. Together. Wouldn't that be great?"

Oliver thumped the table. "Breen has been more than generous with me — not just in financial terms, but with his encouragement and interest in my progress and recovery."

Joseph Breen was one of the most dour-faced, judgmental, morally buttoned-down killjoys Marcus had ever encountered. The idea that he'd been a bleeding-heart sob sister struck Marcus as stretching all bounds of plausibility.

"Oh, come on, Ollie," he said. "You can't possibly think that Breen has your best interests at heart more than I do. Okay, so he's continued to pay your—"

"He told me that he looks upon me as a son."

"He's already got six kids. I hardly think—"

"He said I must end my association with you."

Marcus dropped his fork onto the table. "And what did *you* say?"

"I didn't say much of anything."

"In other words, you didn't say no."

"He's my boss, Marcus. I have to tread carefully."

"Yes, but only for as long as he's your boss."

"How can I quit now that he's paid my salary for so long?"

"Are you sending me away?" Marcus' voice was shaking. "Like you're Humphrey Bogart and I'm Ingrid fucking Bergman and we're standing at the Casablanca airport with the fog rolling in? Is that what's happening here?"

Oliver hurled his plate against the kitchen wall.

Marcus jumped to his feet. He reached his jacket in four strides, then took a sharp turn into the bedroom. He pulled open the bedside table and grabbed one of Dr. Kramer's pill bottles and pushed it into his pocket, then returned to the living room. "This isn't over!"

"I never said it was!"

"Good!"

Marcus slammed the door and took the stairs two by two. When he got to his car, he was too worked up to sit behind the wheel, so he kept walking, and didn't cool off until he'd reached Hollywood High. By then, he was closer to home than he was to his car, so he kept heading west until he saw the twelve-foot sign: GARDEN OF ALLAH HOTEL AND VILLAS.

He slipped his hand into his pocket and pulled out the bottle. He read the label on the back. *The exact ratio of components is confidential.*

"We'll see about that."

CHAPTER 16

When Kathryn slipped on the dark maroon jacket with the black side panels, she knew she'd found the perfect ensemble. She stepped back from the mirror. "That's more like it."

Gwendolyn tugged at the hem to straighten out the lines. "This is the sixth one you've tried on. They all suited you, otherwise I wouldn't have suggested them." She held up a crème blouse but decided it was too light. "I know this luncheon at MGM is a big deal and all, but I can't remember the last time I saw you this agitated over a meal."

Kathryn's appointment wasn't just any old meal — it was MGM's silver jubilee: five hundred guests with fifty-eight stars, a twenty-piece orchestra, and every significant name on the payroll.

She'd dilly-dallied for so long that she'd have to drive straight from Chez Gwendolyn to MGM. "You're right," she admitted, "I'm at sixes and sevens."

"But you'll know everyone there." Gwendolyn held up the clothes Kathryn had walked in wearing. "Shall I take these home for you?"

Kathryn nodded. "It's *because* I'll know everyone there that I'm in such a state."

"It's about this radio show, isn't it?"

The black silk blouse Gwendolyn proposed was a tad frilly for Kathryn's liking, but it was nearly eleven thirty. If she didn't leave soon, she'd be late. She took off the jacket and started putting on the blouse. "Max Factor will have to find a way to reduce their shortlist to a single name, and some heavy hitters will be there."

"You haven't embarrassed yourself in front of any of them," Gwendolyn pointed out. "You haven't hurled drinks in their faces, or thrown up on their laps, or slept with any of them, have you?"

Kathryn followed Gwendolyn into the main salon and pulled out her checkbook. "I just wish I could walk in on somebody's arm. Marcus should be there today. He's done as much as anyone to keep MGM where it is."

"That might be true," Gwendolyn said, "but our dear boy is in no shape to go anywhere. Have you seen him lately?"

"I took him out for coffee and Danish at Schwab's, but I could tell it was an effort." Kathryn thought he looked like he was fresh off a three-day binge, which might well have been true. "He can't win with Oliver these days."

"They'll work it all out, I'm sure."

Kathryn wished she could share Gwennie's confidence, but Marcus looked like a wreck and didn't care who knew it.

Gwendolyn tapped her watch. "You should be halfway to Culver City by now."

* * *

Soundstage Fifteen was the largest in the world, and MGM needed every square foot of it to accommodate the hoards it had invited to celebrate its twenty-fifth anniversary. And they had good reason. Since Dory Schary took charge of production, profits were steaming toward a twenty-two-year high.

Along the far left wall, three tiers of dining tables sat twenty-five each, like the world's most elegant bleachers. It was where the upper echelon of management and movie stars would sit. They faced six trestle tables, each a hundred feet long, where lower management, high-earning cinema owners, and members of the press would sit.

Towering over them was a paddle steamer painted bright pink with white trim and twin smokestacks that rose twenty feet into the air. The perky blonde greeter at the door who found Kathryn's position on the seating chart enthusiastically told her that the set was for Esther Williams' new picture, *Neptune's Daughter*, which meant they were all standing over a swimming tank deep enough to drown in. "Isn't that fun?"

At the far end, perched on a temporary three-level stage, the studio orchestra played a string of MGM's greatest hits. As they transitioned from "Meet Me in St. Louis" into "Fascinating Rhythm," Kathryn surveyed the crowd milling around her. It was as she expected: ninety-five percent of the booze-bloated faces belonged to chumps over fifty hoping to catch an eyeful of high-spirited ingénue types like the Tootsie Roll at the front door.

Still, any of those stuffed shirts could be the exact exhibitor or advertising exec whose opinion Max Factor might enlist. In this town, one never knew who was sleeping with whom.

Backscratching was as popular a pastime as beach volleyball. Kathryn searched for a familiar face and exhaled in relief when she spotted Ginger Rogers.

Ginger had been a resident of the Garden of Allah when she and her indomitable mother, Lela, first came to Hollywood in the early thirties. Ginger was a fervent tennis player Kathryn could barely keep up with. They had remained friends as they ascended their respective ladders, but it had been a while since they'd had a chance to chat.

It took a few waves of Kathryn's purse to attract Ginger's attention. She broke off her conversation with a pot-bellied Midwesterner with a crew cut and hurried away. "How *are* you?" Ginger's sapphire eyes widened with joy. "And what *are* you wearing? That perfume!"

Kathryn had run out the door that morning without applying her usual dab of Tabu. It took her a moment to realize what Ginger could smell. "It's Gwendolyn's."

"She has her own fragrance?"

"Just some concoction she makes up. Tell me, what are you doing here?"

Ginger smiled tentatively. "I'm a last-minute ringer for Judy in *You Made Me Love You*. It seems she's not up to the rigors of filming a musical right now."

The stories of Judy Garland's escalating unreliability had been grist for the gossipmongers ever since *The Pirate*. That picture's screenwriters, Albert Hackett and Frances Goodrich, were frequent Garden residents and had given everyone a blow-by-blow of the on-set troubles and delays. The film bombed at the box office and Judy's troubles reeled from bad to worse.

"You and Fred will be back on-screen together? That *will* be worth seeing."

Ginger nodded. "But not in a movie called *You Made Me Love You*. That title is all Judy's. I'll be livid if they don't change it." She ducked behind Kathryn and held up her purse to cover her face. "As discreetly as you can, look over your left shoulder and tell me if Eddie Mannix is still talking to the man-eater."

L.B. Mayer's right-hand man was fifty feet away, talking to a slim woman in a tight sheath of striking pink overlaid with a bold black leaf pattern. She wore a matching pink Robin Hood cap with a long feather that wobbled as she gabbed at Mannix.

"Who are you hiding from?" Kathryn asked. "Mannix or Pinky McPink-eye?"

"Mannix I can handle," Ginger whispered back. "It's Pinky that makes me break out in hives. Can we move away? But slowly. I don't want to catch her attention."

"I hate to tell you," Kathryn laughed, "but you were built to attract attention."

"You're not helping!"

The two of them slipped down the aisle between two of the long trestle tables until they were hidden behind a knot of exhibitors from Chicago.

"Who did we just sneak away from?" Kathryn asked.

Ginger rolled her eyes. "Howard's been calling me lately."

"Are you and he—?"

"We're just good friends now. But he needed a date for the *Joan of Arc* premiere and he asked me."

"Because Janet Leigh, Cyd Charisse, Kathryn Grayson, and Ava Gardner were all busy?"

"Or made out like they were. Anyway, we were in the foyer chatting about his latest airplane—so what else is new?—when suddenly he darted into the crowd, leaving me stranded. Ol' Pinkie over there descended on me, started barraging me with all kinds of questions, mostly about Howard's love life and his plans for RKO."

"Who is she?"

"Some columnist with *Variety*."

Kathryn craned her neck around the cluster of Chicagoan movie-house owners. "You mean Ruby Courtland?"

"You met her?"

"Twice."

"What's your take?"

"Bit of an eager beaver and a touch naïve, but weren't we all at that age?"

The perky blonde hostess appeared beside them. "Miss Rogers, it's time to make your way backstage. The Parade of Stars will commence soon."

Ginger nodded, then turned to Kathryn. "This is all such a madhouse. Promise me you'll call and we'll have lunch."

* * *

The colossal effort by Mayer and his team impressed the bejesus out of Kathryn. They hired George Murphy as MC and planted him on the *Neptune's Daughter* set, where he introduced the fifty-eight movie stars currently working at the studio.

The line-up was a moviegoer's dream. They were all there: Clark, Judy, Ava, Katharine, Greer, Lena—forced to march across the stage like a pageant of oddities.

Even Errol Flynn, who was currently filming *That Forsyte Woman*, made an appearance. Kathryn hadn't seen him since his last stint at the Garden and was a little shocked at how puffy he looked.

A sumptuous meal followed the parade of stars.

Kathryn was seated in the second row between the foreign correspondent for a London newspaper she had never heard of and the owner of the largest chain of MGM-affiliated movie houses in the Dakotas.

His conversation consisted of one topic: the Supreme Court's decision declaring studio-owned theaters a monopoly. The Justice Department had announced that all five majors must give up their interests in 1400 movie theaters.

Kathryn listened to the man's woes with half an ear. She had a direct sightline to Ruby, who was one row closer to the stars. Kathryn couldn't see Ruby's immediate neighbors, but there was a great deal of conspiratorial whispering.

As the cherries jubilee was served, Mayer approached the microphone at the executive table and addressed the crowd with a flowery soliloquy about the glory of the studio's past, and how their roster of coming films promised an exciting twelve months.

But everyone there knew MGM's crown had slipped; Paramount, Warner, and Twentieth Century-Fox were starting to out-gross them.

Still, it was a superb display designed to dominate countless inches of newspaper columns over the coming days.

They were generous with the wine, too, so by three o'clock, Stage Fifteen was abuzz with tanked-up guests. The London correspondent and the theater tycoon from Fargo stumbled away in the direction of the movie-star tables, which suited Kathryn fine. She wanted to sneak a closer peek at this new version of Ruby. The dolled-up femme fatale with the misguided chignon at Hughes' press conference was bad enough, but what was Ruby shooting for with this pink-and-black concoction?

The bold pink of her dress should have made it easy to track her, but Kathryn's prey proved elusive. She zigzagged around the boisterous crowd until a thicket parted to reveal Errol and Ruby leaning against Esther Williams' paddle steamer—which exactly matched the pink in Ruby's dress. *Surely that's a coincidence.*

Kathryn had been Errol's neighbor and drinking partner long enough to know every maneuver in his playbook, and he was executing one now.

Ruby stood with her back to the set as Errol towered over her, his left arm leaning against one of the pink spokes.

Kathryn skirted around the perimeter of the banquet space and snuck behind the set until she found a quiet nook within earshot.

"Oh, come on, Mister Flynn," Ruby admonished.

"Please, call me Errol."

Ruby let out an artificial giggle. "You and I both know that Mayer's speech was baloney. Tastes have changed, and MGM's been left in the dust. They've had their time. So has Mayer, and so have Louella and Hedda."

"Strong opinions from such a young girl."

Get your mind out of your pants, Errol. She's talking about you, too.

"Louella and Hedda are in their sixties," Ruby pressed on. "They should think about retiring. Meanwhile, I'm only twenty-two, which makes me nearly forty years younger than them."

"I like a girl with ambition."

You like a girl who's barely old enough to vote.

"Even Kathryn Massey," Ruby went on.

"What about her?"

"When she was my age, all she did was answer mail for Tallulah Bankhead, but I'm already being invited to a big wingding like this."

Someone's been doing their homework.

"You make it sound like Kathryn should be put out to pasture."

Ruby let out another giggle, as hollow as the last one.

"I'm just saying that the world is bending toward people with youth on their side. Louella, Hedda, Kathryn, Sheilah, they're all a bit past it. The future belongs to people like me."

"How do you figure that?" Errol's voice had sobered up.

"Over the next few years, the movies are going to see a new surge of customers."

"Who?"

"Teenagers."

"Kids? You're off your rocker."

"If you'd been paying attention, you'd know there's been a huge spike in births since the end of the war. Those babies will grow up in the boom times that follow every major conflict. Look what happened after the Great War. Just you watch: the 1950s will be the Roaring Twenties all over again. And when that happens, who's going to want to listen to a bunch of old bags?"

CHAPTER 17

Gwendolyn figured at least a dozen years had passed
since she'd stepped inside the Hollywood Hotel.

In its 1920s heyday, it had been the epicenter of
Hollywood's social life. Expectant faces glowing with
stardust stayed there when they arrived from the
boonies of Montana and Kentucky hoping for a better
life than the hardscrabble subsistence they'd fled.
Budding moguls inventing the studio system as they
went along struck deals on its spacious veranda. All the
best clubs and charity events held their galas at the
Hollywood Hotel. Rudolph Valentino even spent his
honeymoon there.

Gwendolyn looked around the deserted foyer and
realized its halcyon days were a speck in the rearview
mirror. The splashes of gold and blue in the carpet's
leafy design had faded in the sunlight. The sofas and
easy chairs arranged along the length of the building
sagged from decades of use and gave off the musty
smell of undisturbed dust. The yellowing paint on the
columns had started to peel away in flakes the size of
her thumbnail. Spider webs were left unmolested.

Nobody appeared when she arrived at reception.

A young chap in a deep red bellboy jacket with gold stripes down the arms stood behind a tour desk that advertised bus trips to San Francisco and train tickets to "all points east." As Gwendolyn approached, she could see how frayed the jacket was.

He apologized that there was nobody to greet her, and said he'd see if he could rustle someone up. When Gwendolyn told him she wasn't there to check in, the resigned look in the kid's eyes said, *Hardly anybody does, lady.*

"I'm looking for an employee. His name is Horton."

In desperation, Gwendolyn had gone through the LA City Directory and systematically telephoned each hotel to ask if Horton Tattler worked there. She got nowhere until she hit "H" and was told Horton was employed there, but they couldn't be sure which shift he worked and to try her luck next time she passed by.

The bellhop's face brightened. "Sure, he's here."

"Where might I find him?" she asked.

"Dining room, but it ain't open till eleven."

It was twenty to eleven now. "I want to catch him before the lunch trade starts."

He threw her a jaundiced eye—*What lunch trade?*—and pointed to the doorway on his right.

The dining room was as run-down as the foyer. Threadbare rugs beneath wooden tables pockmarked with neglect, grimy potted plants suspended from a shabby ceiling dulled by decades of tobacco smoke, opaque windows in need of elbow grease.

"Hello?" Gwendolyn called out. "Anybody?"

After a moment or two, a scowl peeked out from behind a swinging door.

"Horton!"

She rushed toward him. His craggy face was blank with surprise.

"I've been looking all over for you!" He pulled at the ragged hem of his ill-fitting white jacket. "I need to talk to you. Do you have a minute?"

They sat down at the nearest table and she ran him through the story of her broken perfume bottles. When she was done, he asked, "Is that what you're wearing right now?" She nodded; he beamed. "You've got yourself a winner."

Leilah had seen to it that her business was doing so poorly that if she failed to turn it around soon, Chez Gwendolyn was a dead duck. She grabbed him by the forearm. "You think so? You really do?"

"And I wish you the very best of luck," he told her. "Now, if you'll excuse me, I have some prep work to do." He went to rise to his feet, but she pulled him down.

"I was hoping we could do this together."

She watched the impact of her words hit his face. "We?"

"Didn't Tattler's Tuxedos have its own product? A cologne, maybe?"

"We had an aftershave balm and eau de cologne set. It was quite the brisk seller."

"Did you develop it yourself?"

"With the help of a professional perfumer, yes, but—"

"I can't do this on my own! I need you, Horton. So here's what I'm thinking: what if you had a stake in this venture?"

His face deflated. "Oh, Gwendolyn, look at me. Look at this scruffy old dining room I'm working in. I have no money to contribute."

"The money, I've got," she told him. "You have the expertise. What if I stake the dough up front, and you take a cut of the profits?" His eyes flashed ever so slightly. "How much do we need to get this off the ground?"

"Getting the formula exactly right takes a professional, and they're expensive. You have to package it right, so figure in the bottle design and box, plus manufacturing costs. Then there's advertising—"

"Roughly."

She watched figures roll through his eyes. "Eighteen hundred, maybe. Do you have that?"

I have precisely one thousand, nine hundred, and sixty-seven dollars in my bank account. It was the last of her Alistair Dunne money. She knew it made poor business sense to pin her entire future on this one idea, but she clung to it like it was the last life vest aboard the *Titanic.*

"Barely," she squeaked. Horton stared at her while she screwed up her courage. "Let's do it."

His eyes misted over. "Are you sure?"

"No!"

"Gwendolyn, my dear, you need to be—"

"I must do something!" Her voice echoed around the dismal restaurant.

He took her hands between his. "In that case, I know the right person."

* * *

Exactly a week later, Gwendolyn stood at her counter, tapping the glass top in apprehension. "How did you find this guy?"

"His father was a master glass blower in Venice who specialized in delicate bottles. When Zap came along, he showed an aptitude for it, so Papa Zaparelli brought him in. By that stage, he was doing very well for himself and was a regular at my store. But Zap got more interested in what went inside Papa's bottles, so he became a perfumer with a knack for packaging."

"He sounds perfect."

"We'll have to play it by ear," Horton cautioned. "The last time I saw him, he'd just started shaving."

Gwendolyn had been picturing a well-turned-out businessman in his mid forties with a self-assured command of the perfume business. "How old is he now?"

"Twenty-five or thereabouts. That men's set he did for us was his very first project."

Gwendolyn felt her optimism trickle out of her. *I'm going to hand over the last of my savings to someone who doesn't even remember* The Jazz Singer?

The silver bell above the door rang, and a tall man with ink-black hair strode in exuding the confidence of a Rockefeller. "Horton, you old son of a gun!" He held his hand out. "What a pleasure to see you again. And how well you look!"

Horton must have spent his last few bucks having his suit pressed and his shoes polished.

The men shook hands and turned to Gwendolyn. "I'd like to introduce Gwendolyn Brick. Gwendolyn, this is Ignacio Zaparelli."

"Call me Zap."

His hands were large and strong, with fingers at least as long as his palms were broad, and reminded Gwendolyn of Alistair.

She took in his three-piece suit. The color alternated between royal blue and deep purple, depending on how the sunlight hit it. In a predictable world of charcoal grays and navy blues, it was a refreshing sight.

"Your suit," she said, "it's so unusual." *No wonder he chose this color — it matches his eyes.*

"I have a cousin, he's a tailor in Rome. I was there at Christmas. You should see that city now. It's coming back to life. Give it five years, and everybody will want to go there." He lifted his arm so Gwendolyn could inspect the fabric. "When he showed me this material, well, how could I say no?"

He swung around to face the store. "What a charming place you have. The colors, the light." He lifted an eyebrow. "So this fragrance, are you wearing it now?"

Gwendolyn nodded, and picked up a cheap little bottle she bought at Newberry's. She popped open the cork stopper and floated it under his nose.

He closed his eyes as he took in a deep breath, then held it until he had to breathe again.

"You've really got something there. But of course how it smells in the bottle is only useful for the sales pitch. What really counts is how it performs on a woman. A *real* woman."

The way he hovered over the word "real" made Gwendolyn blush. Although he had Tyrone Power's dark looks, he wasn't nearly as handsome, but he had a magnetic quality that made the hairs on her arms stand up.

He leaned in, running his eyes along the line of her neck. "May I?"

Gwendolyn nodded, and angled her head to one side. She felt Zap's warm breath on her skin.

Goodness gracious!
He drew in another breath.
He's at least ten years younger than you.
"Mmmm."
So why are you reacting like a silly little Girl Scout?
He stepped back again, his deep blue eyes gleaming with—Gwendolyn wasn't sure how to read it. Admiration? Excitement? Eagerness? Or was it just good old-fashioned lust?

"You came up with this formula yourself?" he asked.

Gwendolyn explained that it was part Chanel No. 5, part Miss Dior, with notes of orange, vanilla, and cinnamon oil.

"Will that be a problem?" Horton asked. "Seeing as how it's mostly made up of perfumes from other couturiers."

Gwendolyn was glad to see Zap shake his head.

"Not once I'm done." He turned to her. "Do you have a name for it?"

"Earthquake—it'll send you staggering!"

"Do you really want to be associated with a natural disaster?"

Gwendolyn began to see how ill-equipped she was for this enterprise.

"Do you have any ideas?" Horton asked.

He took Gwendolyn's pencil and paper and started sketching a bottle shaped like an "S" topped with a palm tree.

"I suggest 'Sunset Boulevard.' It conjures Los Angeles, movie stars, and nightclubs on the Strip. Sunset twists and turns as it heads west toward the ocean, so you're never sure what you might encounter around the next bend. Mysterious. Surprising. Just like the woman who wears it."

A jolt buzzed up Gwendolyn's spine. "That's perfect! How soon can we start?"

He picked up the Newberry's bottle. "If I can take this with me, I'll get on it right away."

She pushed it into his hands. "I don't have much time to lose." *Or money.*

"I'll send a contract by messenger in the morning," Zap said. Horton and Gwendolyn saw Zap to the door. As they watched him climb into a pre-war Pontiac, she hooked her arm through Horton's. "This just might work!"

"For both our sakes, it'd better. But with Zap on board, I have a good feeling about this."

CHAPTER 18

Oliver's Dr. Kramer wasn't listed in the city directory, nor in any of the old ones at the Beverly Hills library. Many of his past and present neighbors at the Garden of Allah were veteran pill-poppers, so he put out feelers, but got nowhere.

Perhaps Kramer wasn't his real name? Or maybe he was a doctor of philosophy pretending to be a doctor of medicine because it was good for business?

Meanwhile, Marcus would visit Oliver from time to time, but not as often as he wanted to. It had taken them weeks to get past the ugliness of that awful night in January.

As January of 1949 became February, and then March, Marcus tried to bring up the subject of Kramer and his shifty pills, but Oliver deflected every time. His skin grew more and more sallow, his fine, brown hair wilted like straw, and his eyes lost their optimistic shine. Somehow he found the strength to return to work, though Marcus didn't know how. Invariably, Oliver would already be in bed when Marcus came around in the evening, exhausted by the day's work defending the Hays Code and barely able to summon the strength to eat.

In the end, it was Charles Laughton who supplied Kramer's address.

———

Laughton and his wife Elsa Lanchester had been occasional guests at Garden of Allah parties ever since the unusually hot summer of '39 when Charles was filming *The Hunchback of Notre Dame*. He would dash from RKO to the Garden during his lunch break in full makeup and keep sane in the swimming pool.

Laughton was off to Europe where he'd been offered the lead in *The Man on the Eiffel Tower*. Elsa invited Marcus to a farewell party in the private room of the Vine Street Brown Derby. Laughton was propped up at the bar knocking back his umpteenth bourbon when Marcus overheard Elsa remind her husband that he ought to see Kramer before they leave for France.

Marcus spun around. "*Doctor* Kramer?"

"You know him?"

"I've been trying to track him down." Suspicion sent Elsa's eyebrows northward. "He's moved offices since the last time I saw him."

Charles gave a throaty harrumph. "It'd take an army of Pinkertons to locate the good doctor Kramer should he fail to apprise you of his latest whereabouts."

Marcus took a chance. "I've never known anybody to move so damn often!"

"I don't have his current address on me," Elsa said. "I'll cable you when we get home."

* * *

Carroll Avenue was lined with gothic Victorian mansions built in the 1880s when Los Angeles was starting to outgrow its boundaries.

Back then, a prosperous middle class that could afford maids and chauffeurs and governesses populated Angelino Heights, but LA's postwar push toward the Pacific and into the San Fernando Valley had left the neighborhood in its wake.

Number 1346 was a two-story house that featured a narrow wraparound porch topped with the sort of witch's hat turret nobody built anymore. If the owner had bothered to keep up the maintenance, it would have looked quite darling, but now its delicate spindle work hung in rotting scraps and the paint on its myriad teardrop shingles had long since weathered away.

The guy who answered the door wore a respectable blue serge suit that was a far cry from the disheveled picture of back-alley shiftiness Marcus anticipated.

"Doctor Kramer?"

The man nodded. He had the full face of someone who enjoyed his pancakes a little too much; an extravagant moustache bisected it from ear to ear.

"Mister Bryant, I presume?" He opened the door wider and directed Marcus into a spacious office that had been a living room at some time. An empty fireplace next to the doctor's desk was bordered by a sheet of pressed metal painted white. A damp chill pervaded the room.

Kramer pointed to a chair and took his seat behind the desk. "How may I help you?"

Marcus pulled Oliver's bottle from his pocket and slammed it on the desk. Startled, the man pitched back. Marcus twisted off the top, shook a couple of pills into his palm, and threw them at Kramer. One of them missed him completely, but the other bounced off a doughy cheek and onto the rug.

"What the—?"

Marcus jabbed a finger toward Kramer. "You're going to tell me what's in these nasty pills of yours, and I'm not leaving till you do."

Within seconds, Kramer had recovered. "My medications are a proprietary blend of ingredients—"

"Yeah, yeah, I read it on the label."

Kramer picked the pill up off the floor and held it between his thumb and index finger. "Where did you get this?"

"A close friend of mine has been coming to see you."

"Doctor-patient confidentiality precludes me from furnishing you with any details whatsoever. This conversation is now at an end."

"I'm not budging until you tell me what's in these things."

Kramer kept his face dispassionate. "Do you really think I haven't dealt with threats far more intimidating than yours?"

"You're ruining his life," Marcus said.

"Exactly who are we talking about, Mister Bryant?"

"Oliver Trenton."

"Ah, the broken legs." Kramer smoothed down his shaggy moustache. "I am not ruining Mister Trenton's life, but saving him from a harsh existence of brutal pain."

"When was the last time you saw him?"

"Doctor-patient confidentiality—"

Marcus jumped to his feet. "Screw your damned confidentiality. If you bothered to care, you'd see that Oliver is unraveling." He grabbed up the bottle. "Whatever's in these damned pills of yours is killing him."

Kramer came out from behind his desk and opened the door to the foyer. "I will not ask politely again."

Marcus plucked an iron poker from the stand next to the fireplace and lunged at Kramer, brandishing it like a sword. He stopped when the tip pressed against the lapel of the blue serge jacket. He willed himself not to blink, but Kramer refused to speak. Several seconds ticked by without a word, so Marcus pressed the poker slightly harder against the man's chest.

"If you lower your weapon, I will tell you what you wish to know."

Marcus lowered the poker but kept his grip firm.

"Those pills," Kramer said, "are comprised of twenty-two different constituents."

"Just tell me the most potent ones."

"Laudanum, cocaine, and heroin."

The poker thudded onto the rug. "But those are all illegal. How can you—"

"Don't be so naïve. Opioids are as illegal as alcohol was during Prohibition, and banning them makes about as much sense as the Volstead Act did. Those three are the most effective painkillers at our disposal. When used safely—"

"But they're addictive!"

"When used *safely*, that is to say when prescribed by a doctor—"

"Are you even a proper doctor?"

"Harvard, class of '28. Would you like to see my diploma?"

Marcus stared at the man, who took his silence as permission to keep talking.

"When prescribed by a doctor, *in* the correct ratio, *and* in appropriate quantities, my proprietary medications are a most effective method of containing Mister Trenton's pain. Without them, he'd be incapacitated. He called me several weeks ago to order a fresh supply and told me he was back at work now. I call that progress."

"When was the last time you actually *saw* him?"

Dr. Harvard Class of '28 sneered. "End of last year."

"You haven't laid eyes on him in three months?"

"Mister Bryant, I have furnished you with the information you wanted, and now my patience is exhausted. Will you leave of your own accord, or shall I be forced to call the police?"

This guy might be Harvard-trained, but he was operating in a legal no-man's-land. It was unlikely that he would go out of his way to have any contact with the police, but he had a point. Marcus had what he came for.

* * *

When he pulled up outside Oliver's apartment, Marcus remembered little of the drive from Angelino Heights. He'd spent it rehearsing the lecture he would deliver when Oliver opened the door. He stomped up the building's gravel path, but stopped at the terrazzo steps when he saw the figure at the top of the stairs.

Joseph Breen lifted his face and narrowed his eyes with suspicion. "What are *you* doing here?"

"I don't see what business it is of yours." Marcus took the steps two at a time and went to brush past Breen, but the man caught him by the elbow.

"I might have known it was you."

"You might have known what was me?"

"Is that his next supply?" Breen flicked his finger at the pill bottle in Marcus' hand. "Do you know what Oliver has been taking all this time?"

So it's 'Oliver' now? "Do you?"

"There's a chap from my congregation. He runs a commercial laboratory. I gave him one of Oliver's pills to analyze. The results were shocking."

"I'm still getting over it myself—"

"What kind of predator are you?!"

"Preda—what?"

"Don't think for a minute that I don't know what you're about."

"What I'm ab—? Tell me, *Joe*, what am I about?"

"Oliver was in *your* car when that accident happened. You were drunk."

"He was—"

"Oliver's life has fallen apart and the blame lies squarely at your feet. You and all your fellow Commie travelers prey on God's lambs, tempting them with every trick known to Lucifer."

Red-faced and running short of breath, Breen looked like he was gearing up to spit in Marcus' face. "That day in Oliver's hospital room. When I walked in on the pair of you. I saw what was going on. I saw you touch him in a way that one man isn't supposed to touch another. You've seduced him into your homosexual lifestyle. Deviants like you make me sick. You've perverted the innocent heart of a preacher's son. You've made him turn his back on God."

"Okay, now that's—"

"Oliver's a broken man struggling to put his life back together. And what do you do? You turn him into a drug addict!"

"I'm not the villain—"

"Degenerates like you don't care about anyone but themselves, just as long as they get what they want." Breen produced one of Kramer's pill bottles from his pocket and shook it in Marcus' face. "Well, I won't allow it! You hear me?"

As a studio scriptwriter, every word Marcus wrote was at the mercy of the man now standing in front of him with the fire of brimstone burning his eyes, but the last strands of patience had slipped from his fingers. *This self-righteous prig no longer holds the ax over my life.* He thought of his own father, too, and the confrontation that took place in the Adlers' front parlor. *If I can stand up to a bully like Roland Adler, I can sure as hell take you on.*

"Who the *HELL* do you think you are?" Marcus planted his hands on the man's chest and pushed him against the wrought iron balustrade. "You're doing what people like you always do. You see one thing and you make a whole bunch of assumptions based on *nothing.* You talk as though you know me. You don't have the slightest notion of who I am."

Breen shoved Marcus' shoulder, making Marcus stagger back to the edge of the top step. "I don't want to know who you are, Adler, but let me tell you this." He shook the glass bottle again. "As soon as I get back to the office, I'm telephoning Clemence Horrall."

"The chief of police?"

"That's right, and I'm going to get him to shut this Kramer charlatan down."

"That's the first sensible thing you've said."

Breen blinked in surprise; his jaw quivered in thwarted anger. "I forbid you from any further contact with Oliver Trenton."

"You can forbid all you like."

"You will not see him, or telephone him, or contact him in *any* way."

Marcus gave Breen his most contemptuous smirk and headed toward his car around the corner. Breen didn't see him collapse into the driver's seat like a rag doll and press his forehead against the steering wheel until his heart stopped pounding against his temples.

CHAPTER 19

Gwendolyn had spent the morning dusting her store. Not that it needed cleaning—she'd only done it two days before—but she had to keep her mind off the doubt nipping at her since Zap called to tell her when the first shipment of Sunset Boulevard would arrive.

She hadn't expected the process to unfold so smoothly, but within a week, Zap was back in her store with the perfected formula, a sample bottle, and a chic green-and-purple box. The very next day they went into production.

The silver bell jangled as Marcus walked in with Horton. "Are they here?"

"Is it noon yet?"

"You look nervous, but you have no reason to be."

"I have plenty of reasons!" She twirled the feather duster.

"You mean that new store opening three doors down?" Marcus asked.

"What new store?"

"Looks like another chi-chi boutique." He jerked his thumb eastward. "It's called Yvette's."

"Not to worry," Horton said brightly. "I know an expert arsonist who works for cheap."

Gwendolyn stared at him.

"I'm kidding!" He grabbed her arm. "You need to loosen—" He broke off when he saw someone come through the door.

It was Miss 35-22-35.

Gwendolyn walked forward to greet her. "How nice to see you again. How are things at Columbia?"

"You remembered!" The girl pursed her perfect lips. "They dropped me in the fall, but that's okay. I've got an agent now. He's with William Morris."

Twelve months ago, she struck Gwendolyn as being one of those girls who didn't realize how pretty she was and simply took everybody's word for it. The intervening year had instilled more poise but stolen most of her wide-eyed innocence. Her hair was a couple of shades lighter, too.

"William Morris?" Gwendolyn said. "That's nothing to sneeze at."

"A real go-getter. He told me, 'Step one, get yourself a bunch of duds to really knock 'em out with.'" She fished in her purse, pulled out an envelope, and showed Gwendolyn its contents.

"How much do we have to play with?" Gwendolyn asked.

"Three hundred. No, make that two hundred and ninety-eight. You ever been to Parisian Florist? Down Sunset, corner of Sierra Bonita? They have the loveliest roses. I love them. They always make me think of that Anne Brontë quote: 'He who dares not grasp the thorn should never crave the rose.' Really makes you think, huh?"

Gwendolyn stole a glance at Marcus. *A stacked blonde who can quote Brontë?* "I've got a bunch of things that'll fit the bill." She'd started to lead the girl to the cocktail dresses when the bell chimed again.

——

"Delivery!"

Gwendolyn directed the guy in a brown uniform and matching cap to the counter, where she signed the docket and thanked him. She ran her hand across the top of the box longingly.

"Aren't you going to open it?" Marcus murmured.

"Not when I've got a paying customer with nearly three hundred clams to spend."

"You want me to open it for you?"

She nodded and returned to the girl, who was ogling a full-skirted dress in red and white with a daring décolletage that she wouldn't have had the confidence to wear a year ago. Gwendolyn could barely concentrate as she listened to Marcus opening the box, but it was impossible to ignore Horton's "OH MY!"

Marcus held up the six-inch box. Zap had called the shade "malachite green" — it reminded Gwendolyn of the copper tower atop Bullocks Wilshire. The edges were trimmed with purple ribbon and on the front in gold lettering:

SUNSET BOULEVARD
Chez Gwendolyn, Los Angeles

The blonde studied the box in Marcus' hand. "What's that?"

The door swung open and Kathryn burst into the store. "Is it here yet?" She noticed Gwendolyn's customer and bugged her eyes. *Moneybags is back!*

"It's my new fragrance," Gwendolyn explained. "This is the first shipment, so—"

"So you've arrived at a very auspicious moment." Kathryn was at the counter now, admiring the package.

"May I smell it?" the blonde asked.

Gwendolyn pulled at the purple bow. "You can be the first!" She flipped open the lid.

Zap had come up with an exquisite bottle.

The final shape was not quite the S he sketched that day, but a more stylized version, "because it looks like those Sunset Boulevard curves." The base was gold— "The sand on Santa Monica beach." —and the top was vivid azure— "A hint of California sky." The stopper remained exactly as it had in Zap's original sketch: a crown of palm fronds in green glass.

"Oh, Gwennie!" Kathryn exclaimed. "It's perfect!"

"Let's see if it passes the schnoz test."

Gwendolyn pulled off the stopper and drifted the bottle under the blonde's nose.

She breathed deeply, held it for a moment or two, then let it out slowly as she opened her blue eyes.

"I've always been a Chanel No. 5 girl, but THIS!"

"So you like it?"

"I *love* it!"

While it was encouraging to hear that Marcus and Horton liked her fragrance, they were just men, so what did they know? Kathryn said she liked it, but best friends are supposed to say that.

However, this girl didn't know Gwendolyn from a bucket of cotton candy.

"May I smell it again?" She took the bottle from Gwendolyn and sniffed. "It reminds me of Chanel No. 5, but with a twist. I *adore* it! How much?"

This was the moment of reckoning. "Twenty-nine ninety-five."

Gwendolyn was almost embarrassed to say the price out loud. A dollar for the bottle, a dollar for the packaging, and three dollars for the perfume itself meant that each unit cost Gwendolyn a little under five bucks. It was Zap who insisted, "Any fragrance retailing for under ten smackers belongs at J.J. Newberry's. Don't you dare sell it for anything under twenty-five. Preferably thirty."

The blonde didn't hesitate. "I'll take two. What's it called again?"

Kathryn held up the box. "Sunset Boulevard."

"Just like Billy Wilder's new movie? That's clever marketing."

Kathryn deposited the box onto the counter. "Wilder's new movie is called *A Can of Beans*."

"I had a roommate for a while. She worked in the typing pool at Paramount. Her first job was to retype the first thirty pages of the script Wilder and Brackett submitted to the head of production. She told me that everybody thought *A Can of Beans* was the silliest name until Billy Wilder revealed it was just a placeholder for the real title: *Sunset Boulevard*."

Gwendolyn watched Kathryn force a smile. If she didn't know about this title change, did Louella? Or Hedda? Or Sheilah? Had she just stumbled onto a scoop?

"You have somewhere to go, don't you?" Gwendolyn asked.

Kathryn gave Gwendolyn a congratulatory peck on the cheek and hurried out of the store. Marcus and Horton took their leave, too, giving Gwendolyn and her customer the time and space they needed to play with the two hundred and forty dollars they had left . . . minus two for roses at Parisian Florist.

* * *

Gwendolyn gave no thought to the boutique Marcus had mentioned until closing time. Selling two bottles of Sunset Boulevard straight out of the box gave her the boost she needed to reconnoiter a potential rival. She locked up Chez Gwendolyn and made her way three doors down.

Planning only to peek in the window then slip away, she hadn't bargained on Yvette herself standing in the window struggling with a mannequin too wide in the hips for the dress she was attempting to pose.

She also hadn't expected Yvette to look familiar.

The two women stared at each other—Gwendolyn on the sidewalk looking up at the abysmal display and a shoeless, resigned Yvette.

She pointed. "I know you."

Gwendolyn nodded. *But I don't associate your face with anything pleasant.*

The woman climbed out of the display and met Gwendolyn at the door. She had the hard look of someone who'd lived a life of heavy drinking and late nights without much thought for consequences. Her attempt to soften it with makeup resulted in too much rouge, lipstick too red, and pencil-thin Harlow eyebrows that hadn't been in fashion for twenty years.

Still, her smile was friendly enough, even if her teeth had suffered.

"I'm Yvette. Where do I know you from? We *have* met, but a while back, though. Under contract at Fox, maybe?"

"I never got that far. Not for lack of trying though. The closest I ever got was talking to Darryl Zanuck—"

OH MY HEAVENS! IT'S YOU!

Gwendolyn couldn't recall the exact circumstances now, but years ago, she'd managed to talk her way into being one of the kewpie dolls that high-flying gamblers liked to have around for marathon poker games. Their job was to ice drinks, hand out sandwiches, and stand around looking pretty.

One night, the party was in the back room of Chasen's and the other kewpie doll was a stringent redhead intent on wreaking revenge on Zanuck for a love affair turned sour. She would have poisoned the mogul if Gwendolyn hadn't intervened.

"You used to call yourself Mae," Gwendolyn said.

"Yes, but not for years—ah! You were that sweet girl who saved Darryl from—" She suddenly blushed. "From me. I was so jealous I couldn't think straight." She slipped her shoes on. "I never got the chance to thank you for heading Darryl off at the pass. I could have killed him!"

"Not really. The bartender told me tippler's bane was poisonous, but not fatal."

"Lord, what a disaster I was back then. He deserved to kick me out on my ass."

"It's all in the past." Gwendolyn turned to face the store. The place was in as much disarray as the window: boxes piled around the floor, half-dressed mannequins, formalwear mixed with daywear, and nothing up to date. "Welcome to the neighborhood."

Yvette let out a husky laugh. "Guess who funded this whole shebang."

"Zanuck? So you and he are still . . .?"

"Christ, no! We managed to put that whole business behind us. We don't hump no more; we're just good pals. Nah, we're just Scrabble adversaries these days."

Gwendolyn suspected this woman had a somewhat elastic relationship with the truth, but Zanuck's love of competitive Scrabble was well known.

"You must be good," Gwendolyn commented.

"There ain't a dame within a hundred miles who can beat me."

"So this store . . . ?"

"About a month ago, Darryl was in a real punchy mood. He'd gotten into a fight with Joe Mankiewicz over *A Letter to Three Wives* — those two are always at war — and he calls me up. Challenges me to an all-night Scrabble tournament. I could tell he'd been throwing them back so I'm thinking, 'Oh boy, easy money, here we come!' He'd started to sober up by the time I got there, but I fixed that. The more I beat him, the angrier he gets. The angrier he gets, the sloppier he plays. I let him win a couple of rounds, so now he's sloppy, angry, and cocky. The final game was winner takes all."

"How much did you win?"

"You're looking at it. But you must excuse me. I'm wrestling with this goddamned window display and I'm opening in two days!"

Gwendolyn knew Yvette was going to have to work forty-eight hours straight to get this place ready. She wished her luck with the opening and let herself out.

The woman she'd known as Mae looked different now. She was still rough around the edges, but the wisdom of hindsight appeared to have tempered the fury she radiated that night at Chasen's.

Outfoxing Darryl Zanuck took balls, but Yvette would need more than that to run a successful boutique on the Sunset Strip. By the time she was ready to close up, Gwendolyn had comforted herself with the thought that Yvette's might not be the competition she feared.

Gwendolyn's finger was on the final light switch when a new thought occurred to her. She cracked open the back door and looked for a red Chevrolet behind Yvette's store, then breathed a sigh of relief. The vehicle parked three doors along was neither red nor a Chevrolet. It was a beaten-up Ford delivery van, probably thirty years old with a hundred thousand miles on it. The sliding side door was open, and Gwendolyn could see a rack of dresses inside. She tiptoed up to it and peeked in. It was the usual assortment of ball gowns, cocktail dresses, sportswear.

"Wait a minute . . ."

Gwendolyn had spent five years working at the high-end Bullocks Wilshire department store. She could spot a Bullocks number with one eyeball tied behind her back.

She reached in, pushing one outfit aside to inspect the next. Every one of them bore the Bullocks label, and they were each a season or two out of date. One floor-length dinner dress in black-and-white zigzags with extra-wide lapels had been a popular item three years ago.

How did Yvette expect to build a business on out-of-date castoffs . . . unless she wasn't there to sell dresses at all.

CHAPTER 20

Kathryn stood under a marble archway bracketed with heavy brocade drapes, turned slowly on her heel, and drowned in Billy Wilder's extravagant set.

A forest of ionic columns led to an ornate grand piano and a towering pipe organ. Sideboards and breakfronts carved out of dark wood lined the walls. Above one of the fireplaces hung a full-length portrait, and over another was an ostentatious gilded mirror so baroque that it must have cost some poor woodcarver his eyesight.

And the photographs! They filled every horizontal surface, each in a different type of frame: Art Deco, Bakelite, sterling silver, Victorian.

Paramount's PR department assigned her a minder whose face matched her plain gray pencil skirt and unadorned jacket. "Are all these photos of Gloria Swanson?" Kathryn asked.

"Mostly. You can tell where they plan to have her or Mister Holden sit; they'll all be in those shots. But Miss Swanson didn't bring enough from New York so Sam—Sam Comer, our set decorator—he rustled up some others from the prop department to fill in the holes."

"Gloria Swanson's character in this movie, what is her name?"

"Norma Desmond."

"I take it she's an actress?"

"From back in the silent era. She's a recluse who lives in the glory of her heyday."

The glory of her heyday. The phrase rolled around Kathryn's skull like a roulette ball. Ever since that morning Gwendolyn's perfume arrived at the store, Kathryn had been wondering if the glory of her own heyday had passed her by.

When Kathryn first heard Billy Wilder's new picture was called *A Can of Beans,* she knew such a crummy title was too inane for a pair of smart cookies like Wilder and his writing partner, Charles Brackett. What bothered her was that she should have known the instant Wilder unveiled its true name. Somehow that news had bypassed her tipsters.

Was her ear no longer pressed as closely to the ground as she assumed? She was still smarting from Ruby Courtland's smug pronouncement at the MGM silver jubilee: *Louella, Hedda, Kathryn, Sheilah, they're all a bit past it.*

Kathryn tapped her shoe on the hexagonal tiles.

Miss PR piped up. "They filmed a scene the other day where Miss Swanson tells Mister Holden that Valentino taught her to tango on this floor. I don't envy the stagehand who had to spend three hours buffing it up, but it'll look great on-screen."

Kathryn pointed to the square table set up in the middle of the floor. Crew members were buzzing around it, setting ashtrays and high-backed chairs into place and hanging a fringed lightshade off to one side. "What are they shooting today?"

"A card game: Miss Swanson, Anna Q. Neilson, H.B. Warner, and Buster Keaton."

"Silent stars," Kathryn mused.

"Mister Holden's got this great line. He calls them 'the waxworks' because they sit around playing cards without talking to one another. But of course, they're all relics from the silent days, so it's even funnier."

Kathryn had covered Keaton's fiftieth birthday party at the Talmadge apartment building on Wilshire, where he moved after his career began to falter. It was a small but thoroughly enjoyable party in a charming apartment—but a long way from the twenty-two-room neo-Tudor mansion he'd lived in with Natalie Talmadge when he was the biggest name in Hollywood.

That party was what, three, maybe four years ago? Which means Keaton's around fifty-four now. And this little blockhead calls him a relic.

"Might Mister Wilder be free for a quick chat?"

The girl winced. "The card game scene involves a lot of setups and lighting. When it gets as complicated as this, Mister Wilder doesn't like to be distracted by the press."

"Miss Swanson, then?"

"She was in makeup last time I checked."

"Perhaps you could ask her?"

Kathryn watched her scuttle away, then wandered past a suite of lugubrious rococo furniture to a long wooden sideboard parked up against a wall. At each end was a two-foot-high Victorian lamp with six inches of crystal fringe on the shade; crowded between the lamps were dozens of framed photographs.

The front row contained portraits of Swanson at the height of her stardom in the 1920s. The back row, however, was a collection of random photos: young children with teddy bears, stern governesses laced into punishing corsets, a pair of identical teenage twins.

But it was a grainy photograph in an austere glass frame that caught Kathryn's eye. A little girl around three years old wearing a starched white linen dress and an enormous bow in her hair sat in the lap of a startled gent exhibiting a hesitant smile. Outfitted in a crème double-breasted vest and a cravat under a dark knee-length cutaway coat, he looked uncomfortable with the youngster on one knee and his black top hat balanced on the other.

Kathryn had no memory of herself before the age of about five, and Francine had never been the type of mother who took snapshots of her growing up. She guessed she had a dress like the one in the photograph. It was the uniform of all pre-school-aged children in the 1910s.

She was still staring at it when a shadow fell across her. The PR lackey was back, her face scrunched into an apology. "Miss Swanston sends her regrets but said it's too close to filming."

Kathryn glanced back at the photo. "Perhaps some other time. I'd love to stick around and watch them film the — what does Mister Holden call them?"

"The waxworks."

"Yes."

"I'm sorry, but this is a complicated day and Mister Wilder has asked that all nonessential personnel be cleared from the set." She made a big deal of looking at her watch. "In fact . . ."

"Don't worry, dear," Kathryn told her. "I can take a hint."

"Perhaps lunch in the commissary? I can recommend the Paramount Special Salad. I don't know what's in the French dressing but it's — "

"Sounds delightful."

"Unfortunately, I can't join you, I have other duties to attend to, but I'll be happy to walk you over there."

"No need, I know the way. I'm sure you have a thousand things to do. You don't need to babysit me." *Even if I am a bit past it.*

* * *

Paramount's commissary was called Café Continental, which sounded swish but was really just a huge room with high ceilings and a half dozen rows of four-tops arranged checkerboard style. Its glass walls let workers who toiled inside the soundstages bathe in California sunshine.

When Kathryn walked in, it was nearly full and the line at the counter was getting longer. When she stopped someone to ask if she could get a coffee and donut without waiting in line, the woman recognized her.

"Normally I'd say no, but—" she bent forward " — but you used to be on my favorite radio show. See that one by the window?" She pointed to a table next to three men in dark blue suits huddled in conference. "It's got a nice view of the water tower. Grab it while you can and I'll bring your coffee soon as I get a chance."

Kathryn's thoughts returned to the photo of the little girl as she sat down at the table and pulled off her gloves. She found herself wondering who the girl was and why the gentleman looked so ill at ease, but was pulled out of her reverie when she heard one of the men next to her say,

"The Pan-Stik team is ready to submit all the finals to the boss. The Max Factor brand needs a new product and it's almost summer. We need to get moving, and soon."

Kathryn stole a quick glance to her right. She'd assumed the men were studio execs—they certainly had that polished gleam about them—but if they were from Max Factor—

"There we go." A cup of steaming black coffee slid in front of her alongside a plate holding two cinnamon donuts.

"Thank you." Kathryn looked up. "Oh!"

Edith Head shouldn't have been the last person Kathryn expected to see on the Paramount lot, but it was a surprise.

"I watched you finagle table service out of Nora and want to know how you managed it."

Edith slid into the seat next to Kathryn with a second coffee. "We've only ever really nodded hello at parties," Edith said. "I thought it was about time we got to know each other better. Especially after I dropped in on Gwendolyn earlier this week—that new perfume is *divine!*—and she told me what you overheard at MGM."

One of the men beside them said "Max Factor" again but Kathryn had to focus on Edith.

"Overheard?"

"Between Errol Flynn and a certain Ruby Courtland. As it happened, I'd received a request for an interview from Ruby but hadn't yet responded, so out of curiosity I set one up for a couple of days later."

Edith had found Ruby sycophantic to the point of nausea, so she baited her with a question about fashion trends. Ruby responded with a speech about catering to the tastes of the moviegoing public's younger members. To someone like Edith, who prided herself on setting trends and establishing tastes, not being a slave to them, Ruby's lecture was a declaration of lunacy. Edith had sent her packing.

Kathryn pretended to give Edith her full attention, but she was actually taking in as much as she could of the conversation next door. One of the men wore a Harvard ring on his right pinky; it glinted in the sunlight as he waved his hands around to punctuate a story about Rita Hayworth and Tru-Color lipstick.

When Edith reached the end of her story, Kathryn leaned in. "I need your help," she whispered.

Edith's eyes widened behind her blue-tinted glasses. "Go on."

Kathryn explained in a rush who their neighbors were. Edith caught on before she even finished. She slapped her hands on the tabletop.

"So, Kathryn, you were telling me about your radio show idea, but of course once you get Betty Hutton started, it's hard to shut her down. However, I'm all ears now."

Kathryn snapped her starched linen napkin open. "Well, as you know, *Kraft Music Hall* is off the air."

"Do you miss it?"

"Terribly! I was intimidated by the prospect of performing to a microphone at first, but there's something about standing in front of a live audience that really got my wheels turning."

"You were so good on that show!" Edith pushed her glasses up her nose and gave a furtive nod to confirm they'd captured the guys' attention.

"That means a lot, coming from you. Anyway, it got me thinking how Louella's show is long gone, and so is Hedda's. You know how popular Hollywood gossip shows are, and now there are none on the airwaves. There's this big black hole desperate to be filled."

Edith held her teaspoon straight up. "You heard about Max Factor offering Sheilah her own slot, didn't you?"

"Oh, yes," Kathryn said airily. "From what I hear, she got greedy and started demanding all sorts of things."

"I'd have thought she would know better after seeing all those stars carry on." Edith wiped her mouth like a disapproving matron. "I've heard there's a shortlist of replacements, and that you're on it."

"I've heard that too, but I'd have to see it typed up on Max Factor's letterhead before I took it seriously." Kathryn wished she could see the Max Factor guys, but they were in her blind spot. "I hear they're thoroughly professional in all their dealings."

"They're missing a golden opportunity, if you ask me."

"I was looking at the radio schedule just the other day. The ideal spot would be Sunday nights on NBC, following *The Great Guildersleeve*."

Edith set her cup onto its saucer with a loud crack. "Perfect! I suggest you find somebody who knows somebody who works for Max Factor before you-know-who steals it out from under you."

Kathryn forced down a mouthful of coffee. "Don't make me say her name," she hedged.

"Then I'll say it. Ruby Courtland makes out like she's all rainbows and bunny rabbits but from what I've heard, she's quite the opposite. I have nothing against ambition—especially in a working woman—but she takes *ruthless* to a whole new level."

"Really?" Kathryn let her spoon slip through her fingers.

"But of course you didn't hear that from me," Edith added.

Her eyes shot to the left. Kathryn heard chairs scrape against the linoleum and said nothing until Edith let out a deep breath.

"Do you think they heard us?" Kathryn asked.

Edith snapped a cracker in two. "They were hanging on every word like I was Moses and you were the two stone tablets."

"But did they buy it?"

"Who knows what goes on in the minds of men. But if I were a gambling woman, I'd bet we just knocked Ruby Courtland out of the running."

CHAPTER 21

When Gwendolyn opened the door and saw the boxes strewn around her workroom, her first thought was, *Did we have another earthquake?*

But when she flicked on the lights, she found every box of buttons and ribbons, gloves and extraneous doodads had been emptied of its contents.

She laid her handbag on the sink and picked her way through the detritus to the telephone. She dialed one of the few numbers she knew by heart and didn't give him a chance to say hello.

"Marcus? It's me. Can you come down to the store? I think I've been robbed."

When she hung up, she picked her way around hatboxes and scarves and walked out into the salon. It was untouched. She unlocked the register. Everything was exactly as she left it.

What kind of robber doesn't go for the cash drawer?

She wondered for a minute what she should do next. Call the police? Tell her neighbors? Marcus arrived before she could decide.

"Christ almighty!" His hair was a bird's nest and he was still wearing his pajama top and what looked like the first pair of pants that came to hand. "Are you okay?"

She nodded and pointed to the open drawer.

He peered at it, puzzled. "So they stole nothing?" The immaculate displays were disturbingly at odds with the wild jumble in the back room. "So if they didn't break in for the money, they figured they'd only find whatever they were looking for in your work room?" They returned to the doorway and stared at the wreckage.

Gwendolyn picked up a large cardboard box in which she kept her broad hat ribbons. "At least they didn't smash my perfume."

"How considerate—or weird."

Gwendolyn dropped the box and crossed to the shelves along the wall. She counted her stock. "Only one is missing."

They stood in silence while they surveyed the debris, Marcus twirling a zipper in his hand like a burlesque dancer. "Maybe we should be asking who wants to see you fail."

Gwendolyn covered her face with the lid of a hatbox. "You really think she'd go that far? Surely they frown on accused felons out on bail committing breaking and entering? Leilah's a ball-breaker, but she's no fool."

"You think someone like that doesn't have henchman to do her dirty work?"

"I thought henchmen only lived in Cagney pictures."

"I must admit," Marcus said, nodding toward her perfume bottles, "they must be mighty considerate henchmen to leave those intact."

Gwendolyn kicked off her shoes and dropped to her knees to start sorting the twenty different kinds of buttons that were scattered across the floor.

Marcus knelt, too, and they got down to returning notions to their boxes, sorting papers into piles, respooling ribbons, and reshelving books and ledgers. As they worked, she asked him about Oliver.

Not long after the confrontation with Breen, Oliver had pulled a disappearing act. Marcus wasn't sure the two events were related, but he suspected they might be. Breen had seemed pretty determined to save Oliver from Marcus' sinful clutches. Marcus confessed he didn't want to believe that Breen had convinced Oliver he could take better care of him than Marcus could, but Oliver was in no shape to think straight, so maybe?

Marcus changed the subject and asked Gwendolyn about Ignacio Zaparelli, whose name had been slipping into her conversations lately. Was romance rearing its soft, fluffy head? Gwendolyn laughed and admitted that Zap had a certain electric charisma about him, but he was at least ten years too young for her.

What she didn't admit was how Zap was one of those guys who added up to a sum much greater than his parts.

His thick, dark eyebrows could do with a judicious plucking. His blue eyes were penetrating and he knew it, but his mouth fell naturally into an unfortunate droop. Those dimples helped, but one was bigger than the other, which gave his face a lopsidedness that worked better than it should have. At the end of the day, none of it mattered much, because the man's innate charm blurred his physical shortcomings. He filled any room just by entering it.

Marcus asked, "Did you pay any attention to your locks?"

After she'd noticed her back door had been tampered with, she got a locksmith to install a second one. She'd felt more secure, but now wondered if she'd been fooling herself. "What about them?"

"I didn't see any signs of forced entry. So either they had the key—"

"I never even got around to giving my landlord the extra one."

"Maybe they got in some other way?" He jacked a thumb in the direction of a metal ladder bolted to the rear wall. "Where does that go?"

Gwendolyn squinted at the ceiling. Most of the lighting was centered over the workbench. She could just make out a rectangular line. "Is that a trapdoor?"

Marcus grabbed one of the rungs.

She pulled at his pajama sleeve. "But what if they're still up there?"

"You've been watching too many Bogie movies."

"I've been broken into!"

Marcus pulled her into a hug. "Someone has broken into your shop, trashed the place looking for something other than money, then pocketed a bottle of perfume on the way out. That's odd, no matter which way you cut it." He climbed onto the first rungs of the ladder. "You got a flashlight?"

She pulled one from under a pile of yellow chintz and handed it to him. "For God's sake, be careful."

When he reached the top of the ladder, he pressed his hands to the trapdoor and gently lifted it. It gave way with no effort. He climbed into the crawl space and out of sight.

"What can you see?" she called.

"It's like an attic up here. It stretches the entire length of the building."

"All six stores?" When he didn't answer, she cupped her hands around her mouth. "Marcus?"

"Give me a second." A few minutes ticked by. When he reappeared in the trapdoor hole, his face was the picture of surprise.

"That woman who opened a boutique three doors down."

"Yvette?"

"Have you seen her lately?"

"We nodded hello a couple of days ago. Why?"

"Each of these stores has a trapdoor, so I peeked through hers."

"And?"

He lowered himself down the ladder. "It's eleven thirty on a Thursday and she's closed."

"Marcus, you're scaring me."

"Isn't she the girl who tried to poison Zanuck? And wasn't she using an alias back then? Or is Yvette her alias now?"

Gwendolyn grabbed her keys, unlocked her front door, and ran three doors down to Yvette's. Not even the window lights were on. The store was shrouded in darkness so impenetrable that she couldn't see through to the back.

CHAPTER 22

Gloria Swanson wore a hat trimmed in white fur with a foot-long white feather pinned to it and a net veil over her face. Her dress was black and a white stole was draped along her left shoulder, around her back, and hung over her right arm. She offered Kathryn a professional smile. "I'm sorry we didn't get a chance to talk the last time you visited."

Kathryn returned Swanson's surprisingly firm handshake. *I hope I look as good as she does when I'm fifty.* "I showed up unannounced, so I hardly expected you to drop everything."

"What were we shooting that day?"

"The card game with H.B. Warner, Buster Keaton, and Anna Neilson. That must have felt like the good old days."

"The old days don't seem quite so golden now." Swanson led Kathryn to a pair of director's chairs facing the set of *Samson and Delilah*. Expanses of fabric hung like a desert tent around embroidered chaise lounges and scattered throw rugs.

"I'm surprised to hear that."

Swanson's face clouded over. "My character has spent years in seclusion reliving her halcyon days." She ran her hand along the white fur. "I want to play her well, but I don't want to *become* her."

In the three weeks since she had last been on the set of *Sunset Boulevard*, Kathryn's thoughts had turned again and again to the photograph of the little girl and her awkward father.

Curiosity plagued her at the oddest times.

When Gwendolyn enlisted her to help clean up the mess in her store, she came across a pale blue velvet ribbon that reminded her of the one in the girl's hair. And when she was listening to radio reports on the start of the espionage trial in New York, every time she heard the name Alger Hiss, she pictured the man in the photograph.

Finally she could stand it no more and asked Paramount for a sit-down with Swanson. When they arranged for an on-set meeting, Kathryn assumed they'd be in Norma Desmond's home. She was disappointed that her PR minder had escorted her to one of the sets left over from *Samson and Delilah*.

Kathryn waved a hand toward the colorful carpets. "Are you recreating one of Norma's movies?"

"No, nothing like that. Norma comes to visit Mister DeMille as he's filming his latest biblical epic. She feels that DeMille must come to her, so she sits and waits, and swats away that pesky microphone." She pointed to a boom mike suspended to their right.

"Norma Desmond is no fan of the microphone?"

"She most certainly is not. At one point she tells Joe, 'We didn't need dialogue. We had faces!' I read that line and thought, That's the key to my character right there."

Over the years, Kathryn had learned that certain types of stars tightened up at the sight of a notebook, as though everything they said could be used against them in the court of public opinion.

So she initiated what appeared to be just a conversation, but was in fact a list of questions based on a mnemonic:

G = Good old days of filmmaking, what were they like?

L = Last time she saw DeMille — when?

O = Oscar — is this role Oscar-worthy?

R = Rekindle — could this role rekindle your film career?

I = Independence — since your fifth divorce, do you prefer your independence?

A = Acting — has your approach to acting changed?

While crew members scurried around them, Kathryn did her best to keep her attention on Gloria's answers. It wasn't hard — they were stock questions to which Swanson was giving routine answers, and Kathryn was relieved when the assistant director approached them to announce Swanson was needed.

Kathryn shook her hand and thanked her for her time, but could see that the actress was already focusing on the scene. She slipped outside and headed for Soundstage Nine.

With only three or four working lights and nobody else around, the overflowing Desmond mansion took on the air of a mausoleum. Kathryn's heels echoed on the tango floor as she approached the sideboard. She ran her eye along the frames, but didn't see the photograph that had been haunting her for days. She made a second, slower pass.

"Can I help you?"

Kathryn let out a yelp and pressed a hand to her chest.

"They're filming on Stage Sixteen today." The guy's voice had a you-shouldn't-be-here edge.

"I've just come from there." She presented him with her sweetest smile. She knew who he was. "I'm Kathryn Massey from the *Hollywood Reporter*." He nodded. "All nonessential personnel were asked to evacuate the soundstage, and I was so enamored by this set, I had to come back and see it again." She raised her hands into the air. "What a feast for the eyes! You guys are a shoo-in for an Oscar nomination, and quite frankly, I can't imagine how anybody could beat you."

That did the trick. His face relaxed into a proud smile.

Kathryn stepped forward. "And you are?"

"Sam Comer."

"That sweet young thing from PR mentioned you specifically. She said you and your team have really knocked it out of the park with this set."

"We're mighty proud of our work here, even if I do say so myself."

"I have a question perhaps only you can answer. I understand all these photographs come from Miss Swanson's personal collection."

"That's right. Except for a few in the back, like here." He pointed to the sideboard.

"There was one that caught my eye. It was a shot of a little girl."

"Sitting on her father's knee? Yeah, I know the one."

"It's not here."

"The sound guy dropped the boom mike the other day. Miss Swanson nearly had a fit. That one took the brunt of the damage."

"It was in a glass frame."

"Yeah, I put it in a new one."

"Where is it now?"

Comer looked around the set. "I think you'll find it on the piano. Look, I just stopped by here to check the tiles, but I'm needed back on the *Samson and Delilah* set. Nobody is supposed to be here, but you're Kathryn Massey, so if you could promise me that you won't stay long . . .?"

Kathryn crossed her heart and swore she wouldn't be more than a minute or two. She hurried to the grand piano, but the photograph wasn't there. She did, however, find it on the pipe organ.

It was just as she remembered. A steady-eyed youngster in Mary Pickford sausage curls sitting on the knee of a starched banker type. The kid had such a self-composed little face. Kathryn wondered what the kid was thinking.

Then the oddest thought popped into Kathryn's head.

That bow was brown.

"And how would you know that?" Kathryn asked herself out loud.

When the answer came to her, it was more like a leaky faucet dropping one word at a time. She opened her purse and slipped the frame inside.

* * *

Kathryn's mother was the head telephone operator at the Chateau Marmont a few blocks from the Garden of Allah. She worked six days a week from eight in the morning to six at night. By six fifteen, she was fixing a brandy and dry in the kitchen of the employee bungalow she rented out back of the hotel.

It was six twenty when Kathryn knocked. Francine opened the door, but Kathryn didn't give her a chance to speak. She held up the photograph she'd just stolen. "You want to tell me about this?"

There was no mistaking the recognition in Francine's flinching eyes. But with it came surprise, and — Kathryn suspected — resignation. She stepped past her mother into the living room and dropped her handbag and gloves on the coffee table.

Francine closed the door slowly; the hinges squeaked as though they were taking her full weight. She turned around, a shade or two paler. "Can I fix you a — "

"I don't want a drink. I want an explanation."

She joined Kathryn at the loveseat, where the two of them sat in a stony silence that scraped Kathryn's nerves raw. She was determined to force Francine to speak first.

Eventually, Francine drew in a breath. "Yes," she said softly. "That is you."

"And the man?"

Long pause. "Your father."

The mantel clock on the curio cabinet behind Kathryn ticked loudly. She counted ten ticks. "Go on."

Francine picked up the photograph, transfixed as Kathryn had been. "Where in God's name did you find this?"

"I want to know when it was taken, and I want to know where."

Francine gripped the frame more tightly.

"You and I had been out here a few years when I received a letter from him. Quite out of the blue. I was using a new name, so how he tracked me down, I don't know. He always was the resourceful type." She laid the photo flat on her lap. "Oh, Kathryn dear, what good does it do to drag this up now? It's all so long ago. Trust me, sleeping dogs — "

"So he tracked you down and — ?"

Silence. Tick-tick-tick. Then, finally, "He said he was coming out west on business and that he wanted to pay a call. In fact, his words were: I want to see my baby."

A fist-sized chunk of Kathryn's heart melted. There were other little girls at school who had no fathers, but they'd been killed in the Great War, so she'd pretended she lost hers in the same way.

"When was this?"

"You were about four." Francine returned to the photo. "Handsome, wasn't he?"

"He doesn't look too comfortable."

"He was quite emotional. He tried to hide it, but I could tell. He sat on the floor and played with you. He'd have stayed all day if I'd let him."

"Why didn't you?"

"Seeing him again was hard. It brought up a flood of memories I'd tried to forget."

"Why didn't you ever tell me about this?"

She ran her finger around the circumference of the frame. "You were so young. I knew you wouldn't remember, so I figured why bother?"

"And the photo? Who took it?"

"I did. He brought along his Brownie, and asked me to take photos. I didn't think it was such a great idea, but I didn't have the heart to turn him down. I snapped a whole roll of film—I didn't really know what I was doing so I assumed none of them turned out. More than a year later, that photo arrived in the mail." Francine tapped the glass. "See this painting behind you, the one of the forest? It used to hang over our fireplace. Is that what gave it away?"

Kathryn saw now that one of the few constants of her childhood was visible over her father's shoulder. "No," she said. "It was the bow in my hair."

"Oh, how you fought me every time I tried to put it on." Francine studied the photograph some more. "That look on your face, it was your 'I'm not happy about this horrid bow' face. You had a name for it: The Brown Horrid."

Francine crossed to the kitchen counter where her brandy and dry sat waiting for her. "Are you going to tell me where you found it?"

"Would you believe on the set of Billy Wilder's new movie? How it wound up at Paramount is anybody's guess. When was the last time you saw it?"

Francine returned to the sofa and took a sip of her drink. "When I moved down to Long Beach. I hired a moving company, but they lost one of the boxes."

"And studios buy lost property from all sorts of companies as a cheap way to acquire more props."

"I guess that's what happened."

"Did you ever hear from him again?"

She shook her head.

"So you don't know where he is now?" Kathryn had pushed the conversation onto thin ice. She'd been harboring a secret about her father since the war ended, but it was time to come clean.

"You're not thinking of trying to track him down, I hope." Francine drew back. "Your father was a decent man, but he only took the trouble to come see you that one time. You've done well without him, so in my opinion, there's nothing to be gained by — "

"I already know where he is."

The ticking clock dominated the room once more as Kathryn and her mother sat staring at each other.

Francine said, "Are you referring to Sing Sing?"

"YOU KNEW?! And you never thought to tell me?"

"Mightn't I say the same?" Francine lobbed back.

It was a fair point. If Kathryn let this conversation devolve into one of their usual yelling matches, the ice beneath their feet might crack. She calmed herself by clasping her hands together.

"How did you find out?" Francine asked.

"It's a convoluted story." Nelson Hoyt never had explained how he learned of Thomas Danford's whereabouts. Then again, she never asked. *And all this time, my own mother knew. How much easier this news would have been to hear if I could have heard it from her?*

"A reliable source?" Francine asked.

"The FBI."

"And I suppose they told you what he's in for?"

"It was the same day the Japs surrendered. There was a lot going on."

"Do you want to know?"

"Is it bad?"

"They don't send you to Sing Sing for shoplifting."

"Maybe I would like one of those drinks."

Francine returned to her kitchen. She said nothing until she was back on the sofa. "He was convicted of treason via the Smith Act."

Kathryn took a long, reluctant sip, putting off the inevitable. Finally she asked, "What did he do?"

"He was convicted of selling secrets to the Germans."

Good God, there's no bouncing back from that.

"It was a sensational trial," Francine continued, "at least as far as New England was concerned, because there was talk of him running for Massachusetts governor after the war. But of course that dream died."

"How long did he get?"

"Twenty-two years, although he could be out in fifteen. Good behavior, and all that."

Kathryn executed some mental math. *He won't be out of jail until the 1960s. So far away it might as well be forever.*

"For what it's worth," Francine said, "I'm not completely convinced he was guilty."

Francine usually assumed the worst in any given situation, so this declaration was as shocking as Truman's win over Dewey.

"Sounds like you followed the case pretty closely."

The hesitation in Francine's face was slight, but Kathryn had grown up learning to decipher every blip on her radar.

"You've been keeping tabs on him, haven't you?" Silence. "All these years, you've been watching him."

Francine kept her eyes trained on her glass. "You make me sound like a stalker."

Kathryn shifted closer to her mother. "I think it's one of the most romantic things I've heard outside a Barbara Stanwyck weepy."

"That's going a bit far." When Francine looked up, her eyes had softened like marshmallows; her smile was tentative and girlish. "I only left Boston because I had to. Because of his family and their standing in society. I never wished him ill."

"You knew where he was all along."

Kathryn didn't mean to sound vindictive, and hoped her mother understood that she was simply coming to terms with how her father had only ever been a question away. "Have you been in contact?"

"I only watched from afar by subscribing to *The Boston Globe*. Their society pages—" Francine hunched her shoulders. "Please tell me you're not thinking of writing to him."

"I've missed out on a lifetime of not knowing my father."

"He was respectable once upon a time, but now he's in prison."

"But you think he's not—"

"I said *I* doubted his guilt, but I'm far from impartial. You must think of your public position, Kathryn. The moment people find out your father is a convicted felon, for treason, no less, it would surely be the end of everything you've built. Imagine what Louella and Hedda could make of this."

"It's just that I have no sense of where I come from. No sense of family history. I feel like everything started when we moved to California."

Kathryn suddenly understood Marcus' plan to go to Russia, and wished like hell that she hadn't told him how thoroughly she agreed with Oliver. But now it made all the sense in the world.

She could also see that her mother had a point. This news that her mother had been monitoring Thomas Danford like a clipping service was a lot to take on board. The sensible option was to do nothing.

"You're welcome to stay for dinner," Francine said. "It's just sausages and sauerkraut, with tapioca for dessert. But it's those pork sausages you like."

"Will you tell me everything you know about my father?"

"If you promise me that you won't be so reckless as to communicate with him."

Please don't ask me to promise that. Kathryn rose to her feet. "If you fix me another drink, I'll cook the sausages."

* * *

Several hours later, Kathryn walked through the front doors of the Garden of Allah, her bloodstream coursing with brandy and her head crammed with Boston society, oversized hair ribbons, and a nervous father's laughter.

The reception desk was deserted. One of the upstairs residents was playing a Wagnerian aria on the phonograph; it wafted down the stairs and encircled Kathryn.

She glanced at her watch; it was nearly midnight and she wondered if Marcus was still up.

From the pool area, she could see the light in Marcus' kitchen. She was halfway to his door when he came running toward her, an envelope fluttering in his hand.

"Telegram! Telegram!"

"Good news, I hope?"

"It's not for me; I just signed for it." He thrust it into her hand.

She stared at the Western Union logo, not sure that she could take any more news today.

If this were a movie, the telegram would be from my father. Or the chief warden at Sing Sing. Or the Massachusetts governor telling me Thomas Danford has been pardoned due to fresh evidence —

"Aren't you going to open it?" Marcus pushed.

Or I could just open it.

She pulled the telegram out.

WE ARE LOOKING TO SPONSOR NEW
PRIME TIME RADIO SHOW STOP
WANT TO KNOW IF YOU ARE
INTERESTED IN HOSTING STOP
CONTACT US AT FIRST OPPORTUNITY
STOP BEST REGARDS MAX FACTOR
STOP

CHAPTER 23

Marcus stood out front of Oliver's apartment building, jiggling his car keys with one hand and flicking a Camel in the other. He'd promised himself that he would knock on the door when he finished the cigarette, but now that he was only a puff or two away, he told himself that he'd go in after he finished a second one.

Tossing the butt aside, he kept his eye on Oliver's window, hoping to catch signs of life. He could see the print of Man Ray's *A Night at Saint Jean-de-Luz* hanging over the mantle. Marcus didn't care for it, but they'd been together when Oliver bought it at an art store in Pasadena during the war.

Surely sooner or later, Oliver would have to come home.

Marcus lit another cigarette.

The morning after his encounter with Breen, Marcus returned to catch Oliver before he left for the office, but nobody was home.

At first, he refused to believe Oliver was avoiding him. He told Gwennie, "Nobody does that to someone they've been with for six years." But there was no call, no telegram, no note.

He ignored his instincts and started calling Oliver at work.

"Mister Trenton is in a meeting. May I take a message?"

None of his messages were returned, so Marcus drove over to Oliver's apartment three or four times a week at different hours of the day and night. The lights were never on and nothing came of his knocking, so he forced himself to face the possibility that Breen had somehow gotten to Oliver first.

Hope faded as his thrice-weekly drive-by dwindled to every other week.

At one point, he even called the city morgue. By June, he'd all but given up. And now he was standing out front of Oliver's apartment block knowing he couldn't go on much longer.

He crushed the butt of his second cigarette under his heel, then swung open the picket gate. Lily of the valley lined the gravel path to the foyer. Bunched so tightly together, the plants gave off a heady scent that reminded Marcus of the previous summer when he and Oliver spent a rare weekend entirely in bed.

They only got out to fetch another bottle of champagne or pop some corn. Marcus remembered an especially satisfying postcoital cigarette he'd smoked at the window as the flowers' perfume drifted up from below.

He arrived at Oliver's door slightly out of breath, and gave himself a moment.

I was nuts to think I could actually go to Russia. You were completely within your rights to tell me so. I was wrong, you were right, and I want you to know it.

He knocked on the door. Three times. Loudly.

He knocked again. Nothing. Down the corridor, a woman peeked out her front door. She had the sort of face Marcus had seen a hundred times. The Betty Boop eyes had probably been her most striking feature, but she ringed them with too much mascara to distract from the crow's feet. The flaming red hair was too bright; the taut curls too uniform to be natural. Her lipstick was supposed to match her hair, but it was several shades off, and even from this distance, it was clear she'd missed the left corner of her lips. He guessed that at her peak she'd probably scored a position in a Busby Berkeley line-up and hadn't been seen on-screen since *Gold Diggers of 1933*.

"Hello, there," she said, with all the coquettishness she could muster. "Looking for Oliver?"

"I am, yes."

She edged outside her doorway, tightening her green kimono. "I haven't seen him in an awful long while."

"Me either, and I'm getting concerned. I'm Marcus."

"Regina Horne." She said her name with such dignity that Marcus wondered if he was supposed to recognize it. He offered her an encouraging smile. *Ah, so you're Regina Horne.*

She jutted her chin toward Oliver's apartment. "I have his key," she whispered.

"You do?"

"Round about Christmastime, I locked myself out. I wasn't the most sober I'd ever been in my life, you understand."

"Haven't we all been there?"

"The building manager forbids us from calling him after ten o'clock, but lucky for me, Oliver arrived. That darling boy shimmied up my drainpipe and opened my balcony door. I should lock it, but I never do."

"It's a good thing you didn't."

"So then we swapped spare keys just in case one of us got caught in a jam."

Marcus wondered why this was the first he'd heard of this woman. "Could I possibly borrow it?"

She didn't answer straightaway, but stepped closer as though to inspect him more thoroughly. At first, Marcus thought she was one of those people who smoked exotic, scented European cigarettes, like the ones Tallulah Bankhead lit up at every party he could remember. But the scent that lingered around this woman had a tang he'd encountered before.

Those Betty Boop eyes widened. "Oliver hasn't been the same since his accident."

"He got banged up something awful."

She studied him some more, then disappeared inside her apartment. When she reappeared, she placed a key and a rolled cigarette in Marcus' outstretched palm. "I owe him one of those."

Marcus had smelled marijuana at the Garden a few times, but it had been a while.

"Thank you, Regina." He held up the key and the cigarette. "For both."

"I have some succotash on the stove I must tend to." As she tottered back inside, she threw over her shoulder instructions to slip the key under the door when he was done.

Oliver's living room looked like the scene of a bar brawl. For a brief, panicky moment, Marcus wondered if Oliver had been broken into—the sight of Gwendolyn's workroom had stayed with him. But no, it was just the home of someone who couldn't be bothered picking up after himself.

Blankets lay crumpled on the floor under empty soda pop bottles; a full ashtray and a rancid bowl of mulligatawny sat on the coffee table.

Marcus called Oliver's name. No response. He hoisted a stack of untouched *LA Times* off the rug and dropped them on the only available space of the dining table. He heard a groan, a few seconds' silence, then another.

Marcus wasn't even sure there was anybody under the tangle of linen in Oliver's bedroom until he saw a foot. The sole was filthy with grime and the nails needed trimming, but he'd know that foot anywhere from the dime-sized birthmark under the anklebone.

He grabbed a fistful of blanket and pulled it toward him. Oliver was face down, his head twisted to one side. He wore boxer briefs, but that was all. His body was pale as paraffin and so emaciated that each bone along his spine jutted out clear enough to count.

"Ollie? Honey? Can you hear me?"

Oliver let out a belch. He lifted his head off the pillow, but kept his eyes closed. "Regina?"

"No, it's me."

The muscles cramped up Oliver's torso. "How did you get in?"

"I got a key—"

"You need to leave."

Marcus sat on the corner of the mattress. He rested his hand on Oliver's ankle, but pulled it away when Oliver jerked his foot. "I haven't seen you in months."

"I thought you'd have taken the hint by now."

Marcus' scalp crawled. "Why don't you get up and I'll fix us a sandwich. You'll feel better with some food inside you. And we—"

Oliver sprang up like a ghost-ride spook in an amusement park. His eyes were hauntingly bloodshot and he hadn't shaved in days. "Yeah, uh-huh," he sneered. "Tuna salad on rye. That's what I need. Didya bring a pickle? Because that'll go with the tuna salad just jim-dandy."

Marcus reached out to grab Oliver's hand but Oliver smacked it away.

"Leave me the hell alone. Just leave me to my . . ." His limbs went rubbery and his back folded in on itself.

"Leave you to your what, Oliver?" Marcus stood up. "To your Dr. Kramer and his little pills?" Oliver's head shot up but he had trouble focusing. "Do you know what's in those pills of his?"

"They relieve the pain."

"Do you know what you're swallowing?"

A burst of anger propelled Oliver off the bed and onto his feet. "Yes, Marcus, I do. Breen had them analyzed. They've got laudanum and cocaine and . . . and . . ."

"Heroin, Oliver. *Heroin.* That stuff is treacherous."

Oliver pushed past him and staggered into the living room. "It wasn't too long ago that you could get heroin over the counter."

"They banned it for a reason."

Oliver rummaged through the mess on his coffee table. "Kramer's stuff kills the pain, that's all I care about. Nothing else works. Well, besides . . ." He pushed the *LA Times* off the dining table.

"Looking for this?"

Oliver made a grab for Regina's marijuana cigarette, but Marcus got to it first. Instead, he clung to the back of a chair to stop himself from stumbling over. "Give it to me."

Marcus wanted desperately to toss the reefer out the kitchen window, but he could see the hunger in Oliver's eyes and found he didn't have the heart. "You heard what happened to Mitchum. He got two months in jail. How long do you think Uncle Joe will keep you on if you get arrested for marijuana possession?"

"You got to walk away from that accident just fine. Lucky you! The doctors say that my bones have all healed, but I'm in agony. Every. Waking. Moment." The pleading in Oliver's voice tore at Marcus. "Breen's taken me to doctor after doctor. You know what they all say? 'It's in your head, Mister Trenton. Mind over matter, Mister Trenton.' One of them told me I should grow a backbone and go cold turkey."

"Maybe he was right."

"Maybe he doesn't know what he's talking about. And maybe you don't either. Screw them, and screw you."

Marcus gripped the back of a kitchen chair. "I don't pretend to know what it must feel like—"

Oliver stared at the reefer. "You going to give me that, or do I have to fight you for it?"

Marcus dropped it onto the table. Oliver scooped it up and lit it with a nearby lighter, then took a deep drag. As he slowly breathed out, he dropped onto one of the dining chairs and let his head sink onto his chest.

They were on a precipice; any ill-chosen word could send them toppling over the edge. Marcus decided to let Oliver speak next, even if it meant sitting in silence for the rest of the afternoon.

On the other side of Oliver's kitchen wall, Marcus could hear Regina Horne singing along with "That Lucky Old Sun." She was surprisingly in tune. Maybe she got further than a walk-on in some kaleidoscopic extravaganza. Then her parakeet started squawking and Regina yelled at it to shut the hell up.

The minutes crawled by as Oliver puffed through the marijuana cigarette. He pitched the stub into one of the putrid soup bowls. "It's time you left."

Marcus rounded the dining table. "Okay, but let me fix you a bite to eat. You've gotten so thin." He opened the refrigerator to find there was nothing inside but a lone bottle of milk—and even that was nearly empty.

"I mean go . . . and not come back."

Marcus gripped the refrigerator door. "You're in terrible shape and you need help."

Oliver was on his feet now. "I've seen every doctor in the book."

"Then we'll go farther afield. Up to San Francisco if we need to."

Oliver reached the front door and grabbed the knob. "There is no 'we,' Marcus. Not anymore."

Marcus felt himself starting to go pale. "I'm not leaving."

"I'm not giving you a choice." A steely edge cut through Oliver's words. "You need to get your life on track."

"It isn't *off* track."

"You haven't worked in a year and a half."

"I haven't wanted to."

"It's time you went back to work."

"*I'll* decide when it's time." Marcus strode toward Oliver. "You need me far more than Hollywood does. So here's what's going to happen: We're going to get this place shipshape; I'm going to make some dinner; then we're going to start listing every doctor registered in California, and we're going to—"

"YOU'RE NOT LISTENING TO ME!" Oliver shoved Marcus away, but the attempt sent Oliver lurching against the door. "We're at the end of the line, you and me."

"I refuse—"

"I don't know what my future holds, but I do know that it no longer involves you."

Oliver's ragged face began to warp and blur through Marcus' tears. "You're not alone!"

"But I want to be. And I want you to get on with your life. Without me." Oliver threw open the door and it hit the wall with a bang. He gripped Marcus and shoved him out into the corridor.

"I'll come back every day, and I'll bang on your door until—"

"You'll be wasting your time. I'm moving out."

"Where are you going?"

"Goodbye, Marcus, and good luck."

"I love you!"

Oliver smiled sadly, tears in his eyes. "I know," he said quietly. "That's the problem." He stepped back and closed the door.

CHAPTER 24

Kathryn pressed her palms to her forehead. She didn't need to look at the clock—she'd just consulted it less than a minute ago.

"Where the *hell* can she be?"

"You've got an hour till showtime," Marcus said. "Will this help?"

She eyed the chrome hip flask in his hand. She thought Marcus was a darling for even showing up tonight. He'd been shattered by the bombshell Oliver dropped on his head and hadn't left his villa all week. But he knew this was a big night for her so he pulled himself together and offered, soberly if somewhat ashen, to drive her to the NBC studios.

Kathryn looked at the clock above her dressing room door. It was now twelve past seven. Forty-eight minutes to air and no special guest. She thanked him, but said she needed to keep her head clear.

Two days after she got the telegram from Max Factor, she was in a meeting with all the honchos discussing a fifteen-minute chat show they wanted to call *Window on Hollywood*—the same title as her column. Twenty-four hours later she had a contract and ten days to put a show together. Life felt like a montage from a Lubitsch picture.

She'd hoped to precede *The Great Guildersleeve* on Sunday night, but NBC gave her Friday evenings when people were at nightclubs or dinner parties. Even worse, they inserted her ahead of a new police whodunit nobody had heard of, *Dragnet*. But she did have her own radio show, so she was thankful for that.

When she telephoned Bette Davis to call in her promise, Bette said, "Of course! And I can give you your first scoop." Kathryn gripped the receiver. Bette had almost cackled with glee. "After nineteen years of indenture, my final day at Warner Brothers is to be August ninth!"

Without Bette, the show would kick off with a whimper, not the brass band she'd hoped for.

Gwendolyn walked in with Bertie and Doris trailing behind her. "Any word?"

"How could she do this to me?"

"Can't you get a replacement?" Gwendolyn asked.

"With less than forty-five minutes to air?" Kathryn knew how shrill she sounded, but there were now five of them crowded into her dressing room and she was starting to panic.

"What about Tallulah? She's always game."

"No go," Marcus said. "I read in *Variety* that she's touring *Private Lives* around New England."

"You read *Variety*?" Kathryn asked pointedly.

"I read everything."

Wallace Reed poked his creased brow into the room. "I'm getting worried."

Reed had been the unflappable producer on *Kraft Music Hall*. During the *Kraft* years, they'd had very few disasters, but when they did blow up, his composure got them through.

Kathryn realized she was squeezing her hands together and consciously unlaced her fingers. "I know it's getting late."

"You told her it's a one-hour call, right?"

"She's done a million of these things. She knows how it works."

"But it's seven twenty—" he consulted his wristwatch "—two."

WHERE THE HELL IS SHE? "Probably just stuck in traffic." Kathryn flapped her hand around in an attempt to sound airy. *I'M GOING TO THROTTLE HER.* "You know how bad traffic's gotten lately."

"And if she doesn't show?" Reed asked. "You've got a backup, haven't you?"

"Several, so no need to worry!"

Reed appeared to be satisfied with Kathryn's bald-faced lie, and withdrew.

"This is going to sound extreme, but I have an idea." Bertie said. "I do a pretty damn good Tallulah Bankhead impersonation."

"In front of three hundred people?" Kathryn burst out.

Marcus held up his hand to stop her and turned to Bertie. "Show us what you can do."

Bertie flicked her head back. "Dahling! I simply can*not* begin to tell you how *excited* I am to be your very first guest! Why, just yesterday, I was saying to Noel Coward, 'Noelie! Dahling! One of my absolute *favorite* people in the world has her own radio show and she's asked *me* to be her first guest. Isn't that simply *mah*velous?!'"

What Bertie was proposing was outrageous—but damn, if she didn't sound just like Tallulah.

"That's really quite uncanny," Kathryn admitted, "but I don't see how we could get away with it."

Seven twenty-four.

"What if we billed her as The World's Greatest Tallulah Bankhead Impersonator?" Marcus suggested.

Kathryn ran her fingers through her hair. "Reed would have a fit!" *I'm about to have one right now.*

"If it comes down to the wire," Bertie said, "he won't have much choice."

"Isn't there anyone else we can get? Preferably with a picture to promote."

"What about Gable?" Gwendolyn exclaimed. "He's got a new movie coming out with Alexis Smith."

Kathryn turned to Marcus. "Weren't you on good terms with him when you left MGM?"

"Sure," he replied, but she could already read his mind: *You might as well be asking for God.* "But someone from the Garden of Allah would be more likely to jump in."

Doris snapped her fingers. "What about Bogie?"

"That's not a bad idea!" Kathryn dove into her little black book.

"But they live way up Benedict Canyon." Bertie said. "Even if he left right now, could he get here in less than thirty minutes?"

"He doesn't have to," Doris said. "He's filming *Knock On Any Door* with us."

Doris had recently started work at Columbia, which was only three blocks away.

"He'll still be there?" Kathryn asked.

"He's producing the picture under his own company. He's always the first one to arrive and the last to leave."

Kathryn laid her hand on the telephone. "Do you know the number?"

Doris shook her head. "But the main switchboard doesn't go off until nine."

Seven twenty-eight. *If this is what it's like to head your own radio show, I don't think I've got the stamina.*

Kathryn flipped to "C" and dialed Columbia's main switchboard. When the operator put her through to the Santana production office, Kathryn could scarcely believe it when Bogie himself answered.

"Hi there, it's me, Kathryn. Sorry to do this to you, but I'm in the most terrible bind. My new radio show starts tonight. Half an hour from now, in fact. My guest was supposed to be Bette Davis, but she hasn't shown up. So I'm hoping—no, *pleading* that you—"

"Bette? She's right here." Bogie let out a slurred giggle. "She dropped in to see how we're going on our independent picture. Personally, I think she's trying to avoid going home to her husband. You want me to put her on?"

Kathryn heard more giggling before Bette's voice boomed down the line. "Kathryn, my sweet, are you in a tizzy?"

"What are you doing there? You're supposed to be *here*!"

"Why? Where are you?"

"At NBC. Remember? My show?"

Bette took a leisurely drag of her cigarette. "But you start next week."

"No! Tonight!"

"That's what I thought, but Ruby Courtland insisted I had it all wrong."

Kathryn wanted to bash the receiver into the wall. "Ruby? From *Variety*? Is sitting there right now? And she told you my show starts *next* week?" She was repeating this out loud for the benefit of the others in her dressing room. *That conniving little bitch.*

"She was, yes. She just left."

Marcus got to his feet. "My car's out front. I can be at Columbia in two minutes."

Kathryn nodded furiously and mouthed, "Go! GO!" He sprinted toward the exit. "Bette?" Kathryn drew in a ragged breath. "We go to air in twenty-seven minutes."

"Oh, Kathryn, no! I feel terrible."

"You remember my friend Marcus? He's going to be out front in two minutes. He's in a yellow Buick."

"But I've come straight from the studio!" Bette croaked. "I look a fright. I can't appear wearing this getup in front of a live audience."

Kathryn looked at Gwendolyn. She was in a sundress, tiny green checks with white lapels. It looked more like one of Joan Crawford's costumes from *Mildred Pierce*, but it'd have to do.

Gwendolyn whispered, "I have safety pins in my purse if it doesn't fit."

"We've got that covered," Kathryn yelled down the line. "Just get here!"

She hung up as Reed appeared in the doorway again. "I heard yelling. Please tell me it's the good sort."

"Bette got stuck at Columbia and—"

"What was she doing there?"

Ruby goddamned Courtland is what she was doing there. "She's only three blocks away." Kathryn silently begged the guy to leave.

"As long as everything is in hand."

"It absolutely is!" Kathryn swallowed hard so she wouldn't sound like she was hopped up on bennies. "We'll meet you in the wings in a few minutes."

Nobody breathed until Reed left.

"Bertie," Kathryn said, "park yourself at the stage door. I need you to hold it open for Bette. Meanwhile—" Gwendolyn was already pulling at her side zipper. "Do you think it'll fit?"

She'd sewn a dress for Bette once before. "If her measurements are the same, it'll be a bit loose around the bust, but the waist should be close enough, give or take."

Kathryn collapsed onto her vanity stool and looked at herself in the mirror. "Is this really all worth it?"

"Of course it's worth it!" Doris joined her at the mirror. She crumpled her round little face so earnestly that it made Kathryn smile. "How many women on the radio have their own show?" She started kneading Kathryn's knotted shoulders. "You're a role model and a trailblazer! This business with Bette Davis is just a last-minute snafu. And she's a trouper—you know that. She'll jump into Gwendolyn's dress, run a brush through her hair, and she'll be good to go. You'll see."

Kathryn couldn't bring herself to check the time. "On *Kraft Music Hall*, all I had to do was show up. I'll never live it down if this blows up in my face."

"Hey now!" Doris dug her thumbs into Kathryn's shoulder muscles. Her hands were surprisingly strong. "Nothing's exploding in anybody's face."

"Yet."

"Worst-case scenario is Bertie goes on as Tallulah Bankhead and everybody gets a big laugh."

"What is it you do at Columbia?"

Doris rolled her eyes. "I started out as a grunt. But now they've got me reorganizing the prop department. It was a junk shop in there."

"You should be in PR," Kathryn said. *Seven forty-three.* "You've got a very human touch about you."

"GANG WAY!" Bertie's voice boomed down the corridor. Running footsteps followed.

Doris closed the door as soon as Bette came in. The next five minutes was a flurry of apologies, hairbrushes, zippers, safety pins, lipstick, and cuss words. Before Kathryn could get nervous, she and Bette were standing shoulder to shoulder on the wings of the NBC stage.

* * *

Kathryn turned out of the NBC parking lot and headed north up Vine Street. For reasons Bette hadn't bothered to explain, her car was still at Warner Bros.

Bette fell back into the passenger seat and let out a long sigh. "It went off rather well, don't you think?"

"I'm glad *you* think so. That was the longest fifteen minutes of my life."

Bette patted Kathryn's knee. "Congratulations on a job well done. *Window on Hollywood* got off to a flying start. You should be thrilled."

"I'll be thrilled when I get some whiskey in me. Right now I feel like one of those poor souls who got trampled on by King Kong."

"Trust me," Bette said, "in my dressing room there is puh-*lenty* of fortification."

"*Beyond the Forest* still not going well? Even with King Vidor directing?"

"They should retitle it *Beyond the Pale*. Put it this way: my character attempts to induce an abortion by throwing herself off a cliff. Who *does* that? After eighteen years, this piece of trash is going to be my final Warners picture. But you know what? I'm so fed up that I don't even care. I'm counting the days."

The two women rode in silence as the shadows of Hollywood passed by. It was after nine o'clock now and hardly anybody was on the street.

"Those guys who follow your timeslot," Bette said, "my goodness but they're a serious bunch, aren't they? What's their show called?"

"*Dragnet*."

Bette blew a raspberry.

"Sounds like something one of Gwendolyn's clients would throw over his wig once it's set."

Even Kathryn was surprised by the laugh that erupted out of her. It came from deep inside her belly, cathartic as a purgative, and brought tears to her eyes until she had to pull over in front of a court of bungalows at the top of Vine.

She dabbed at her eyes. "Oh, Lord, I needed that."

Bette reached into her purse. "I was going to hold off until we got back to the studio, but screw it."

As Bette rummaged around her purse, Kathryn said, "I need to talk to you about Ruby Courtland."

Bette lit a cigarette and held out one for Kathryn. "I must say, I'm surprised she's a friend of yours."

"What on earth makes you think that?"

"You should have heard the way she was gushing about you back in Bogie's office. It was all Kathryn this, and Kathryn that. 'I look up to her so much! Of all the careers in Hollywood, it's Kathryn Massey's that I want to emulate!' Oh, brother! She laid it on so thick I nearly gagged. No offense."

Kathryn paused to enjoy the hit of nicotine. "She was there to sabotage me this evening. I do not know how she knew you'd be there."

Bette rolled down her window. "What does she have against you?"

"She wants what I've got."

"But without having to work for it, I suppose?"

Kathryn tossed the idea around for a moment. "There might be some truth to that."

"Ugh. I've been fighting rich bitches like her my whole life. Entitlement, entitlement, entitlement."

"She comes from money?"

"King's wife, Elizabeth, visited our set the other day to cheer him up, and she mentioned how Ruby was some sort of big-deal debutante back East."

Kathryn pictured Ruby that day on the *Samson and Delilah* set, with her dull, straight hair and her insipid outfit. "What else did Elizabeth say?"

"Something about her father earning a fortune during the war. I didn't know who she was talking about, so I changed the subject. Then she popped up in Bogie's dressing room tonight, all sweet as pie and fawning like Ruby of Sunnybrook Farm. Now that I know otherwise, I wish I'd paid more attention. I can't believe I fell for that story of hers. You're not going to let her get away with it, are you?"

Kathryn turned the key, disengaged the clutch, and pulled back onto the deserted street. "Not a chance in hell."

CHAPTER 25

Gwendolyn felt the thrum of the engine as she ran a finger along Marcus' dashboard. The setting sun shone directly into their faces, and she was glad to see Marcus losing the pallor he'd acquired since his relationship with Oliver went south. He'd gently rebuffed her attempts to draw him away from his sofa, so their destination tonight felt like a tiny ray of hope.

He pulled his eyes off the traffic for a moment. "What's going on with you?"

"I'm pleased you said yes tonight, that's all."

"No, it's not. I know you, so out with it."

"Well, now that you ask," she admitted with a shy smile.

"Is it the store?"

"In a way," Gwendolyn replied.

The week someone broke into Chez Gwendolyn, a producer on the new Marx Brothers movie sent his secretary for "a bottle of that Sunset Strip stuff." Three days later, a snappily dressed gent in charge of screen tests at Fox walked in. He said he'd recently encountered a starlet wearing a most arresting perfume and asked her where she got it.

The very next day, a trio of women came in, each flaunting the black-coffee-for-breakfast sleekness of ex-showgirls who'd made good by marrying front-office yes-men.

The one with the flaming Maureen O'Hara hair announced that she'd heard about Sunset Boulevard, and squealed when Gwendolyn wafted it under her nose. The three of them ran her ragged with fittings for everything from hats to gloves, blouses to evening gowns. Two hours and four bottles of Sunset Boulevard later, they exited amid a tumult of air kisses, darlings, and checks totaling fifteen hundred dollars.

She had been waiting for the right moment to tell Marcus about Zap, but she felt it was cruel to talk about it while he was still piecing himself together.

The first inkling that Zap looked at her as more than just a client came the day after the first shipment of Sunset Boulevard. He sent her an extravagant bouquet of tulips in a wicker basket backed with peacock feathers. Attached was a note saying how deeply he'd enjoyed working with her.

The next week, a messenger delivered a pair of pearl drop earrings. The note attached assured her that he was sending them "for no other reason but that they'd look heavenly on those exquisite lobes of yours."

Then he asked her to be his guest at the final episode of *The Fred Allen Show*, which was ending its eighteen-year run; it was black tie and invitation only.

His last-minute request implied he hadn't given it much forethought, but the way he pressed his hand into the small of her back as they located their seats caused her to wonder if she was heading for trouble.

After all, he was born the year she entered junior high.

Halfway through that broadcast, he inched his leg rightward until his knee touched hers. He applied a gentle probing pressure, pressing his thigh, then his calf against hers. She felt the heat of his leg through her stocking, and when she felt his elbow press against hers, she was running short of breath.

By the time the DeMarco Sisters were singing "Doin' What Comes Natur'ly," neither Gwendolyn nor Zap were paying much attention. They barely exchanged a word as he drove them up Beachwood Canyon and into a secluded cul-de-sac.

After an hour of enthusiastic necking, they drove into Hollywood for cheeseburgers at Simon's Drive-In.

She waited until the last of the fries were gone, then admitted that she was "steaming toward forty." His response—"You're the type of woman who'll still be turning heads at seventy"—sounded sincere enough to warrant a second date.

A week later they were snuggled into a booth at the Formosa Café, after which they indulged in a session of window fogging while parked on Mulholland Drive overlooking the lights of Universal Studios.

She promised herself they wouldn't go all the way until they'd had at least three dates, although she wasn't entirely sure why. It wasn't like she didn't know her way around a man's body. A pretty girl at the Garden of Allah was rarely the cloistered type.

Zap must have sensed what was in the cards: he went all out by taking her to dinner at Perino's, a swanky French restaurant where the waiters wore white gloves.

He ordered for them: oysters Rockefeller, followed by breast of guinea hen. But they were too worked up to bother with coffee, and raced back to his place. They'd been going at it like jackrabbits ever since.

As the Sunset Strip gave way to residential Beverly Hills, Marcus said, "You don't have to tell me if you don't want to."

"It's just that I feel funny talking about it while you're still —"

"Have you met someone?"

"I think so, yes."

He landed a hand on top of hers. "Gwennie, honey, don't ever feel like that. I want to kno v all about him, including when do I get to meet him?"

"In about an hour."

"*Tonight?*" He shot her a sideways look. "Is there something wrong with him?"

"I wouldn't say *wrong*, necessarily."

"What would you say?"

"He's younger than me."

"So?"

"By twelve years."

"Now I *am* intrigued. Who is it?"

"The guy who put my perfume together."

"Tapa . . .? Papa . . .?"

"Ignacio Zaparelli."

"I hope he knows movies. Albert and Frances are going to be drilling us."

Albert Hackett and Frances Goodrich were back in LA for the summer, putting a great deal of effort into their latest project, a musical called *In the Good Old Summertime* starring Judy Garland and Van Johnson.

Neither was convinced it worked as well as it should, and they'd asked Marcus to attend a sneak preview. It was held on the night Kathryn did *Window on Hollywood*, so Marcus recruited Doris, Bertie, and Gwendolyn.

The Bay Theatre was a new place near the western end of Sunset, close to where it ended at the Pacific. Its enormous sign spelled out *BAY* in twelve-foot neon; cool white light saturated the outdoor foyer. Bertie and Doris were sharing a cigarette in front of a Coming Attractions poster for *The Heiress*, but Zap was nowhere in sight.

Gwendolyn was still looking for him when Albert and Frances arrived in a taxi. She'd come to think of them as a single unit: Albert-and-Frances. But as they marched toward her, she saw them in a whole different light. It had been years since Gwendolyn gave any thought to how Albert was ten years his wife's junior and that Frances looked ten years older than fifty-nine.

She wasn't sure exactly how long Albert-and-Frances had been married, but she figured they must be close to their twentieth anniversary.

Who cares if Zap's twelve years younger than me? I haven't had a steady beau since Linc. That was four years ago. What am I? A hermit?

Almost on cue, Zap emerged from the shadows of the parking lot wearing a charming smile and his smart Italian suit.

I'm my own woman, and my own boss, with nobody to answer to but myself. Why in God's name have I been so preoccupied with what other people think?

She grabbed his hand. "Everyone, this is Ignacio Zaparelli, but for heaven's sake, call him Zap. Shall we go in?"

——

* * *

Zap didn't ask if he'd passed muster until he and Gwendolyn were in his car driving back to Hollywood.

Gwendolyn chuckled. "What do *you* think?"

He'd charmed Albert-and-Frances by quoting several of their wittiest lines verbatim. He'd won Doris over when he complimented her taste in jewelry. "One carefully chosen brooch says so much more than a glut of earrings, pendants, and bracelets." He achieved the same result when he told Bertie he wished more women were as in tune with their most complimentary colors as she was. And as for Marcus, well, all he had to do was flash that Tyrone Power smile of his.

"I've learned it's smart to never assume." He drove several more blocks. "We're coming up on Doheny."

She knew what he was hinting at, but he was a little smug at having gone over so well at the Bay, and she wanted him to work for it. She agreed that they were and left it at that.

It took him several more blocks to say, "If we're going back to my place, it's easier to take Doheny to Melrose than all the way to Vine."

"And if we're going to mine?"

They sailed through the Sunset and Doheny intersection without speaking. He hadn't been to her place and she knew he was curious as hell.

"There's a parking lot off Crescent Heights—"

"I know," he said. "I may have driven past once or twice."

* * *

As they walked through the Garden of Allah, Gwendolyn counted three different parties, which wasn't unusual. Sundays were still the weekend, and the weekends were for the letting down of hair, regardless of how early the alarm clocks went off in the morning.

The Garden's management had recently doubled the number of lights along the meandering paths, strategically positioning them in ways that cast intriguing shadows and made the foliage glow extra green.

As they approached her villa, Zap spun her around and pulled her into a clinch with a fervor she didn't see coming. She leaned into the kiss and felt her body melt against his. When they broke apart, she looked up into his face.

"Where did that come from?"

"I like kissing you with your clothes on." He took the key from her hand and inserted it into the lock. "I also enjoy kissing you with your clothes in a trail to the bedroom. Ah! The sweet promise of things to come." He swung the door open and stepped aside with a ladies-first motion.

Gwendolyn flipped on the lights.

Instinctively, she reached out behind her. Zap took her by the hand and pressed his chest against her back. She felt his lips press her right ear. "Either you're the world's worst housewife—"

"Or I've been broken into."

* * *

When Gwendolyn returned with Marcus, Kathryn, Doris, and Bertie, Zap had cleared away the jumble of hurled books and upended drawers from her sofa and dining table.

So you're stylish, smart, sensitive, obedient, and good in a crisis. But will you stick around when you learn that Leilah's got her knives out for me?

Gwendolyn introduced Zap to Kathryn as they all took a seat.

Kathryn rubbed her forehead. "Leilah's gone way too far."

"Leilah *O'Roarke*?" Zap's unblinking gaze conveyed his alarm.

"Did you ever meet Horton Tattler's son, Linc?" Gwendolyn asked. He shook his head. "He and I used to date. He died recently and I received a box of personal effects. Leilah is convinced that her client cards were inside."

"The ones that Winchell talked about?" Zap asked. Gwendolyn searched for signs that he wanted to run a mile, but he looked more fascinated than apprehensive. "Are you sure they weren't there?"

"It's hard to miss a box of five-by-three index cards. I thought I'd managed to persuade her, but then my store was broken into, and now this."

"We should track her down and tell her again," Marcus said.

"Could I have been any clearer at Mocambo?"

"Maybe it is time to tell the police," Bertie said. "Or the FBI. Or someone." She swept her arms over the trash heap of Gwendolyn's apartment. "This is too close to home."

"If this is her handiwork, she's obviously determined," Zap said.

"Desperate is more like it."

"But what if this Linc guy took them out of the metal box?"

Gwendolyn could feel her patience running out. "I don't have them!" she said. "Even if Linc had, I would've seen them. But there was nothing in that cardboard box Horton gave me but mementos."

Doris gasped. "You don't suppose—?" She jumped to her feet. "I'll be right back."

"Should I follow her?" Marcus stood up and went to the window. "I've always felt so safe here, but now that this has happened . . ."

Nobody knew quite what to do, least of all Gwendolyn. "I wish I *did* have them!" she declared.

"No, you don't." Marcus returned to his seat.

"I could give them to Leilah and wash my hands of this whole situation—"

"Is she coming back already?" Kathryn cut in. They listened to the sound of running feet crunching the gravel. "That didn't take long."

Doris burst back into the room clutching Linc's copy of *Magnificent Obsession*. "When I put this on my bookshelf, I thought it felt heavy." Still panting from her sprint, she laid the book on Gwendolyn's coffee table and opened it up.

Someone had cut a rectangle into the middle of the pages, just enough to fit a stack of cards.

"Hell's bells!" Bertie exclaimed. "I've seen that in the movies but I didn't know anyone actually did it in real life."

Gwendolyn's fingers trembled as she picked up the book, tipped it toward the light and read out loud the name written along the top of the first card. "Yardley Aaronson."

"I know him," Zap said. "He makes props. Specializes in mirrors with ornate frames and frosted glass, like for bathroom scenes." He snickered. "He's a devout Catholic. Five kids. The whole nine yards."

Gwendolyn snapped the book shut. "I'm taking this to Leilah."

"You've got Pandora's Box in your hands there, Gwennie," Kathryn warned.

"I don't want this! It's brought me nothing but trouble."

"Give it to Leilah and she'll ruin the reputation of every man in town."

The book felt like a ticking bomb. Gwendolyn slid it onto the coffee table. "Then I'll burn them. The whole damn lot!"

"You can't do that, either," Zap said.

"Why not?"

"Because she's been charged with pandering, and that's a felony." He pointed to *Magnificent Obsession*. "If anyone hears that you've destroyed crucial evidence, you could find yourself up on charges of evidence tampering."

"I'm damned if I do, damned if I don't?"

"He's right," Marcus said. "You're going to have to keep these hidden away until you can figure out the best way to handle all this." He looked at the group huddled around the room. "Meanwhile, we all keep mum. Not a word. Right?"

CHAPTER 26

Marcus hadn't seen Trevor Bergin for days. Whenever a Garden resident disappeared without notice, everyone assumed they'd taken off with a trunkful of whiskey and locked themselves away in some divey motel.

Earlier that summer, panicked whisperings had circulated that a new, secret FBI report mentioned a bunch of Hollywood names. One theory said it was part of the Alger Hiss trials in New York. Another one insisted that HUAC had commenced closed-door sessions in Washington. According to a third version, a California State Senate Committee was looking to pick up where HUAC left off a year ago, investigating anyone in Hollywood who might have links to the Communist Party.

The rumors mutated with every lap around the grapevine, so Marcus paid only passing attention. Whenever he spotted the word "Commie" in Louella Parsons' and Hedda Hopper's columns, he often skipped to the next page. He didn't even bother with Ruby Courtland's column—what a right-wing loose cannon that little humdinger was proving to be.

But when he did pay attention, Marcus noticed that the names often changed. First it was John Garfield and Edward G. Robinson. The following week, Katharine Hepburn, Gregory Peck, and Orson Welles were the bad guys. But the name that surfaced with every iteration was Trevor Bergin. Marcus knew how it felt for the world to think you were a Red, so he didn't blame the guy for disappearing.

With half the residents taking off for the long Fourth of July weekend, the Garden was unusually quiet. After a blissfully solitary swim, Marcus was toweling himself off when he heard smashing glass coming from Trevor's villa.

He knocked on the wall and called out Trevor's name. When he heard a dull thud followed by a terrific belch, Marcus rounded the corner and pounded on the front door. "I know you're in there! I'm not stopping until you open up."

"It's not even locked."

Marcus let himself in expecting to see what Gwendolyn's place had looked like a few weeks ago, but Trevor's living room was as tidy as it had always been. Trevor sat in the dead center of his sofa, his face wiped clean of expression.

Marcus kept his voice even. "I heard the sound of breaking glass." *Which can come in handy if you're looking to open a vein.*

"It was the crystal vase I gave Melody for our first anniversary. She didn't take it with her when she moved out, and I hated it so . . ."

"So you dropped it on the floor?"

"I was aiming for the trash can. The point is, I don't have to look at it anymore."

Marcus looked at Trevor's bare feet. "That could prove dangerous the next time you need to walk around your apartment."

"You want to clean it up? Be my guest."

He joined Trevor on the sofa. "We haven't seen you in a while, buddy. I was hoping to see you at Frances and Albert's preview. You should see Judy! She looks great, especially in this dress Irene designed—"

"I think I've been fired."

Outside the window, a raucous gang of holidaymakers burst randomly into laughter.

"You have, or think you have?"

"I've been taken off *Three Little Words*." The biopic about the songwriting team of Kalmar and Ruby was one of MGM's big hopes for 1950; it would have ensured Trevor's continued perch atop the heap. "They're replacing me with Red Skelton."

"Oh, come on! You know what that means." Marcus chanced a friendly leg nudge. "Replacing you with Red is like swapping Garbo for Sonja Henie. They just decided to go in a different direction."

"This week, I turned up for fittings on *The Toast of New Orleans* and nobody could look me in the eye. Come to find out that Joe Pasternak had called Walter Plunkett a whole week earlier. Everybody knew but me. It was humiliating."

"There can be a ton of reasons why people get recast—"

"David Niven's getting my part."

Although Trevor possessed a sportier barrel-chestedness than Niven, and Niven's screen persona had a worldly playboy charm that Trevor's lacked, the two men were somewhat interchangeable.

Marcus clamped his hand on Trevor's knee. "I was going for a drive down to the beach. Come with me."

"I'm not ready to face the world."

"I'm not asking you to face the world. Just the ocean. It can be soothing for a troubled soul. I've been where you are."

* * *

The stretch of sand where Sunset met the Pacific was deserted. Scarcely a handful of people roamed the beach — an older couple with their Labrador puppy, a tanned beachcomber Marcus often spotted collecting driftwood, and a quartet of teenagers lugging a picnic basket toward the rocks at the northern end.

Marcus pulled his key out of the ignition and opened his door. The sun was already high, but not nearly so scorching as the forecasters had predicted. In fact, it was pretty much as perfect as California perfection got.

He pulled off his topsiders and jumped onto the sand. That was his favorite part of what had become a thrice-weekly ritual. He loved to feel the warmth squelch between his toes as he headed for the water. The ocean was always bracingly cold, and he loved that too.

The two men stood at the shoreline. "See?" Marcus asked. "The waves come in, the waves go out. It has a comforting rhythm, don't you think?"

Trevor grunted.

"With all the uncertainty and impermanence in our lives, it's nice to know there are some things that don't change. Jobs come and go, relationships come and go, some years we have scads of money, some years we're broke, but whatever's going on, the tide ebbs, the tide flows, the tide ebbs again."

"And you find that comforting?"

"It puts things into perspective," Marcus said.

"My life is going down the drain and you bring me here to look at water?"

"Yes. To help you see this too shall pass."

"AND WHAT THE FUCK DO YOU KNOW?"

The picnicking teenagers turned around and stared.

"I know better than anyone else what it feels like."

"The hell you do." Trevor picked up a stick of driftwood and hurled it into the ocean. "Quentin hasn't returned my calls in weeks."

Quentin Luckett had been Trevor's boyfriend for as long as Marcus had known either of them, going on seven or eight years now.

"I haven't seen him since Easter. Meanwhile, my career's ground to a standstill. All the rumors about me being in that secret FBI report, you know it's just a matter of time before I'm canned. And don't tell me you know how it feels. I have a very public career whereas yours . . ." He picked up a stone and skipped it across the water's surface. "Nobody cares about the writers."

It was a callous way to put it, but Trevor wasn't far off the mark. Writers sat at the bottom of the Hollywood pecking order. They were considered the least valuable and most expendable, which only made the idea of a blacklist even more ludicrous. Nobody listened to the writers.

"Are you forgetting how public my downfall was?" Marcus asked. "I was forced to defend myself in front of HUAC, *in* Washington, *with* the entire press corps shoving their microphones *and* cameras in my face. That's about as public as it gets, Mister Pity Me."

Trevor had six inches on Marcus and used every one of them when he stepped forward to tower over him, terror and fury crinkling his face. "My entire career is based on my popularity with the public. Once I've lost that, I have no career."

He'd always played the dapper idealist who got the girl in the final reel. His looks were tailor-made for moviegoers searching for an Adonis on whom they could pin their romantic dreams. But as Marcus felt Trevor's spit hit his face, he thought of the guy's unnaturally neat apartment and realized this was the first time Trevor had let himself go. It was time his perfect façade came down, and if he didn't do it soon, he might implode.

"That's true," Marcus conceded. "But if you do get fired—*if,* mind you—burying yourself in your apartment and wringing your hands won't accomplish diddly."

"Oh yeah? From where I'm sitting, you got no job and Oliver told you to take a hike. Where has the last year and a half gotten you?"

Marcus backed away—not from Trevor's red-faced browbeating but because his question had slugged him in the rubber parts. "I just don't want you to waste as much time as I have."

"When I want your advice I'll ask for it." Trevor scooped up his shoes and pounded them together. "And the next time you want to shove your opinions down someone's throat, don't leave them stranded so far from home."

"I'll take you back," Marcus said, turning to the car. "We don't have to talk—"

"I'll find my own way, thank you. And fuck you."

Marcus turned back to the waves. Their steady pulse now seemed empty and monotonous. He dropped his butt and scooped the sand into his hands. It felt almost liquid as he let it slip through his fingers.

"That didn't go so well, huh?"

Driftwood Guy was standing with his back to the sun, endowed with a golden radiance usually seen in religious paintings.

Marcus gave a weak smile. "Not so much."

"Mind if I join you?"

"Pull up a sandbank."

"Reuben."

"Marcus."

This was the first time Marcus had seen Driftwood Guy up close. He was well into his fifties, with the tanned face and sun-bleached hair of someone who'd spent a great deal of time outdoors.

Marcus sighed. "What you witnessed was a case of 'Do What I Do, Not As I Say.' I only wanted to help, but I guess I won't try that again."

"As a matter of fact, I think you're pretty good at helping people."

"What makes you say that?"

The guy broke into the sort of smile someone makes when they're trying hard not to. "You don't remember me, do you?"

Marcus quickly ran through the carnival of faces belonging to people he'd slept with, but came up blank.

"It was a while ago." Reuben ran a fistful of sand from one fist to another. "The night they raided that log cabin bar up in Mandeville Canyon."

That was where Oliver and I had one of our worst fights. "Hermit's Hideaway."

"Yes! I must have blocked it. They say we do that with traumatic events. Do you remember the fool who shouted, 'I didn't survive the Battle of the Somme, the polio epidemic, and Prohibition to put up with this shit' and then got thumped with a billy club?"

It had been dark inside that bar, and with vice cops stampeding in, Marcus only had scant memories of what that guy looked like. "For a minute there I thought you were a goner."

The smile dropped from Reuben's face. "You were the only one there who showed me kindness. All the others backed off like I had the bubonic plague."

"Every homo for himself."

"But you escaped."

"I had a friend who had a friend who pulled some strings."

"You got a swell break. They made us wait for hours until the press started sniffing around to see who was in lock-up. By then, they had our names, addresses, and employers typed up and ready for distribution."

"Did you lose your job?"

Reuben nodded. "But it turned out to be the best thing that ever happened to me."

That would explain the tranquility that radiates from you like candlelight. "How come?"

"It got me to thinking about what I was doing when I was happiest."

He nodded toward the canyon behind them.

"You know what this used to be? We called it Inceville. Thomas Inceville leased this land when he needed more space to make his movies. I was a set builder for him. It was the best time of my life. With my name in the papers, I could no longer work for the studios, so I turned my hand to building furniture. Now I have a store down the road apiece in Santa Monica. We make custom furniture—any size, any style, any wood. You should come by and visit us."

"Us?"

"My lover is a wood wholesaler. We joke how we should send those cops a thank-you note. We'd never have met if it hadn't been for them."

"I love a happy ending."

"And I never got a chance to thank you for your kindness."

Marcus leaned back on one elbow. "I see you here all the time."

Reuben grimaced, revealing two rows of bright movie-star teeth. "A while ago, I saw someone else from that night. I could tell he recognized me, so I approached him, but he ran off. I didn't want to take the same chance with you, but then I saw you and Trevor Bergin—that was him, wasn't it?"

"He's my neighbor." Marcus started drawing triangles in the sand with his finger. "I don't know that I did much that night but check you were okay."

"Under those circumstances, it was a lot. You're lucky that your life went on as normal."

"Yeah, until HUAC got its teeth into me."

"You lost your job, after all?"

"When MGM throws you to the HUAC lions and you tell everyone to go to blazes, it doesn't leave you with much in the way of career options."

"And now?"

And now I feel like I'm floating with the current like that driftwood you collect. "Still figuring it out."

"You a screenwriter?"

"Is . . . was . . . it's a blurry line."

"What about television? I have a friend who works on *Colgate Theatre*. He's in casting, but I could talk to him for you."

A television show? Sponsored by a tube of toothpaste? Marcus couldn't think of anything worse. "Thanks. That's kind of you, but I don't think so."

"If you change your mind, you can find me on Third Street." Reuben started collecting up his sticks of wood as he got to his feet. "What you did that night was the one bright spot of humanity that got me through a very dark time, so thank you."

Marcus watched him hike across the sand and dump his driftwood into the back of an old truck speckled with rust. He climbed behind the wheel, roared his engine to life, and steered onto Route 1 without a backward glance.

Marcus stared out to sea. The waves lunged forward and withdrew again, lunged and withdrew. Twenty feet from the shore, a pair of seagulls swooped in for a perfect landing. They bobbed up and down toward the surface of the water for only a minute or two before one of them unleashed a piercing shriek and took off again, leaving his pal to float around on his own.

"Did you hear him?" Marcus asked the bird. "*Colgate Theater.*" The bird turned his head toward Marcus and stared at him unblinkingly. "I can do better than that, don't you think?"

The seagull had nothing to contribute.

CHAPTER 27

Kathryn had been to the Polo Lounge at the Beverly Hills Hotel so often she was on a first-name basis with the maître d'. She wasn't sure where Lukas was from, but he had the eternal tan of an Argentine playboy and the dyed black hair to match.

"Miss Massey! How enchanting you look today!" He welcomed her with his customary continental kiss to both cheeks.

"Is he here yet?" she asked.

He nodded.

"You didn't put him at my usual table, did you?"

Kathryn typically preferred the one near the center so everyone could see her lunching with Gene Tierney or Betty Grable.

Lukas shook his head. "I sensed some privacy might be required."

She pressed her cheek to his. "You're a treasure, and I suspect a little bit psychic."

He accepted her compliment with an enigmatic smile. "I put him in number seven."

"Perfect." Booth seven was tucked away behind a cornucopia of palm fronds. "Oh, and I need you to come over at three o'clock and remind me of the time. I have another appointment in Burbank."

A table of four luncheon ladies followed her through the maze of tables. As she rounded the greenery, she slid her professional smile into place.

Walter Winchell was more handsome than the craggy journalist she expected. In person, his face had a pleasant shape to it, with features in tidy proportion. His hair was graying now, but his firm skin showed no signs of sagging.

When he looked up from his menu, the razor-sharp eyes caught her like headlights.

He got to his feet and presented her with a professional smile of his own.

"Right on time," he said, shaking her hand. "I like that."

"How nice to finally meet you." Kathryn ducked under the shady umbrella and into the booth.

"I ordered us martinis, or was that presumptuous?"

Kathryn peeled off her gloves and told him martinis were fine, and trusted that Lukas was clever enough to send her a diluted one.

It took some effort to meet Winchell's penetrating stare, but she knew if she didn't, he'd have her at a disadvantage.

"What brings you out to the coast?"

"A sizable chunk of my items originate in Hollywood, so I figured it might be wise to stick my nose out here once in a while. You're only as good as your last broadcast, as I'm sure you're starting to discover."

He smiled at her, but it was mechanical.

He's come to check out the competition.

Kathryn had been on the air for a heady six weeks now. Her disappointment over being lumped with a cop show soon turned to celebration—*Dragnet* was the runaway hit of the season, pushing her show into the top twenty nationwide. Broadcasting on a Friday meant she had five days to scoop Winchell, whose show aired the previous Sunday.

A waiter arrived with their drinks and departed with their lunch orders. They clinked glasses.

Kathryn said, "I was wondering if perhaps the Battle of the Sunset Strip lured you here."

Last week, unidentified gunmen had opened fire on Mickey Cohen as he left a restaurant called Sherry's, not far from Chez Gwendolyn. The press burned through inches of columns, dubbing it the "Battle of the Sunset Strip" as though the Strip was the new OK Corral. Fortunately for Gwennie, the whole scene had played out at four in the morning, so she was nowhere near the place, but it had driven extra traffic into her store.

Winchell was known for his vitriolic anti-mobster/pro-FBI stance, so Kathryn's question was an educated guess.

"It was the catalyst," Winchell admitted smoothly.

She took stock of the man opposite her. *The last time I felt this intimidated, I was sitting next to Hoover down at Howard's Spruce Goose flight.* Hoover exuded raw power and used it to unnerve people. There was a cold ruthlessness to his speech, the way he gestured, and his ramrod posture. Winchell was like this too, but he masked it with a veneer of worldliness and studied indifference.

He asked about several people they knew in common: radio celebrities he'd worked with, moguls and stars she'd interviewed. By the time lunch arrived—swordfish for him, chef's salad for her—and a second martini supplanted the first, Kathryn noticed that he'd brought up nothing that he couldn't have by telephone.

Time ticked by. She had to be out of there by three to wish Bette Davis well on her final day at Warner Bros. Finally, Kathryn disrupted his monologue on *The Fountainhead.* "Have you asked me here for a reason. A specific one, I mean?"

He drew back, unaccustomed to being interrupted. She relaxed a little when he smiled. "I was planning on bringing it up over dessert."

"I have somewhere to be at four o'clock."

He planted his elbows on the table and interlaced his fingers. "I have a hunch. A very strong one. About Leilah O'Roarke."

Don't blink. Not in front of him. "What about her?"

"I believe you know the location of her client cards."

Winchell was the number-one journalist in America, so surely his network of tipsters and informers stretched the entire country. There could be any number of ways he connected the dots from Leilah to Gwendolyn to Kathryn.

"What makes you say that?"

"What I said just now was an outrageous accusation and you didn't even flinch." He pushed aside the remnants of his lunch. "If you tell me what you know about Leilah and her cards, I'll share with you what I know about Ruby Courtland."

Kathryn tried to keep her poker face intact but it was a losing battle. She brought what was left of her martini to her lips and pondered how Ruby figured in all this. "I hear she comes from serious money."

"Nouveau-riche money."

"Out here, everybody's dough is nouveau riche, so I don't hold that against her. And besides, it's not like your money came over on the Mayflower." She knew a jab like that was a risk, but she'd survived Hoover, the FBI, and William Randolph Hearst, so what the hell.

He glowered at her for a moment, then gave her the first genuine smile she'd seen. "Touché," he conceded. "But there's nouveau riche, and then there's *nouveau riche.*"

"The difference being . . .?"

"The way you flaunt it."

"I assume the Courtlands are the flaunting kind?"

"In the worst possible way. Her father, Otis, is a military contractor who spent the war amassing a fortune in New York. Started out as a men's haberdasher, reasonably successful on a middling scale, but he managed to wrangle major deals with both the army and the navy to manufacture uniforms."

"Somebody had to."

He studied her through narrowed eyes. "I was led to believe you were not a fan."

"I'm not."

"And yet you're defending them."

"I'm trying to figure out the connection between Ruby and Leilah."

"I didn't say there was one."

Kathryn's glass was now empty. Lukas had made sure her martinis were weak, so she signaled the waiter for a third. "No, you didn't."

234

She caught the four Beverly Hills housewives staring openly at her and gave them a little wave, which sent them diving behind their menus.

"So what do I need to know about Ruby Courtland?" Kathryn asked.

"She was very prominent in the debutant and society pages."

"Her job with *Variety*; is it legit?"

"Probably the result of some pulled strings courtesy of father, dear father."

From the wry look on Winchell's face, Kathryn had been hoping for something juicier. "He's hardly the first schmo-made-good to buy his daughter's way into high society."

"What's interesting isn't that he did, but that he *had to*."

"'Had to'?"

"Darling little Ruby was one of the most notorious victory girls in Manhattan."

In a city the size of Los Angeles, it was hard to ignore the phenomenon of victory girls: women who offered "comfort" to servicemen heading out to war. During times of peace, girls like that would be written off as tramps, but war blurred judgments. At worst, victory girls were generous; at best, they were patriotic. But this was no longer wartime, and perceptions had a way of shifting. Just as Russia was once seen as an ally but was now the evil face of Communism, victory girls were just floozies looking for an excuse to sleep around.

"How notorious?" Kathryn asked.

"Admirably. Fearlessly. Nightly."

"So he bought her respectability?"

"Tried. Failed. Hence the move out west." Winchell lit up a thin cigar and obscured himself in a cloud of white smoke. "I'll leave you to exploit that information however you see fit."

Kathryn's gaze wandered back to the wives. They'd lost interest in the Massey-Winchell meeting and were now enthralled by a story one of them was telling with scandalized eyes and flashing nail polish. Probably about what the maid discovered in her husband's pockets, or maybe the purchase of a new fur coat at *such* a good price. For a fuzzy moment, Kathryn envied them. Their lives were a shiny bubble, floating on ocean breezes, passing the time with lunches and shopping and bridge parties, maybe a charity function to fill their days. They never had to worry about conniving victory girls, or ratings. Or Sing Sing, for that matter.

She heard Winchell clear his throat. "We have a bargain."

"We do?"

"I traded Ruby Courtland for Leilah O'Roarke."

"Ah!"

Kathryn realized she was slouching and straightened her back. She tried to clear her head by breathing in deeply, but the sweet haze of bougainvillea distracted her.

"Your hunch was right. I know where Leilah's cards are. Or rather, were. There is someone I know —"

"Gwendolyn Brick?"

You've been talking to Leilah O'Roarke. The two of you are in cahoots because . . . because . . .

Kathryn pictured Linc's hollow book. Gwennie had only shown them the top card before shooing everybody out. Kathryn understood why Gwendolyn had come unglued at the sight of Leilah's cards, but now she wished she'd convinced Gwennie to pull out the entire stack for them to paw through. If they'd dug as far as the W's, might they have unearthed Winchell's name?

"Yes," she admitted, "they came to Gwendolyn. She wasn't aware she had them for the longest time." Kathryn held her hand up to cut Winchell off. "I know that sounds unlikely, but you'll have to trust me. They were very well hidden, and when she found them, she took a match to them straightaway."

Kathryn watched Winchell's shoulders relax slowly, almost indiscernibly.

A sudden movement on her far left caught her attention. It was Lukas pointing to his wristwatch.

She picked up her handbag and gloves. "I imagine that's better news for you than it is for Leilah." His eyes darted away. *Bull's-eye!* "Thank you for lunch. It's been . . ." *Educational? Frightful? Soul destroying?* She went with "memorable" and glided out of the booth.

* * *

Kathryn was halfway up Coldwater Canyon Drive before she realized that it wasn't the greatest idea to attempt the winding trek over the Hollywood Hills and into the San Fernando Valley with three martinis swirling inside her. Maybe they weren't as weak as she'd assumed. But a promise was a promise, so she pressed forward.

She reached the crest, where Mulholland Drive traced a meandering line, and braked for a moment to take in the vastness of the Valley. The citrus orchards that once carpeted the land as far as the eye could see were giving way to a patchwork of suburban neighborhoods built to accommodate the postwar boom.

Ruby Courtland was the Tramp of Manhattan. Kathryn knew that this sort of information could come in handy, but she balked at pointing the finger at a woman whose Achilles' heel was that she behaved like most men. Girls aren't tramps all by themselves, and Leilah was in hot water because she was guilty of making a buck out of helping men behave like men. *Guys who sleep around are Casanovas; if women do it, they're just cheap. This is nearly the 1950s, for crying out loud. Isn't it time we heaved those old rules out the window?*

A skunk raced from behind a manzanita and scuttled across the bitumen as a Cadillac careered around the corner and roared past Kathryn, missing the critter by inches. She watched the skunk freeze up, then slowly continue its route to the safety of the other side and disappear behind a flowering rhododendron. Kathryn let out the handbrake and pointed her blue coupe into the Valley.

* * *

The security guard told Kathryn that Miss Davis left word that she was looping dialogue. It was already past four when Kathryn found the recording studio and let herself in.

A couple of men were seated at the control booth. One of them was the director, King Vidor. Kathryn was surprised to see him there. Vidor was big man on campus, having directed more than his share of important pictures. The chore of redubbing poorly recorded lines with an actor was considered assistant director stuff, especially as — according to Bette — *Beyond the Forest* was "an undercooked, overstuffed turkey." Maybe he was there because this was Bette's final task after nearly twenty years.

Bette was in a small booth, earphones perched on her head, her eyes trained on the screen in front of her. Vidor leaned into his microphone.

"That's not quite it. Come in a split second earlier, please."

Bette nodded without taking her eyes from the screen.

Vidor pressed a button. Bette appeared on the screen in a preposterously dark shoulder-length wig that would have looked more at home on Dolores del Río. On Bette, it just looked ten years too late. A chime rang out, then three beeps.

Bette leaned into her microphone. "I can't stand it anymore!"

King Vidor conferred with his technician, who nodded his approval. "That's it, Miss Davis. You're free to go."

Bette removed the headphones, smoothed out her hair, and picked up her handbag. By the time she exited the booth, both men had left.

Bette jutted her chin toward the door. "Did you see that? My last task on my last day on my last picture and the bastard didn't even say goodbye."

"Maybe he—"

"Nobody's said jack shit to me."

"They're probably waiting until you've finished—"

"No 'Best of luck, Miss Davis.' No 'It's been grand working with you, Miss Davis.' I'd settled for a 'Kiss my ass, Miss Davis,' but I'm not holding my breath."

They walked into the warmth of the late afternoon. A matronly woman with a tape measure around her neck and arms loaded with black nuns' habits waddled a few yards ahead of them.

"I must have made a dozen pictures with that one," Bette said, "I've met all her kids *and* her grandkids. Signed every request for an autograph she's put in front of me. Did she even so much as look in my direction?"

"Maybe she's not aware that this is your last day."

"Ha!" Bette barked. "The entire studio knows this is my last day."

"And nobody's wished you well?"

"A few have, sure. But I was expecting . . ." She watched the studio workers bustling about their jobs, her face falling into a glum scowl. She lifted a shoulder. "I'm no longer queen of the lot."

"But you didn't want to be," Kathryn reminded her. "You've fought to break free of Sing Sing."

Bette laughed. "You're right! Why am I wallowing? The queen is dead. The crown's already been handed on to my successor." She hooked her arm through Kathryn's. "And brother, Doris Day can have it."

Kathryn thought about those four Beverly Hills wives back at the Polo Lounge, with their superfluous degrees in art history, their mink stoles from I. Magnin's, their wedding albums stuffed with bridesmaids and their interminable bridge parties, and wondered why she'd been jealous of their insulated lives for even so much as a split second.

"I've just come from lunch at the Polo Lounge with Winchell."

"OH MY! I do want to hear about that. Preferably someplace dark and dim."

"Ever been to the Sahara Room at the Garden of Allah?"

"Just what the doctor ordered!"

"Get in."

Kathryn backed out of her parking space and headed for the exit. As they approached the security barrier, Kathryn hit the brakes. "One final look?"

"Did you hear that line I looped just now?"

"'I can't stand it anymore.'"

"My sentiments exactly." Bette waved her hand at the guard to raise the gate. "Drive on, MacDuff."

Kathryn pulled out of the studio lot just as the last of the sun ducked behind the hills, leaving a sky flecked with purple and gold. She kept an eye on her passenger, wondering if she might be tempted to take a parting peek at the place she'd called home for almost two decades, but Bette Davis kept her eyes fixed on the road ahead.

CHAPTER 28

Early in the summer of 1949, Gwendolyn hid *Magnificent Obsession* in the narrow space behind her headboard and tried to forget that she was sleeping next to a powder keg.

Chez Gwendolyn bustled with customers most days, but if sales started to flag, she'd subtly spray the store with Sunset Boulevard. Customers invariably remarked on it, launching Gwendolyn into her sales spiel, and the cash register would sing like Dinah Shore.

She also had an attentive boyfriend who'd fashioned her life into a dreamy blur of dinners, picnics, and movie dates. Nobody at the Garden gave two hoots that she was dating a much younger guy, and she didn't give two hoots if she caught some malicious glances. But Zap did. He'd ask her a little louder than necessary, "Have you seen that new movie, *The Giggling Gigolo*?" On such evenings, his lovemaking took on a more vigorous brio.

It turned out that Zap had a penchant for making love in adventurous places. Shadowy alleys got him especially worked up—like the one out back of the Warner Bros. Theater on Wilshire. After seeing *Flamingo Road*, they were filing out of the place when Zap pressed his hard-on against her backside.

"They have an alleyway."

She hadn't encountered such an enthusiastic lover since Alistair Dunne, and it was thrilling to have someone so bursting with passion.

But as lovely a summer as it had been, down in the murkiest corners of her mind, Leilah's stack of cards lurked.

For a while she toyed with the idea of knocking on the door of each customer and giving them their cards. If they put a match to them, then *they* would be guilty of destroying evidence. But surely word would get back to Leilah or the vice squad, so she did nothing . . . until Zap appeared at her store with a copy of the *Examiner* and a scared-rabbit look on his face. He laid the paper on her counter.

WB SECURITY CHIEF ARRESTED OVER BROTHEL SCANDAL

"Aiding and abetting, huh?" Gwendolyn said. "They must be spitting mad. Is there enough to make the charges stick?"

"The DA says the lynchpin would be your client cards—"

"Leilah's cards."

"—and the paper suggests that Clem's arrest is the prosecutor's attempt to force the cards out into the open."

"But Leilah and Clem think they've been burned."

"*If* they believe Winchell, which assumes Winchell believes Kathryn."

Gwendolyn strummed her fingernails. "So I'm back at square one."

"You still hold all the cards—literally."

"Oh, Zap, this is no joke."

He ran his hand up her arm. "Just trying to inject a little humor."

"I wish I could just make them all disappear."

"Speaking of disappearing, I see you've mowed down the competition."

"I've what?"

"Zanuck's old squeeze. The one with the French name. Her store's emptier than a kosher deli on Yom Kippur."

Gwendolyn dashed out the door. Yvette's was deserted—no racks, display cabinets, mirrors. Even the sign was gone. She drifted back to her store.

"That whole setup was weird," Zap said. "I never did trust her."

Gwendolyn realized that she hadn't, either.

"You want me to go in there and snoop around?" he offered.

"What are you going to do? Break down the door?"

Zap pointed to the ladder Marcus climbed up to get into the crawl space. She wondered now if Yvette broke into Chez Gwendolyn using *her* ladder.

Zap scaled the rungs and disappeared through the trapdoor.

She let a few minutes tick by, then climbed the ladder and poked her head through the hole in the ceiling. A faint shaft of light penetrated the dark. "Zap? Are you there?"

"You rang?" Zap stood at the base of the ladder, grinning like a monkey.

She started climbing down. "Where did you come from?"

"Her door wasn't even locked." He held a crumpled matchbook out to her.

"You went through her trash?"

"The trash can was all she left behind, and it's lucky I did."

She took the matchbook from him. "The Flaming Rose, 1905 Sunset Boulevard. That must be near downtown."

A smirk curled Zap's lips. "It's right near Aimee Semple McPherson's old temple."

"Have you been to this—" she read the name again "Flaming Rose?"

His smirk softened into an indulgent smile. It had been a long time since Gwendolyn had felt like a noob.

"It's a hooker hangout," he said. "Sort of a sisterhood thing, I guess."

Gwendolyn pictured a college sorority, but with fishnet stockings and much shorter skirts. "So if Yvette had a Flaming Rose matchbook, then . . ." The thought of seeing the inside of a shady hooker bar thrilled her in a twisted sort of way.

"You're not thinking of going down there, are you?" Zap asked.

"Naturally you'd come with me, but we'll do better if we brought someone along who knows the lay of the land, so to speak. I know just the gal. Have you met Arlene in Villa Twelve?"

"One of your neighbors is a hooker?" Zap looked so scandalized that Gwendolyn almost laughed.

"I do live at the Garden of Allah, you know."

* * *

Arlene Curtis had led an interesting life, even by the Garden's standards. Her parents' passing put her so deeply in debt that she'd resorted to making "the quickest buck available to a single girl short of gold-digging her way into the Jonathan Club."

Marcus met her when Eddie Mannix took him to a cathouse on his fortieth birthday. He'd picked the least battle-hardened girl in the place, a young ingénue called Opal, whose real name was Arlene. When he learned that she was halfway through legal secretarial school, he finagled her a job at MGM, and before long, she moved into the Garden. It wasn't until much later that Gwendolyn learned that the cathouse where Arlene got her start belonged to Leilah O'Roarke.

Arlene was in the middle of her après-work sherry when Gwendolyn and Zap arrived on her doorstep. When Gwendolyn filled her in and showed her the matchbook, Arlene snorted.

"That's where Leilah got her start. She ran her first operation in the back room, managing her stable of OGs."

So Leilah and Yvette know each other? Why am I not surprised? "OGs?"

"Outcall girls. Real high-class. Very pricey. She sent them out on appointments at one of the hotels where Leilah had an arrangement."

"Did you ever go there?" Zap asked.

"To the Rose? Once or twice."

Gwendolyn folded her hands as if in prayer. "Will you take us there now?"

Arlene flipped the matchbook through her fingers. "You think maybe this Yvette woman was one of Leilah's OGs?"

"I believe in connections more than coincidences."

"But what is it you think Yvette's connected to?"

Arlene hadn't been around when Doris discovered the cards, and Gwendolyn believed the less people knew, the better, but she figured this girl had already seen it all.

Arlene shook her strawberry blonde curls when Gwendolyn was done telling her about the cards and their connection to the recent break-ins. "It'd sure explain a few things."

"So you'll take us?"

"It's awfully seedy. You might want to brace yourself."

* * *

The Flaming Rose sat one block north of the Angelus Temple in a stretch of pawnbrokers and fifty-cent barbershops. It was one of those bars with no windows facing the street—just a brick wall in dire need of a paint job. Over a black door, in place of a sign, there was a small picture of a faded red rose engulfed in flames.

Zap pushed it open. "Ladies of the night first!"

Gwendolyn nudged him. "Remember, you're our muscle. If things get dicey, your job is to vamoose us out of here intact."

The interior was every bit as murky as Gwendolyn expected.

The bar ran along the left-hand wall with wooden stools that probably hadn't seen daylight in a dozen years. Along the opposite wall sat a line of eight small square tables. None of them matched, nor did the chairs. They were all battered relics, many of them held together with ragged strips of duct tape and punctured with cigarette burns. They looked wobbly as hell.

Gwendolyn felt Zap's lips against her ear. "This is where barflies come to die."

It was nearing six o'clock; all the stools were occupied, mostly by women clustered in twos and threes. They looked up to see who'd walked in, gave them the once-over, then returned to their conversations. Every one of them had caked their faces in makeup and cinched themselves into tight outfits that showed too much cleavage.

"Do you recognize anyone?" Gwendolyn asked Arlene.

"Nope. Let's take that table in the corner and figure out a game plan."

The hangdog bartender — unshaven, with greasy hair and teeth too straight and white to be his own — approached them. "You three in the right place?"

"I'm looking for Bunny," Arlene told him.

He pushed his cigarette to the corner of his mouth. "Platinum-blonde Bunny?"

"Uh-huh," Arlene replied, all casual as you please. "She still come in?"

The bartender nodded. "What'll it be?"

They ordered a round of beers.

"Bunny's nice," Arlene said, "for an over-the-hill hooker. When I was working the house above the Strip, she was the oldest girl there. She'd get the virgins who couldn't afford much or the guys with a mommy fixation, but even *I* knew she couldn't last much longer. She'd worked for Leilah for fifteen years, but do you think she even blinked before putting poor old Bunny out to pasture? Not a chance."

"What makes you think we'll find her here?" Gwendolyn asked.

"I bumped into her over the zippers at Kress's five-and-dime a couple of months ago. She told me working the streets is a whole lot tougher than a brothel, but it's the only thing she knows. She said to me, 'At least I have the Flaming Rose. I remember thinking, God, is that place still open?"

The bartender delivered their order with a bowl of heavily salted peanuts. "How long should we give her?" Gwendolyn asked. Her rickety chair was sticking to her dress for reasons she didn't want to contemplate.

"Until we can't stand the taste of this turkey piss any longer."

A hand-lettered flyer tacked to the wall caught Gwendolyn's eye.

CHERRY TAN
SEAMSTRESS – COSTUMES
ANY STYLE
MEN & LADIES & IN BETWEEN

The "& IN BETWEEN" piqued her curiosity. She went to the bar and asked the guy about the flyer. He pointed to a door at the rear.

Back at the table, Zap offered to go with her, but Gwendolyn told him to keep Arlene company.

The door led to a short corridor, which opened onto a windowless room with a low ceiling, twice the size of her apartment. Six industrial sewing machines were set up in two rows of three; bent over each of them sat a diminutive Asian woman sewing together panels of sparkly orange material.

Gwendolyn knew a Licketysplitter outfit when she saw one. "Is Cherry Tan here?"

A woman at a machine in the last row stood up. She was barely five feet tall, but possessed a bulldog sturdiness to her: thick neck, hunched shoulders, and a don't-screw-with-me scowl. "Me," she said.

As Gwendolyn walked down the center aisle between the whirring machines, Cherry closed her fist around a pair of scissors. Gwendolyn stopped in front of her machine and planted her hands on her hips. "I'm Gwendolyn Brick."

Cherry's suspicion mutated into recognition, then shifted into comprehension. "You no how I picture."

"You put me out of business."

Cherry lifted one of her broad shoulders. "I make for less money. Not personal. Only business." She narrowed her eyes and started nodding. "I see your work. Customers show me. You *very* good." She turned to the seamstress to her right and rattled off a speech. The only word Gwendolyn caught was her name. The other woman, taller than Cherry but much older, addressed Gwendolyn in a rapid-fire foreign tongue.

"She says you famous in lady-men. She try to make lady-men costumes like you because you make the best."

"Tell her thank you."

"She also say you work here too?"

Gwendolyn's resentment began to melt. "Thank you, but no."

"Pity. We have too many works." Cherry nodded her head toward the Flaming Rose. "We make costumes for them too. You know. Girls who sell." Her eyes took on a mischievous gleam as she cupped her breasts and hoisted them up. "Big! Big! Big!"

Gwendolyn laughed. If she had to lose her Licketysplitters, she was glad it was to someone who took it all in stride. "I didn't come here to fight with you," she said. "I came here looking for one of those girls."

"Which girl?"

"Bunny."

"AH!" Cherry and her co-worker nodded. "She nice." The scowl resurfaced. "Too old. Bunny should stop."

"Do you know where she lives?"

Cherry shook her head, then pointed to the woman working directly behind Gwendolyn. "This for Bunny. She come later."

"Here? Today?"

"You come back. Midnight. Yes?"

* * *

Neither Zap nor Arlene were keen on spending the next six hours drinking turkey piss, so they headed six blocks down Sunset to a Chinese restaurant the bartender recommended. After six egg rolls and a dubious bowl of chicken chow mein, they were back at the same table, downing what were supposed to be old-fashioneds when a pale woman, unmistakably past fifty with scrawny arms and a helmet of white-blonde hair, walked in.

Arlene waved her over and hugged her, then Zap bought Bunny a drink and Arlene got down to business.

"We're hoping you might be able to help us out. Do you know someone called Yvette?"

"You might know her as Mae," Gwendolyn put in.

"A working girl?"

"Most likely back in the days when Leilah was conducting business in the back room."

Bunny flapped her lips. "Now you're pushing it. What does she look like?"

Gwendolyn described Yvette as best she could.

"Sounds like Hilda. God, I haven't seen her in donkey's years."

Hilda? Yvette? Mae? How many aliases does that woman have? "So she and Leilah go way back?"

"She was one of Leilah's original OGs, but they'd parted company by the time Leilah opened her first house."

"They had a fight?"

"Oh, sweetie." Bunny yawned. "It was such a long time ago."

"Perhaps another highball might jog your memory?" Zap signaled the bartender.

"Thanks, handsome. Best as I can recall, there wasn't no bad blood. Those two were cut from the same cloth. Nah, I think she just moved to a sweeter deal."

Like Darryl Zanuck. "So if we were trying to track her down, what name do you think she'd use?"

"That's anybody's guess, but if I were her, I'd go back to my original. Nobody's called her that since Garbo learned English."

"So what's her real name?"

"Saperstein." Bunny chortled. "Ain't it a lulu?"

"Are you sure?"

The hooker looked at her with dull eyes. "Ain't nobody on purpose chooses to call herself Hilda Saperstein."

CHAPTER 29

Marcus stretched out his arms and wondered if he'd chosen the most uncomfortable chair in the reading room of the Los Angeles Public Library. He closed his eyes. Immediately, Kathryn's face appeared, her brow furrowed in that I-mean-business-Buster way she had when she was intent on getting her point across.

A week ago, she'd knocked on his door. Before he had a chance to say hello, she marched past him. "Enough!" she announced. "Enough with the Gloomy Gus routine. You've been through a lot—I know that. Your breakup with Oliver was awful and wrenching and I wouldn't wish it on anyone. But it's been nearly six months. Dear God in heaven, Marcus, do you plan on spending the rest of your life staring at the ocean and pining for days that aren't ever coming back?"

He appreciated what she was trying to do, albeit in her typical steamroller way. But in truth, time was doing what time was supposed to do: lend distance and mend scars. What Kathryn took as sadness was closer to frustration.

Reuben's suggestion of moving into television irked Marcus, but it compelled him to see that he should do more than sit on his ass waiting for everyone else to come home so he could crack open the bar. And his money wasn't going to last forever.

He always thought best when in motion, but it's hard to carry pen and paper doing laps in the pool, so he took to walking: along Sunset to Hollywood Boulevard, along Hollywood to Vine Street, down Vine to Sunset and back home. It took him the best part of two hours, but it gave him time to bounce a germ of an idea around his imagination, examine it from all angles to see where its fatal flaws might lie.

However, nothing appeared that quickened his heartbeat. Inspiration had always gushed out of him, but now he couldn't even summon one scene for a *Saturday Evening Post* short story. It was frustrating beyond endurance, but he didn't get a chance to explain any of this because Kathryn had a speech and a solution, and charged ahead like a Super Chief locomotive.

"I have a mission for you!" she declared.

When Kathryn first told him of the circumstances surrounding her father's incarceration, she made out like it was a *fait accompli*; there was nothing she could do about it; and she didn't really care one way or another.

But he knew her better than that, and he wasn't the least bit surprised when she asked him to find out everything he could about what had happened to Thomas Danford.

"All I've got to go on is what my mother told me," she said, her face twitching in irritation, "and we know how reliable she is."

And so he spent a week trooping to the central library downtown to comb through back issues of *The Boston Globe*. He discovered that Francine had pretty much told Kathryn the truth, but by the end of the week he had a notebook filled with the facts, and a butt that couldn't sit on those tortuous chairs any longer. He left the building and dawdled on the front steps to feel the sunlight warm his bones.

"There you are!"

Marcus hadn't seen Melody Hope since she'd moved out of the Garden a year ago after she and Trevor waged the mother of all screaming matches at two in the morning. The Gardenites had breathed a collective sigh of relief—her dipsomaniacal unraveling had been painful to witness, but she'd rebuffed any olive branches they'd extended.

But now a whole new woman was standing opposite him. Her large brown doe eyes that had charmed a million moviegoers shone again. Her skin, once distended and sallow, glowed with reinvigorated youth. Her smile, once so twisted in bitter resentment, was relaxed as a spring morning.

The last time she made the papers was when MGM announced they would not be renewi. ɡ her contract "due to contractual conflicts." Everybody knew it was code for "She's too difficult to work with, so let her be someone else's problem." Hedda Hopper's column carried an unflattering photograph of Melody leaving through the studio's main gate—no lipstick, hat askew, one glove missing, and a large smudge on the front of her dress. But this Melody was somebody he could like again.

"You're looking remarkably healthy," he told her.

She leaned in to whisper, "I owe it all to AA."

She smelled of Lux soap flakes. "AA?"

"Alcoholics Anonymous. It's this group where people help strangers get through the next twenty-four hours. A burden shared is a burden halved, and all that. I'm happier now than I've been in a very long time."

Marcus had heard vague references to Alcoholics Anonymous but had envisioned a bunch of hopeless down-and-outers barely able to cling to the bottom rung of life's ladder. He had no idea it could turn someone around like this. "I'm very happy for you."

"How's Trevor?"

"MGM canceled his contract, electing to enact his morals clause. Translation: We're taking no chances with this rumor that you're a Commie. Please leave your career with the security guard on your way out."

"He's had a rough time of it."

"There's a lot of that going around."

This Melody reminded him of the girl he first met years ago, full of fresh-faced, take-on-the-world piss and vinegar. "It's been nice to see you," he said and took a step around her.

"Actually, I came here looking for you," she said. "I didn't think I'd be welcome at the Garden, so I dropped in on Gwendolyn at her store. She told me what you were up to, so I came straight here."

They fell into step along Hope Street. She wore a dark tweed swing coat with the narrow collar turned up to protect her from the November breezes. "I have an idea that I want to run past you."

"Okay."

"Seems to me like you and I are in the same boat. Both dumped by the same company, both out of work, and both keen to get back in the game."

"Go on."

"Since MGM pushed me out the door, I've had a lot of time on my hands, so I've been working my way through all those books I wanted to read but never got around to. One of them was Amelia Earhart's memoir, *The Fun of It*. Have you read it?"

"No."

"It's got everything: a plucky heroine, adventure, drama, obstacles. It's a thrilling read, and I think it would make a hell of a movie."

She let him absorb the idea, then said, "Remember how well we did way, way back with *The Pistol from Pittsburgh*? I think we could do it again. You'll need to read the book first, but I just know you'll see what I mean. I've got a ton of ideas myself, but of course you're the screenwriter, so I'll bow to your superior judgment. But the whole thing is simply loaded with potential—"

He raised his hand to halt the babble pouring out of her. "You don't have to convince me."

She let out a little squeal that reminded him of his favorite scene from *I Spy with My Little Eye*, a movie she made with Ray Bolger before the war. She'd been so gosh-darned endearing in it—sort of a 1930s Clara Bow with a generous dollop of good-girl Ruby Keeler. It was delightful to see that version of Melody Hope had returned.

"Your instinct is right on the money," he continued. "I'm surprised nobody's done it already."

She clapped her hands. "My copy of the book's got notes scribbled all over it like a madwoman, but I could drop it by—"

"Hold your horses." He pulled her into the recessed entrance of an empty millinery store for refuge from the honking traffic. "We'd be wasting our time."

"Are you talking about HUAC? Pish! You're not one of the Hollywood Ten; you haven't been officially blacklisted."

"I'm a Commie by association in the eyes of anyone with the clout to approve a project like this. And—" he added before she could insert another protest "—so are you." She clamped her mouth shut. "You were married to Trevor Bergin, and he's been named as a suspected Communist. Ergo, you are also deemed Commie by association. You and me together? We make a potato so hot we're virtually radioactive."

She crossed her arms. "Are you quite finished?"

"In addition to which, everybody knows why MGM booted you out. People don't forget that sort of thing in a hurry."

"Don't you think I've considered all that? Mayer was right to fire me. I'd have fired me if I were him. But I've pulled myself together, and if there's one thing the American public can't resist, it's a comeback. And this Amelia Earhart idea's a pip!"

Marcus used the boisterous rattle of a passing streetcar to gather his thoughts. "I suspect you're right about the comeback, but that doesn't get around the sticky issue that we're both suspected Commies. The guys who run the studios all signed the Waldorf Statement. They can't be seen entertaining the idea of hiring someone with even so much as a hint of pink. Melody, you have to be realistic."

"There's one studio head who didn't sign it."

"Who?"

"Howard Hughes. He doesn't give a fig about what anyone thinks. Plus, he's an aviator." She gripped his arm. "We're already pariahs! What've we got to lose? This could be our ticket back, Marcus. It's a solid idea; you said so yourself. Look, I know I've done nothing to earn your trust, but I'm asking you to take a chance. With me."

Marcus felt a film of sweat collecting under the brim of his hat. *How long has it been since I've felt that?* He wiped his hand down the side of his pants and presented it to Melody. "Is a handshake good enough?"

"We can make it formal. Write it up into a contract, all official-like."

"If we're going to do this, I think I want to fly by the seat of my pants."

"The seat of *our* pants?"

He nodded, grinning now.

She grabbed his hand and shook it like a truck driver. "I won't let you down."

CHAPTER 30

On some days, it was a challenge for Kathryn to fill all fifteen minutes on her radio show. But on others, it was hard choosing which items to drop. Her first show for 1950 was like that. So much had happened in the past few days.

Louis B. Mayer had returned from his honeymoon with his new bride, Lorena; a romance between Frank Sinatra and Ava Gardner appeared to have sprung up at the Broadway opening of *Gentlemen Prefer Blondes*; everyone was ravenous for morsels about Ingrid Bergman's pregnancy by her director Roberto Rossellini; and the premiere of Paramount's *Samson and Delilah* went over so well that industry watchers were predicting it might become the biggest picture of the year. In addition to which, the antitrust consent decree requiring the studios to divest their ownership of theaters had gone into effect, but none of the studios had taken any action.

And then came the news that HUAC head J. Parnell Thomas had resigned from Congress after being handed an eighteen-month sentence for fraud, which he'd serve out at Danbury prison. That's where two members of the Hollywood Ten, Lester Cole and Ring Lardner Jr., were serving time. Oh, the delicious irony of it all.

Kathryn's drive to the NBC studios gave her a chance to sort through the items.

I'll start with Bergman, then Sinatra and Gardner, then Mayer, Samson and Delilah, *and then close with two-faced rat-fink jailbird Thomas. Perhaps if we're running short, I could improvise about the antitrust decree. Betty Grable will sing a number from her remake of* Coney Island, *which — oh! This is perfect. Her costar is Victor Mature, and he plays Samson. So maybe swap it with Mayer, so we can segue into the song.*

She pulled into the parking lot, where her producer was standing as though he were waiting for an overdue bus.

"Wallace!" she exclaimed. "What are you doing out here in the cold?"

"I tried to call you at home, but nobody picked up."

"Is everything okay?"

"It's Max Factor. They've pulled their sponsorship."

"In the middle of a season? We signed contracts. Can they just up and leave like that?"

The glow of the electric NBC sign on the wall above them gave his face a ghostly pallor. "They'll only say that they've elected to invoke their morals clause."

When Kathryn's lawyer asked if she wanted him to negotiate the removal of that clause, she'd told him not to bother. "It's not like I'm a girl with a shocking past."

But now she wondered if she was.

She leaned against the stucco wall and stared up Vine Street. Her first thought was of Ruby Courtland. This smacked of sabotage. Or was it Winchell's doing? The man was as ruthless as Attila the Hun, but their lunch at the Polo Lounge went well — didn't it? Or had she offended him? Did he want her out of the way in case she got bigger? Surely he didn't see her as a threat.

She turned back to Reed. "So where does that leave us? We're due on the air in an hour and a half, and we can't go on without a sponsor. Can we?"

He smiled bleakly. "I've already lined up a replacement."

"What are you, Superman?"

"My wife and I are a fixture on the pro-am bridge circuit. We were playing in a tournament in Pasadena a few weeks ago. At the end of the evening, this guy comes over to introduce himself. I knew his face but didn't know who he was. He tells me he's head of marketing at Sunbeam and they're about to relaunch their Mixmaster. He asked if we were happy with our current sponsor arrangement. I told him we were, thank you, and he said if ever an opportunity arose, to keep him in mind."

"Did you call him?"

"He's sitting in your dressing room waiting to meet you."

They started toward the stage door. "But don't we need to sign contracts?"

Reed's face took on a disconcerting ambivalence. "I've already signed them."

"Without consulting me?"

He pulled open the door and let her into the corridor that led to dressing rooms, rehearsal rooms, and ultimately the broadcast studio. "I couldn't reach you. I had to make a decision. They came with the papers all prepared. The standard deal, not much different from what we had with Max Factor. I know Sunbeam doesn't carry the same prestige, but our largest demographic is housewives between thirty and fifty. And you can bet most of them own a Mixmaster — or want to. I figured it was a good fit — "

"It's fine," she told him. "Is there anything I need to know before I go in there and turn on the charm?"

"The Mixmaster relaunch involves pairing up with Betty Crocker for a print and advertising blitz. Betty Crocker's coming out with a new and improved cake mix. Mrs. Homemaker just has to add water and two eggs to keep the cake moist and tender."

"That's my kind of cooking."

"I'm glad you said that." Kathryn's *uh-oh* antenna quivered as a tuba player and a cellist squeezed past. "The deal involves you participating in a cooking demonstration at the Wilshire May Company's homewares department."

"You want me to cook? In public?"

An imposing figure stepped out of the doorway of her dressing room.

"Ah," Wallace exclaimed, "we were just coming to see you. Kathryn Massey, I want you to meet our new sponsor from Sunbeam, Leo Presnell."

Kathryn knew she'd heard that name, but it wasn't until she saw his face that she was able to place the man standing in front of her, hand extended, a toothy smile stretched across his face. The last time she saw him, they were at a USO fundraiser during the war. He'd made it clear that if she wanted to be on the Pepsodent Show, she'd have to sleep with him first.

She shook his hand and matched him smile for smile. "How nice to see you again."

"You two know each other?" Wallace asked. "Leo, you didn't mention that."

He kept his gaze directed at her. "I wasn't sure if you'd remember."

She said, "We last saw each other at The Players, if I'm not mistaken."

The gleam in his eye told her that she wasn't.

"I'm a big fan of your show, Miss Massey. Coming on board as your sponsor is exactly the sort of opportunity we've been seeking."

For the briefest fleeting moment, Kathryn wondered if Presnell had engineered this disruption. Who has a sponsorship contract ready in his briefcase unless he knows the other guy's already backing down the driveway?

She decided she'd read too many Raymond Chandler novels.

"You must excuse me," Wallace broke in. "But I need to make sure the writers have the new sponsorship wording. Fifty minutes until places!" He retreated down the corridor.

Kathryn skirted around her new benefactor and stepped into her dressing room, leaving him to follow. "Mister Presnell," she started.

"Please, call me Leo."

She wasn't sure she was ready for that, but it seemed snippy to correct him.

"And may I say that I heard the apprehension in your voice when Wallace told you about the cooking demonstration. I want to reassure you that it's nothing to get worked up about. The whole point of this new cake mix is that anybody can open a box, add water, a couple of eggs, and hey presto—a perfect cake every time!"

"I'm not the kitchen type."

"Me either. But then my wife left me. And I ask you: How's a guy supposed to live without cake?"

She looked at him properly for the first time and found he wasn't the arrogant huckster she remembered. *So your wife left you, huh? Is that the tint of humility I can see in your eyes?* Kathryn hated to admit it, but the way he confessed a failed marriage and a baking success in the same breath was appealing.

"You must excuse me," she told him, "but I've got a show to prepare for, and this news has broadsided me."

"Of course." He stepped out into the corridor. "I'll be in the control booth if you need me."

"Exactly when is this cooking demonstration?"

"Next week."

"You don't give a girl much notice."

"Can you see how anxious we were to clinch a sponsorship deal?"

Okay, so maybe you're not directly responsible for Max Factor's bowing out, but I'm still wary of the way you operate, mister. She gave him a bland smile as she closed her dressing room door.

* * *

Kathryn had only ten minutes to prepare for a show that wasn't the one she'd planned an hour ago. By the time she emerged, Betty Grable had arrived, glittering in a silver and white floor-length dress and matching jacket. She fingered one of the white leather buttons. "You want to take a stab at where I got this?"

Kathryn knew Sunset Boulevard when she smelled it. "A certain boutique on the Strip?"

A harried stage manager shepherded them toward the stage where Kathryn could hear the chatter of the audience. "Eight minutes to air."

"She's a good friend of yours, isn't she?" Betty asked. "She has some wonderful stuff. And that perfume! One whiff and I was sold."

When they walked out onto the stage, the audience erupted into applause and wolf-whistles. Kathryn was happy to let Betty take the spotlight while she organized her notes.

> *New sponsor*
> *Bergman*
> *Sinatra & Gardner*
> *Mayer & Lorena*
> *Song, "Wilhelmina" from* Wabash Avenue
> *Chat with Betty, mention Victor Mature*
> Samson and Delilah
> *J. Parnell Thomas going to the slammer*

She went over the order a couple more times, then glanced up at the huge clock at the rear of the studio. Four minutes and fifty-one seconds.

Although Kathryn had been on the air for years now, she still had to settle her fluttering nerves. As she took a deep breath, she surveyed the audience to pick out a face that would help her forget about the twenty million listeners NBC claimed were tuning in.

It usually wasn't hard to find someone who fit the bill, often a kindly widow gussied up in her Sunday best, but tonight the widow proved elusive. Three minutes and twelve seconds. She continued to scan the crowd.

Ruby Courtland. Fifth row. Far end. Kathryn kept her eyes moving.

What is she doing here? Tonight of all nights?

Kathryn cast a quick glance back at Ruby, just long enough to take in the annoyance plastered across her face.

Were you expecting us to cancel the show because we had no sponsor?

Kathryn glanced at the broad window in front of the control booth, where Leo Presnell stood behind the team of technicians. He shot her a thumbs-up sign, which Kathryn wasn't sure how to interpret, but it did give her an idea.

She leaned into the mike. "Ladies and gentlemen, just a quick word before we begin. I'm very happy to announce that Sunbeam is now our sponsor. And to celebrate, one lucky audience member is going home with a brand-new Mixmaster!"

As the crowd burst into applause, Kathryn looked at Ruby, raised her eyebrows and pursed her lips.

Nice try, bitch.

CHAPTER 31

Gwendolyn couldn't stand to look at Kathryn's twitching fingers any longer, and clamped her right hand on top of them. "Anyone would think they were sending you into the Battle of Midway."

Sunbeam had sent a car and driver to take Kathryn to the Mixmaster-Betty Crocker promotion. Less than an hour before it arrived, Kathryn appeared on Gwendolyn's doorstep begging her to come along.

"I know!" Kathryn let out an uncharacteristic whimper.

"This coming from the woman who yelled 'Rosebud!' at Hearst in the middle of the Biltmore? But a cooking demonstration sends you into spasms? And it's not even real cooking. It's a cake mix, some water and eggs. Blend 'em together and throw it into the oven. What's the big whoop?"

When Kathryn failed to respond, Gwendolyn pressed her hands more firmly against the fidgeting fingers. "Come on. Get it off your chest." When Kathryn still didn't respond, Gwendolyn went with her gut. "Is it about that Presnell skunk?"

Kathryn's head popped up.

"Mister Hearst didn't make you nervous, but Mister Sunbeam does?"

"I'm not so sure that he is such a skunk."

"What is he, then?"

"Not nearly as full of himself as he used to be."

"So you're nervous because . . .?"

"I don't want him to think I'm useless in the kitchen. If there's a way to burn water, I'll find it. This isn't a cake recipe; it's a disaster recipe, and he's going to be standing there watching it all unfold like the Long Beach earthquake."

They had only half a dozen blocks to go. "Recite the sales pitch for me," Gwendolyn said. "They'll want you to get it right."

Kathryn put on a Happy Homemaker smile. "The Betty Crocker method guarantees a perfect cake every time you bake, cake after cake after cake. Bake a Betty Crocker cake right now. Perfect every time."

"See?" Gwendolyn scoffed. "Such a fuss over nothing."

"Gwennie, honey?" Kathryn sounded distant. "I'll feel better if you're in my sight line."

"You got it. Just so long as I don't have to talk to the skunk." She watched Kathryn screw up her nose. "What?"

"I was hoping you'd talk to him. I think he's changed, but I want a second opinion."

"I've never met the guy."

"At the very least, I want to know if he looks like he's disappointed in me, or laughing at me, or is relieved I haven't burned the store down, or—"

"Or happy he's made the right choice?"

Kathryn's shoulders relaxed a full two inches. "Or that."

* * *

Gwendolyn was floored to see three hundred women milling around the May Company's homewares department just to witness the baking of a cake.

A white cloth covered a long table bookended with Betty Crocker cake mixes in a range of flavors. Suspended from the ceiling was a huge sign: *Today only! Sunbeam Mixmaster and Betty Crocker present Kathryn Massey! Live demonstration!*

A gracefully lanky man appeared. "Right on time!"

"Leo Presnell," Kathryn said, "this is my friend Gwendolyn Brick. I've brought her along for moral support and general cheerleading."

Gwendolyn took him in. Was that a cashmere jacket? "You must be pleased at the turnout," she allowed.

"We are." He turned to Kathryn. "That script I sent you, think of it as a rough guide. Remember, we're not here to sell cakes."

"We're not?" The strain in Kathryn's voice had started to evaporate.

"We're selling convenience without compromising quality. And we're selling it to women who take pride in their ability to bake a perfect cake from scratch. But you don't have to worry about any of that."

"I don't?"

Presnell leaned in to ensure he'd make himself heard over the growing din. "We want you to have fun, and if you can slip in the words 'Sunbeam Mixmaster' and 'Betty Crocker' and 'perfect cake' a couple of times, everybody will go home happy. Okay?"

Kathryn nodded.

Gwendolyn slipped her fingers around the handles of Kathryn's purse and tugged it away from her. "You're not going to need this. Good luck, and I'll see you afterwards."

As Presnell led Kathryn to the stage, Gwendolyn made her way to the back wall of the demonstration area. By the time she located a spot that ensured a clear sight line, Presnell had introduced Kathryn to a round of applause.

"You know what, ladies?" Kathryn began. "I feel like a fraud!" Her confession reaped a tentative laugh. "I'm serious! I can't bake a cake to save my life." She planted her fists onto her hips. "I'd bet my last dime that any one of you could bake a better cake than me while blindfolded, one hand tied behind your back, a hungry kid screaming in the next room, and your mother-in-law due on the doorstep in the next five minutes."

The cheers of several hundred enchanted women filled the hall. Gwendolyn watched Presnell retreat into the background. She groaned inwardly when he began to inch toward her.

"Which makes me the perfect person to tell you about Betty Crocker's new cake mix," Kathryn continued, "because the Sunbeam Mixmaster-Betty Crocker method guarantees me a perfect cake every time I bake. And if I can do it, you'll have your mother-in-law eating out of your hand before she's had time to take off her hat and criticize the way you're spoiling the baby."

The crowd broke into more applause as Presnell drew alongside Gwendolyn. His aftershave balm hinted at sandalwood and musk. He tilted his head so she could hear him. "I didn't figure her for the nervous type."

"She's not, normally. But she is the type who always gives her all."

"That's why I wanted to sponsor her show. You wouldn't believe how unreliable on-air talent can be." He pointed to Kathryn as she held up a mixing bowl. "She was always my number-one choice."

Gwendolyn drew back to study this man again. *If I didn't know his history, I'd say he's a bit of a catch.* "She was, huh?"

Her question pulled his attention away from the stage. "What does that mean?"

"Kathryn told me about that proposition you made to her back when you were Mister Pepsodent."

Presnell cringed. He looked at her with a reticence that a guy like this—so well put together, so confident and professional—would rarely let slip publicly. "I've often thought about that night."

"That gives us something in common."

"And when I do, I mentally kick myself so damn hard."

Kathryn warned her audience that they might want to stand back. "Because ladies, when I flip the switch on my Sunbeam Mixmaster, I'm giving fifty-fifty odds you'll end up wearing Betty Crocker Honey Spice cake batter."

Presnell kept his eyes on Kathryn. "After the end of the war, I was transferred to the New York office for a big promotion. I'd only been there a month or two when I met a gorgeous socialite. I fell for her the moment I saw her. She said, 'Me too!,' so we got married. Everything was great for the first couple of years . . . or so I thought. Then evidence started mounting that she had been cheating on me the whole time."

"That can't have been fun."

"Do you believe in karma?"

———

272

"I'm not sure what that is."

"It's an idea they have in the Far East, like fate, but more along the lines of 'Reap what you sow.' I was an unconscionable philanderer in my first marriage, so I was determined to get it right in my second. But instead, I learned what it was like when the shoe gets rammed onto the other foot."

"Are you still married?"

"I got out by giving her everything. Then I quit my job, left New York, and returned to LA divorced, broke, and jobless. Eventually I talked my way into Sunbeam. A couple of weeks later, I listened to Kathryn's first *Window on Hollywood* and made it my business to pursue her."

"When you say 'pursue her' . . .?"

"Is she single?"

Ah, so this is the ol' sidling-up-to-the-best-friend tactic. On the other hand, a guy who can talk about Far Eastern philosophy . . . "What if she were?"

"I'm hoping for a second chance."

Kathryn rarely talked about her romance with Nelson Hoyt. As far as Gwendolyn knew, he wasn't coming back any time soon.

"She doesn't trust you."

"She has no good reason to—and neither do you—and that's my karma."

"Kathryn's had a rough time of it, romance-wise, and after that stunt you pulled at The Players, you're going to have to work hard."

"Just tell me how, and I'll do it."

Gwendolyn could feel her resistance softening. "You spent time in New York among the social set; ever come across a Ruby Courtland?"

Ruby's name brought forth a disdainful growl. "My wife was an alley cat, but she was strictly amateur hour in comparison."

"Bad as all that?"

"Ruby seduced my college roommate during his stag party at the Waldorf-Astoria, gave him a social disease, which he then passed to his bride, who subsequently sued him for divorce."

"She's even worse than I thought."

"Why are we talking about her?"

The crowd whooped over some crack Kathryn had made about licking the bowl. She hadn't glanced at Gwendolyn since her mother-in-law gag. Gwendolyn led Presnell behind a display of rolling pins and flour sifters.

"Did you know Ruby Courtland lives out here now?"

He rolled his eyes. "Columnist with *Variety*. What a joke. She fled to LA after she burned every bridge in all five boroughs."

"Kathryn has an idea that Ruby was behind Max Factor dumping her."

"How is that possible?"

"The evidence is circumstantial, but sure adds up to something stinky."

"Does Kathryn want to get Ruby out of the way?"

"I certainly would if I were in her shoes."

"The best way to neutralize an enemy like that is to make her an exile. I'll happily give that moll the cold shoulder."

"If you want to get on Kathryn's good side, it might take more than turning your back on Ruby at a cocktail party."

"Count me in. Nothing would give me more pleasure." A hearty round of applause spilled over them. "We should probably get back. I don't want her to think we've deserted her."

She made an *after you* gesture. As he turned around, she reached for the bottom edge of his jacket and let the material slide through her fingertips.

Cashmere. I knew it.

CHAPTER 32

The outer office of Howard Hughes' executive suite at RKO was sparsely furnished. A pair of underworked secretaries in tight sweaters faced each other behind matching white desks on either side of a rosewood door whose unembellished brass handle was its only decoration.

Marcus waited on a sofa long enough to seat five. Beside him, on a low square end table stood the only other sign of life — a potted plant with long spindly branches and spiky leaves. It gave off a strange odor, like overly peppered Spam.

Ever since Hughes bought RKO, the rumors reported increasingly bizarre behavior: chronic hand-washing, 3 A.M. telephone calls, an army of private investigators hired to keep tabs on a revolving platter of beauties: Susan Hayward, Elizabeth Taylor, Mitzi Gaynor, Barbara Payton, and even European actresses like Gina Lollobrigida and Zizi Jeanmaire.

But Marcus tried not to dwell on any of those things as he sat on the sofa with the plastic covers and the smelly plant. When he accepted Melody Hope's proposal that they work on Amelia Earhart together, he'd expected her to flake, figuring she'd fall off the wagon or get bored with the undertaking and stop returning his calls.

To his surprise, though, she collated her notes on *The Fun of It* into fifteen typed sheets and called every other day to share ideas or check on his progress and came up with several remarkably insightful suggestions.

Three months ago, in front of the library, Marcus wouldn't have bet ten bucks that he'd be sitting outside Howard Hughes' office with an outline for a project he was excited about—let alone that he'd be feeling desperate to come in from the professional cold.

The telephone on the desk of the right-hand secretary rang. She picked it up before it clanged a second time. She listened for a moment, then replaced the receiver and pointed to the rosewood door.

Hughes' office was as austere as his reception area. In fact, it looked like he'd just moved in and the van had misplaced all his belongings.

It was a long room, maybe forty feet, and ended in a semicircle with windows that extended from waist height to the ceiling. His desk was as plain as the rosewood door. A bank of five telephones sat on one side, a pen and paper were the only things in front of him.

Kathryn knew Hughes better than Marcus did, so he'd prevailed on her to make the call. When she reported back that Hughes had agreed to see him, she reminded Marcus that he now eschewed the practice of shaking hands.

When Hughes saw Marcus approach, he nodded, but made no effort to stand. He pointed to one of the three chairs in front of his desk. "I can give you seven minutes."

Suspecting this might be the case, Marcus had rehearsed a tight pitch. It highlighted the aviation aspects of the project and included enough technical jargon to thrill the pilot in his audience of one. Hughes said nothing as Marcus moved through the story, but from the tics that twitched Hughes' pale and marred face, Marcus could see he'd hit the mark.

"The final shot," he concluded, "is Earhart's Lockheed Electra 10E flying over a vast and empty ocean—and into history."

Without realizing it, Marcus had worked his way to the edge of the seat. He slid back and waited for a response.

He didn't have to wait long.

"I love it," Hughes declared. "Great story. Great idea. Great job, Adler. Absolutely first rate."

Breathless with anticipation, Marcus pushed out, "Thank you. I appreciate that." He reached into his briefcase and extracted the outline.

Hughes's face clouded over. "But I can't make it."

"You just said—"

"A movie like that will have to pass the Breen Office."

Marcus gripped the armrests. "I am very familiar with every single rule in the Hays Code, and I can assure you there is nothing in this story that contravenes them." He tried to push the outline across the desk, but Hughes waved it away.

"I know who you are, and what you're capable of. That's not why I'm saying no."

I knew I shouldn't have counted on this. I shouldn't have let myself get carried away. I'm not back on square one, because I never damn well left it.

It took some effort to look at Hughes in the eye again. "Why are you knocking me back?"

"Because you occupy the number-one position on Joseph Breen's personal shit list."

Marcus took the news like a slug to the chest. "How do you know that?"

Hughes jumped out of his chair and walked over to a narrow basin Marcus hadn't noticed. He wet his hands under the faucet and started lathering them with a fresh bar of soap. "You've heard of *Stromboli*, right?" Who hadn't? It was the movie Ingrid Bergman left her marriage and Hollywood career to make with Italian director Roberto Rossellini. "Did you know that I secured most of the funding in exchange for distribution?"

Marcus told Hughes he wasn't aware of that.

"Yeah, well, I did. And now I've got a boatload of cash tied up in that godforsaken white elephant and if I've got a snowball's chance in hell of seeing a dime in profits, I need Breen on my side. But now of course Bergman's going to have Rossellini's bastard any minute now, and Rossellini's recruited the help of the guy who wrote the screenplay, who—wouldn't you know it—is some sort of goddamned priest. So of course Breen just loves that. I tell you, Adler, the whole thing's a nightmare. I cannot afford to get Breen offside—"

"But what makes you think I'm on Breen's shit list?"

Hughes' hands were coated in thick soapsuds. If there'd been any germs when he started, there couldn't be any left now. He started to wash them off with the deliberation of a surgeon.

"He showed it to me. That prick has literally typed out his shit list. Can you beat that? I was in his office a couple of weeks ago about *Stromboli* and things became heated. We got into this argument about who's qualified to write screenplays and who's not, and suddenly he's planting his shit list in front of me. I recognized your name because you're good friends with Kathryn. Given your turn in front of HUAC a while back, I wasn't too surprised to see your name on his list. But number one?" He let out a whistle.

"Why did you even agree to see me?" Marcus asked.

"I was intrigued."

He grabbed a towel and started drying his hands so thoroughly that it looked like he was out to remove the top layer of skin.

Marcus grabbed the handle of his briefcase and got to his feet. "Well, thanks anyway. I appreciate your time." *Even if it was a complete waste.*

"Sit down," Hughes ordered. "I've got a suggestion." He dumped the used towel in a trash can below the basin and returned to his desk. "You know who's desperate for writers and not real particular about the whole Red Menace distraction? Television. With your experience, you'll automatically be the most experienced guy in the room."

Marcus didn't have it in him to say *Thanks but no thanks,* so he just stared at Hughes.

"I'm friendly with the producer of *Texaco Star Theater.* You know, Milton Berle and all that."

"Yes, I know."

"It's number one in the ratings. You'd be going into a hugely popular show. I could make a call. That's all it'd take and you'd be hired."

That show is sketch comedy. Hardly up my alley. At least when Reuben from down at the beach brought up television, he was talking about drama.

"I appreciate that," Marcus said, standing. "How about I give it some thought?"

He went to offer his hand to Hughes, but at the last second remembered Kathryn's advice, and kept the momentum going and scratched a pretend itch down his right cheek, knowing full well that he wasn't fooling anyone.

CHAPTER 33

Kathryn wished she hadn't volunteered for flower-arranging duty. The fluke of her successful cake-baking demonstration notwithstanding, she was about as good with flowers as she was with recipes. Surely there was somebody at the Beverly Hills Hotel who could do a far better job?

She wrapped the white silk ribbon around the neck of the small vase and tried to tie it into a bow, but the damned thing kept slipping through her fingers.

Wilkerson is sixty-one, for crying out loud. What the hell is he doing marrying a girl in her twenties? She yanked the ends of the ribbon. The bow was a bit droopy and if she had time, she'd do it over, but there were eleven more of these suckers. *And what does he think this Tichi girl has that none of his previous five wives had?*

Despite her misgivings, Kathryn rather liked Wilkerson's new bride. Tichi was inappropriately young, and the fact that her mother was Wilkerson's maid seemed indecorous, but the dark-eyed lass was smart, articulate, and approached everything she did with gusto. So when she asked Kathryn to help her with her wedding luncheon, Kathryn couldn't say no. Especially after what had happened in Sun Valley the previous month.

Wilkerson's involvement with Bugsy Siegel had spun out of control so badly that he'd fled to Paris until it was safe to return after a hit man gunned Siegel down in his girlfriend's living room. That was three years ago, so Wilkerson was completely unprepared when he and Tichi were enjoying a ski vacation in Idaho and a drunken Virginia Hill approached their table, screaming accusations that Wilkerson was responsible for Siegel's death.

Hotel security quickly bundled Hill away, but the episode shook them and Tichi wanted their wedding to go off without a hitch. Kathryn imagined it was a lot for anyone to take on, particularly for the maid's daughter who'd married into the spotlight. Kathryn felt she couldn't say no. And besides, a happy boss at home was a happy boss at work.

The second ribbon-tying wasn't a great improvement over the first, but it took Kathryn half the time.

"How's it coming?"

Kathryn hadn't seen Tichi approach. "It's coming. Let's leave it at that." She grabbed another vase and length of ribbon. "Did they put out the sign directing everyone to the Sunset Ballroom?"

"I didn't notice it."

"You don't want seventy people meandering around the lobby, wondering where to go."

"I'll check."

Kathryn called her back. The fascinator Tichi wore was an explosion of blue-and-red feathers of unidentifiable origin. The colors contrasted boldly with the safe beiges and pale blues of the ballroom. It was striking, but it looked like it was about to fall off the side of her head.

As Kathryn hitched it up and readjusted the clip, Tichi whispered,

"I can't believe how nervous I am."

"It's your debut into Hollywood society," Kathryn replied. "It's natural to be jittery."

"So many big shots!"

Kathryn placed a soothing hand on Tichi's shoulder. "They're just people who happen to be very successful. Now scoot out there and see if they've put that sign where people can see it."

Kathryn returned to her tiny vases and decided to try holding them steady with her thighs. She extracted the bouquets of miniature tulips and gypsophila and began to test her theory while thinking about what she'd just said to the boss's wife.

They're not "just people" at all. They're quagmires of neuroses and ego who assume their opinion is the only one that matters.

Her mind flew back to an incident she'd witnessed the previous week at an industry preview of *Sunset Boulevard*. She still couldn't get L.B. Mayer's reaction out of her head.

After the show, she was chatting with Edith Head and Barbara Stanwyck in the foyer when Mayer came striding across the carpet toward Billy Wilder.

"You bastard!" he screamed. "You have disgraced the industry that made you and fed you! You should be tarred and feathered and run out of Hollywood!"

Kathryn admired how Wilder kept his anger in check, replied with a curt "Fuck you!" then left the building without another word. She also couldn't understand Mayer's reaction.

Back in May when she visited the opulent set, she'd suspected Wilder was crafting a remarkable film, but she was unprepared for the audacious way he told such a wry and darkly comic story.

She wanted to tell Mayer to wake up.

Sure, *Sunset Boulevard* showed audiences what happens when an adoring audience forgets its idol, but everybody knew movie stars weren't flawless models of unimpeachable perfection, so why pretend otherwise?

Thoughts of that movie had been haunting her lately. Gwennie hinted once that maybe it was because Kathryn was forty and time was marching ever onward. And maybe that was true. Norma Desmond was supposed to be fifty, and fifty loomed disturbingly on her horizon.

There was another reason though, one she hadn't shared with anyone: that photo of her father.

She'd first put it on top of her bookcase—out of easy reach, but still in view. It stayed there for weeks until Marcus came back from the library. He'd taken copious notes that confirmed what Francine had told her.

After that, she put it in the bottom drawer of her filing cabinet.

In the limo drive home from the department store demonstration, Gwennie related her exchange with Leo Presnell. Kathryn's knee-jerk reaction was to keep her guard up until Gwennie started talking about the guy's sincerity. "You should give him a chance," Gwennie told her.

So she'd wrangled him an invite to today's luncheon to see how he handled himself among the big cheeses.

Kathryn's improvised method of accelerated flower arranging proved a success. She finished her final vase just as the first guests — the top three members of Twentieth Century-Fox's publicity department — wandered into the ballroom.

Soon the guests started streaming in, keeping Kathryn busy schmoozing and entertaining studio executives, a smattering of stars, and just enough regular folks like Wilkerson's accountant and Tichi's mother to keep it grounded. When Leo Presnell entered the ballroom, he headed straight for her.

The guy sure had good taste in clothes. His dark charcoal suit had a pinstripe so faint that it was barely noticeable unless he was close enough for her to smell that in his sandalwood aftershave. The pinstripe made him look taller than he was, and slimmer, too. It was subtle, but effective.

"Have you seen the afternoon papers?" he asked.

"I've spent most of the day in here."

"Leilah O'Roarke held a press conference this morning. She's petitioning the court to have her case dismissed on the basis of the Cohen bombing."

Earlier that month, Los Angeles awoke to the news that a bomb exploded inside the house of Mickey Cohen in Brentwood. By sheer dumb luck, Cohen and his wife escaped unharmed, causing Cohen to brag that he was unkillable. Still, he'd hired a bodyguard, a small-time hood called Johnny Stompanato who everybody knew and nobody liked.

Leilah had done well to keep her case from going in front of a judge for this long, but now she was getting desperate. "How does she figure Cohen's bomb and her charges are connected?"

"She says rumors have run rife that she's responsible for the explosion, which means she can't get an impartial jury."

"Sounds like someone's running out of tactics."

Presnell's smile dropped suddenly. "Don't look now, but *Variety*'s newest columnist just walked in."

Kathryn pulled a glass of champagne from a passing waiter. She and Tichi had gone over the guest list two days ago, and Ruby Courtland was not on it. "What's she doing?"

"Giggling with Dore Schary and Vincente Minnelli like it's the senior prom and they're competing to be next on her dance card."

"Are either of them buying it?"

"Minnelli doesn't know where to look, but I'd say Schary's lapping it up."

Kathryn snuck a peek. Ruby was in a tight-waisted dress of aqua moiré silk with a matching bolero jacket designed to barely contain a bulging bosom whose sole purpose was to pull the focus of every man within fifty feet.

She turned back to Presnell. "Gwendolyn told me what you said that day at the May Company about helping me get Ruby out of the picture."

"And I meant it."

"Good, because now's your chance."

"You want me to steal behind enemy lines and reconnoiter?"

"She's a sneaky one, so tread lightly."

As he sauntered in and around the guests, Kathryn sought camouflage behind Howard Hawks. She was only halfway to him when a large gong resonated through the room. It was the signal that the newlyweds were arriving.

The guests turned to the double-wide front doors of the Sunset Ballroom and applauded as Billy Wilkerson and his — literally — blushing young bride paraded in. It was also the signal that the guests take their seats.

A phalanx of waiters appeared, scattering through the room, handing out champagne coupes from their trays. As soon as everyone was holding a glass, Wilkerson got to his feet.

"Welcome! Welcome! And thank you all for helping me kick off what I have no doubt will be a joyous new adventure." He was beaming like a bridegroom at his first wedding reception, not a sixty-year-old, five-time divorcé. "As you all know, Tichi and I had a quiet civil ceremony in Phoenix last week, but somehow it didn't seem right to not share the moment with the people I love and admire the most."

Kathryn knew her boss well enough to know that he had already enjoyed several snorts before making his big entrance. He prattled on for a while about the joys of marriage and the "indefinable feeling of satisfaction that the right union with the right person can bring."

Kathryn paid only intermittent attention to his long-winded soliloquy. She was too distracted by the presence of the baby elephant in a bolero jacket.

Is Leo sitting next to Ruby? He can be pretty charming when he wants to be — did he have a chance to coax her into conversation? Would she remember him? Did she see me with him? Would she be on guard?

By the time Kathryn tuned back into Wilkerson, he was starting to wrap things up.

"I won't bore you too much longer," he said. "But I do have a couple more things to say. First, a vote of sincere thanks to my lovely new bride, who organized today's festivities. And she tells me she couldn't have done it on such short notice without the capable assistance of my favorite radio star, our very own Kathryn Massey."

He asked Kathryn to rise and acknowledge the applause he'd coaxed from the crowd.

"I want to finish by making a professional announcement. I'd like to take this opportunity to welcome to the *Hollywood Reporter* team a new member who I'm sure will inject a burst of excitement. Please join me in greeting our new columnist, who I've cunningly managed to lure away from *Variety.*" Kathryn's champagne coupe almost slipped from her fingers. "Ladies and gentlemen, please give a round of openhearted applause to Miss Ruby Courtland."

While Ruby beamed at the crowd and waved, Kathryn scanned the room for Leo Presnell. She spotted him a table away from Ruby, looking at Kathryn, his hands raised in doleful apology. *At least he was game.*

She returned to Wilkerson, who was glowing as though he'd just stolen the Hope diamond out from under Harry Winston.

As long as I live, I'll never understand how otherwise smart and clever men can be so easily bamboozled by a nice bust. And it's not even a nice bust. It's a pull-me-up, push-me-out, shove-me-in-your-face-so-you-can't-look-away display of brazen trampiness.

She flagged down a waiter and took another glass of Help Me Get Through This Ordeal and drained half the glass in one gulp.

CHAPTER 34

Gwendolyn slipped her hand into Zap's and fell in step behind his parents as they walked up the aisle. The Church of the Recessional was a simple sandstone building with a sloping roof and four pairs of stained-glass windows. When they stepped outside, Gwendolyn was surprised to see how many people had gathered to hear George Jessel's touching eulogy over the loudspeakers. There must have been hundreds of people milling around. It was far more than what poor old D.W. Griffith got.

"How did your parents know Sid Grauman?" she asked Zap.

"Pop had a little store around the corner from the Egyptian. Uncle Sid loved Pop's decorative glass bottles. He'd give them as gifts and people'd always ask him, 'Sid, where did you get this gorgeous bottle?' and he'd send them to Pop."

Mr. Zaparelli had a round, genial face punctuated by bright blue button eyes and shaggy brows that appeared to move independently from each other. "I don't like to think where I would be without Sid."

Gwendolyn wasn't fond of the idea of meeting her much-younger boyfriend's parents at all, let alone at a memorial service. It took Zap two days to convince her. "Trust me, they'll be pleased to finally meet the girl I've been talking about for so long."

She kept an eye out for signs of disapproval or hesitation, but they were polite, if perhaps somewhat distant. Then again, she was hardly meeting them at their best.

"Sounds like he was a wonderful person," Gwendolyn said.

"Sidney was a terrific guy." Mrs. Zaparelli dabbed at her eyes.

A quartet of swarthy Italian men greeted the Zaparellis in rapid-fire Italian peppered with dramatic gestures that made Gwendolyn feel excluded. Even Zap didn't notice her draw away.

She looked around for Kathryn, who'd said she'd try and make it, but now that Ruby Courtland was on the payroll, she had to maintain her vigilance to prevent little Miss Snake-in-the-Grass from gaining any more territory.

There were a few distinguished faces among the crowd, but the one that caught Gwendolyn's eye belonged to Darryl Zanuck. She hovered on the periphery of his iron-jawed yes-men until Zanuck sized her up with a quizzical look.

"We've met, haven't we?" he asked.

"Years ago, but I'd hardly expect you to remember."

"Try me."

"Poker game in back of Chasen's. A certain someone had it in for you and—"

He slapped one palm against the other. "You saved me from getting poisoned! What a screwy night that was. How've you been?"

Gwendolyn told him that she had a boutique on the Sunset Strip, and how it was doing well, thanks to the sales of her own perfume.

"Sunset Boulevard? That's *you*? I keep hearing about it."

"From Yvette?"

"My secretary. She wears it—" He fixed her with an unsure eye. "Who did you say?"

"Yvette. The one from that poker game, who tried to—the one with the tippler's bane. She called herself Mae back then."

It took Zanuck a few moments to conjure the woman's face in his mind. "I haven't seen that conniver in years!"

"How long?"

"After that stunt she pulled at Chasen's, we got ourselves into a knock-down, drag-out free-for-all like you wouldn't believe. Jesus, did we go at it!" He winced as he lowered his voice. "I'm ashamed to admit this, but she got me so worked up that I punched her. Right in the kisser."

Gwendolyn took an involuntary step backward, raising her handbag as a barrier.

"Don't feel too badly. She knew just how to play that one: I ended up buying her a goddamned apartment."

His eyes drifted away for a moment or two, lost in the recollection of what Gwendolyn assumed was a painful memory, but a smile dawned on his lips. Though barely five foot six, he carried himself with the assurance of John Wayne. The charisma the man exuded was almost palpable, although Gwendolyn wasn't sure where self-confidence ended and ego picked up.

His eyes focused again. "To tell you the God's honest truth, I kinda miss her. Mae's a real good sport. Fun to be around. She taught me more than a trick or two in the bedroom, I don't mind admitting. And she wasn't into man-trapping as a sport, which is why that stunt with the poison threw me off. I said a bunch of things I probably shouldn't have."

"Mister Zanuck." Gwendolyn knew she wasn't going to like the answer she was about to hear, but she had to ask anyway. "When was the last time you saw Mae?"

"Must have been when I became a colonel and went to show her my Army Signal Corps uniform."

"You haven't seen her since the war?"

"Nope."

"The two of you don't play Scrabble together?"

"Hell, no!"

"Do you know if she still lives in that apartment you bought her?"

"With the real estate boom, that place's gotta be worth a small fortune now. She'd be a fool to sell it, and that gal ain't no fool."

"I don't suppose you recall the address?"

"Sure I do. Listen, if you go see her, will you let her know that I'd be up for a reunion?"

"Are you sure? The two of you sound pretty combustible."

A droll look crept into his eye. "You say it like that's a bad thing."

* * *

The Talmadge was a ten-story brown brick building on Wilshire, just down from the Ambassador Hotel. Gwendolyn had always thought of it as a home to silent-era celebrities, the haut monde, and loaded dowagers whose husbands invested well. But as she sat in Zap's Pontiac and took in the crumbling façade that was grubby with car exhaust, she wondered if she had the right address.

"If you've changed your mind," Zap said, "we could go for prime rib at the Derby."

"Don't wait," she told him. "I might be three minutes or three hours."

He tugged his keys out of the ignition. "You're not going up there by yourself."

"I most certainly am."

"This woman sounds like she's off her rocker."

"I'm more likely to get the truth out of her if there are no menfolk in sight." He stared at her glumly. "Wait fifteen minutes. If she's not home, we'll go to the Derby."

She kissed him on the cheek and climbed out of the car. The directory inside the dingy foyer with the desiccated maidenhair ferns listed a "Saperstein, H. (Miss)" on the fifth floor, Apartment 502.

The elevator door opened onto a threadbare carpet running down the center of an empty corridor. Number 502 was second from the end. The door had once been painted dark brown, but it had been years since it felt the stroke of a paintbrush. Gwendolyn heard the muffled sounds of Glenn Miller and heels clacking on tile. She banged as hard as she could.

"Yvette? Hilda? Mae? I know you're all in there. It's Gwendolyn Brick. From the store on Sunset."

The brass handle squeaked and the door cracked open a couple of inches. A dull green eye, bleary with fatigue and caked with days-old mascara, stared at her. "What do you want?"

"I've just come from Sid Grauman's memorial service."

"What of it?"

"Zanuck was there. You came up in conversation."

The woman had nothing to say.

"Yvette—Hilda—Mae, I don't even know what to call you."

Long pause. "It's Hilda."

"Can I come in? Please?"

Hilda let out a breathy groan and swung the door open. She was dressed in a red robe with a stork motif printed along the hem, too shiny to be real silk. At one time, it might have matched her hair, but it had been a while since she'd bothered with a henna rinse.

The living room enjoyed a view of the Bullocks Wilshire tower, whose burnished copper crown glowed in the sun. Gwendolyn doubted Hilda spent much time admiring it. The room stunk with stale air and cheap cigarettes. Newspapers and magazines were strewn about; the remains of last night's pork chops were on the coffee table.

"Zanuck told me he hasn't seen you since the start of the war." Hilda pretended to stifle a yawn. "Zanuck didn't set you up in that fake store, did he?"

"*Fake* store?"

"Your entire stock was from three seasons ago." She pointed to the Bullocks Wilshire tower. "I used to work there. I want to know who put you up to it, and why did you break into my store?"

"Break into—? That's a hell of an accusation, I must say. If that's what you came in here to—"

"Cut the act, Hilda. You're not fooling anyone."

The woman wavered like a stalk of corn. She blinked slowly and tilted her head back.

Gwendolyn placed her handbag on the least-stained chair. "It was Leilah O'Roarke, wasn't it?"

Hilda maintained her unruffled mien for a few seconds, but then her crinkled brows pointed into the center of her face, her eyes clamped shut, and her lips all but disappeared as she clenched them tight.

Gwendolyn said, "I think we could both do with some coffee."

Hilda jerked her head up. "Irish?"

"I'm happy to make it if you want to put some clothes on."

"This is about as dressed as I get these days." Hilda made a token gesture of tightening the sash around her waist and told Gwendolyn to follow her.

The kitchen overlooked Wilshire Boulevard. Intermittent Sunday drivers in both directions sped up, then stopped for traffic lights.

Hilda heaped coffee into her percolator and stood staring at it for a while. "Yep," she said, "that story about Zanuck was a bunch o' bull." She wagged her coffee scooper at Gwendolyn. "But I want you to know that I said yes to Leilah before I realized who you were. Swear to God, I nearly died when you came into my shop."

"You hid it well."

"The whole time we were chatting I was thinking, 'Are you kidding me? Of all people, did it have to be her?' If it wasn't for your quick thinking that night at Chasen's, I might be doing hard time for murder."

Gwendolyn could feel her resistance begin to dissolve just as it had with Leo Presnell that day at the May Company store. "I don't think you can actually kill anyone with tippler's bane."

"But I wanted to. I was nutty back then."

"If it's any consolation, not only did Zanuck have complimentary things to say, but he wants to see you."

Hilda looked away. "That's nice to hear, but I'm past fifty now, and he's still in his forties."

"You'll never know unless you make that call." *And a trip to the beauty parlor wouldn't be a waste of time.* "Or I could make it for you."

"You would?" Hope glimmered in Hilda's eyes.

"But first you have to tell me about Leilah O'Roarke. The two of you go back a ways, huh?"

"All I've ever done is lurch from one regret to another."

Gwendolyn could see it was going to be tough to keep this woman on track and truthful. "She was after those client cards?"

"I was hard up for cash, so I put this place on the market. Next thing I know, Leilah's on the line telling me I wouldn't have to sell if I could do her a favor. She said, 'I've got this shady character I need to keep an eye on, and I need the right someone to do it for me.' She dangled a whole wad of bills in my face. I only said yes 'cause I figured I could use her to get myself set up in a legit business. Who knew what it took to make a real go of a store like that? Honey, I take my hat off to you."

The percolator reached the end of its cycle. Hilda started to pour the coffee into a couple of genteel porcelain cups, but her hand shook and she spilled some onto the counter.

"Leilah O'Roarke is one cool customer, but as time went on, she'd jump on the horn again and again, getting more and more rattled."

She poured some cheap Irish whiskey into her cup; Gwendolyn lifted hers to her lips before Hilda had a chance to spike it.

"Is that when she told you to break into my store?"

Anger flared in Hilda's face. "I want you to know that I told Leilah 'Absolutely not!' But she jumped off the deep end, so I went ahead with it. Me and a coupla schlubs she recruited."

"The ones with the red Chevrolet?"

"How did you know?"

"I'm not blind."

"Yeah, well, anyway, I was glad when we couldn't find anything."

"Did you like the perfume?" Gwendolyn asked with a smile.

"Sorry about that, but I couldn't resist." Hilda started looking around. "I want to pay you, though. My purse is around here someplace."

Gwendolyn laid a hand on top of Hilda's. It was clammy, and more than a little dirty, and she wished she hadn't. "Think of it as a gift."

"I don't deserve it."

"You will if you can tell me what Leilah's plans are. Has she shared them with you?"

"Oh, brother!" Hilda let out a nicotine-coated chuckle. "I sure dreaded having to tell her we came up empty-handed. I half-expected her to sucker-punch me right in the puss, but she took the news pretty well. Then she told me she was looking for someone to get drunk with, and hey, I've never said no to an open bar."

"What did she tell you?"

Hilda looked down at her hands clenched in her lap; her chest rose and fell raggedly. Gwendolyn grabbed the whiskey bottle and added a generous splash to Hilda's cup. "I have Zanuck's number in my purse."

Down on Wilshire, a pair of drivers erupted into a honking match.

"Leilah plans on using them to bargain her way out of jail."

"That much I already figured."

"Yeah, but she's going to make copies first, and sell them off to the highest bidder before skipping bail and disappearing to South America."

"She wants to have her cake and eat it, too."

Hilda slurped her coffee. "Did you know her trial's been set?"

"I'd started to wonder if she could keep getting one continuance after another indefinitely."

"Trust me, that gal's got more legal connections than the attorney general. Her trial starts June fifth."

Three months was plenty of time to maneuver and connive.

"And if she doesn't have her bargaining chips by then?" Gwendolyn asked.

"I guess they'll ship her and that sleazeball husband of hers down the river."

"Leilah O'Roarke's too cunning for that."

"Ah, so you *do* know her."

Hilda reached for a half-empty pack of Luckies. She lit one with a smirk and offered another to Gwendolyn. The two of them stared out the kitchen window as the weekend traffic lazed its way eastward through heavy yellow smog until it disappeared in the haze.

CHAPTER 35

Marcus was still drunk when he pulled up to the security gate of Republic studios. Not slurringly, staggeringly, four A.M. drunk, but nowhere near as sober as he ought to be. He wished he'd taken a few moments to clear his head during the drive over the Hollywood Hills, but he was there now and the security guard behind the gate had seen him.

Thanks to Quentin Luckett, he was already two martinis in when the call came an hour ago. Quentin had been Trevor Bergin's boyfriend for a number of years, but all that went the way of the dodo bird with Trevor's Pinko branding-by-innuendo. Not long after that day at the beach, MGM kicked Trevor out on his ass. Without a word to anyone at the Garden, Trevor packed his things and disappeared into the night.

Suddenly, Quentin had decided he couldn't bear to be alone, and invited himself over for an afternoon of wallowing in heartache. He arrived at Marcus' door, gin in one hand, vermouth in the other, a jar of olives in his pocket and a grim look in his eye.

When the call from Republic came, Marcus' first reaction was to laugh. What would the head of Republic Pictures want with him? But when the secretary on the other end of the line told him Mr. Yates wanted to see him at three o'clock, he stopped laughing.

———

"Yes, Mister Adler," the guard said, "we've been expecting you." Until that moment, Marcus had only half-believed it. "Mister Yates' office is the first building on the right. Follow the sign, you can't miss it."

The corridor was lined with posters of Republic's typical B-movie fare: *Desperadoes of the West, Carson City Raiders, Ghost of Zorro.* The door at the end opened into a reception area where a humorless woman pounded at a typewriter. She told him that Mr. Yates wouldn't be a moment.

He took a seat, leafed through a copy of *Life* magazine and breathed in deeply.

Oxygen in . . . martini out . . . oxygen in . . . martini out . . .

The door with Yates' name on it opened and a guy in his late sixties strode toward him. He wore an unadventurous bowtie, and a friar's ring of white-gray hair around the back of his scalp.

"Glad you could come in at such short notice."

He headed back the way he came, leaving Marcus to follow in his wake, and indicated that Marcus should take a seat on the other side of his expansive desk. Sitting in front of Yates were some typewritten pages. Marcus squinted to read the title: *Skybound.*

How the hell did Amelia Earhart get HERE?

Yates pointed to the outline. "I understand you wrote this."

"I did, although I'm not sure how you got a copy."

"Vera Ralston. Have you heard of her?"

The name rings a bell . . . wait, isn't that the ice skater from . . . where was it? Czechoslovakia? Yugoslavia? The one this guy brought to America to be the new Sonja Henie, only she couldn't speak English or act worth a damn.

"Yes," Marcus replied. "Of course."

"I have her under contract and am looking for a project to showcase her talents. She did a movie with John Wayne last year, *The Flying Kentuckian*, and—" Yates tapped Marcus' outline "—I want this to be her next project."

So that's it. You want to jump into her drawers, and this is your way to do it. Or maybe you already have, and this is how you stay there. Either way, it'll be fascinating to hear how you plan to sandwich a glittery ice-skating number into a movie about an earnest aviatrix.

"I think she's ready to take on a lead role," Yates declared. "She's going to be thrilled that I got this for her!"

"How exactly did you get this?" Marcus asked. "I can only assume Howard Hughes gave it to you."

"Hughes? Never met the man. No, no, this came to me via a chap by the name of Purvis."

Marcus pushed his glasses onto his forehead and rubbed his eyes as his head spun from three martinis mixed with stupefaction. "Purvis?"

"He told me the two of you used to work together."

"We did, but—"

"You did write this, didn't you?"

"Yes, but—"

"All righty then!" He rubbed his hands together like a cartoon character. "Let's talk turkey. How much are you asking for this?"

The guy had the square-headed, square-jawed, square-shouldered look of a straight shooter, and Marcus didn't have the heart to stick him with a project he couldn't use.

"I've got to level with you. I used to head up the writing department at MGM."

"Do you think I live with my head stuck up my ass?"

"Are you aware I appeared before the HUAC in Washington in what became a very sticky situation—"

Yates cut him off with a dismissive gesture. "Yeah, yeah, I know all that Commie bull."

"If it comes out that you made a picture written by an accused Pinko, you'll probably be hounded. Most likely by Hedda Hopper. She's on a rampage and is taking no prisoners—"

"Just answer me this, Adler: Are you a Commie?"

"No, sir, I am not. But gossip and innuendo—"

"Screw that. You're not on the blacklist, that's all I care about. Now, give me your price."

There was still a decent amount left in Marcus' bank account, but it'd recently dropped from five figures to four.

"*Skybound* is pretty much already written in my head. I could knock out a great script in a few weeks."

"Nah. I've already got more writers than I know what to do with. All I want is your outline. How does five grand sound?"

* * *

The Tahitian Restaurant—"Catering! Banquets! Luaus!"—was the first place Marcus spotted that would likely have a public telephone. He was going to wait until he got home to call Anson Purvis, but by the time he swung onto Ventura Boulevard, he knew he couldn't. In addition to which, it seemed a sure bet that the Tahitian had a decent bar. He turned into the largely empty lot and walked inside.

It was a typical Polynesian joint: lots of bamboo, coarse rattan, and tiki gods suspended from the ceiling. At a quarter to four, it was too late for the lunch rush and too early for the pre-dinner cocktail crowd.

He found Purvis' number in the telephone book and was relieved when the guy picked up.

"I've just met with Herbert Yates at Republic," Marcus spat down the line.

"Already? Oh, shit."

"You want to explain to me why? And how? And when? And what the hell?"

When Purvis asked where he was, Marcus read out the address from an empty matchbook on the floor of the phone booth. Purvis told him to sit tight.

Marcus hung up and headed for the bar. He was the only patron in the place, which suited him fine. Taking the barstool closest to the wall, he ordered a navy grog from the bartender and contemplated what had just happened.

I guess I'm back in the game.

He'd thought he'd be thrilled, but he found scant comfort. Three years ago he was the head of MGM's writing department, and now he was selling outlines to a poverty-row studio for the purpose of getting into some starlet's panties.

His drink arrived. The grapefruit bit into his tongue; the rum soothed it.

Oliver would have asked, "Why the long face, Cyrano de Bergerac? You just earned five grand for a story idea. If you split it with Melody, which you should, that's still two and a half grand. See? Ya still got it, baby."

Oliver had moved out of his apartment the week after he sent Marcus packing. Desperate, Marcus called the Breen Office but was told Mr. Trenton was on an extended sabbatical. A few weeks later, a picture postcard arrived from a town billing itself "The Redwood Gate to the Golden State." On the back, Oliver scribbled, *Doing okay. Don't worry. Don't come looking.*

Marcus was on his second round when Anson Purvis pitched himself through the front doors.

When Purvis started at MGM not long after the war, he'd come at the recommendation of the devious bastard who'd penned a reprehensible roman à clef. But the guy proved to be a first-rate screenwriter so Marcus gave him a job. He'd later come to regret it when he learned that Purvis had curried favor with Mayer so effectively that when Marcus exited, Purvis replaced him.

Marcus said nothing as Purvis took the stool next to him and motioned to the bartender to have whatever Marcus was having. He was panting like he'd run the last five hundred yards.

"Yates and I only talked yesterday morning. I can't believe he moved so fast."

"Imagine my surprise," Marcus said.

"I was going to call you tonight. Give you advance warning, but, well, look, I'm sorry. This isn't the way I planned it."

"So there was a plan?"

Over the PA, a mournful whine started singing about tears mixing with raindrops on Waikiki Beach. Purvis took a sip of his navy grog and inhaled sharply until the sting subsided.

"How did it go with Yates?" Purvis asked. "Did he like *Skybound* enough to buy it?"

"He did."

"That's terrific, right?"

"The more relevant question is: How the hell did that schlemiel end up with my outline?"

Purvis looked at Marcus blankly. "Howard Hughes," he said, as though it were sufficient explanation.

"What about him?"

"At RKO."

Marcus could feel his face turn the shade of the lava-red carpeting. "I know where Howard Hughes works."

Purvis did a double take. "You didn't even see me, did you?" When Marcus gaped mutely at him, he continued. "A couple of months back, you had a meeting with Hughes at RKO, right? You were his one o'clock, right? Well, I was his two o'clock."

"You were there?"

"I said hello. I assumed you saw me—"

"I was pretty steamed."

"You looked it. I figured your meeting hadn't gone well, so when I went in to see Hughes I asked him about it. He told me about your pitch, and how he couldn't do anything with it, so I took it off his hands. When I read it, I thought, Wow, this is classic Marcus Adler. Solid idea, terrific execution, it was all there."

"I'm surprised you didn't keep the idea for MGM."

"I'm not there anymore."

Marcus slouched over his drink, feeling the three different rums soften the coarse edges of his ego. *Have I been so out of touch that I didn't even know my replacement got replaced?* "What happened?"

"You name it. Interoffice politics, monstrous egos, paranoia over the blacklist. I don't know how you stood it. I quit the Motion Picture Alliance for the Preservation of American Ideals, too, by the way."

Back at MGM, Purvis had been one of the few hard-line right-wingers in Marcus' life. "I'm surprised to hear it."

"After the HUAC hearings, their heads swelled up bigger than the Lincoln Memorial. It all got too jingoistic for me. I don't have anything to do with Clifford Wardell, either. He earned a lot of dough from *Reds in the Beds* and *Deadly Bedfellows*, and he started spending it like water, most of it on beer, broads, and blackjack in Las Vegas."

Marcus felt pleasantly gooey but knew he wasn't so drunk that he could be easily misled. "So you took *Skybound* and gave it to Yates? Why would you do that?"

A flicker of hesitation shot through the guy's Nordic blue eyes. The sugar in his smile dissolved until a thin-lipped pucker settled in its place. "Fact is, I feel guilty."

"About what?"

"I wanted your job and I was convinced you were a Commie playing the innocent, so I said some pretty terrible things about you to people of influence. Wardell suckered me in and preyed on my ambition. It wasn't until much later that I realized I'd been duped. Now, of course, I know you're nothing of the sort." He swiped his forehead with a cocktail napkin.

"This is all about your penance?" Marcus wasn't sure if he liked that or not.

"I hoped you might be more open to doing me a favor. You've got to believe me—I was going to call you tonight and lay it all out for you."

A year ago, Marcus wouldn't have crossed the street to piss on Purvis if he was on fire.

Purvis flagged the bartender and signaled for another round. He watched a couple of booze-hardened businessmen in shiny suits take up residence at the other end of the bar. "I need you," he admitted.

It had been a long time since anyone had told Marcus they needed him. Kathryn had her radio show, and Gwendolyn had her store. They both had budding romances and their lives were now busy and successful. Meanwhile, Oliver was MIA and might never come back.

"Need me for what?" Marcus asked.

"Have you ever watched *The Lone Ranger*?"

"I wouldn't waste my time even if I did own a television set—which I don't."

"I used to talk about television like that. But then the *Lone Ranger* producer asked me to be their head of writing. It's steady work, pays well, nice offices. My bosses are very trusting and don't interfere much. Now I run the show on a day-to-day basis. I'm very happy."

Marcus took the fresh glass thrust in front of him. "Then I'm happy for you. I mean that, by the way. No hard feelings."

Purvis slid off his stool and propped an elbow on the bar. He angled his body away from the businessmen and leaned in closer to Marcus.

"I'm not asking you to write for the show."

"But I can't ride a horse, so . . ."

"*The Lone Ranger* is such a massive hit that George and Fran brought up the possibility of making a feature just when my best writer got lured to Desilu."

"What's Desilu?"

"Christ! You really don't keep up, do you? I need someone who knows what he's doing, and has the imagination to come up with fresh ideas. That poor masked son of a bitch can't lasso the baddies over and over and over forever."

Marcus always thought that writing for television was scraping the bottom of the barrel. But writing a stick-em-up Western television show? That was scraping the layer of crud *underneath* the bottom of the barrel. Fortunately, he had an out.

"Listen," he told Purvis, "I appreciate the gesture, I do, but even if I wanted to sign on, you're forgetting about the blacklist."

"Trust me, nobody cares."

"Are you kidding? Plenty of people care, especially Hedda Hopper. She cares a hell of a lot."

"Yeah, about *movies*. Television flies under the radar. So what do you say?"

Marcus had never put much stock in the concept of fate. He preferred the idea that men created their own luck. But now he wasn't so sure. First Reuben, then Hughes, and now the guy who'd slithered into his chair at MGM while it was still warm.

He swallowed his bitter drink and lowered the glass to the cardboard coaster. Knowing he couldn't procrastinate any longer, he looked up at Purvis, but the guy was gripping the edge of the bar, knuckles straining through the skin. His teeth were clenched together, pale lips pulling at the edges of his mouth. He started emitting a strangled groan.

"What's wrong?" Marcus asked.

"It's my stump." Purvis had lost a leg at Iwo Jima, but in the whole time he'd worked for Marcus, he'd never once referred to it. "Been giving me trouble," he panted. "Not usually this bad, though."

"What do the doctors say?"

"I've seen enough doctors to last me ten lifetimes."

"But they —"

"They don't know shit!" Another wave of pain rocketed up his leg, through his spine, to his neck.

Marcus turned to the bartender. "Call an ambulance!" He wrapped his arm around Purvis' shoulder. "Let's get you on the floor."

"Great." Purvis attempted a smile. "Flat on my back in a bar and it's not even cocktail hour. So will you think about it?"

Marcus helped ease him onto the carpet. "About what?"

"My offer."

"Jesus, pal, you've sure got a one-track mind."

"Tell me you'll think about it."

The medics arrived within minutes, bundling Purvis onto a gurney and wheeling him out to the ambulance on Ventura Boulevard. Marcus pulled his car keys from his pocket, unlocked his door and dropped into the driver's seat. By the time his engine growled to life, he knew what his answer was.

CHAPTER 36

Kathryn first heard about Bette Davis' new movie when she bumped into Edith Head at the party Lucille Ball and Desi Arnaz threw to celebrate bringing Ball's radio series, *My Favorite Husband*, to television. Bette had specifically requested Edith's services for a picture at Twentieth Century-Fox, then jumped on an airplane two days later to start shooting in San Francisco.

When Joseph Mankiewicz first announced his backstage theater movie, it was called *Best Performance*, and was going to star Claudette Colbert.

But now it was called *All About Eve*, and Kathryn couldn't imagine Bette playing anything written for Claudette. Kathryn wondered if she was getting desperate about her next paycheck

Rather like Marcus, in a way. She was still surprised he'd said yes to *The Lone Ranger*.

Bette had returned none of Kathryn's messages, so she waited it out. When Bette resurfaced, she explained that the role of Margo Channing was a once-in-a-decade part. Kathryn was perplexed that it wasn't even the title role, but Bette was unconcerned.

"I've got bigger fish to fry!" she declared over the phone.

Her voice was deep and scratchy, like a Licketysplitter's.

"My marriage has completely fallen apart. We had the screaming match to end all screaming matches before I flew up to film my first scenes. The quack said I screamed so loud that I broke a blood vessel in my throat."

"Mank can't have been happy."

"Are you kidding? He loved it and told me to keep it that way. And that isn't everything. I'm having an affair with my costar. We've been screwing all over the goddamned place!"

The whole thing sounded like a shambles. "So it's going well, then?"

"Fabulous!" Ice tinkled against glass. "Except perhaps tomorrow."

"What's tomorrow?"

"Could you come to the set? We're on Stage Eleven. Please say yes."

Kathryn wasn't sure she wanted to witness this train wreck, even if it'd make for a juicy item in her column. "Does it have to be tomorrow?"

"YES! We're filming a cocktail party. All the leads will be there, plus dozens of extras. Zingers flying in *all* directions."

"Won't I be in the way?"

"I need you there for moral support," Bette insisted. "Anne Baxter and I are getting along famously. George Sanders, too. And of course Gary and I are—well, we're whatever we are. What I'm worried about is this blonde they've cast. A real knockout. She's only got a small part, but she's the type who can unravel me."

"Oh, Bette, there isn't an actress born who can throw you off your game."

"In the past, maybe, but I'm over forty, my third marriage is kaput, I'm having an affair with a married man, and now I live from picture to picture."

"But isn't that what you wanted? Independence?"

"All I thought about was wriggling free. I gave absolutely no thought to what that freedom would mean."

It was unsettling to hear Bette sound anything less than a hundred percent sure of herself. "Stage Eleven? I'll be there."

* * *

The set looked like the sort of penthouse apartment that Kathryn imagined rich New Yorkers called home.

A mezzanine balcony loomed on the right. A curved staircase with a wrought iron balustrade led to a split-level living room featuring an ornate mantelpiece, high-toned artwork, a crystal chandelier, and the biggest monstera Kathryn had ever seen. Or was it a philodendron? She'd killed pretty much every houseplant entrusted to her care.

Either way, the thing was monstrous. Kathryn wrote down "monstrous monstera?"

She tried to stay inconspicuous among the dress extras in cocktail attire who stood around making small talk as they waited for the star.

Frankly, Kathryn was glad to be out of the office. She hated to admit it, but the *Hollywood Reporter*'s new columnist was starting to bamboozle her. In the two months she'd been on staff, Ruby had presented an immaculate picture of charm and modesty.

When Senator Johnson from Colorado charged Ingrid Bergman with moral turpitude, Ruby leapt to Ingrid's defense in the newsroom before Kathryn could open her mouth. When the Supreme Court announced its decision not to review the cases of the Hollywood Ten, Ruby didn't bring it up, which enabled Kathryn to publish a rant blasting the court for constitutional cowardice that garnered her widespread attention.

Ruby sought her advice on everything from dressing tips to grammar, and as far as Kathryn could determine, wasn't chasing after any of the available men at the office. Ruby Courtland had banished the sour-faced bitch Kathryn saw in the audience the night Max Factor pulled their support, and reverted to the sweet debutant from the *Samson and Delilah* set.

Kathryn had no hard evidence that Ruby was responsible for Max Factor dumping their sponsorship, and Ruby's face could have been read a number of different ways. On the other hand, neither Walter Winchell nor Leo Presnell were fans.

Kathryn's gut sensed something wasn't quite right, but there were enough men ready to cut a girl off at the knees; the last thing a working woman needed was a female colleague helping to sharpen the blade. And if Ruby had left New York to escape her mistakes, she'd hardly be the first girl to do it.

Kathryn wasn't sure what to think anymore. All she knew was that she needed to put some distance between the two of them.

"There you are!"

Bette approached Kathryn in an off-the-shoulder cocktail dress of heavy brown silk with sable lining the three-quarters cuffs and around the pockets. Her shoulder-length hair was parted at the side.

"Don't you look great!" Kathryn told her. "That dress!"

Bette pursed her lips. "Poor Edith! She's mortified at how it's turned out." She shimmied her shoulders. "It's not supposed to be like this, but when I put it on just now, the whole top sagged worse than an old stripper's G-string."

Kathryn pictured Edith crouched in a corner somewhere, pounding her head against a wall.

"So I yanked the neckline off my shoulders and hey presto." Bette checked herself in a full-length mirror standing just off the set. "Turned out pretty well, huh?"

Kathryn had been around long enough to know that when a production was floundering in a sea of directorial indecision or star truculence, a tense grittiness permeated the set. People darted about, rarely looking each other in the eye or stopping to crack a joke. This was the sort of set Kathryn had expected to encounter today, but she found instead a relaxed atmosphere, busy with people focused on the work at hand, but at the same time cozy and unruffled.

"Dress mishaps aside, you look fairly happy."

Bette ran her fingers over a glittering piece of costume jewelry pinned above her left breast. "Everything's marvelous! And the script! It's so goddamned witty."

"And Gary Merrill?" Kathryn whispered. "Is he around?"

Bette put negligible effort into suppressing a smile. "I may have mussed up his tuxedo a tad. I imagine he's still in his dressing room . . . unmussing."

"And what about the blonde you mentioned?"

"We had an eight o'clock call, so naturally she showed up ten minutes ago. They're stitching her into her dress as we speak."

Joseph Mankiewicz and his ubiquitous pipe appeared to their right in a cloud of fragrant smoke, surveying the penthouse with a critical eye.

"You'll have to excuse me," Bette said, turning away from the mirror, "I want to be sure that Mank is okay with this dress before we start." She gave Kathryn's hand a quick squeeze. "Just knowing you're here, it's settled my nerves considerably." She marched away.

Kathryn spotted a line of paintings hanging on the wall that led to the mezzanine and headed toward it.

After the experience of finding her own photo in the Norma Desmond mansion, Kathryn had taken to inspecting props. She knew it was unlikely that she'd find another that looked like her, but she couldn't help herself. The thought of a man she didn't remember sitting in a prison cell was starting to haunt her.

She was inspecting a painting of an aristocratic woman on a wooden throne when a flash of glittering white caught her eye.

Standing at the bottom of the stairs in a strapless gown gathered over a hip into a fabric orchid was Gwendolyn's customer with the big bucks.

"Hello," the blonde said meekly. "I'm not sure if you remember me."

"Of course!" Kathryn joined her at the bottom of the stairs. "But I don't know your name."

"It's Marilyn."

Sunset Boulevard radiated off her. "You're wearing Gwendolyn's perfume."

Marilyn gurgled like a baby. "I simply adore it! People are always asking me what it is, so I send them to the Strip."

"She'll love hearing that."

"But it's Gwendolyn I talk about the most. What she's doing is practically revolutionary!"

Gwennie? A revolutionary? "How do you mean?"

"Whenever I can't decide between one outfit or another, she'll ask me, 'Who will you be wearing it for? Yourself, or some man?' It made me realize us women dress entirely for men. We accentuate the bosom, narrow the waist, lengthen the leg, enhance the silhouette. It's all about catching *their* attention." The girl slanted her head to one side. "But now I think, 'If there were no men left in the world, would I even wear something like this?'" She let out another baby-doll giggle. "Of course there are times when you *do* want to impress a casting director, or photographer, or that handsome stranger across the room. But I look at clothes differently now, and I have Gwendolyn to thank. I tell everyone about her."

Marilyn's tentative smile faded when Bette's barking laugh shot across the set. "I saw you talking to Miss Davis."

This is the blonde? "I got to know her quite well when I volunteered at the Hollywood Canteen."

"She doesn't particularly like me."

"There are lots of people she doesn't like."

"I admire her so much that I go completely to pieces whenever I'm around her. She's intimidating and she knows it, and uses it to her advantage."

"I suspect you might be right."

Marilyn fidgeted with the bracelet around her left wrist. "I want a career just like hers."

Standing on an A-list movie set, in full costume and makeup, the girl had even more charisma than she did in Gwennie's store. She glowed with an inner allure that Kathryn had seen in only a few women. Vivien Leigh had it, and so did Greer Garson. Ingrid Bergman, too, even if she was persona non grata in Hollywood these days. But with that angelic face and enviable bust, Kathryn doubted she was fated for a Bette-Davis type of career. Betty Grable, maybe, but Bette Davis? No.

"Who do you play in this movie?" she asked.

"Miss Caswell, the girlfriend of George Sanders."

Sanders had third billing in this movie. "*Eve* Caswell? As in *All About Eve*?"

Marilyn shook her head in alarm. "Oh, heavens no! I'm a long way from being able to pull off a role like that!"

"Why?"

"Eve Harrington is so devious, so treacherous, so— so—Machiavellian!"

Kathryn hadn't expected a word like that to come out of a girl so amply endowed with such physical charms. She went to ask what made Eve Harrington so Machiavellian but an assistant director called for the set to be cleared.

The key lights came on, drenching the penthouse. Kathryn positioned herself next to the full-length mirror and watched Bette stand with Celeste Holm, Gary Merrill, and Hugh Marlowe. The two women held martinis and stood in place until Mank called, "Action!"

Celeste twirled the olive in her martini. "We know you. We've seen you like this before. Is it over, or is it just beginning?"

Stone-faced, Bette drained her glass in one gulp, handed it to Merrill, then swanned to the foot of the stairs. She ascended to the first step and swung around to survey the crowd. "Fasten your seatbelts; it's going to be a bumpy night."

Mankiewicz got her to do it several times more until he felt she'd delivered the line with the level of blithe menace he was looking for. The blazing lights were switched off as the crew got to work setting up the next shot. Bette beckoned Kathryn to join her at the bottom of the steps.

"What do you think of our Little Miss Bombshell?"

"You must admit, she's very pretty."

"I overheard someone in makeup say she could play Helen of Troy." Bette curled a lip. "The face that launched a thousands *shits*—and all of them mine! I suppose she bitched about how rude to her I've been."

Kathryn skipped over Marilyn's comment about Bette's intimidating presence, and told her that the younger actress admired her very much. It provoked a *So what?* raise of the eyebrow. Then Kathryn asked, "This Eve Harrington character, what makes her so Machiavellian?"

"Didn't I tell you what this movie's about?"

"I haven't heard from you in weeks."

"I'm playing a—well, let's call Margo a *seasoned* actress who's approaching the upper limits of credibility for romantic parts. And then in creeps mousy little Eve Harrington, who's all 'I'm not worthy to be in your presence, Miss Channing.' She insinuates herself into Margo's life so cunningly that nobody realizes until it's far too late that Eve's intention all along was to replace Margo completely."

Kathryn felt heat prickle her scalp.

Bette grabbed Kathryn by the hand. "My dear! Do we need to find you a chair?"

"How does Margo dispense with Eve?"

"She doesn't! Eve gets everything she wants: starring roles, her own dressing room, acting awards. Meanwhile, all poor old Margo gets is older and wiser."

"But surely Eve gets her comeuppance?"

Bette snickered. "I suppose she does, in a way. Right at the end, Eve gets an Eve of her own, but doesn't recognize it." The assistant director called the cast back to the set. "Really, Kathryn, you should take that seat near the prop table. I wish I could join you but I have to deal with Miss Copacabana School of Dramatic Art."

Bette took her place on the set with Baxter, Sanders, and Marilyn. Mankiewicz asked for quiet. Marilyn looked like she was about to face a firing squad. Kathryn winked. She mouthed the words "You can do this!" and showed her a discreet thumbs-up.

Maybe Margo doesn't drop Eve through a trapdoor, but life doesn't have to imitate art. Not my life, anyway.

"And—" Mankiewicz paused for a moment " — ACTION!"

CHAPTER 37

Gwendolyn held open the door of a second-string theater down on the fleapit end of Hollywood Boulevard for Kathryn and Doris. "What a stinker!"

The three of them stopped in front of the poster of Ingrid Bergman pressing against her dark-haired costar above an exploding volcano. Below it: *This is it! The place: STROMBOLI. The star: BERGMAN. Under the inspired direction of ROSSELLINI.*

"Hughes tried his best before word got out," Kathryn said.

Doris pretended to gag. "Dressed-up mutton by any other name."

They turned away from the poster and headed down the sidewalk.

"It's Ingrid I feel bad for," Gwendolyn said. "She's completely thrown away her career. It might've been okay if a decent movie came out of it."

"I thought the eruption scene was pretty good," Kathryn said wistfully.

"You didn't actually like that movie, did you?" Gwendolyn asked.

Kathryn jolted herself out of her revelry. "God, no! I was ready to leave after the first fifteen minutes."

"Penny for your thoughts, then? Or a root beer float? I've got some Wil Wright's ice cream at home."

"In a funny sort of way, I almost identified with Ingrid's character — living in the shadow of a volcano that's likely to erupt at any moment."

The previous week, Gwendolyn had been at home finishing up a capriciously tricky suit of mustard crêpe de chine when Kathryn came knocking, straight from the set of *All About Eve*. "I assume your volcano is named Ruby?"

They were at Kathryn's Oldsmobile now. She unlocked it and the three of them climbed inside. Kathryn dropped her hands into her lap and stared out the windshield. "I feel like I'm sitting next to a powder keg."

Doris tsked from the back seat. "You can't let Ruby worm her way any more deeply into your life."

"But how do I stop her?" Kathryn pulled into the traffic heading west.

"By figuring out what she wants."

"She wants to replace me!"

They fell silent until they were passing the Egyptian Theatre. Kathryn said, "Last night, I found out for sure that she was behind Max Factor dropping me."

"How did that happen?"

"Leo and I were at the Vine Street Derby. Max Factor's head of PR came in. He was by himself, and headed straight for the bar. He looked like he was waiting for someone, so I handed Leo some excuse and went straight up to him. I told him he'd do me the biggest favor by being straight about what happened."

"So it really was her?"

"He didn't know her by name, but he described the person who told him."

"And what did she tell him?"

"All about my father and Sing Sing. He assured me he'd keep it to himself, but with a scandal like that, they felt they could no longer put themselves at risk."

"But how could Ruby know?" Gwendolyn asked. "You'd only just learned that yourself."

Kathryn strummed her fingernails along the top of her steering wheel. "All I know is she and Winchell are both socially prominent New Yorkers."

"You think they're in cahoots?" Gwendolyn began to feel nauseous. "But that means Winchell knows about your father. So . . . you think Winchell and Leilah *and* Ruby are all in cahoots together? I don't know, Kathryn, that sounds a bit far-fetched, if you ask me."

They'd had a straight run down Hollywood Boulevard to the Garden of Allah without much traffic. Kathryn pulled into the residents' parking lot.

"I don't believe in coincidences." Kathryn started counting off with her fingers as they walked down the gravel path. "I've got some debutante upstart trying to worm her way into my life. Meanwhile, from out of the blue, I've got Walter Winchell inviting me to the Polo Lounge because he's been coerced by Leilah, who's hell-bent on getting her client cards back from you. These are not random events."

A party was in full swing at Lucius Beebe's villa. He and Charles were in town, finalizing their permanent move to Nevada. Prohibition-era jazz music floated across the courtyard. "Everything Is Hotsy-Totsy Now" blasted through the open door as they walked past. Gwendolyn was pleased to see Marcus dancing with Natalie Schafer, an actress who'd been floating in and out of the Garden for years.

"Shall we go in?" Gwendolyn asked the girls.

Kathryn shook her head. "You promised me a root beer float."

They were inside Gwendolyn's villa, pulling off hats and gloves and raiding Gwendolyn's icebox when Doris said, "Let's be logical about this. Winchell and Leilah know each other. Also, Winchell and Ruby know each other."

"All Winchell said was that Ruby's reputation preceded her."

"But there is a possible connection," Gwendolyn pointed out. "So if Ruby and Winchell know each other, it's possible he told her where Leilah's cards are."

"I told Winchell that Gwennie burned them," Kathryn said, "so even if he did, as far as she's aware, they don't exist anymore."

Gwendolyn scooped out a ball of vanilla ice cream and let it plop into a tall glass. "But I didn't burn them."

"Nobody knows that except us," Kathryn said.

"And Zap," Doris added. "But he wouldn't have blabbed, would he?"

"I don't think so."

Gwendolyn knew it was time to confess what she'd discovered a few nights ago after the first going-away party at Lucius and Charles' villa. It'd started as "just a few quiet drinks" but of course went the way of every "just a few quiet drinks" at the Garden.

Before she knew it, two dozen people had appeared, champagne was flowing like the Colorado River, and someone nearly broke their dentures on the diving board.

Gwendolyn stumbled home sometime around midnight, but she didn't feel sleepy. Instead, curiosity rose inside her. She hadn't looked at Leilah's cards since the day Doris produced them. It all seemed so sordid and she didn't want to know whose names appeared there. But sitting on her sofa, lightheaded from French champagne, she sensed an overwhelming tug pulling at her.

She opened up *Magnificent Obsession* and flipped through the cards, one by one.

Virtually every name was familiar. If she hadn't served them as the Cocoanut Grove's cigarette girl, she'd encountered them at Mocambo or the Trocadero, or volunteered alongside them at the Hollywood Canteen.

Every studio head was there, and their second-in-command, and often their heads of publicity, casting, and distribution. And their lawyers. And their bankers. And even their former bootleggers-turned-restaurateurs.

But it was the movie stars that shocked Gwendolyn. Any of them could snap their fingers, and women would come running with their skirts flapping over their heads.

And then she came to the card at the very bottom of the pile, and suddenly she wished she hadn't.

ARTURO ZAPARELLI

She pictured Mr. Zaparelli's well-fed face and laughing eyes, and couldn't imagine him in the sort of place Marcus had described.

"What do you mean, you don't think Zap would blab?" Kathryn asked.

Gwendolyn hollowed out two more scoops and returned the ice cream to the Frigidaire. She told the girls to wait as she went to her bedroom and pulled Leilah's cards from behind her headboard. "Until the other night, I'd never looked through them." She picked up the floats and led the other two into her living room.

"*Never*?" Doris asked. "I've been dying to take a gander at those things!"

"I was worried that I might not be able to look any of these guys in the eye again."

"Is my revered boss there?" Doris asked.

Harry Cohn was a rough-talking risk-taker who ran his domain as a dictatorship Mussolini would have admired. Gwendolyn flipped to the Cs and held up Cohn's card. She laid the pack in front of Kathryn and told her to look at the last card.

Kathryn's mouth formed a perfect O when she read the name written across the top. "Does Zap know this?"

"Not that I know of. Jump back to the Ws."

Doris peered over Kathryn's shoulder and then giggled when Kathryn arrived at Wilkerson's card.

Kathryn skimmed the information listed below his name. "I'm surprised he didn't go more often."

"Look at the next one," Gwendolyn told her.

Kathryn stared at the card for a moment. "Winchell, huh? These men would die if someone made them public."

"Someone like Leilah?"

"Or Ruby."

Gwendolyn had barely slept the night she went through Leilah's cards. Now that she knew who was involved, she could see how revealing them could cause a scandal as big as the Fatty Arbuckle trial or the William Desmond Taylor murder. Those incidents had outraged the moralists and led to the Hays Code, which most film industry folk considered another word for censorship.

"And get a load of this." Gwendolyn took the cards from Kathryn and flicked back to the Cs. She withdrew one from the pack and held it up: Mickey Cohen.

Kathryn flopped back onto the sofa. "No wonder Leilah's so desperate."

"Can you imagine what Ruby would do with them?"

Gwendolyn took the cards from Kathryn. "Which is why I think we should burn the whole lot. Tonight."

"That's a drastic move, Gwennie," Doris warned.

"You really need to think about this," Kathryn added.

Gwendolyn pulled out Wilkerson's card and waved it in the air. "Depending on which way things play out, it could also spell the end of the *Hollywood Reporter*."

Kathryn nodded soberly. "Arlene made a valid point about destroying evidence, especially with Leilah's trial coming up, but so many lives could be damaged should this come out."

The three of them stood in silence while "Button Up Your Overcoat" floated in from Lucius' party.

"I have some brandy," Doris said, "if you want to be sure they get good and toasted."

Gwendolyn had some in her cupboard.

They moved back to the kitchen, where Gwendolyn tossed the cards, one by one, into her sink. When she got to Zap's father, she wondered if she should hold onto it, just in case.

At the last moment, she decided, *Nah*, and dropped Mr. Zaparelli's card onto the top of the pile. She unscrewed the brandy bottle; the tang of Courvoisier filled her nose. She held the bottle almost horizontally, but not quite.

"Second thoughts?" Kathryn whispered.

The bottle didn't move. "I've tried not to judge," Gwendolyn said. "Men will be men, and all that. It's just that some of them pretend they're such moral pillars of integrity."

Doris grunted. "If there's one thing I've learned since I moved here, it's that those words are more malleable in Hollywood than they are elsewhere."

The bottle grew heavy; Gwendolyn struggled to keep it above the cards.

Kathryn sighed. "Personally, I think if the menfolk don't want to be caught out, then they shouldn't frequent places like that." She took the bottle from Gwendolyn and returned it to the counter. "But even I wouldn't burn these things. We need to be smart."

Relief swamped Gwendolyn as she collected up the cards and juggled them back into a neat pile. "So I'm not being a coward?"

"Having leverage is smart. What bothers me is Ruby knows who my father is, and that he's in Sing Sing."

"If Ruby can find out, so can Winchell."

"Or worse—that Ruby would *tell* Winchell."

"I thought you said there's no love lost between those two," Doris said.

"That's the impression I got, but I wouldn't put anything past either of them."

Gwendolyn sorted through the cards until she came to the one she was looking for: *Arturo Zaparelli.*

"In this town," she murmured, "it's best not to put anything past anybody."

CHAPTER 38

Marcus read the piece of paper in his hand: *General Service Studios, 1040 N. Las Palmas Ave, Hollywood.*

"Christ," he muttered, "could it sound any more boring?"

He knew he should probably drive there; this was his first day on *The Lone Ranger*, after all. But when he looked up the address, he saw that he could walk. Now that he was no longer free to drive down to the ocean for his beach runs, it was a good way to get some exercise.

Plus, he had another reason to walk the twenty-odd blocks along Santa Monica Boulevard. En route, tucked away behind the Formosa Café, were the offices of Dudley Hartman, private investigator for hire.

Marcus had only spoken to him over the telephone, and was vaguely disappointed that he lacked the bourbon-ripened growl of Bogart's Sam Spade. In fact, the guy sounded so cheery and chipper that he could have voiced a rascally raccoon for Disney. But he'd come recommended by his new neighbor, a film editor at Columbia whose deadbeat husband had failed to pay eighteen months' alimony until Hartman tracked him down in freshly rechristened Truth or Consequences, New Mexico.

It was only twenty past eight when Marcus arrived at the guy's office. The front door of the converted bungalow was open and the sign in the window lit with a single bulb.

Inside, the place smelled of pine-scented Air Wick, which probably helped mask the smell of the café next door. Hartman was in his fifties, thinning on top, thickening in the middle, nattily dressed in a tie, collar, and jacket as though he'd come from a court appearance.

"I'm Marcus Adler. We spoke on the phone last week about a missing person."

"Of course." Hartman motioned for Marcus to take the nearest of two seats in front of his desk.

"I was literally passing by and was wondering if you had any news."

"As a matter of fact, I do." He waited until Marcus was settled in the chair. "Mister Adler, locating people is only difficult when they don't want to be traced." He offered up a jovial smile that wouldn't have been out of place in *Bambi*. "Your Mister Trenton is not such a person."

Marcus ran a finger along the crease in his pants. "Meaning?"

"He's in a facility outside Santa Barbara."

Just a couple of hours up the road? "What kind of facility?"

"If I may ask, what is your relationship with Mister Trenton?"

Marcus guessed that Hartman had pounded his portion of the seedier side of the street, but his round, pink face seemed unaffected. Still, Marcus wasn't sure what sort of reaction he'd get if he revealed the full nature of his relationship with Oliver.

"He's one of my best pals. Why?"

"Mister Trenton is in a sanatorium."

Sweat collected in Marcus' underarms. "He's in a nuthouse?"

"It's the sort of place where people check in to . . . ," Hartman rotated his hands as he struggled to summon an upbeat slant to the news he had to deliver, "get back on their feet."

"I'd prefer you just give it to me straight."

"Your pal is a dope fiend."

Marcus turned away. On the opposite wall was a silver pistol mounted onto a stained wooden frame. Underneath it was branded in rough letters

GENE AUTRY
"In Old Santa Fe" (1934)

"That was the first gun Gene used on-screen," Hartman said. "He gave it to me when I did a job for him a few years back."

"Even Gene Autry has problems."

"We've all got our secrets."

"I start a new job today. I'm going to be writing for *The Lone Ranger*."

"Hi ho, Silver, huh?" Marcus heard the guy breathe out. "If you want my advice, get on with your life and forget about your friend. These dope-fiend cases, they rarely have a happy ending."

Marcus kept his eyes on the pistol. "Surely some of them turn out all right."

"I spoke to the head doctor there, and also the nurse in charge of his ward. He's in a bad way. He'll only get better if he wants to."

If.

Marcus faced the guy again. "What's this place called?"

"I'd strongly discourage you from going to visit him. The nurse said—"

"I'll feel better if I knew where he was, that's all."

Hartman flipped open a folder. "It's called Cloverleaf Sanatorium."

Sounds peaceful. "Outside Santa Barbara, you said? Okay. Well. Thank you for your efforts."

"Good luck with your new job, Mister Adler."

Marcus stumbled out into the thin morning sunshine. It wasn't warm yet but it would be soon. He had fifteen minutes to get to Boring Generic Studios, and was considering calling in sick.

The last thing he felt like doing was sitting down to a typewriter to compose a scene where the Lone Ranger lassoes some grimacing bad guy and hauls him off to the local jailhouse.

The morning traffic whizzed by him, horns honking, paperboys calling to drivers at red lights. Somewhere off in the distance, an ambulance siren screamed.

Forget about your friend.

Marcus knew Hartman was right. Chases on horseback and scatterbrained gold miners with tattered maps were better than sitting around the Garden waiting for everybody else to get home.

He headed toward Las Palmas Avenue. "But I'll be damned if I'm going to forget about him."

* * *

The *Lone Ranger*'s production offices were painted a calming light desert orange and had a linoleum floor whose shade of eucalyptus Anson joked was "horse-hockey green." Posters featuring Clayton Moore and Jay Silverheels in heroic poses adorned the walls, but when Anson showed Marcus to his own office, he said Marcus was free to replace them with anything he wanted.

"I think it's ironic that you've ended up here," Anson said with a lopsided grin.

The word I'd have used was 'depressing.' "How come?"

"Some people think your best movie was *Free Leningrad!* But for my money, it's *William Tell.* What a terrific picture!"

"Why is that ironic?"

"Have you seen our show?"

"I told you: I don't own a television set."

"Our theme tune. It's the *William Tell* Overture! It's like you belong here, right?" Anson beamed his eager-beaver face at Marcus until he saw how little of an impact he'd made. "So this'll be your office."

The corner office Anson had assigned him was larger than the one Marcus had at MGM. Windows on two sides let in the early summer light, and in front of the soundstage across the way, a crew member was pushing a costume rack past a hand-lettered sign that read "The George Burns and Gracie Allen Show." Marcus looked at it wistfully.

"Let's go to our projection room," Anson said. "I'll set you up with a bunch of episodes so you can get the feel of it."

Sounds tedious. "Sounds good."

The screening room had sixteen seats in two rows of eight. It was a fraction of the size of MGM's.

How about you stop comparing this place to your old life? You can like it or lump it or leave it, but at least give it a fair shake before you abandon ship. It's not as though anybody is sitting at home waiting for you.

A few minutes later, Anson reappeared with paper and pens so Marcus could take notes. He'd gathered the first three episodes of season one and the six latest episodes of the current season.

As he turned to go, Marcus called him back and pointed to his new boss's wooden leg. "You seem to be doing okay."

Anson clenched his jaw. "It was an infection. Pretty bad. They've got this new class of antibiotics. The nurse called it 'Superman in a hypodermic.'"

"Did it save the day?"

Anson see-sawed his hand. "Jury's still out." He left Marcus alone in the screening room.

By the end of the fourth episode, Marcus had grasped the formula. Open with the Lone Ranger and Tonto; cut to the bad guys discussing their evil plot; discover the vital clue to undo the villains; if possible throw in a damsel in distress, a horse chase, a daring stunt and/or rope trick; end with a bravery-wins-out battle. It was kiddie stuff compared to the complex movie plots he was used to at MGM.

By the fifth episode, Marcus' mind started to wander. Did Oliver have his own room? What did he do all day? Did they make him lie on a sofa with a psychoanalyst? The word *sanatorium* conjured sadistic nurses in starched uniforms ignoring pleas for sympathy.

The image of Oliver tied down with straps was too much. Marcus forced himself to watch the screen, where a stagecoach was hurtling through the desert, hijacked by an outlaw called Knife Norton. All the bad guys had names like that: Blackie Kane, Butch Cavendish, and Marcus' favorite: Baron Von Baden.

Surely I can do better than this.

A couple of hours later, Anson returned to the screening room and fell into the seat next to Marcus. "How'd you get on?"

"I've got an idea I think you'll like."

"Shoot."

"How about we give Tonto a backstory? The two of them return to the village where Tonto nursed the Lone Ranger back to health. While they're there, a posse attacks. It's like history repeating itself, only this time Tonto has taught his tribesmen how to fire—"

Anson held up his hand. "Sounds great. Have it on my desk by Wednesday lunchtime."

"It'll only take a few hours."

"To write a whole episode?"

"I'm talking about the movie outline," Marcus said. "You brought me on board to write a feature."

"Yeah, but to get the hang of things, I need you to write some episodes."

"That's not what you said. It's not what I agreed to."

Anson gestured toward the television set. "You've seen the show. Come on, you can write this stuff in your sleep."

You better believe I could. Marcus jumped to his feet. "I'm here under false pretenses. And I'm *this* close to telling you to shove your hi-ho-silver up your ass."

"If you sit down, I'll come clean with you."

Anson's admission piqued Marcus' curiosity. He dropped to his seat.

"Fact of the matter is, I don't have an infection." Anson glanced back toward the screening room door. "I've got me a whole pile of diabetes."

"How bad?"

Anson sighed. "Prognosis: Screwed nine ways to November. Evidently, planning my fortieth birthday party is likely to be a waste of time."

"That's a tough break."

Anson slumped in his seat and started rubbing the nub where his stump met his wooden leg. "I don't know how much longer I can wear this thing."

"Don't, then. If your wooden leg aggravates it, come in on—"

"On crutches?" Anson groaned. "And have to ignore the looks of pity while they wonder if I can do the job? No thanks."

"But what if you can't?" It felt cruel to ask, but necessary.

Anson didn't reply for the longest time. "That episode you mentioned, with Tonto's backstory, if you can get it to me by lunchtime on Wednesday, I can fine-tune it before I hand it over to the production department on Thursday. That gives them three days until they start filming."

"The show I start writing today will go into production next Monday?"

"And will air two weeks after that. Not like the good old days when we could spend months getting a script right, huh?"

The image of Oliver stretched out on a nuthouse bunk in a padded room swam through Marcus' mind, only it wasn't Oliver's face he saw, but his own. *I've been recruited to replace my own boss.*

CHAPTER 39

The marriage of Elizabeth Taylor and Conrad Hilton Jr. had been the topic of cocktail chatter for months. Taylor had been around since *National Velvet*, but she was now blossoming into a ravishing beauty. Even though studio moguls liked to keep their sex symbols unattached, it could hardly have surprised L.B. Mayer that Taylor would catch the eye of a prominent bachelor—and there was no bachelor in America more prominent than the son of its most famous hotelier.

Taylor was only eighteen and Gwendolyn couldn't see why a rich, beautiful movie star would want to give up her independence, even to a dashing heir whose fortune dwarfed her own. But that was between Taylor and Hilton. What interested Gwendolyn most was The Dress.

Such was the focus on Taylor's wedding dress that columnists across the nation had started to refer to it in capital letters. The facts and figures poured from MGM's PR department:

Twenty-five yards of shell-white satin! Fifteen-yard train! Twenty-inch waist! MGM designer Helen Rose was in charge! The $1,500 price tag was Mayer's gift! The bugle bead and seed pearl detailing took fifteen people three months to complete!

Gwendolyn found that last part hard to swallow, but it did pique her curiosity so that by the time the wedding day arrived in May, Gwendolyn decided she had to see The Dress for herself. Kathryn scored an invite, but Gwendolyn's only opportunity was to wait outside the Church of the Good Shepherd in Beverly Hills with the rest of the hoi polloi.

When Gwendolyn stepped off the bus and spotted hundreds of onlookers spilled across the steps and front lawn, she wondered if she'd even get close enough. She hung back. Eventually, some people were peeling away and heading back to their cars, while others were getting sick of being sardined into the areas cordoned off by the police and sought shade under the trees.

Gwendolyn spotted a gap near the top of the stairs that would offer her an uninterrupted view of The Dress as the couple exited. She was more than halfway there when a familiar face caught her attention. Horton Tattler was on the other side of the steps, several people in from the perimeter.

It pleased Gwendolyn enormously that the success of her Sunset Boulevard perfume had helped Horton back on his feet. He no longer lived in a ratty apartment, and now rented a place at the Brevoort residential hotel near Vine Street. She suspected that he rather enjoyed living in a place now slightly infamous as a former address of the Black Dahlia.

She gently elbowed her way to the edge of the crowd. As she scuttled across the steps, she waved at him until she caught his eye. His quietly mournful expression contrasted sharply with the enthusiasm permeating the lookie-loos.

She greeted him with a kiss to the cheek. "Yours is one face I wouldn't have expected to see today."

"There was a time when all the men in the wedding party would have asked me to fit them for tuxedos."

Gwendolyn had forgotten the heights he'd reached long before she met his son. It was no wonder he looked like someone just ran over his dog.

"So why are you here?" she asked.

"Schadenfreude, I guess."

The church bells pealed, and a surge of excitement rippled over the throng. The press photographers and newsreel cameramen jostled for position at the bottom of the steps as the white doors opened and the couple emerged. Hilton looked handsome in his one-button morning suit but his bride appeared slightly overwhelmed by the tumult around her.

Gwendolyn strained to see the beading. A line of creamy bugle beads contouring Taylor's décolletage caught the sun and glittered like stars. The Dress wasn't nearly as elaborate as she'd imagined. Its off-the-shoulder neckline tightened into a tiny waist, then flared out into a full skirt, giving the bride a darling silhouette.

The couple lingered at the top of the stairs long enough for the photographers to capture the moment, then were hustled into a waiting car. The crowd began dispersing as soon as the limo was out of sight. Gwendolyn turned to Horton.

He'd thrust his hands into his pockets and quietly studied his shoes.

"Nothing good can come from pining for the past," she told him.

"Today reminds me of Eleanor Boardman's wedding to King Vidor. What an exciting week that was. We had so many orders for custom-made tuxedos that we had to hire three extra—"

"Wasn't that supposed to be a double wedding with Garbo and Gilbert, only Garbo didn't show?"

Horton blinked at her.

"And later, Mayer found Gilbert crying his heart out, and told him to sleep with Garbo but don't marry her, so Gilbert punched Mayer in the face, and Mayer yelled, 'I will destroy you!' *That's* the wedding you're mooning over?"

He kicked a pebble off the sidewalk and onto the road. "Mooning is an overstatement."

"It's not worth romanticizing." She hooked arms with him. "I'm taking you to lunch. Your choice, but it has to be close." She lifted a foot to show her three-inch heel.

* * *

A line of brown leather booths ran down the middle of Nate 'n Al's delicatessen, with counter service along the side and a glass takeout display filled with cream cheese, tuna salad, and blintzes. The whole place smelled of pickles, brisket, and short ribs.

Gwendolyn and Horton ordered pastrami with the works from the middle-aged waitress in an unflattering red-checked uniform. An abandoned *Los Angeles Examiner* in the booth next door caught Horton's eye. He pointed to it. "Did you see the big news?"

MISTER MADAM HANGS HIMSELF IN JAIL

Gwendolyn craned forward to see the photo. "That's Clem O'Roarke!"

"Tore his bed sheet into strips and tied a noose. Good riddance, I say."

"I assumed he was out on bail."

"My neighbor runs the mail room at Warners. He told me that studio's a rat's nest of rumors lately. You know those client cards everybody's been in a flap over? When they didn't surface, Leilah went to the DA." He ran his thumbnail across his neck.

"She double-crossed her own husband?"

"Musta been quite a pile of goods she had on him. That guy's every bit as crooked as the LAPD."

The waitress arrived with a bowl of miniature pickles. Gwendolyn selected a pale yellow one and bit into it. "You don't know what some people are capable of until they're cornered, huh?"

"I was reading the *Hollywood Reporter* the other day."

"You still read the trades?"

"When I'm feeling nostalgic," Horton admitted. "I see they've got a new columnist."

"Yes, and Kathryn's none too happy about it."

"Nor should she be. I wouldn't want Otis Courtland's daughter within a hundred miles of me."

"You know Ruby's father?"

Horton's mouth curdled into a scowl. "He started a tailoring business on the Lower East Side around the same time I did. I came west when *The Jazz Singer* hit big, but he stayed and cultivated the swanky trade. It was the twenties, so everybody had plenty of dough to throw around on three-piece suits and tuxes. By the time the stock market crashed, he had fifteen stores over the tri-state area. He was smart with his money, all cash, no credit, so he survived the Depression better than most. By the time the war came along, he was in the best position to contract with the military to make uniforms."

"Isn't that what you did?"

Their pastrami sandwiches arrived, steaming. Horton stared at his. "He amassed the fortune I should've made by hogging all the high-quality cotton and wool, leaving people like me with the shoddy stuff. It gave my product a second-rate reputation, so the military went to him more and more. I had the same setup costs but had to be thankful for a fraction of the business."

"So if he'd played fair—"

"It was called the war effort. We were supposed to be all pulling together to beat the Nazis, remember? Otis was only in it for himself." Horton bit into his pastrami like a snarling dog would a postman. "The heartless bastard lowballed me on my machinery after I was forced into bankruptcy. Pennies on the dollar. Goddamned heartless son of a bitch in heat."

Gwendolyn had never heard Horton swear. "So what can you tell me about his daughter, Ruby?"

"You mean apart from the fact she's a cheap slut with a thing for colored men in uniform?"

Gwendolyn laid her chin on her left palm. Her days at the Cocoanut Grove had come into her thoughts more and more often lately. Every night she'd observe the behavior of some of the richest men in the country. They'd be all charm and savoir-faire when they walked in, but pour half a dozen scotches down their gullets, and they'd turn into letches. And now she owned a store where their wives shopped with *I'm-sorry-please-forgive-me* money.

"The ways of the well-heeled often astound me," she told Horton. "Why do they think the rules don't apply to them?"

"Ah, but that turned out to be his undoing."

"Is this a comeuppance story?"

"By the end of the war, Courtland was richer than Solomon, so of course his daughter became spoiled—and loose. Some dowager died and her enormous apartment came on the market. Walter Winchell was desperate for it, but Courtland was, too. So they set him up."

"Setting up Winchell takes chutzpah."

"As daddy was closing the deal, Little Miss Chip Off the Old Block was entertaining him at the Algonquin."

"I bet he went to town in his column."

"That's where they miscalculated. They figured he couldn't say anything considering he was married, but they never figured Walt was happy to bide his time."

"Walt? You sound like you know him."

"He was a big client of mine back in the day. Not for the formal stuff, but most of his casual wear."

"So you're friends?"

"In a way." Horton pushed strands of pastrami around with his fork. "If I'm going to judge someone, I'll do it by their actions. Walt's one of the few people who hasn't treated me any differently since my luck went kaput. We had drinks just the other day. He's in town for the big wedding."

Gwendolyn wished Kathryn was hearing all this. "There's something you ought to know."

He looked up.

"Those client cards of Leilah O'Roarke that everyone's talking about? She forced Winchell to help her track them down."

"Nobody forces Walt to do anything he doesn't want to."

"His name was on one of them."

Horton seemed to roll the news around in his head like a pair of dice. "How would you know that?"

"Remember the box of Linc's stuff you brought to me? Leilah's cards were hidden inside."

"Wait, so *my son* had them?"

"He did, and Leilah had her suspicions. She tried to bully me into handing them over, only I didn't know I had them at the time. So then she arranged for my store and then my home to be burgled."

Horton stared at Gwendolyn for a moment, then wiped his paper napkin across his face. "My place has been broken into as well."

Gwendolyn glanced around to see if anybody was paying attention. "I suspect her goons were watching the day you delivered that box to my store."

"Oh, my dear, I'm so very sorry you got dragged into all this. I just assumed Linc sent you a bunch of mementos. I had no idea—"

"Neither did I, but Leilah's trial is coming up. She's double-crossed her own husband, for crying out loud."

"How can I help?"

"Do you think maybe Winchell might be willing to do you a favor?"

"He might. But what's in it for him?"

"What if I gave him his card?"

Horton gave a weary snort. "Leilah must have put the fear of God into him."

An idea started to bloom. "What if we sweeten the pie by taking down Ruby Courtland, too?"

"Now you're talking."

"How often does Winchell come to LA?"

"More than he used to." Horton raised his eyebrows comically high. "Between you and me, he's been worrying about Kathryn ever since her show hit it big." Much had been made in the trade press when *Window on Hollywood* broke into the top ten prime-time radio shows. "A couple of years back, he wouldn't have traveled out here for a wedding. Katharine Hepburn or Greer Garson, perhaps, but never for some starlet."

"And now?"

"It's only May and this is his third trip."

Gwendolyn signaled the waitress for their check. "If we can find a way to be rid of both Leilah and Ruby—"

"Killing two birds with one stone is Walter Winchell's favorite blood sport."

CHAPTER 40

Kathryn stood on the wings of NBC stage number two and felt the tingle of nervousness kick in. She turned to Fanny Brice.

"Do you get nervous before going on?"

"Used to." Fanny pulled at the enormous ribbon in her hair until she was satisfied. She'd shown up for her special-guest spot in costume: soft pink baby-doll dress with tiny white polka dots, matching oversized hair bow, black Mary Janes and white ankle socks. "But then it dawned on me that I knew what I was doing. I told myself, 'You're a professional, so what are you panicking for?' After that, *meh*."

"You go all out to stay in character, don't you?"

Fanny pulled the sides of her dress wide apart. "Studio audiences expect to see Snooks, but if I show up as myself, they don't laugh so much. I lose the flow, and that ain't so good. I put on the getup and everybody's happy — me, the audience, the sponsors." She nudged Kathryn with an elbow. "But you've been at this radio thing long enough to know that it's all for show. I may be the one in a goofy dress, but I'm sure you have a character."

"I try to be myself. I think audiences appreciate authen—"

"Authenticity, yeah, yeah, I know. But there must be a version of Kathryn Massey that's just for your audience. You gotta hold back, otherwise that well's gonna run dry as the Mojave. And besides, it's all showbiz. Ain't we all putting on an act when we step outside our front door?"

This wasn't the sort of conversation Kathryn liked to have before going on air. She preferred to keep the atmosphere light and bubbly so that when she walked out onstage, the champagne ambiance flowed into the show. And she especially needed someone to buoy her spirits right now. After learning that her last sponsor knew of her father's incarceration, she decided it was only fair that her current one should know, too. Especially seeing as how she was sleeping with him.

It was inevitable, really. He was handsome, stylish, well read, and not at all the man she took him for years ago. Sleeping with her sponsor was hardly the most ethical thing to do, but she could count on one hand the number of genuinely decent, romantically available guys she had met in Hollywood. As far as she was concerned, there was a lot to be said for a guy who could mend his ways when he realized life was slapping him across the face.

Plus, he was pretty damn good in the sack. He took his time; he was considerate of her needs over his; and he curled up with her afterwards.

A guy like that deserved to know about Thomas Danford, but telling him was a tall order. Kathryn planned to lower the boom tonight after the show, but meanwhile, it was fifty minutes to airtime. There'd be enough time later to get nervous about that.

"Sorry I'm late!" Humphrey Bogart was sweaty and his tie was askew. "I know you said call time was one hour, but Junior started puking—"

Kathryn waved him quiet. "We've still got fifty minutes. Have you met Baby Snooks?"

Fanny did a little-girl curtsy and grabbed Bogie's necktie and straightened it. "How did your missus let you outta thuh house looking like that?"

Bogie glanced at Kathryn. "Speaking of the missus, I've got a scoop for you. Warners is letting her out of her contract."

"I bet that'll cost a pretty penny," Kathryn said.

"Fifty grand. They're taking half her future earnings until she pays it off."

Last month MGM let Judy Garland go, and this month Warners was releasing Lauren Bacall. It was like they were all being put out to pasture.

Animated chatter began to fill the auditorium as the audience took their seats. Kathryn let Bogie and Fanny run through the skit Fanny had written in which Bogie played Snooks' father, a vindictive screenwriter. The joke was that he'd played one in his latest movie, *In a Lonely Place*. Ordinarily, Bogie wouldn't parody a movie that hadn't fared well at the box office, but Kathryn knew he was proud of his work in it.

She scanned the audience for three specific members; she'd decided it was time to introduce her mother to Leo. She knew enough about men to know that introducing them to family was a good litmus test. She was prepared for him to start backing off, but he was all for it. "Mothers love me!

Just in case, she'd asked Gwendolyn to come along. Francine had always approved of her, especially now that she was a successful businesswoman. If Leo passed the mother test, she'd tell him about Thomas Danford and Sing Sing.

Kathryn found Gwennie and Francine in the fifth row, half a dozen seats in from the right. She was still looking for Leo when her stage manager tapped her elbow and told her fifteen minutes to air.

Spirited applause greeted her when she walked out on stage. Although the lights blinded her to everything beyond the first few rows, she acted as though she could see everyone. She put on her professional smile and waved at the audience. *Maybe Fanny's right – we're all acting.*

She stepped in front of her microphone. "Hello, everyone! And welcome! Now, listen up, ladies and gentlemen. You need to be extra nice to me this evening because my mom's in the audience. If you start throwing tomatoes at me, you'll have to answer to her!"

This brought a huge laugh.

"And now I want to introduce my first guest. She's a shy little tyke, so you're going to have to clap extra loudly to coax her out here. Ladies and gentlemen, Miss Baby Snooks!"

* * *

Fanny and Bogie landed every joke to booming laughter. When Bogie lost his place in the middle of their sketch, the crowd lapped it up. Afterwards, when he said yes to Kathryn's offer of a post-show drink in her dressing room, he was as relaxed and charming as she hoped he'd be when Gwendolyn and Francine walked in. When Kathryn introduced her mother, Francine beamed.

By the time he left, Francine was giddy as a sophomore at her first school dance, so when Leo proposed the four of them go out for dinner, Francine accepted immediately. Kathryn suggested Nickodell a few blocks away, and the four of them piled into his Cadillac.

Although Kathryn made out like she'd randomly selected Nickodell, Gwennie knew her choice was deliberate.

Several weeks after the Taylor-Hilton wedding, Horton called Gwendolyn to tell her Winchell was very interested to hear that Leilah's cards still existed, but was cagey about his next visit to Los Angeles. When Horton pressed him for specifics, Winchell admitted that he was getting together with Jack Webb in early July, adding how Webb liked to down a few post-show drinks at Nickodell.

It stood across the street from Paramount and RKO, extending nearly a whole block. It was notorious as a place where studio personnel could swill as many stiff drinks as it took to get them through an afternoon of endless retakes.

The maître d' showed them to the last open table. Like most steakhouses, Nickodell was fitted out with brown leather booths whose low backs facilitated the Hollywood institutions of table-hopping, schmoozing, and flirting.

Their waiter was dropping off a second round when a tremor of anticipation circulated down the long dining hall. Kathryn sensed a celebrity-spotting, but she had her back to the entrance.

"Kathryn, honey?" Gwendolyn swirled the ice cubes in her gin fizz while she made with the Clara Bow eyes, directing them toward the bar.

"It's Walter Winchell!" Francine exclaimed. "But who's that with him? The one without the hat."

"Jack Webb," Gwendolyn said. "He stars in *Dragnet*."

Francine looked unimpressed. Kathryn swallowed her excitement.

Leo tilted forward. "*Dragnet* delivers a huge audience to your daughter's show. It's one of the reasons *Window on Hollywood* is such a success."

"I'd have thought my daughter was the reason for her show's success."

Francine seldom praised her daughter, and Kathryn savored this rare moment. She turned to Leo. *All right, Mister Mothers Love Me, show us what you've got.*

"I said it's *one* of the reasons; all the others have everything to do with your remarkable daughter. Sponsoring her program is the best decision we could have made."

Francine's pressed lips softened into a mollified smile. As far as Kathryn was concerned, that counted as a victory. She ached to turn around. "I've only met Jack once—the night my show kicked off. He's usually on stage when I'm leaving the studio. I really ought to go up and say hello."

"I'd love a chance to meet him," Gwendolyn said.

Kathryn turned to her mother. "We'll make it quick."

Leo slid out of the booth to make way for Kathryn. "Don't worry about us," he said. "I've got a hundred questions for this lovely lady."

Yes, but is she going to blab about my father before I get a chance?

Kathryn and Gwendolyn picked their way to the bar where the golden boy of radio gossip and the golden boy of radio drama pretended not to notice that half the eyes in the place were trained on them. They sat at the bar like a couple of regular Joes knocking back a round of stingers after a day at the savings and loan.

Halfway there, Gwendolyn tugged at Kathryn's wrist.

"Just to be clear, you still need me to be a decoy, right? You want me to distract Webb while you drill Winchell?"

Kathryn waved to Ann Miller, who was filming *Two Tickets to Broadway* at RKO. "I owe you for this," she told Gwendolyn through a controlled smile. *Look at me – acting again.* "If you're stuck for conversation, tell Webb you saw a preview of *Sunset Boulevard* and you thought he was great as Artie. Okay? Chin up, chest out."

Gwendolyn complied. Kathryn was impressed; her new push-up bra from Fredrick's of Hollywood enhanced her clingy dress and plunging neckline.

The men feigned surprise when the women stepped into their periphery. A round of introductions was followed by a perfunctory exchange of professional admiration. When Gwennie angled away from Winchell, Kathryn took her cue. But before she could say anything, Winchell cut her off.

"You're lucky I'm talking to you."

"Why is that?"

"Rossellini and Bergman were supposed to be *my* exclusive."

Back in May, Kathryn scored a huge story with news that Roberto Rossellini and Ingrid Bergman were married in Mexico by proxy. Landing such a huge scoop meant there'd be ramifications. Louella and Hedda would freeze her out for a while, but she could cope with that. Winchell, on the other hand, was wholly unpredictable.

She took a leaf out of Snook's book and tried the baby-doll approach. "Are you frightfully angry with me?"

"If you'd been in the room when I read your column, I'd have clobbered you with the heaviest frying pan that came to hand."

"I have a hard time picturing you in anybody's kitchen."

The smile hinting at the edges of Winchell's lips helped Kathryn see that he was probably quite a Dapper Dan during his salad days. He clamped the smile down fast. *Ain't we all putting on some sort of act?*

"Come on!" She nudged him like a kid sister. "You'd have done the same."

"That's not the point. Rossellini's agent assured me I had the exclusive."

"Then don't blame me if nobody told Ingrid's agent." She laid a placating hand on his forearm. She doubted he was the touchy-feely type, but she wanted his full attention, which was straying toward Gwendolyn's bosom. "How about I make it up to you?" Those intense eyes darted back to her. "I believe Horton Tattler called."

Winchell pulled a Havana from his inside pocket. He bit the end off and spat it onto the carpet. "You told me she burned those cards."

"I made an assumption I shouldn't have."

Winchell tried to camouflage his interest with a slow, deliberate draw on his cigar. He drained the rest of his stinger and motioned to the bartender. "Being careless with your facts can get you into trouble."

"Turns out she lost her nerve at the last moment."

His eyes drifted back to Gwendolyn. "She still has 'em, then?"

Kathryn saw Spencer Tracy bee-lining in their direction. "Uh-huh."

"Might she be willing to give them to me?"

"We had a better idea."

In fact, it was Leo who came up with it. Make a set of fake cards, he suggested, then get word out to Ruby that they're up for grabs. When she tells the world about them, her credibility will be shot to hell and she'll be laughed out of town.

"Better, how?"

From the other side of the room, Ann Miller was hacking a path through the diners toward them, too. "How long will you be in town?"

"As long as I want."

"You know Walter Plunkett, don't you?"

"The costumer?"

"He's giving a party the weekend before Leilah's trial starts. I'll be in need of an escort. There's bound to be tons of people there you'll know."

"Anyone in particular?"

"Ruby Courtland."

"WINCHELL, YOU SON OF A BITCH! WHY DIDN'T YOU TELL ME YOU WERE IN TOWN?"

Spencer Tracy reached out for the edge of the bar to steady himself, but missed. Winchell caught him as he sprawled toward the floor.

Kathryn whispered, "You staying at the Beverly Hills Hotel?" Winchell nodded as he hauled Tracy to his feet and guided him toward a barstool. "I'll be in touch. By the way, the number you want is Bradshaw 9-7071."

"Who's that?"

"Katharine Hepburn. She'll be worried."

CHAPTER 41

It was weeks before Marcus understood that his new job wasn't quite the creative wasteland he'd assumed.

Initially, he battled to conceal his feelings of superiority toward the *Lone Ranger* staff. Then he felt guilty for being so arrogant, so he kept to himself. Sometime during the second week, he ventured out of his office and found that they had him on a pedestal on account of his MGM pedigree. Oliver would have told him to get off his goddamned high horse, so he did, and saw they were a decent bunch, fun in a let's-have-drinks-after-work-on-Friday sort of way.

And just as he allowed himself to relax into the job, Anson suffered what he called a "diabetes attack." Marcus didn't know what that was, but it was severe enough that he asked Marcus to take over his duties until he could recover.

Marcus expected someone to object, but Anson told him, "Just walk in there like it's a done deal, because it is."

The following Monday, Marcus called a staff meeting, told everyone what happened over the weekend, then assigned new episodes to the writers, told the crew to bring him any questions, and planned out a production schedule for the next month.

"It's business as usual," Marcus told them, "until Anson's back on his feet," then sat in his office and waited for someone to ask who'd died and made him boss.

Not one person did.

Marcus assumed Anson would return soon, but week after week sailed by without any word. So Marcus plugged away, figuring the job out as he went, happy he had the masked man to distract him from missing Oliver so much.

Meanwhile, his feature screenplay had a name now: *The Lone Ranger and the Battle for Spirit Mountain*. It had pretty much written itself.

"See what happens when you get back into the saddle?" Kathryn asked. "Pun intended."

Marcus' response was to trounce her at the game of cribbage they were playing at the time. That summer, cribbage around the pool by torchlight had become everyone's favorite way to spend the balmy evenings.

Late in July, Marcus was playing with Doris, Kathryn, and Bertie when Kathryn peered over her cards. "I'm seeing it with my own eyes and I still don't believe it."

They took in the sight of Trevor Bergin and Melody Hope stepping through the French doors that opened from the back of the Garden's main house onto the pool patio.

Melody waved like a cheerleader. "Not interrupting anything, I hope."

Marcus rose to his feet. "This is a surprise."

Melody smiled sardonically. "Surprised that we're within spitting distance of each other and yet not spitting *at* each other?"

Kathryn laid her cards on the table. "You don't even look drunk."

"I haven't touched a drop in six months," Melody announced. "Isn't that a miracle?"

Marcus hadn't heard from Trevor since the night he did his midnight run, and he hadn't seen Melody since the day he told her Hughes rejected Amelia Earhart. She'd taken it on the chin with a surprisingly genial, "That's showbiz."

"And you?" Kathryn asked Trevor. "You're looking better than I've seen in eons."

"How ironic." He pulled up chairs for the two of them. "Considering."

He flicked his eyes down to Melody's large alligator skin purse. She pulled out a slim book. The title—*Red Channels*—was emblazoned across the top, then *A Report of Communistic Influence in Radio and Television.* Below it was a hand, gloved in red leather, reaching to grasp a microphone. Below the mike, "Published by Counterattack, the newsletter of facts to combat Communism," then a New York address, and the price tag of one dollar.

Marcus locked his eyes on *Red Channels.* "Are we still not done with all that?"

Trevor handed him the book. "Not by a long shot."

Marcus opened to the first page and read a quote by J. Edgar Hoover about how the Communist Party had stopped depending on the printed word as its medium of propaganda and had taken to the air. When he flipped through the pages, what he saw horrified him.

"Dashiell Hammett, Lena Horne, Gypsy Rose Lee, Arthur Miller, Zero Mostel, Dorothy Parker, Edward G. Robinson, Artie Shaw, Orson Welles—" He threw the book onto the table.

Trevor said, "According to this idiotic drivel, they're all Reds and should be blacklisted along with the Hollywood Ten."

"At least three of those people have lived here at the Garden," Gwendolyn remarked.

Kathryn was now flipping through the book. "Writers, actors, singers, film, radio, television. Burl Ives? Oh, come *on*. What is this, the Spanish Inquisition?"

"I'm starting to suspect that's where they're taking their inspiration," Melody said. "You missed a few important ones."

"Who?"

"Trevor Bergin and Melody Hope."

"Holy mother of God! This is terrible!"

"Yes and no," Trevor said. "We've both been offered work."

"But this booklet is tantamount to making the blacklist official," Marcus said.

Melody shrugged as though she couldn't care less. "Ever heard of Cinecittà?"

He shook his head.

"It's just outside of Rome, kind of like the MGM of Italy, if you rolled MGM together with Fox, Warner, and Paramount into one huge back lot. The Fascists built it, but it got blown to smithereens during the war. It's taken the Italians all this time to rebuild it, but now that they have, production has started up. All the studios have their pre-war profits stuck in Europe — they can't transfer the money stateside, so the mountains have to go to Mohammed."

"So, what, you're moving to Italy?" Kathryn asked.

"I'm doing a movie there called *The Cross of Light.* It's about the transition of the Roman Empire to Christianity under the reign of Constantine."

"Who will you be playing?" Marcus asked.

"Constantine."

"The lead?"

Trevor nodded.

"You've beaten them at their own game!" Kathryn exclaimed. "Well done!" She turned to Melody. "And you?"

"I'll be playing a Judean queen called Berenice, who was the mistress of the Roman emperor Titus in an Italian-French coproduction about the building of the Colloseum. Apparently, it took three emperors to finish the job, but they're squeezing it down to just one." She clapped her hands like a gleeful toddler. "We're both on the same flight, staying at the same hotel, working at the same studio, at the same time, and we both speak not one single solitary word of Italian!"

Kathryn announced that this called for champagne, then caught herself, declaring that offering booze to people on the wagon felt inappropriate. Melody said it was fine and to go right ahead because this was worth celebrating.

As Kathryn disappeared into her apartment, Trevor eyed Marcus. "We think you should come with us." It was more than a suggestion.

Marcus flinched. For a moment or two, he'd envied Trevor and Melody, and their *Screw you, Hollywood!* second chance. But he felt like he'd finally gotten the tiniest toehold on life again.

"And do what? Stand around in a toga and yell 'Death to the Christians!'? Besides, I'm working now and, surprisingly, it's not bad."

Kathryn arrived with champagne and orange juice.

As she filled the glasses, Trevor pushed *Red Channels* across the table toward Marcus. "Flip back to the beginning."

Marcus read the first name. "Yardley Aaronson. I don't know him."

Gwendolyn let out a yip.

"Couldn't happen to a nicer bastard," Kathryn said. "But what's he got to do with Nero and togas and death to the Christians?"

Trevor kept his eyes on Marcus. "Read the next name."

MARCUS ADLER, *screenwriter, MGM, William Tell, Free Leningrad! . . .*

All his movies were there, even ones for which he'd received no screen credit. These Counterattack pricks had really done their homework.

Marcus tossed the book onto the table for a second time. "This is more like the French Revolution. It's enough for someone to stand up and say, 'J'accuse!'"

"They must have listed a hundred names," Kathryn said. "Do these blockheads expect us to believe *all* these people are Commies? Well, guess what I'll be writing about in my column tomorrow."

Marcus loved to see the fire of indignation light Kathryn's eyes. He saw it when she was defending Orson's right to make *Citizen Kane*, and when she tried to steer her boss clear of the mob. But he feared the tide was turning.

"And I'll certainly be talking about it on my show," she added. "Do you know how many people tune in to me each week?"

"I do," Marcus countered, "but you might want to run this past your sponsor." *You know, the one you're sleeping with. He's a nice guy, and I like him, but this is where it starts to get sticky.*

"I know Leo's politics; he'll agree with me."

"Yes, but he answers to a boss, who answers to a board, who answers to the stockholders. And they might not be so gung ho about the defense of free speech. Not when it comes to risking profits."

He watched her wrestle with this prickly reality until the fight in her eyes subsided.

"What are you going to do?" Doris asked Marcus.

"I have to show this to Anson." He looked at Trevor. "Where can I get a copy?"

"Keep it. By this time next week, I won't give a flying duck who's saying what about me."

Trevor and Melody declared they had some packing to do, so they promised to write once they were settled in Rome, and left the four of them to stare at their abandoned cribbage board. Kathryn read out more names until Marcus decided he had to tell Anson before everything hit the fan.

"If I'm the one bringing it to his attention," he told the others, "I can shape the way he gets the news."

* * *

Anson Purvis lived in a mock Tudor house on Woodrow Wilson Drive atop the Hollywood Hills. The front porch light was on, as though Anson was expecting company.

When Marcus rang the bell, the German shepherd next door started barking, but Anson didn't respond. He pressed the bell again.

—

364

The dog stopped barking just as the door swung open to reveal Jack Chertok, the *Lone Ranger*'s producer. Jack was older than Marcus by fifteen years. He wore the distracted smile of producers who had fingers in many different pies.

"Hello, Adler," he said darkly.

Marcus looked past Chertok to Anson's sparsely furnished living room. He knew Anson hadn't lived there long, but figured he'd have made an effort to decorate. A lamp shoved in the corner was the only source of light. In the center sat a mismatched pair of occasional chairs.

Chertok opened the door wider. "I thought you were the ambulance."

"What's happened?"

"I'm putting together a new show and wanted Purvis' thoughts." He shook his head. "I was here maybe ten minutes when the guy started sweating like a pig. Then he passed out."

He took Marcus into the bedroom where Anson was sprawled on a double bed, breathing lightly and drained of color. Marcus took his hand—it was cool to the touch. He called out Anson's name, but the guy didn't stir.

"I think he's in a coma. The ambulance said they'd be—"

A siren cut the air. White and blue lights flashed through the Venetian blinds. Marcus told his boss to stay with Anson and dashed outside to guide the two men into the bedroom. They stepped back and watched as Anson was strapped onto a gurney and wheeled outside. By then, neighbors had emerged from their houses to watch the vehicle shoot away, leaving Marcus and Chertok on Anson's front lawn.

"I've never seen anybody in a coma," Chertok said. "I don't even know what causes them."

"Diabetes," Marcus told him. "It's pretty bad."

Chertok ran his hand over the top of his head. "Cheese and crackers! He could have told me."

"I guess he didn't want to alarm you."

Chertok let out a deep sigh. "Hell of a way to find out. Well, congratulations, Adler, you've just been promoted. Meet me in my office tomorrow. Nine o'clock."

"Not so fast."

Marcus led Chertok back inside and over to the solitary lamp, where he pulled *Red Channels* from his jacket.

Chertok leafed through it. "Arthur Miller? Edward R. Murrow? This smacks of the Motion Picture Alliance. God, what a rat's nest."

"Still, we can't ignore it."

"It'll blow over soon enough."

"The Spanish Inquisition lasted three hundred and fifty years," Marcus replied. "Look at the cover. 'A Report of Communistic Influence in Radio *and Television.*' It's no longer just the movies."

"Goddamnit."

"Page three, second name down."

Chertok grunted when he saw the name listed after Aaronson.

"So," Marcus began, but he had to stop. Two months ago, the idea of working for a hokey television show felt like the act of a desperado with no viable options. He hadn't quite realized how much his feelings had changed until he was forced to resign. "Clearly, I cannot continue to work for you."

Chertok slapped the book shut. Marcus expected him to say something, but he didn't.

"You've got a good thing going," Marcus told him. "You don't want to endanger it."

"But the Lone Ranger is as all-American hero as it gets."

"Think about it: Red-baiters maintain that Commies all wear a mask of respectability. And what does the Lone Ranger wear across his face? These Counterattack people see connections everywhere. Why put yourself through—"

"What if there was a way to get around it?"

"How?"

"You have a contract with us, right?"

"Yes."

"Suppose we bring a formal end to it. Nice and legal. Then you go out and start a company."

"What sort of company?"

"I don't care. Props. Costumes. Horses—yeah! That's it. Horse wrangler. Give it a name that's broad and forgettable, like Screen Animal Services. Anything'll do. We bill you for your services but in fact we'll be paying—"

"You'll be leaving yourselves open to a whole mess of trouble."

"Anson showed me the script for *The Lone Ranger and the Battle for Spirit Mountain*. He was vague about who wrote it, but I can see from the look on your face it was you."

Marcus nodded.

"It's a mighty fine piece of work, Adler."

"Thank you, but your horse-wrangling scheme, it's not going to work."

"This whole Red Scare, it's a dung heap on top of a shit hole on top of a cesspit."

"I'm not disagreeing with you, but I've been through this before. It kills me to say it, but those dung beetles on top of the shit hole? They've won."

Marcus found it heartening to see the conflict in Chertok's eye, but he waited for the skirmish to evolve into indignation, and then sag into resignation. He raised his hand to shake Marcus' with a firm grip. "I'm sorry, Adler. I wish there was a way around it."

Marcus thanked him and returned to his car. Through the gap in a pair of cypress pines, the lights of the San Fernando Valley glinted like fireflies.

That's the problem with this place. Klieg lights, searchlights, neon lights, sunlight, key lights. He pulled onto Mulholland, then turned left onto Laurel Canyon Boulevard, where the road banked steeply down and down and down. *So much damned light. It's enough to blind a person.*

CHAPTER 42

When Winchell's black limo pulled up outside the Garden of Allah, it took Gwendolyn a moment to realize that neither he nor his chauffeur had any intention of doing the gentlemanly thing.

She opened the door herself and climbed in.

Winchell was dressed in a cream linen suit, with a crimson carnation boutonniere and a meticulously matched silk tie. He nodded hello and told the driver to turn up Laurel Canyon.

"You have the cards with you?" he asked.

Gwendolyn tapped her purse. "Right here."

"And what about mine?"

She pulled it out and placed it in his palm. He slid it into his jacket and kept his gaze on the passing view.

Gwendolyn wasn't sure if she should attempt idle chitchat. She wasn't supposed to be here. She was *supposed* to be back at the Garden working on Kathryn's gown for Bette's *All About Eve* premiere. Sewing its six petticoats required the whole weekend, but then last night Kathryn twisted her ankle dancing with Gene Kelly at a party for *Summer Stock*. So now Kathryn was at home with her leg up, and Gwendolyn was sitting in a limo next to Walter Winchell.

As the driver rounded the corner onto Wonderland Avenue, she couldn't bear the silence any longer. "Horton tells me you and he go way back."

"We've had some fun times—especially during Prohibition." He flicked on the cabin light. "Let me see the rest of those cards."

They were taking a huge chance tonight. Leilah's trial was set to commence after the weekend. If those cards were going to do any good at all, there were only a couple of days left.

Kathryn had spent the day making up a stack of fake cards, imitating Leilah's handwriting as best she could, making up a bunch of names, throwing in a few people who had passed away, and sprinkling it with the likes of Errol Flynn and Harry Cohn, who Winchell would expect to see.

He flipped through the cards, grunted, then handed them back. "Are you sure Ruby'll take the bait?"

"Kathryn thinks so."

The driver pulled into a tight curve.

"Have you ever met Walter Plunkett?" Gwendolyn asked.

"He did all those *Gone with the Wind* costumes, right?"

"I doubt I'll be able to corner him for more than a moment or two, but if I can, oh boy do I have some questions."

"You're not going to act like a teenaged movie fan, I hope."

The driver pulled up at 8715 Wonderland Avenue. Gwendolyn did a last-minute lipstick check before they mounted the stone steps to the open front door. The unmistakable voice of Judy Garland beckoned from somewhere deep inside.

* * *

Of all the costumers Gwendolyn admired — Adrian, Orry-Kelly, Irene Lentz, Dolly Tree, Helen Rose — the two at the top of her list were Edith Head and Walter Plunkett, and they couldn't have been more different.

Gwendolyn revered Edith's clean lines and her less-is-more approach to character-led design.

However, she adored Plunkett's work for the opposite reasons. The detail! The fabric! The buttons and bows and feathers and lace! He designed an autumn-leaf dress for Elizabeth Taylor in *Little Women* that Gwendolyn went back a second time just to see again.

And now I'm in his house! So close! With so many questions!

She had the perfect conversation starter. The owner of the Trocadero had hired her to wear his Scarlett barbeque dress to *Gone with the Wind*'s post-premiere party. Fainting on the sidewalk was a moment she decided to keep to herself.

Plunkett had decorated his postcolonial home in pastels: pale green swirl in the carpet, billowy drapes in light mauve, pastoral prints and still lifes filling the walls, lamps on corner tables and sideboards. The windows were bracketed with white shutters that were all open to let in the late summer air perfumed with bougainvillea.

To the right, pairs of loveseats arranged for intimate conversation dotted a sunken living room. At the far end, Harold Arlen was seated at a glossy Steinway. To his left stood Judy Garland singing "You Wonderful You."

Gwendolyn was surprised to see her there. Over the summer, Mayer had taken Judy off *Royal Wedding*, precipitating an attempted suicide that birthed speculation that Judy was washed up at twenty-eight. But then *Summer Stock* opened to huge crowds, proving her detractors wrong. When she hit her final note, it came out clear and strong, and her halo of admirers gushed with applause.

Gwendolyn couldn't see Plunkett anywhere. She turned to leave the room when she felt Winchell's hand on her arm. "Where are you going?"

"It's polite to say hello to the host."

"And tell him how much you admire his work?" *For the most listened-to man in the country, you really are a toad.* "We have a job to do. Let's circulate."

Gwendolyn poked her head into Plunkett's office. It had the agreeable hint of expensive pipe tobacco. Two walls were lined with floor-to-ceiling bookcases; a pair of French doors opened onto a patio paved with broad flagstones.

"There he is."

She was halfway through the office when Ruby came into view. She had engaged Plunkett in a one-sided conversation and was oblivious to the futility of her cleavage.

Everyone knows he doesn't swing that way, you little nitwit.

At forty-eight, the rakish Plunkett was on the precipice of going gray. He had the cultured face of an English literature professor. When Winchell distracted him with a broad wave, he turned from Ruby and held out his hand.

"Mister Winchell!" he exclaimed. "Welcome!"

The two men shook hands. "May I present Miss Gwendolyn Brick?"

Plunkett turned toward Ruby. "Allow me to introduce—"

"Ruby!" Winchell exclaimed. "Delighted to see you again." He landed a kiss on her right cheek.

His charade was convincing, but Ruby's eyes were wary with alarm.

"Plunky!" June Allyson's raspy voice rang out across the patio from the French doors. "Judy has a special song she wants to sing in your honor."

Plunkett swung back to them. "There's a buffet in the dining room; please help yourself." He headed inside.

As soon as he was gone, Ruby threw off her smile.

So did Winchell. "I'm glad we've bumped into you. I have a hatchet I wish to bury—and not in your back."

Ruby gave him a once-over, then Gwendolyn. "Oh yeah?"

"That wretched business about the apartment."

"Mmm."

"I want you to know that I don't hold anything against you or your father for the way that whole situation unspooled."

"You don't, huh?"

"Oh sure, I was mad as hell when I found out you'd snapped it up, but it wouldn't have suited me. Geographically it was all wrong, and the place I bought is perfect for my needs. In a way, you did me a huge favor, and I want to thank you."

He let out a hearty laugh that caused several guests around Plunkett's landscaped patio to glance in their direction.

"I'm glad to hear it." The caginess in Ruby's eyes waned.

A waiter with a tray of champagne appeared; they each took a glass.

"A toast!" Winchell beamed a mouthful of surprisingly strong white teeth that showed no signs of the late-night drinking and chain-smoking that he was famous for. "To your father!"

"My *dad*?"

"I miss the old cuss!" He turned to Gwendolyn. "Otis and I go way back. So many people are intimidated by my reputation, and most of the time it works in my favor. But with Ruby's *paterfamilias*, I could always just be me. No putting on the Winch costume. I miss that and I want to rebuild the bridges by telling you that the biggest scoop of your career is right here."

Ruby stiffened and cast her eyes around at the guests wandering in and out of the patio. Gwendolyn played along and looked around as well, but she wasn't prepared to see Zap stepping through the French doors with an exceptionally pretty girl on his arm.

She was at least fifteen years Gwendolyn's junior and wore her blonde hair in cascades around her shoulders. She had a neat little figure and wore a deep blue dress designed to show it off in a way that advertised it was available to the right guy. The way she gazed at Zap made it clear that he was that right guy.

He could have turned her around and retreated back into the house, but to his credit, he didn't break his stride.

"Hello, Zap." His timing was terrible, but there was nothing she could do about that. *At least you have the decency to look embarrassed.*

"May I introduce you to Graziella Lombardi?" *Italian? Now, there's a shocker. I'm guessing she's a highly appropriate twenty-two, twenty-three at most.*

Zap looked taken aback at meeting Winchell, but Leda barely noticed him.

"I know you," she told Gwendolyn. "Well, I don't *know you* know you, but I was there that night at Romanoff's."

"Which night was that?"

"Or Mocambo?" She pressed a hand to her cheek. "New Year's Eve. Not the last one, the one before. Remember? Humphrey Bogart asked you to dance. Then later you yelled at that madam." She elbowed Zap in the ribs. "The one that everybody's talking about."

Oh my God, Zap, she's dumb as dirt.

"You marched over to her like you were General MacArthur!" the girl continued. "It was a better floor show than what's-his-name Nougat."

"Xavier Cugat?"

"Yeah, him. So how do you and Zappy know each other?"

Zappy, is it? How adorable.

Zap studied the contents of his drink. "I designed a perfume bottle for her."

"He's so talented, isn't he?" *Oh, just you wait. You'll find Zappy is talented in so many ways. If you haven't already.* "Hold the presses! Are you the gal with the boutique up on the Strip? Très something?"

"Chez Gwendolyn."

"Yeah! You sell that perfume. What's it called? Hollywood Boulevard?"

Gwendolyn could feel the heat of Winchell's glare. "Did you hear Judy Garland?" She pointed to the French doors. "If you hurry, you can catch her singing live in person."

Zap wasted no time in wrapping his arm around the ninny's irritatingly slender waist and pulling her away.

"You were saying?" Ruby said. "The scoop of my career?"

Winchell turned to Gwendolyn. "Show her."

Gwendolyn popped open her purse and pulled out the fake cards.

"I knew it!" Ruby hissed. "Leilah's been wailing on my shoulder, convinced you'd torched 'em, but I told her you wouldn't dare."

"You and Leilah are chums?" Winchell asked.

"I've been visiting her in lock-up." Her eyes narrowed, bleeding suspicion. "Why are you telling me this? And why are you coming forward with only two days till Leilah's trial?"

"I had them all along, but I didn't know it," Gwendolyn said. "They were hidden inside a copy of *Magnificent Obsession* like some Hitchcock movie." Kathryn told her to throw in that detail if Ruby wasn't swallowing her story. "Yesterday I was looking for something to read but instead I got the shock of my life."

"What did Kathryn say when you showed them to her?"

"I didn't."

"Hogwash!"

Gwendolyn pursed her lips at Winchell. "I told you she wouldn't believe me."

Ruby's eyes were glued to the cards. Gwendolyn raised her hand so Ruby could see them better. "These men deserve to be publicly humiliated."

"So expose them."

"I don't have the access to the media that you do."

"Kathryn does."

"I don't want her to be caught up in a scandal like this."

"But you don't mind if *I* am."

"You're not afraid to get down and get dirty, and you're not the type to shy away from standing your moral ground." She pushed the cards into Ruby's chest.

Ruby took them and jiggled them as though gauging their weight for a carnival prize. "Is Wilkerson's name here?"

Gwendolyn and Kathryn had had a long discussion over whether or not to include it. Gwendolyn won the debate, arguing that it lent authenticity. She nodded.

"Do you have any objection to my taking it from the pile? Mister Wilkerson's been real good to me."

"They're yours to do with what you will."

"I could hand them over to Leilah."

Gwendolyn could see the greed and glory ignite behind Ruby's eyes. "An exposé like this will be the making of your career."

"What's the catch?" Ruby asked.

"If there's a catch at all, it's that you can't use my name, or Kathryn's."

Winchell flicked the cards with a finger. "If you don't want them, I'll be more than happy to take—"

Ruby yanked them beyond his reach. "I've already started writing the article in my head." She shoved them into her pocketbook and closed it with a sharp click.

Gwendolyn watched her walk inside. "She could've at least thanked me."

"Bitches like her never thank anybody for a damned thing." Winchell deposited his glass on the tray of a passing waiter. "We can go now."

Gwendolyn wondered where Plunkett was. Surely they could do one circuit of the house, even if it meant bumping into Zap.

"But you must know plenty of people here."

Winchell jammed his hands in his pockets. "Near as I can figure it, this swelegant soirée is filled with daft doxies without a brain between them, refugees from the Girls' Friendly Society without a friend between them, and MGM fags who've never had a girl between them. We're leaving."

She had no choice but to trail behind. She searched for Plunkett but neither saw nor heard any sign of him. When Winchell stepped out onto the front porch, he stopped.

Gwendolyn almost collided with his back. "Change your mind?"

"The way you handled yourself back there, you were very good."

"Thank you."

"Ruby Courtland is a cunning little vixen but you convinced her." Something drew his attention. "Oh, Jesus."

It was Zap, this time without Little Miss Whoever That Was. He wore a pale, sheepish *Can we please talk?* face.

"I'm sorry," Gwendolyn told Winchell, "this won't take long." She joined Zap at the bottom of the stone steps leading to the driveway.

"Who was that you were with?" Zap asked.

"How could you not recognize Walter Winchell?"

"Not him, the girl."

"Speaking of girls, who was that on *your* arm? Let me guess—she's the daughter of your dad's second cousin because your parents took one look at me and immediately found someone far more suitable."

"Can we forget about Graziella? She's nothing."

"Did you see the way she looked at you, *Zappy*?"

He bunched his hands into fists and pressed them together like a prizefighter about to pray. "That girl with Winchell, it wasn't Ruby Courtland, was it?"

The way he bit down on his lower lip made Gwendolyn see he was far more concerned about Ruby than Miss Nougat. "It was."

Zap started to rub his forehead like it was punishment. "I've done a very bad thing. Get ready to punch me. I deserve it."

"Just tell me what you did."

"A few weeks ago, I got invited to an advance screening of *Sunset Boulevard*—"

"Did you take what's-her-name?"

"Forget the girl. She's just a favor to my folks. Afterwards, Billy Wilder hosted a party at Musso and Frank's. And you know how strong they pour their drinks."

"So you got drunk."

"And I got to chatting with some girl I didn't know from a bottle of Bromo-Seltzer. She was all giggly and flirty and—I don't know, I found myself trying to impress her."

"You look like you're about to hang yourself."

"Because—because I'm the one who told her about Kathryn's father being in Sing Sing." The words came out in one long string.

"Are you telling me that the girl at Musso and Frank's was Ruby Courtland?"

"I was drunk! She has this way of wheedling information out of a guy. I feel terrible. I'm *such* a stinker."

Gwendolyn stepped forward until their faces were almost touching. "Do you realize what you've done?"

"I'd give anything for a do-over."

"They only happen in Capra movies. What you've done is unfixable."

He ran his hand through his hair. "You think I don't know that?"

"Goodbye, Zap." She turned to go, but he pulled her back.

"That sounded final."

"It was meant to."

Zap looked like he was about to burst into tears. "Jesus! I'm the worst person in the world!"

The whole time Gwendolyn was looking at the girl on Zap's arm, she couldn't understand why she kept thinking of Hilda Saperstein. It wasn't like she resembled Hilda in the least.

But looking at Zap with his stricken don't-hate-me face, she now understood why.

"That business with Ruby is unforgiveable," Gwendolyn told him, "but seeing you with Grenada—"

"Graziella."

"I don't care what her name is, Zap. The point is that sooner or later, you'll be ready to settle down and have babies, and if that happens in ten years' time, I'd be fifty."

"You want kids?"

"You'd pack your things and leave me in a cluttered apartment in the Talmadge building wondering how life passed me by."

"Miss Brick?" Winchell called from the top of the stairs. "Tick tock!"

Zap went to respond but she pressed a fingertip to those soft lips of his. "You've done enough damage. Just go. I mean it, Zap."

As she watched the guy retreat down the hill, she heard Winchell's footsteps on the stone.

"Touching as that scene was, I've got better things to do. If we could —"

"YOU MISERABLE LITTLE SHITS!"

Ruby's unmistakable voice shot at them from across the street. She marched out of the shadows, the cards gripped in her hand.

"This is a pile of CRAP!"

She flung the cards at them; for a moment they quivered in the air like stunned moths, then fell to the ground. "Did you really think you could get away with this?"

Winchell looked at the cards scattered at his feet, then up at Gwendolyn. "What is she talking about?"

We should've made a contingency plan. Kathryn should have taught me how to handle —

"Those aren't Leilah's," Ruby said. "They're phonies. Don't make out like you didn't know."

There was, however, one tactic Kathryn had taught Gwendolyn.

"What makes you think they're fakes?" she fought back. "Have you ever seen Leilah's cards?"

"No—"

"And yet you feel entitled to throw accusations—"

"When I was practically the only one visiting Leilah in jail, she told me all about them. Like how on the back of *her* cards, she drew a little symbol in the top right-hand corner."

Winchell picked up the card closest to his shoe. "What kind of symbol?"

"She'd find out what zodiac the guy was, like a Taurus or a Scorpio or whatever, and she'd draw the astrological symbol for that sign, real tiny, on the back of his card. She's into all that sort of stuff. Got her own astrologer and everything. She told me, 'When you find out a guy's astrology sign, that's pretty much all you need to know about what he likes between the sheets.' And those—" she waved her hand over the cards "— don't got no symbols."

Winchell scooped up a handful of cards and inspected the back of each one. He looked up, practically breathing fire through his eye sockets. "You care to explain this to me?"

"I don't know about any astrological signs!" Gwendolyn burst out. She knew people were peering out of windows, but she didn't dare look at them. "All I can tell you is those are the cards I discovered hidden in a book that Linc sent me."

"And who's Linc?"

"He's the one who stole them from the O'Roarkes in the first place."

"So let's ask him."

"We can't," Gwendolyn said. "He's dead."

"How convenient." Ruby jabbed a finger at Gwendolyn. "I don't trust you." Then turned to Winchell. "And I especially don't trust *you*."

The two of them stood in silence as she steamed back to her car, then careered down the hill.

"You just made a fool of me," Winchell said, his voice intimidatingly low. "I'm not the sort of person you or Kathryn Massey want as an enemy."

"I'm well aware of that, Mister Winchell." Gwendolyn had to force the words; they came out hoarse with panic.

Winchell stomped up the hill toward his waiting limo. "You can make your own way home."

CHAPTER 43

As July of 1950 melted into August, then dissolved into September, some of the entertainment industry's most celebrated names found themselves trapped in the glare of *Red Channels*.

Some of them faded into the night. Others took to jousting windmills to an audience immobile with panic.

Still others got while the going was good and decamped for England.

Marcus was surprised how much he missed working for the masked man.

He'd grown to enjoy hearing his dialogue on Gwendolyn's television set two weeks after he wrote it. During his days at MGM, so much time would pass that he'd almost forget what he'd written.

Kathryn was preoccupied more and more with Leo Presnell now, so Marcus and Gwendolyn spent more time together. She sprang for a Magnavox Playhouse with a sixteen-inch screen and a high-fidelity speaker and they often sat on her couch watching *Arthur Godfrey's Talent Scouts* or *You Bet Your Life*. Or rather, half-watching.

Gwennie was always working on a sewing project and Marcus couldn't take seriously anything on a screen the size of his oven's window. So they'd sit there with half an eye on the flickering screen and talk about that awful night at Plunkett's house, about Winchell and Zap, and Oliver, and Leo, and all the men who'd preceded them.

Sometimes Doris joined them if her job at Columbia allowed.

On Saturdays, when Gwendolyn was busy at her store, Marcus and Doris often drove to the beach at Inceville. They were sitting on the sand one Saturday in October, the wind gusting off the Pacific with a noticeable chill, when he recalled Reuben telling him about his store. Its name escaped him, but there couldn't be too many furniture stores in Santa Monica. When he suggested they hunt it down, Doris looked at him, puzzled.

"Can you afford new furniture?"

Doris was as broadminded as a guy could hope for in a sister from a small town where everybody knew what everybody else had for breakfast, but he avoided mentioning that horrible night he got caught up in the Hermit's Hideaway raid.

"I know the guy who owns it." He brushed the sand from his elbows and grinned. "Reuben told me I should go into television, and I want to tell him how fantastically well it worked out for me."

They parked near the pier and walked the length of Third Street until Doris spotted a sign: *Santa Monica Custom Furniture.*

It was a spacious store, with huge windows on three sides, and filled with chairs, tables, and sofas fashioned in the new style people were going for these days — clean lines, minimal detailing, slung low to the ground. Marcus preferred wingback chairs that looked like they'd sat in a private club since before Rockefeller had three dollars to rub together. But Reuben was in the business of selling what he made, so why wouldn't he produce the sort of furniture people wanted?

Marcus ran his hand along the back of a loveseat, admiring the craftsmanship. The guy sure knew what he was doing.

"I thought that was you." Reuben's white teeth contrasted with his deeply tanned face. "You here alone?"

"I'm with my sister." Marcus scanned the store but Doris was nowhere in sight.

"I haven't seen you at the beach lately," Reuben said.

"I got a job. In television, as a matter of fact."

"Really? It was my impression that you weren't overly enthralled with that idea."

He nodded as Marcus took him through the events surrounding his foray into chronicling the adventures of heroes on horseback and how *Red Channels* cut it short.

"I'm sorry to hear that. I know several of our brethren whose lives have been ruined by that nasty piece of trash. What are you doing now?"

"Back to napping on square one."

"So you have time to inspect my latest commission."

He led Marcus through the labyrinth of furniture to the back room. It was three times the size of Gwendolyn's and smelled of raw wood and fresh lacquer. Near the far wall stood a six-foot mahogany chiffonier. The left side featured four deep drawers; the right side was an unfinished space.

Marcus ran his finger down it. The wood was so smooth it almost felt like vicuña. He pointed to the empty space. "What's this for?"

"I'm trying to convince my client it'd be more useful as a dresser for hanging suits, but he wants a place to display his Oscar. Say, you were at MGM, right?"

The *LA Times* had recently announced that Los Angeles was fast approaching two million residents, but it always surprised Marcus how often he'd bump into someone he knew.

"I'm building this for Mervyn LeRoy," Reuben said. LeRoy was one of MGM's leading directors, and had directed some of Marcus' favorite pictures, including *Waterloo Bridge* and *Madame Curie*. "He's coming over to check on the progress."

"Here? This morning?"

"You should stick around and say hello."

Marcus grew hot with panic. They'd had a number of crises during the production of *Thirty Seconds Over Tokyo*. Although it was based on a true story, it was filmed after the attack on Pearl Harbor, which made it pro-war propaganda, much like Marcus' *Free Leningrad!* Dalton Trumbo, the most prominent of the recently imprisoned Hollywood Ten, wrote the screenplay, and yet somehow, LeRoy glided through the HUAC quagmire unscathed while Marcus' career crash-landed into quicksand.

"I must find my sister."

Marcus hurried into the showroom; Doris stood near the street entrance. He headed toward her but swerved off course when he saw LeRoy's handsome face appear at the front door. He kept his back to him, pretending to inspect a dinette set in pale wood while Reuben greeted his customer and steered him into the back room.

Doris sidled up beside Marcus. "I really can't see this at your place."

"What?"

She pointed to the dining table.

"Let's go."

Marcus hustled his sister onto Third Street, where Saturday afternoon shoppers strolled the sidewalk. Marcus turned right.

"But you parked thataway," Doris reminded him, pointing toward the pier. She stopped walking and planted her hands on her hips. "You okay?"

"My past was about to catch up with me and—"

"Adler! ADLER!"

Marcus put on a who's-that-calling-me face.

LeRoy pulled him into a firm handshake as Marcus introduced his sister. "I've been searching for you," he said.

"Looks to me like you two have business to discuss," Doris broke in. "When you're done, you'll find me at JC Penney's." She merged into the crowd, leaving Marcus to face his past.

"Searching for me, why?" he asked.

"I'm hoping you might be free to take a job."

"I'm available, but I'm not exactly employable."

"The hell you're not."

Marcus tugged LeRoy into the shade of the awning over Reuben's store. "Have you seen *Red Channels*?"

"Of course."

"My name was the second one listed. So you must know that—"

"That it's all bullshit?"

" —that I'm now one of the scary red lepers."

"I don't care. Neither does L.B. And if he doesn't, you shouldn't, either."

Marcus blinked. "L.B.? As in *Mayer*?"

LeRoy's face crinkled into a dry grin. "Now do you want to hear about this job?"

"L.B. knows you're talking to me?"

"L.B. could stand for all sorts of people. Lucille Ball. Leonard Bernstein. Lauren Bacall."

Marcus was confused. Then he saw LeRoy's delicate lift of an eyebrow, and realized of course Mayer knew, but only on the QT, and who knew whose ears were listening.

"I'm currently prepping *Quo Vadis*," LeRoy said. "Have you read the book?"

"Years ago."

"I'd like you to read it again."

"Screenplay not progressing well?"

LeRoy winced. "The guys I've got working on it, they've got tons of experience, but they have two very different approaches. That can work well when they complement each other, but it's just not . . ."

"Meshing?"

"Exactly. I need someone who can take each of their versions and turn them into a filmable picture. That *Red Channels* pile of horse manure has decimated the screenwriting talent pool. There's nobody left at the studio with enough experience to grapple with such a huge project. I've got over twenty-five speaking parts. Some scenes will need a thousand extras."

This made Marcus' heart beat faster in a way the Lone Friggin' Ranger never had. "We passed a used bookstore a couple of blocks back."

"I've got a bunch of copies at home. Where do you live?"

"The Garden of Allah."

"Someone told me you'd moved out."

"Nope, still there."

LeRoy sighed. "I wish I'd known. I'll get it to you later this afternoon if I have to drive it there myself."

A dreamlike veil dropped around Marcus, throwing the shoppers and strollers around him into soft focus. "I want to be clear. All this has the okay of L.B.?"

"He just bought my house on Benedict Canyon. We're like this." LeRoy crossed his fingers. "He's the one who told me to track you down."

Marcus pressed his hand against the warm brickwork as this astonishing morsel of information sunk in. *That crusty old son of a gun, he's got a heart, after all.*

"However," LeRoy said, "there's just one wrinkle." *Isn't there always?*

"Preproduction—costumes, sets, casting—it's almost done. I'm leaving in two weeks."

"Two? Mervyn, there isn't enough Benzedrine in the state of California—"

"I need you to come with me on location."

"You're not filming on the back lot?"

LeRoy let out a barking laugh. "We had to build the Roman forum—and I mean the whole damn thing. My budget is seven and half million. This picture makes *Gone with the Wind* look like an Molière drawing-room comedy."

"Where are you filming this monster?"

"Cinecittà. No other place could accommodate us. I'm leaving on the tenth and I need you with me. We'll be able to work on the screenplay together. We don't have a day to lose. And I mean literally not one day. Please tell me you're on board, because if not, I don't know what the hell I'm going to do. I'm running out of options. I need an answer, Adler, and I need it right now."

* * *

Doris and Marcus were passing Malibu, heading north on Route 1, when Doris spoke up.

"Are you sure about this?"

"You think I'm on a fool's errand, don't you?"

"I think you should do whatever's right for you. Pursuit of happiness and all that." Doris fidgeted with the map they'd purchased at a filling station. "I just don't want to see you disappointed if your big romantic gesture doesn't come off the way it would in the movies. Chances are, this might not be *Love Affair*."

Marcus mustered a smile. "Does that make me Charles Boyer or Irene Dunne?"

"You've got your sense of humor. That's good to hear."

He tapped her knee. "Don't worry, sis, I know the chances are slim that this will work out the way I want."

"He might not even be there anymore."

Anything could have happened in the six months since that private eye tracked down Oliver. Marcus eased off the gas a touch while he tempered hope with reality.

Several miles down the highway, Doris said, "I have some news. Columbia's getting into the television business."

"Everyone else is pretending like it doesn't exist, but Harry Cohn's going after it? That bastard always did have the biggest balls in town."

"He says television's only going to get bigger, and any studio that thinks otherwise is a bunch of ostriches. He's formed this new production company called Screen Gems. I'm going to be in charge of juggling soundstage and personnel logistics between feature production and television shows."

"Sounds like a big job."

"It is, *and* they've given it to a woman. I've heard there's been rumblings from malcontents in the men's room."

"Do you care?"

"I probably should, but I can't come up with one good reason why."

"Then don't," Marcus told her. "I've wasted so much time trying to convince myself that I'm happy not working; happy not being challenged; happy to be single again."

"We could see you weren't."

Marcus figured he could guess who "we" were. "When LeRoy told me he wanted me to help him fix *Quo Vadis*, my heart nearly jumped out of my chest. I've missed that feeling."

"So you really are going? Regardless of what happens in the next couple of hours?"

The sign for Oxnard flashed past them; they were halfway there.

"Let's just take this one grand gesture at a time."

* * *

Cloverleaf Sanatorium sat at the end of a winding, dusty road behind a chain-link fence. The guard looked like a wizened forty-niner from straight out of *The Treasure of the Sierra Madre*. He treated Marcus' request to "see whoever's in charge" with respectful disinterest and directed them to an office inside the main building.

Marcus parked in front of the two-story lump of whitewashed stucco and told Doris he preferred to go in alone. She pulled a paperback of *A Tree Grows in Brooklyn* from her beach bag. "Go get him, tiger."

The Whoever's In Charge turned out to be a middle-aged woman with a wide-open midwestern face and gray overtaking what had once been white-blonde hair.

"Oliver?" She seemed shocked to hear his name. "Of course you may see him. How delightful!" After what that private eye had said, Marcus was expecting a wholly different response. When he asked her where he might find Oliver, she pointed through her office window to a rose garden.

The beds were laid out in the careful arrangement of a formal English garden: three concentric semicircular rows bordered with chunks of brick, eight rosebushes per bed, all of them devoid of petals. Oliver was squatting over the outmost bed, churning the earth with a small garden fork.

"I guess I'm too late in the season."

Oliver shuddered when he recognized Marcus' voice. He pressed his shoulders down as he gathered himself. After a long pause, he rose to his feet.

His collarbone poked through the loose white t-shirt that hung off him like worn-out bed linen; his face and arms were tanned to a deep brown. His jaw hung loose. "How did you . . .? Where have you . . .?"

"You think you're so mysterious that you're impossible to track down?"

The shock on Oliver's thin face melted away. "And you drove straight up here?"

Marcus felt his smile start to quiver. "I've known where you were since May, but I figured I'd give you time."

"To recover?"

"Have you?"

Oliver cast his gaze across his stark rosebushes. "Yuh-huh."

Marcus took a step. "So why are you still here?"

Oliver dropped onto the grass and drew his knees to his chest. He motioned for Marcus to do the same.

Marcus desperately wanted to throw his arms around Oliver and let a hundred questions burst out of him, but this moment was delicate as a snowflake. He parked his butt on the soft grass and waited.

Oliver kept his eyes on the horizon. "Places like these, they don't come free. Or cheap. Breen wanted to pay, but he didn't realize how long it took to get well."

"Neither did I."

"It doesn't help when you've got pushers lurking just beyond the perimeter."

"They actually do that?"

Oliver threw him a look that said, *Don't be so naïve.* "If you've got a product to sell, you go where the market is. Dope fiends stuck in a place like this are sitting ducks."

"Didn't you report them to the authorities?"

"When all you want in the world is another fix, and there's someone dangling it in front of you, trust me, you're not going to tell them to take a hike."

And I thought being listed in Red Channels was the worst thing that could happen.

"Rock bottom isn't a pretty place. I hope you never have to see it." The late afternoon light caught a spider as it jumped from one branch to another, connecting them with a silver thread. Oliver dropped onto his elbows, and then his back, and stared up at the cloudless sky. "Then you arrive at the point where you want to get better."

Marcus lay back too. "But when you do?"

"*Then* you tell the bigwigs about the pushers. That's when you start the hard slog of getting clean."

"That must have been hell."

"Let's just skip to the part when you realize that you've slept through the night without waking in a cold sweat wishing you could die. You can think clearly for the first time in you don't know how long. And *that* is when you realize how much you owe the people who have clothed and washed and fed you for months, to say nothing of mopping up your vomit and taking you to a doctor when you punch a brick wall so hard you break a bone in your wrist."

Marcus heard the whir of a hummingbird several seconds before it appeared, hovering several feet above their heads. It stayed suspended in the air for a while, then zipped out of view.

Marcus rolled onto his side to face Oliver. "It breaks my heart to hear—"

"So I'm working off my debt." He indicated the naked rosebushes. "I'm quite the gardener now. You should have seen these babies a few months ago. The fragrance was enough to make you woozy."

"I wish I had."

"Why are you here?" Oliver asked. "I mean, why now?"

"MGM is doing *Quo Vadis*, but the script needs work. Mervyn LeRoy wants me to go with him to Rome so we can punch it into shape."

"That's a heck of a break."

"Come with me."

Oliver let out a soft gasp. "Why?"

"Because no matter how hard I've tried, I can't unlove you." Marcus reached out and gingerly took Oliver by the hand. He expected him to pull back, but instead, he let Marcus' fingers intertwine with his. "Because you pursued me once, now I'm pursuing you."

A single tear seeped out of the corner of Oliver's eye and trickled down his temple.

Marcus moved closer so that he was only inches away. "We each need a fresh start. Where better than the land that invented spaghetti?" Marcus' heart just about burst when Oliver let out a laugh. "Come with me?"

Oliver turned his head, his hazel eyes roiling with emotion. He leaned forward and pressed his lips to Marcus' and kissed them three times.

CHAPTER 44

As Kathryn walked out of the Roosevelt Hotel with Gwendolyn, she realized her nerves had already burned through the two whiskey sours she'd just downed in the bar. She surveyed the throng on both sides of Hollywood Boulevard and wished they had time to run back inside for a third.

"Heavens!" Gwendolyn exclaimed. "And this isn't even the world premiere!" She adjusted her tangerine scarf so that it sat more squarely around her neck.

Kathryn thought it was cute that Gwennie considered it her lucky scarf, but it wasn't luck they needed tonight—it was *pluck*.

As they jostled their way to the north side of Hollywood Boulevard toward Grauman's Chinese Theatre, everybody looked back at the Roosevelt. The hotel had dimmed out all but three of the letters in its sign on top of the building, leaving just *E V E*.

An usher handed Kathryn the special program.

Presenting the Hollywood Premiere of
"ALL ABOUT EVE"
Grauman's Chinese Theatre
November 9, 1950

Kathryn loved that it was the size of a *Saturday Evening Post*, making it an effective fan. They were running behind schedule, and that made for sweaty armpits.

The tumult outside subsided as they walked into the theater's foyer, where guests gathered in groups awaiting the star's grand arrival.

Since the night Bette's movie celebrated its debut in New York, superlatives like "sensational" and "whip-smart" had been bandied from coast to coast. Earlier that day, over the phone, Bette had confided to Kathryn, "This picture is so good that I'll be shocked if tonight doesn't prove to be my comeback moment."

Bette hadn't been away from the screen long enough to need a comeback, but Kathryn knew that actresses measured their careers in terms of *successful* pictures. She'd promised to be there in time for Bette's arrival, but she made sure to be there well before.

Gwendolyn pointed to a life-sized cardboard cutout of the movie's six stars in the center of the foyer; Leo was standing next to it.

Despite how well things went that night at Nickodell, Kathryn hadn't been able to summon the courage to tell Leo about her father. But a few weeks later, she knew the time was right after a particularly delicious dinner at Romanoff's followed by a session of moonlight parking and smooching in a leafy alcove on Mulholland Drive.

She felt so comfortable and safe with him that she blurted out everything. To his credit, he hadn't even blinked when she mentioned Sing Sing. Instead, he'd confided that his own father was a violent drunk whose only selfless act was to fall into the town quarry and fatally split open his head the night of Leo's fourteenth birthday. And when Kathryn recruited him as a decoy tonight, he agreed without hesitation.

"He sure fills out a tux well, doesn't he?" Gwendolyn commented.

"He gives Gary Merrill a run for his money."

When Kathryn had asked Bette if she was happy now that she and Merrill were married, Bette let out a guttural shriek. "At forty-two, I should've known better than to equate sex with love. We don't have a marriage. We have a battleground with cessation of hostilities conducted in a demilitarized no-man's-land that normal people call the bedroom."

Kathryn caught Leo's eye just as Ruby walked through the front doors with a white fox stole draped around her shoulders. She was alone.

She couldn't even drum up an escort?

Kathryn and Gwendolyn retreated behind a wax mannequin in traditional Chinese armor. They watched Leo approach Ruby, who shook his hand like it was last month's lettuce. Kathryn could tell which part of the spiel he was up to by the changes in Ruby's face.

Hello, I'm Leo Presnell, head of marketing for Sunbeam.

I know.

May we have a word?

What about?

We sponsor Kathryn Massey's show, but we're not happy with her stance on the issue of stamping out Communists.

You and me both, pal.

We're a conservative company with traditional American values, and Miss Massey's views do not align with ours. We are thinking of pressuring NBC into replacing her.

Even from halfway across the foyer, Kathryn could see the hunger in Ruby's eyes.

A couple of weeks ago, Kathryn and Marcus had been at Grauman's to see a Fox picture called *No Way Out*. Kathryn wasn't terribly interested in noir crime dramas, but this one featured a black actor from the Bahamas called Sidney Poitier, and she was keen to see what all the fuss was about. As they were exiting the theater, Marcus gently prodded her up a flight of stairs she'd never noticed before. They led to a balcony four rows deep and eight seats across. It was perfect.

Leo pointed to the stairwell. Ruby blinked rapidly.

Kathryn muttered, "Go on, go on."

Whatever Leo said next was enough to quell Ruby's hesitation, and she trailed him up the stairs.

Kathryn counted to ten, then followed with Gwendolyn at her back. By the time Kathryn arrived at the top of the stairs, Leo and Ruby were standing at the balcony's edge, looking across the auditorium. The low hum of the crowd filtered up from the main floor, anticipation thickening the air.

A dull thud echoed up the stairs. Kathryn peered behind her. Walter Winchell stared back. She told Gwendolyn to stay put, then shot down the steps to meet him halfway.

"What's going on up there?" he asked.

"Just a last-minute gown snafu." She hated the way her voice shook. "I didn't know you were in town for tonight."

"I'm not." He rotated a black homburg in his fingertips. "I already saw it in New York. I was supposed to head out today, but some information fell into my hands and I thought I'd stick around. Figured you'd be here tonight."

Kathryn held up her purse. "I'm the one with the emergency safety pins, so maybe I can call you—"

His eyes hardened. "Thomas Danford."

Danford? And you want to have this conversation RIGHT NOW? "Bette's about to arrive any moment. Perhaps later—"

"He's your father, isn't he?" She could only gape at him. "Are you aware he's in Sing Sing? I just wanted to be sure you knew."

Be sure that I know where my father is? Or that YOU know where he is?

"It took quite some digging," he said. "I've had my man working it for months."

"Digging? For what? Dirt on me?"

He took another step up so that their faces were level. "I like to know who my competition is."

"You did all that for radio ratings? You're Walter Winchell. You have no competition." He eyeballed her, sly as a cobra. "Sorry to disappoint you," she said, "but I've known about my father for years. The question is, what do you intend to do with this information?"

"I have no specific plans. For now."

Kathryn faced him squarely, her arms folded and her mouth turned down into a pout. "It's like that, is it? Hide it away in your file marked 'In Case of Emergencies' until—what? My show is number five? Number three? At what point am I considered a menace?"

Thankfully, Winchell said nothing in reply—she was all out of smart retorts. He gave her a jaundiced once-over, then headed back down the stairs as Kathryn returned to the balcony.

"Leo's been improvising for the last couple of minutes," Gwendolyn told her. "You're on."

Ruby didn't see her approach until Kathryn joined Leo at the balustrade. "Say, what is this?"

"We want to have a little chat," Kathryn said.

"Then why do I feel cornered?"

"Ruby, it's time you left."

"Left what?"

"California."

"I'm not leaving this theater, let alone the state."

Kathryn pointed to Leo. "Do you remember him?"

Ruby took her time studying him from head to foot. "Should I?"

Leo jutted out his chin. "I'm sure you've attended more than one stag party in your time, but you might recall one at the Waldorf."

Ruby didn't even need time to think about it. "Right at the end of the war? The guy whose dad was some Ivy League mucky-muck?"

"Chancellor of Cornell. I was there that night, and had to endure the sight of you dragging him off to the bedroom."

"So?"

"You gave my pal a dose of the clap, which he passed on to his bride, who then sued him for divorce. The scandal nearly ended the mucky-muck's chancellorship."

"Nobody forced your buddy into that bedroom. If you ask me, it's a case of bachelor beware."

Leo looked at Kathryn. *Over to you.*

"Ever heard of the Truman Committee?" she asked Ruby.

Slow blink. "Vaguely."

"More formally known as the Senate Special Committee to Investigate the National Defense Program."

"Sounds dull."

"The original one disbanded a couple of years ago, but there's been a fresh round of allegations that some military contractors manipulated wartime resources to bring about an artificial monopoly. And guess what?"

The cords on Ruby's neck strained as she swallowed hard.

"The guy you infected with gonorrhea is now the senator heading the reformed committee."

When Gwendolyn told Kathryn about Otis Courtland's wartime shenanigans, she told Leo, who in turn told his buddy. Technically, his pal wasn't a senator yet, but he was planning to run in the next election and was looking for a way to make his mark. So the story they were spinning was at least partly true.

"I don't believe a word of it."

"I took the precaution of writing out his name and telephone number." Leo produced a slip of paper from his pocket. "He'll be very happy to accept your call."

"Oh, we're all very clever, aren't we?" Ruby's face burned with resentment. "You think you've got it all figured—Jesus Christ! Who else you got back there? Jack the goddamned Ripper?"

Winchell stepped into Kathryn's peripheral vision; she could hear him breathing deep and fast.

"Hello, Ruby," he said evenly. "I'd say it's nice to see you again, but we both know that would be a whopper."

"Yeah, because the sight of you brings up only the cheeriest of memories. Like for instance that last time in New York. Remember? I did all the work while you just lay there."

Kathryn nearly yelped. *These two sharks are made for each other.*

Winchell lunged forward. "Thanks for all your hard work, you little tramp! I had to endure all kinds of hell to be rid of what you gave me that night."

"I'm sorry, Walter. Did I forget to mention I had gonorrhea? Must have slipped my mind while you were plying me with enough whiskey to sink the *Bismarck*."

"Again with the gonorrhea?" Kathryn said. "That's quite a pattern, Ruby."

She wondered if Winchell had heard about the fabricated Truman Committee and prayed that Gwendolyn had distracted him long enough for him to miss it.

Ruby looked at the paper in Leo's hand. "I'll be making a phone call all right, but it won't be to some stick-up-his-ass senator from Connecticut. I'll be calling Mickey Cohen."

Is this little chiseler bluffing our bluff? "You don't know Mickey Cohen."

"I didn't . . . until he called me."

"Mickey Cohen? Called *you*?"

Kathryn was reassured that Winchell didn't believe Ruby any more than she did.

"Who do you think convinced me to come to the West Coast?"

"Did you give him the pox, too?" The quiver in Winchell's sneer told Kathryn he knew Ruby was telling the truth now. "I doubt he'll take too kindly to that." It was well known around LA that Cohen was a hypochondriac who washed his hands dozens of times a day.

"My dad and Mickey go way back." She turned her marbled eyes on Winchell. "Prohibition in New York, it was quite a time, huh?"

"Cohen has his hands full with the Kefauver Commission. I doubt he'll want to get tangled up in a whole other senatorial investigation."

The Kefauver Commission had recently been making inroads into the world of organized crime. Many people believed it spelled the beginning of the end for the mob, but Kathryn wasn't so sure. People like Mickey Cohen and Ruby Courtland always knew how to squeeze out of a thorny situation.

"If that's all you people have," Ruby had taken on a haughty Queen of Sheba tone, "then I'm afraid it's game over."

"Not so fast."

Gwendolyn emerged from the shadows and took the stairs one by one. She reached into her purse and pulled out a stack of cards tied together with a white ribbon.

Kathryn tried to smother her panic. Why would Gwennie bring Leilah's cards with her?

Gwendolyn wiggled her hand. "Every mover and shaker, how frequently they visited Leilah's fleshpots, and what they liked to do when they got there."

Ruby had her beady little eyes fixed on the cards. Leilah had been sentenced to twenty months at a women's prison in northern California, but her cards were still a potential flashpoint, and everybody there knew it.

"You were right," Gwendolyn teased, "they've got little astrological signs on the back."

Ruby's mouth dropped open. "I'm listening."

"Your father is on one of these cards."

"My father's never been west of the Mississippi."

"Apparently, Otis Courtland doesn't share everything with his daughter."

Kathryn looked across at Leo, who raised his eyebrows. *You didn't tell me about this.* Kathryn shot back, *Plan B?* The chatter downstairs ratcheted up a notch as people poured into the auditorium. Kathryn touched Gwendolyn's elbow. "Honey," she murmured, "we didn't talk about this—"

Ruby stuck her hand out. "My dad's card. I want to see it for myself."

"I'll go you one better, Ruby, and give it to you—if you're on the next train heading east. Whatever it takes to get you out of town. That's all I want."

"I don't care what any of you want!" Ruby snapped. "I've got plans." She faced Kathryn. "Your job, for starters."

Otis must be a fine piece of work—his chip off the old block is a real pip. "And how do you plan on getting that?"

"Because I'm going to have the goods on every mover and shaker in this town. Gwendolyn here is going to give me Leilah O'Roarke's cards. All of them."

"And why would she do that?" Kathryn asked.

"Don't push your luck, Ruby," Winchell broke in. "You know the damage I can trigger with a few calls."

Ruby turned on Winchell with scorn. "Just you try it, and I'll dial J. Edgar Hoover so damn fast. I know his direct number off by heart."

"Bullshit."

"National 6—"

Winchell took a step closer. "You'll call him and say what?"

"I'll tell Hoover how Senator Joseph McCarthy has a new list of suspected Commies and degenerates, and it's going to blow his Wheeling speech to kingdom come."

"Why would I care about that?"

"My dad and Senator Joe went to the same college — Marquette in Wisconsin. They're old pals, and Hoover knows it. I'm going to tell him your name is on the list."

"It won't take long to establish McCarthy has no list," Winchell said.

"There's a list all right, but by the time Hoover gets his hands on it, most of America will know about it. I'll make sure of that."

Kathryn, Gwendolyn, Presnell, and Winchell looked at each other. *This little schemer has covered all her bases.*

Without warning, Winchell lunged at Gwendolyn, trying to snatch the cards out of her hand. Ruby blocked him with her shoulder and rammed him hard enough to send him staggering. Quick as a whip, she grabbed the cards and ripped off the ribbon. She glanced at the top one. "Walter Winchell! Just as I suspected."

Winchell turned on Gwendolyn. "If that's my card, then what the hell did you give me back at Plunkett's?"

Gwendolyn looked at him with the best poker face Kathryn had ever seen.

Ruby started to laugh — a cynical, mean-spirited noise. She leaned backward and extended her arm so the stack in her hand hovered over the audience. "Don't push your luck, any of you."

"Half the people in those cards are probably sitting down there," Kathryn whispered. "Including our boss. You drop those and you'll be throwing away your career. You might even bring about the end of the *Hollywood Reporter*."

"And I had you down as one of the sharp ones," Ruby said. "The *Reporter* is just a stepping stone. I don't care if it lives or dies."

Winchell dove again, this time for Ruby, his hands flailing like a drowning man. She raised her left foot and planted it dead center in his stomach. She grunted as she thrust her leg forward, sending Winchell sprawling onto the steps.

"Last warning," she panted, "I will not hesitate to drop these overboard."

Kathryn glanced from face to face. They were each frozen with uncertainty. Nobody on the balcony doubted for a second that this devious bitch would let those cards go. She had them over a barrel, and she knew it. Kathryn glanced at her watch. The show would be starting in fifteen minutes.

The crowd below burst into applause. "Bette! Miss Davis! Bravo!"

Kathryn swore under her breath. Crowning achievements for actresses over forty were scarce, and she wanted to be around when Bette made her big entrance. She was about to ask Ruby what she wanted when Gwendolyn spoke.

"You ain't nothin' but a conniving little coward!" Kathryn wasn't aware Gwennie possessed such malice. "You don't have the guts. Cowards never do. You have no morals, no scruples, and worst of all, no friends. You couldn't even drag up a date for the biggest premiere of the year. You don't care what happens if you toss those cards over the edge, because nobody you care about will be the slightest bit affected. And that's because the only person you care about is yourself."

Ruby held up a hand; the other hovered over the crowd. "I'm warning you! One more word!"

Gwennie! Stop! We'll figure out some other way!

"Just one?" Gwendolyn jeered. "Bitch! Tramp! Whore! There's three. Take your pick."

Ruby flicked her wrist and pitched Leilah's cards into the air. They shuddered like snowflakes caught in an expected updraft, then wafted down onto the unsuspecting crowd below.

Winchell turned on Gwendolyn. "YOU IMBECILE!"

In response, Gwendolyn produced another card, just like the ones Ruby had dispersed into the glittering audience. Kathryn saw Gwendolyn's quiet smile and breathed for the first time in what felt like a month.

"That's because," Gwendolyn said, "what Ruby just pitched into the crowd were all exactly like this one." She handed it to Kathryn. "It'll sound better coming from you."

Kathryn held the card up to the light. "Hello, everyone!" she read out loud. "My name is Ruby Courtland, and I would like to take this opportunity to declare that I am a devious little slut who spreads venereal disease wherever I go. You can trust nothing I say, and nothing I do. I am, in fact, a real-life Eve Harrington, and if you don't know what that means, you will by the time you finish watching *All About Eve*."

People below started to laugh. Someone gasped, then someone else, too.

Gwendolyn wore a perky smile as she leaned over the balcony and cupped one hand to her ear and the other to the base of her throat. "Never underestimate the power of a lucky scarf."

The lights dimmed for a moment, then an announcer came over the PA. "Ladies and gentlemen, tonight's motion picture will commence shortly. Please take your seats."

Kathryn stepped up to confront Ruby square in the face. "I suggest you go home and start packing."

CHAPTER 45

Marcus pulled the two suitcases from the trunk of his Buick and set them next to Oliver on the sidewalk out front of Union Station. He was proud of himself that he hadn't started with the waterworks, but he could feel them coming.

Kathryn and Gwendolyn stared at him — *Please don't go. PLEASE.* — and was glad for the distraction when a porter appeared.

"We're on the Super Chief," he said. "Palm Star sleeper, roomette number five." He handed the guy a quarter. "Thank you."

He turned to the girls. Kathryn used the wide brim of her hat to shield her eyes as Gwendolyn dabbed her cheeks with a handkerchief.

The four of them had barely said a word during the drive downtown. Marcus wasn't sure he could speak without crying, but the train would be leaving soon. He watched the porter cart his life away.

"Not taking your Remington?" Kathryn still wasn't looking at him.

"They have typewriters in Italy."

Oliver took the car keys from Marcus. "I'll go park it in the lot over there and be right back." He eyed Kathryn and Gwendolyn. "On second thought, I want to get a newspaper and gum for the trip. I'll meet you on the platform."

Thank you for reading my mind. "And cigarettes. Four packs of Camels, filtered if they have it."

Marcus watched Oliver drive away into the chaos of the railway station parking lot. For a fleeting second, panic gripped him. *What if he doesn't show up on the platform? What if he bails on me at the last moment?*

Kathryn took his right elbow and Gwendolyn hooked his left. Through the double doors that opened onto the main concourse was an information booth, and beyond that, a sea of waiting chairs.

"I'm only going to ask this once," Kathryn said, her eyes dead ahead. "But I need to say it out loud, if only for my own piece of mind."

"Shoot."

"Are you sure you're doing the right thing? I mean, *really* sure? This is such a drastic step."

"You think I don't know that?"

Marcus wanted to gather the three of them into a quiet nook, but somehow their forward motion was keeping the emotions at bay. Maybe it was because they couldn't look into each other's eyes if they were all heading in the same direction. Or maybe they weren't ready to face this awful moment.

"I ran out of options the day *Red Channels* came out. At least here in LA."

Kathryn tightened her grasp. "Maybe you could— perhaps there's—I don't know, somebody who'd . . ."

He let her arrive at the same conclusion he'd been forced to face after days of thinking about nothing else.

The wide corridor leading to the train platforms stretched ahead of them. He could feel Gwendolyn slowing down, pulling at his arm. He laid his hand on top of hers and hauled her forward.

"I'm one of the Invisible Men now," he said. "I've got three choices. Stay in LA and do what? Pump gas or sling hash? Or I could run away to Mexico and sell screenplays to guys who haven't been blacklisted."

"I know that's not a great option," Kathryn said, "but at least we can drive to Mexico!"

"We can't drive to Rome," Gwendolyn put in.

The writers who'd migrated south of the border were working, but for a fraction of the salary they used to command.

"Or I can go with LeRoy, do the work I love, and get paid decently. I won't receive screen credit, but two out of three ain't bad, and I get to see some of Europe."

The sign for the Super Chief came into view. They stopped in front of it, staring at the arrow pointing up a walkway to the platform where the train would whisk him away from the last twenty years.

"Is this where we say our goodbyes?" he asked.

"The hell it is!" Kathryn tugged them up the ramp. "We're spending every second we can with you."

"I'm going to Europe, not Jupiter! It's not *that* far away."

"Any place that takes a week to reach is what I call far away."

The train almost filled the entire platform. The front of the engine glowed fire-truck red; a gold stripe ran down its center with the name of the railway line—SANTA FE—spelled out in black.

They pulled alongside the sleeper car Marcus had booked. They only had a few minutes left. He pulled the girls close so he could smell their hair and feel their tears against his cheeks.

He spotted Oliver at the top of the ramp, heading toward them. As he drew closer, Marcus realized he was with a girl in a low-brimmed hat and sunglasses. She pulled the glasses off. "Surprise!"

Oliver laughed. "Look who I found wandering the concourse like a lost little lamb."

Marcus pulled his sister into a tight embrace and inhaled Gwendolyn's Sunset Boulevard. "You said you weren't going to come."

"And then I came to my senses."

"I'm glad," he told her. "Our goodbye this morning at the Garden didn't seem right."

"Why do you think I'm here?" She slapped his shoulder playfully, but he could tell it was just camouflage.

Oliver tapped his wristwatch. He hugged each of the girls goodbye, then handed Marcus his car keys. "I'm going to make sure our luggage is there and see if I can book a table for dinner."

He climbed up the stairs and disappeared.

Marcus took Gwendolyn's hand and dropped his keys into her palm. She'd resisted earlier when he said, "It's time you had a car of your own." But now she just nodded silently and wrapped her fingers around them. "Is it too late to stage a kidnapping? Because now I have a trunk to stuff you into."

"I'm not just doing this for me," he said quietly. "Oliver needs a fresh start just as much as I do."

"He can't do that here?" Gwendolyn asked.

"It's the dope pushers. He said they have ESP when it comes to sniffing out addicts. I need to go where I'll be respected, and he needs to go where he can't be tempted."

"Of course you do." Kathryn was looking him in the eye now. She pressed her hand to her mouth. He read her thoughts: *It all makes perfect sense, but don't expect me to like it.*

"He needs me," Marcus added. "And I've discovered it's nice to be needed."

"We need you, too!" Gwendolyn blubbered.

Kathryn gripped her shoulder. "But not like Oliver does."

Gwendolyn sighed. "I know. I'm just being a selfish so-and-so. Listen, I need you to do me a favor." She pulled a brown paper bag out of her purse and handed it to him.

"What's this?"

"Somewhere between here and New York, I want you to dump the contents out of your window."

Marcus opened the bag; it contained a mound of ashes. "Is this what I think it is?"

"We may or may not have gotten drunk last night," Doris said, "and had a little bonfire, like Macbeth's three witches."

Gwendolyn resealed the bag. "Leilah's in jail, Clem's dead. Let everybody else deal with their own karma."

"ALL ABOARD!"

"And you?" Marcus asked Kathryn.

"What about me?"

"Winchell knows about your dad. What are you going to do about him?"

She lifted a shoulder. "What can any of us do about Walter Winchell? Try not to piss him off? Cross that bridge if I come to it? Try and forget I ever found that goddamned photo? All of the above?"

Marcus pulled each of them into a tight hug before tearing himself away and jumping onto the steps. As the sliding door closed behind him, the commotion on the platform receded, leaving him alone with his doubts.

Outside, a sharp whistle sounded and the train shunted to life. As it started to chug along the track, he rushed to the window. The girls were still there, arms linked in a chain. He pulled the window down and reached out as a shot of steam gushed from under the carriage. "I LOVE YOU!"

Kathryn was the first to burst into tears; the other two followed suit.

The train inched away from them, then caught momentum. The figures along the platform started to blur. He groped his pockets for a handkerchief and found he'd neglected to pack one, and had to make do with the back of his hand.

As Los Angeles slipped past, he thought of the day he first arrived at the Garden of Allah. He'd had no way of knowing he was walking into a pair of friendships that would mean more to him than he ever suspected possible. And now he was walking away from everything he knew.

He looked up to find Oliver a couple of feet away. "How long have you been standing there?"

"Long enough to know you were having second thoughts."

Marcus wiped his eyes again. "Nonsense."

Oliver looked at Gwendolyn's paper bag. "What's that?"

"History."

They watched the edges of downtown disperse.

"We can get out at Pasadena," Oliver said quietly. "Or San Bernardino. There's bound to be a bus back to LA."

"So what if there is?"

"I feel like I'm taking you away from everybody who loves you."

Marcus looked down the corridor to make sure it was empty. He grasped Oliver's hand and gave it a quick squeeze, hard as he could, before letting go. "We're not leaving a place *behind* so much as heading *toward* somewhere we can start over. We've both been dealt a shitty hand. But it's how you play your shitty hand that counts."

Under their feet, the train chugged over an unending expanse of track.

Marcus turned back to the window. Suburban Los Angeles started to give way to the leafy outskirts of Pasadena. He could already feel the Garden wrenching him back, and knew that his rousing speech about heading toward a new place with fresh starts and poker hands wasn't just directed at Oliver.

Oliver joined him, standing close enough for their shoulders to touch. It was a comforting feeling, like putting on a favorite sweater.

Oliver prodded him. "Do you even know where the Trevi fountain is?"

"It's Europe. I don't know where anything is."

Chugga-chugga.

Chugga-chugga.

Chugga-chugga.

"In that case, we'll need this." Oliver produced a foldout map of Rome. "The kiosk where they sell papers and candy, who knew they have a whole shelf of maps?"

They kept their eyes on the passing vista.

"So no Pasadena?" Oliver asked.

"Nope."

"San Berdoo?"

"God, no! It's Rome or bust."

The connecting door behind them slid open and a pair of businessmen in bowler hats squeezed past. Marcus waited until they disappeared into their roomette, then breathed against the window, fogging it up. He drew a heart onto the cold glass. Oliver pressed his pinkie finger and made three little dots.

Their secret code. Dot, dot, dot. I love you.

Chugga-chugga.

Chugga-chugga.

Chugga-chugga.

The Super Chief let out a long blast.

Marcus pushed himself away from the window.

"We better get settled in. It's going to be a long ride."

THE END

Did you enjoy this book? If you did, could I ask you to take the time to write a review on the website where you found it? Each review helps boost the book's profile so I'd really appreciate it. Just give it the number of stars you think it deserves and perhaps mention a few of the things you liked about it. That'd be great, thanks!

Martin Turnbull

ALSO BY MARTIN TURNBULL

Hollywood's Garden of Allah novels:

Book One: *The Garden on Sunset*

Book Two: *The Trouble with Scarlett*

Book Three: *Citizen Hollywood*

Book Four: *Searchlights and Shadows*

Book Five: *Reds in the Beds*

ACKNOWLEDGMENTS

Heartfelt thanks to the following, who helped shaped this book:

My editor: Meghan Pinson, for her invaluable guidance, expert eye, and unfailing nitpickery.

My cover designer: Dan Yeager at Nu-Image Design

My beta readers: Vince Hans, Nora Hernandez-Castillo, Bradley Brady, Matthew Kennedy, Beth Riches and especially to Royce Sciortino and Gene Strange for their invaluable time, insight, feedback and advice in shaping this novel.

My Proof Reader Extraordinaire: Bob Molinari

My thanks, also, to Susan Milner and Andie Paysinger for providing verisimilitude. I can only dream of these lives but Susan and Andie lived it.

VISIT MARTIN TURNBULL ONLINE

www.MartinTurnbull.com

If you'd like to see photos of Los Angeles and Hollywood back in its heyday, be sure to visit the Photo Blog on MartinTurnbull.com where old photos are posted daily: http://www.martinturnbull.com/photo-blog/

Facebook.com/gardenofallahnovels

The Garden of Allah blog: martinturnbull.wordpress.com/

Goodreads: bit.ly/martingoodreads

If you'd like to keep current with the Garden of Allah novels related developments, feel free to sign up to my emailing list. Fear not! I won't be clogging your inbox. I only do an email blast when I've got something relevant to say, like revealing the cover of the next book, or posting the first chapter. Go to http://bit.ly/goasignup

CPSIA information can be obtained
at www.ICGtesting.com
Printed in the USA
FSOW02n1947091216
28401FS